VOID WHERE PROHIBITED

VOID WHERE PROHIBITED

◆

A STORY OF LOVE AND MURDER

Mike Borgos

iUniverse, Inc.

New York Lincoln Shanghai

VOID WHERE PROHIBITED
A STORY OF LOVE AND MURDER

iUniverse books may be ordered through booksellers or by contacting:

iUniverse
2021 Pine Lake Road, Suite 100
Lincoln, NE 68512
www.iuniverse.com
1-800-Authors (1-800-288-4677)

This is a work of fiction. All of the characters, names, incidents, organizations, and dialogue in this novel are either the products of the author's imagination or are used fictitiously.

ISBN: 978-0-595-43587-6 (pbk)
ISBN: 978-0-595-87914-4 (ebk)

Printed in the United States of America

Acknowledgements

My deepest and most profound debt of appreciation goes to my wife Michelle, whose wise and patient guidance in this project was invaluable, and whose persistence in overcoming my resistance to her proposed improvements to the manuscript was unflagging and immensely beneficial. My thanks also goes to the many others who have read and commented on the work in progress. This includes Joy, Jennifer, Seth, Eric, Tana and other members of my family. It also includes many of our friends in "The Theater Group," too numerous to mention individually, for whose support and feedback during the process of writing <u>Void Where Prohibited</u> I will remain eternally grateful. Among many others whose help I have welcomed and valued are Rev. John Tackney, Joan Borgos, George and Marilyn Price, Debbie Burke, and Jim Wilkinson.

1

I got involved in all this through Sandy.

This is how I met her: It was dusk, about 7:30, I'm starting for home. This was downtown Boston, the financial district, not many people on the street by that time. I heard some noise, a scuffle, and when I turned around I saw this guy yanking a purse from the arm of a woman. The woman was frozen, petrified. This was happening about thirty feet away from me. I was frozen too, a bit petrified myself. Getting the purse free, the guy started running.

The thing is, the woman was beautiful. I mean really beautiful. My type beautiful. The other thing is, the guy was running in my direction.

To this day, I have no idea what possessed me to do what I did. Come on, you're thinking, you obviously wanted to meet the woman. That's true, yes. What I mean is, I don't understand what possessed me to even begin to imagine that things would turn out OK. That I wouldn't end up beaten to a pulp, or worse.

Anyway, I was on the corner of Water and Kilby. It's a neat spot, by the way. There's a square there which is really a triangle where some streets come together. It's small, just a few car lengths on each side. But in it is one of those minor surprises which makes me love living in a city. There's a statue commemorating, of all things, the uprising in Hungary against the communist oppressors in 1956. I relish it because it has this wonderful quixotic attitude. It is topped by a revolutionary holding a baby aloft (the future!) in triumph above the pain and death of the rebellion. In actual fact, the rebellion was crushed when Budapest was overrun with Soviet tanks.

So that's where I was, on Kilby looking across Water Street, trying to look harmless, and it became clear that this guy was going to run right past me. Apparently I've succeeded in looking so harmless that he doesn't care. He crossed Water and raced by me to my left. Just as he did, I turned toward him and gave him a big shove forward and sideways. Believe me, I was just as surprised as he was.

Now, he was sprinting at top speed—that's what for a healthy guy in his twenties, 12, 15 miles an hour? So he careened off my shove at an angle and smashed into the corner of the building at one hell of a clip. Bam! He tried to put his hands out in front to protect himself, but he was off balance so the effort was largely ineffectual. Fortunately his face avoided hitting the sharp right angle corner of the building head on, but his shoulder slammed right into it. His face bashed into the wall right next to the corner. Smack!

Instantly he was down on the sidewalk writhing. Blood was spurting from his nose, the right side of his face was raw with abrasions and contusions, but his big hurt was in his shoulder. His collarbone or an upper rib or something else in there was broken. Fifteen miles an hour is a serious collision. Think of the damage in an automobile bumper test at only 5 miles an hour.

The purse lay forgotten on the sidewalk. I ran around him, grabbed the purse, and trotted across Water Street to the woman, who had been watching from the opposite corner. I held it out and said, "Here." She took it, and then I said, "My name is Barry. Can I buy you a drink?"

She just stared at me.

"Can we get out of here?" I said. "I think we need to get out of here."

She nodded.

All right, now what? My plan—if you can call improvising in a state of panic a plan—was first to disappear as fast as possible and then blend into a crowd. Just behind the woman, who I noticed hadn't yet volunteered her name, was a break between buildings. Hoping it was an alley going through to the next street, I pointed and said, "In there."

To my vast relief, it was indeed an alley through to Congress Street. I started trotting down it, and to my further relief she was keeping up with me. Soon we made it to the far end, and I dared to venture a glance backwards. So far so good; no one was following. Kitty corner to the right across Congress, opposite Exchange Place, there's another alley, and we headed in that direction. "Walk, don't run," I cautioned. Out in a street I didn't want to attract attention.

Across Congress, we ducked left into this second alley and there was more good luck. This one twists right, then left, and it let us out on Devonshire Street. Across Devonshire, there's a street level passage through an office building which leads to Washington Street. As we went through it my plan was jelling. Washington is a shopping street and I was hoping for a crowd. Also, the perfect place had occurred to me to go get that drink.

I was rather surprised, and definitely delighted, that the woman was staying with me. She didn't have to. She could have peeled off at any corner, said, "Thank you very much. I'm going that way," and fled in a different direction. End of story. But there she was, at my side step for step. So I stopped and said to her, "I have a place in mind to get that drink. Still with me?" She hesitated, sizing me up, but just briefly, and answered, "Yes." This was the first she'd spoken.

"I'm sorry," I added. "I didn't get your name."

"Sandy. Let's keep moving," she answered.

And that is how I met Sandy.

So far I had seen no sign that we'd been followed. By now, we were no longer trotting, just walking briskly. The crowd on Washington was thinner than I had hoped, but it didn't seem to matter. My anxiety was receding, and as it ebbed, the space was filled with a blooming euphoria. This balloon would be burst soon enough, but for the moment I was experiencing the unfamiliar luxury of soaking in a warm bath of self satisfaction. I had foiled a crime, inflicted frontier justice on the criminal, restored the victim to her prior state of wholeness, and I was fading into the sunset, literally, side by side with the "girl." This was a whole new, astonishingly new, utterly unexpected new me. I gotta' admit, I liked it just fine.

A few more twists and turns and our destination was in sight. The place is called The Expansion Joint. EJ's to the regulars and semi-regulars. Back then I was in the latter category. The name is a play on words. It alludes to the presence of several architectural and engineering firms in the office floors above, and elsewhere on the block. It's a construction term. An expansion joint is a feature designed into large structures that allows building materials room to expand with the heat and contract with the cold as the weather changes. At the same time, the name—Expansion Joint—evokes the picture of an informal, unpretentious hangout where you can relax, let your hair down, and feel better.

You would expect Howard to think up a great name like that. Howard Tu owns EJ's, and he is very, very smart. Born in China but raised in the U.S., he retains a slight accent which is a part of his charm. I've always thought he did that deliberately to spice his persona with a taste of the exotic. Anyway, he was trained as an architect in the U.S. and years ago he worked for one the firms upstairs. But he grew really bored really fast. Architecture sounds like a glamorous profession, but Howard has assured me it is not. According to him, ninety five percent of architecture is toiling over minutia like stair construction details and concrete mix specifications. Only a lucky few get to be celebrities who enjoy the satisfaction of leaving their personal imprint on the cityscape. Howard quickly lost hope that he would ever be one of these people. So, when the bar and liquor license downstairs went up for sale, he borrowed every cent he could from family, friends and the bank, and took the plunge.

Howard Tu had a vision and he made it happen. What he lacked in business education he more than made up for in common sense and an innate gift for marketing. It shows in the presentation. When you come in, the bar fills your field of vision. The inventory is displayed in munificent profusion, with multiple tiers of bottles in a glorious array of shapes, sizes and colors. Highlighted by dramatic lighting, the glassware is sparkling and the brass fittings glow. Through a low archway, you can glimpse the dining room in back, which is quite different. The back is warm and cozy, with oak wainscot, forest green wallpaper, soft lights, white tablecloths, and comfy chairs in impeccable condition. Even if it's pub style food, Howard makes sure you feel like you're out for a special evening.

Greeting customers at the lectern by the door is Howard himself. No hostess. It's not that he can't afford one. This is his management technique. He knows his customers because he greets them personally. He knows how well his bartenders and wait staff are performing because he's out there watching them work. He never asks customers if they enjoyed their meal because he knows most people are too polite to tell the truth. Instead, he keeps close tabs on how well his kitchen is doing by monitoring the food on peoples' tables as he shows customers to their seats.

When we finally arrived that first evening, Howard was there as usual to greet us by the door: "Hey Barry the T! How you this evening?"

There's another regular named Barry, so I am Barry the "T", for Thomason.

"Hi, Howard. Tonight, we are in desperate need of a drink. But we'd like to go in back 'cause we may stay for dinner."

"First you introduce us. Then we see."

"I'm sorry. Howard, this is Sandy. Sandy, this is Howard. He owns this hole in the wall."

Howard held out his hand. "Pleased to meet you, Sandy. Barry is a good man. No money but big heart!"

Sandy took the hand and shook it. "A pleasure. I have no doubt about his heart. It's his brains that are at issue at the moment."

Howard's face lit up with a smile. "You not only beautiful, you perceptive too. For you I choose the best table in the place!" Talk about a charm offensive! One look at Sandy and it wasn't hard to figure out why.

By grace of good timing there were several tables empty. The after-work crowd was clearing out and the out-for-the-evening throng was still in its incipient stages. Howard took us to the back, made eye contact with a waiter in a look that signaled "treat these people well," handed over the menus with a flourish, and as he said, "Enjoy!" treated me to a wink.

In no time the waiter arrived with pen and pad poised. I turned to Sandy: "I'm going to have a real drink. But they have a great wine and beer list if you'd care to look at it."

Sandy looked toward the waiter. "I'm not particular. A glass of a nice Pinot Grigio would be fine." "Yes ma'am," said the waiter and turned to me. "Grants on the rocks." I hesitated while I debated what Sandy would think if I made it a double. Then I added, "Make it a double," because I very much needed a double. "Yes, sir," said the waiter.

Neither one of us picked up a menu. We just looked at each other. Face to face for the first time, without distractions, just us, I tried to figure out how to begin. I needn't have worried. Sandy solved this problem right away.

"Barry," she said. "I don't want you to think I'm ungrateful. I am definitely grateful. You saved my purse, and it would have been awful to lose it. You took chivalry to a level that was beyond my imagining. And I'm flattered that you think I'm attractive enough to do that for me, and then take me here. But ..."

"But?" I prompted.

"But what you did was ... profoundly dumb. It was foolhardy at best, and maybe criminal."

"Criminal? I foiled a crime."

"I'm not a lawyer, but it seems to me that what you did to that guy was an assault. At least. You were not in actual danger. I was no longer in danger. You attacked him physically with intent to do bodily harm. I don't know how else shoving him into the corner of a building at breakneck speed can be construed. I think you're very fortunate he didn't end up worse. A cracked skull. Blind. Dead."

"I didn't think of it that way."

"That's my point. You didn't think at all. I called that foolhardy. A prosecutor might call it reckless."

Luckily the waiter arrived with our drinks right then. I was reeling from what she said, not because she attacked me but because she was right. The waiter's business of setting the drinks down gave me a few seconds to get my bearings. He stayed at the table in case we were ready to order. "We'd like a few more minutes," I told him.

Then I looked at her. "I don't know what happened. That's not like me at all. I never get physical."

Her expression and tone were ironic: "Never say never."

"You don't believe me."

"The strange thing for me is that I do."

"You do? I'm delighted, but you don't know me. How can you know whether to believe me or not?"

"You passed a test. Something you didn't say."

Now I was bewildered. "What?"

"After I said, 'You're lucky he isn't dead,' most guys would have said, 'HE'S lucky he isn't dead.' But you didn't. You knew what I meant, and accepted it."

Again, she was right. Wow. I gulped down half my scotch. She was way ahead of me. Demurely sipping her wine, she was enjoying it too. "So," I said, "Are you telling me you set me up? You were testing me?"

"Oh no," she answered. "Nothing like that. I just said what I thought, but then when I heard myself say it I was eager to see how you would respond. You done good."

"You're something else," I blurted.

Sandy shrugged. And grinned. A loopy, self aware, positively wonderful grin, a grin á la Sandra Bullock, the actress. A grin that said, "Yeah, I know." A grin that said, "Whatever my problems, poor self esteem is not among them."

"Hey, wait a minute," I said. "If I'm such a dummy, how come you came here with me? You could have said 'thanks' and gone your own way. But here you are, having wine and dinner—I hope—with an alleged dimwit."

No hesitation: "That's because you're kinda cute."

"Well thank you. But are you supposed to tell a guy something like that? It sounds so … I don't know, so … so retro."

"OK," she said. "Chalk it up to post-feminism. Post-feminists are allowed to be retro."

"OK. I'm glad you think so. I mean …" I stammered.

She put up her hand in a stop gesture. "Let's make a deal. I won't patronize you and you won't patronize me. Each of us is sitting here for exactly the same reason. You wouldn't have done anything to that purse snatcher if you didn't think I'm attractive, isn't that right?" She cocked her head, forcing me to respond. I had to nod yes. "And equally, I wouldn't have come here with you if I didn't think you're cute. And I don't think you're stupid, I just think you did a stupid thing. There's a difference. But my bullshit detector is a finely tuned instrument. If you don't set it off, we may get along. Besides, what you did *was* spectacular. I may not approve, but it did get my attention."

"Wow. OK. Deal. No patronizing, no bullshit. I promise."

"Accepted. Now let's look at the menu. I'm hungry."

And so we did.

"Everything here is well prepared," I told her. "You might want to try the onion soup," I added. "It's intense. They understand onion soup here." Another thing I like at EJ's is that every item is listed in both "lunch" and "dinner" sizes with prices to match, and you can order either at any time. One of the great mysteries of life: why haven't other restaurants done that? It's like the checkout line mystery. At banks, airport ticket counters and car rental stations, there is one line and the first in that line goes to the next available clerk. Why don't retail stores work that way?

The waiter came back, and Sandy ordered a small onion soup but the large cheeseburger. I went with onion soup and a steak, both large. It tickled me that she had an appetite. You would hardly think so from looking at her. She's on the small side, trim. But not too skinny, not like a model. She has regular features. They're perfect. Short brunette hair, soft and lustrous, not unlike a model in a shampoo commercial. And skin. Oh, that skin. Incredible. Gorgeous. Think Catherine Bell, from the TV program JAG, with a dash of Audrey Hepburn thrown in.

"I want to tell you," I ventured, "I'm impressed at how you speak your mind, especially with a guy you don't know."

"You mean I have spunk? Like Mary?" She was teasing me, but in a nice way.

I got the "Mary" reference and nodded to show her that I did. "Lou Grant I am definitely not. I *like* spunk."

"OK, then," she parried, "In that case, what do you think of feisty?"

"Feisty is good. So is pluck."

"Is pluck as good as grit?"

"It is most assuredly better. Pluck is right up there with mettle."

We were both enjoying this. She kept it going: "I say mettle be damned. Why settle for mettle when you can have moxie?"

"Settle for mettle? Good grief!" I was laughing.

"I couldn't help it." She was smiling too. "It just came out."

"So," I said, "Where did you get yours?"

"My moxie?"

"Your spunk."

She shrugged. "Survival strategy, I suppose. I have two older brothers."

"Tell me about them," I urged.

"You want to hear about my family?"

"I do. What's more important than your family?"

"True, but it's boring."

"I don't believe you believe that. We agreed, remember? No BS."

"Point taken," she admitted. "All right, my family. My brother Jim is three years older than I am. He's a priest." She caught my eyebrows lifting. "It's not a disease," she scolded me. "You would like him. He's devout, but not holier than thou. Jim is very much in the real world."

"I'm sorry," I said. "I was stereotyping. Forgive me?"

"Jim would tell me that's what good Catholics are required to do. Forgive, that is." With a wry expression, she held up her hands in *what can I do?* gesture. "I guess I have no other option."

"I like your brother already!" I said.

It was her turn for raised eyebrows: "You think you're going to meet him?"

"Assuming too much?" I backpedaled.

"More like too soon," she amended.

"Did anybody ever tell you that conversing with you is like walking through a minefield?" Sweet Jesus. It just came out.

As you might expect, this stopped the conversation cold. Sandy sat there thinking, although, to my surprise, she really didn't seem that angry. All things considered, it was a good time for onion soup to arrive, and that's what happened. In short order, her interest in the food took precedence. Even before mine, her spoon was poking through the cheese crust and she was taking a small careful sip of the deep brown broth to see how hot it was. She glanced up: "You're right. This is good."

Pleased, I started on mine. Relieved that Sandy hadn't bitten my head off, I was revved up to savor Howard's really good onion soup, when I was blindsided by a whole new anxiety. The cheese. As in any good restaurant, Howard's onion soup is topped by a crust of cheese. When you try to lift some in your spoon to eat it, a tissue of cheese stretches out and ties it to the remaining crust. Pulling the spoon toward your mouth attenuates the strands but doesn't break them. I had never found a satisfactory solution to that problem. In the past, I had put the spoon in my mouth, and used my teeth in combination with the spoon to break the strands. It was dorky, but who cared? Now I cared. Thirty six years old and here I was, reduced to a quivering globule of jitters over onion soup decorum.

So I ate the broth and the onions, and waited to see what she would do. Sandy, of course, had no problem at all. She held the spoon close the to soup, deftly used her fork to separate the excess cheese, and brought the food to her mouth in a graceful, continuous motion. Another mystery of life: how do people adept in the social graces get to be that way? Is it a genetic message which is present in their DNA but somehow missing in mine? Is it perhaps a hidden cultural subtext my parents forgot to decode on my behalf? Sometimes I feel so lacking in the know-how of cool that I wonder if there isn't some secret society of savoir faire, some clandestine freemasonry of the felicitous, to which people like Sandy are initiated and I am not.

I copied her technique to the best of my ability, with equivocal success. And as the liquid in my bowl dwindled, I struggled with steadily increasing apprehension to think of how to rectify my "minefield" *faux pas* and get things back on track. Again, I needn't have worried. Sandy, after polishing off her onion soup with the most beguiling gusto, gazed in my direction and asked in a voice of ineffable gentleness, "Am I coming on too strong?"

With that, my heart dissolved into mush.

I shrugged, having no idea what to say.

"Look," she continued, "if I'm more blunt than you might expect, it's because I like you."

"I'm very glad to hear that." I couldn't help blurting it out: "I like you too."

"I hope this makes sense to you," she went on. "Usually when people first meet, they stick to safe topics. Their jobs. Their home towns. Where they went to school. Topics with no emotional weight."

"It makes sense," I said. "You have to begin by finding common ground."

"Yes," she continued, "and the point of common ground is to start building a basis of trust. But with you, somehow, I felt that kind of trust right from the beginning. I'm not sure why. And that led me to let my guard down. To be more open in expressing myself than I should have been. More candid than was appropriate."

"I like your candor," I offered. "It's spunk."

"But it's candor I'm not entitled to because it presumes a level of trust I haven't earned. The proof is that I frightened you."

"Frightened me?"

"Talking to me is like 'walking through a minefield'?"

"I'm sorry I said that."

Her hands waved back and forth. "No, don't you see? You have nothing to apologize for. I was out of line. You had every right to be put off."

"I'm not put off in the least. The thing is," I countered, "you were right every time. I *did* stereotype your brother as a priest. I *was* presumptuous when I assumed I would meet him someday. And as for shoving that guy into that building ..."

"But right there is why I like you," Sandy said with emphasis. "You're not defensive the way most guys are. When I called you on something and I was right, you acknowledged it. You know what that tells me?"

I shook my head no.

"It tells me that you're emotionally strong. I mean, you're secure in your sense of self. You're not automatically threatened by criticism. You don't react by lashing out. You listen to what is being said and consider it objectively. Am I right?"

"That I'm secure?" I paused to think about that. The word certainly could not apply during my onion soup moment. But on a deeper level, maybe she had something. Surprised and pleased, I put away the thought for later contemplation. "I suppose I am. I never thought about myself in those terms," I told her.

"Most guys don't think about it consciously. Still, men are generally all wrapped up in defending what they think of as their manhood. I don't sense that you're like that. That makes you unusual." She was looking right at me. Her voice earnest, her eyes open wide. She was so, so lovely. I was thinking about my manhood all right.

I said, "Do you know what I like about you?" She shook her head. "Your intelligence." It was her turn to be surprised and pleased. She cocked her head to one side—I could see now it was one of her signature gestures—and waited for more. So I said more. "It's true. I think most guys are threatened by intelligence in a woman. I am not. I like it. It excites me. For me, it's an aphrodisiac."

There was that grin again. She radiated amusement. "Why Barry the 'T', I do declare," she teased, "are you making a pass at me?"

I put my head in my hands in mock anguish. "Sandy, Sandy, Sandy …"

"What?"

"How can I answer a question like that?" I wailed, milking the histrionics. "If I say yes, you could be upset that I don't respect you enough. If I say no, you could be upset that I don't find you attractive enough. Either way I lose."

Sandy settled back in her chair, beaming with wicked glee. "Uhhh Huhhhh." She drew it out. "Sooooo …?"

"Sooooo … you have it all wrong."

She made no attempt to contain her delight. She relished watching me squirm. "Wrong?" she said. "Moi? How is such a thing even remotely possible?" Now she was making fun of herself. At first I was simply delighted that her sense of play, as well as her ability to avoid taking herself too seriously, was very much like my own. Suddenly it struck me as more than that. I realized that I connected with Sandy, that I understood how she thinks and feels, in a way that I had never experienced with anyone else before. And clearly she understood me in return. She knew just how to find and push my buttons. Did she really mean it when she said that I was secure and emotionally strong? That she trusted me? I didn't know and it wasn't important. What got to me was, one, that she evidently wanted to make me feel good, and two, she knew, instinctively, just precisely how to do that. This was no longer about her appearance. It went far beyond pheremones. I was falling hard.

So naturally, fool that I am, I got myself in deeper. "Here's how you're wrong. I was praising your intelligence, which is not a pass. But at the same time I was actually praising your beauty. It's your modesty—which is most becoming, by the way—which led you astray. The truth is that you are not merely attractive. You are without question stunningly gorgeous. Therefore, in your case, no aphrodisiac would ever be needed. If you acknowledged how beautiful you are, you would have understood that."

Oh God. That was worse than ridiculous. It was incoherent. But Sandy was kind and came to my rescue. Eyes full of mirth, she said, "Let me get this straight. You like my intelligence. But when you said intelligence is an aphrodisiac you weren't making a pass because that part didn't apply to me. And that's because I'm so gorgeous you don't need an aphrodisiac. Which I would have understood if I weren't so modest."

"Exactly," I said. "Is it politically incorrect to tell a woman she's beautiful?"

"You mean, can the man change the subject before the woman catches on to how deep a hole he's digging himself into?"

"Exactly," I admitted.

"Well, Barry," she said, "Not too many women really object to being told they are attractive." She reached out and put her hand on top of mine. "Relax. You're very sweet."

And so it went.

The food arrived, the food disappeared, and I hardly noticed. We were talking. We got back to talking about her family. She told me about her other brother Jeff, a marketing executive in Portland, Maine. Jeff and his wife Sharon have two kids, who were in grade school at the time. She told me about her kid sister Bonnie, living at home, working as an administrative assistant at a software company, dating one of the programmers. Home for Bonnie was their parents' split level in Westborough, one of Boston's outer suburbs. That's where the family had grown up, and still gathered for holidays. Dad is a civil engineer, Mom manages a retail gift shop.

We also talked about my family. About my brother, an auto salesman at a Lexus dealership who does so well at it he won't consider moving on to anything else. About my Mom, a high school English teacher who finally found happiness with my stepfather. He's an airline pilot, of all things.

We talked about work. About movies. About television. About college. Suddenly the waiter arrived with the check. I looked at my watch and discovered it was 10:30. Two and a half hours gone at warp speed. I put my debit card on top of the check. Then I looked at Sandy and asked if I could see her again. She smiled, nodded, and said, "Oh yeah." I suggested that I call her Wednesday to make plans for next Saturday. That was fine. She gave me her number. All at once, we became self conscious and didn't talk much before the waiter returned with the charge slips. I wrote him a large tip because we had occupied one of his tables for quite a long time.

On our way out, we passed by Howard at his lectern. On it he had his mini TV, tuned to the ball game. He waved and said, "Red Sox down by two. Pitching stink!" Howard Tu is a devoted baseball fan. He also uses his interest in the game as a marketing tool. He keeps a membership in the .406 Club, the premium box section at Fenway Park, and four season tickets. Executives at companies that use EJ's to cater their business functions, or have business dinners and holiday parties there, tend to find themselves as Howard's guest at one or two outings each season. But this utilitarian element doesn't contradict his genuine love for the game. Combined with his puckish sense of humor, this passion can have some quirky results. For example, he named his son Owen, after the no balls, two strikes count in baseball: Owen Tu.

I was telling Sandy about this on as we left the restaurant. She knew baseball well enough to appreciate the pun. On the sidewalk she was still tickled by it, and as she giggled she hung on to my arm a while longer than she might have. I was thrilled to receive this message in body language, and thus encouraged I offered to accompany her home. However, she said that she never let anybody know where she lives after just one date. Too many strange and dangerous people out there. I understood that. So I hailed a cab, gave the driver a twenty, and said, "Talk to you Wednesday." "Wednesday," she said. We hugged briefly, then she got in the cab and was gone.

I watched her taxi round the corner, and started for home on foot. I was singing out loud. "I have often walked ... down this street before ..."

2

Sandy and I swiftly became a couple. There is no mystery in that. We understand each other. We appreciate each other. The things we have in common are the things that are important, and at the core of it all is agreement on the fundamentals of what is right and what is wrong. No wonder, then, that by the time we headed off to the Legato's for Thanksgiving dinner six years later, we had courted, dated, lived together and married. After three years of matrimony, we were still on a honeymoon that showed no signs of abating.

No kids. I was not interested, and Sandy was ambivalent. Sandy's mom, after staying home to raise her four children in the pre-feminist mode, understood. As attentive and loving a mother as Gladys is, she was nevertheless happy to see her kids reach the age when they could be left alone to take care of themselves. It was, however, an issue with Ken, her father. Ken's participation in the child rearing process had been good natured but minimally invested. His limited exertions produced little appreciation of the effort involved in child rearing. He wanted grandkids. He thought he deserved them. And besides, it was the natural order of things, wasn't it? Jeff and his wife Sharon had two daughters, but they were hers from a previous marriage. Ken enjoyed them and liked having them around, but from the perspective of perpetuating the line they didn't count. He was chagrined that so far none of his own brood had delivered.

Ken was not reticent to express his impatience. With regard to Sandy, he assumed that I was the culprit. There was a kernel of truth in this. Had I been intent in the opposite direction, Sandy's ambivalence might have tipped in the direction of having a baby. As it is, we agreed that ambivalence is a poor motivation for pregnancy. But I never got into that discussion with Ken. I took all the heat. I'd rather Ken be aggravated with me than disappointed in Sandy. She was my coconspirator in this, and it earned me credits.

The topic was on our minds as we drove west on the Turnpike on our way to Westborough. It was sure to come up over dinner, since Sandy's sister Bonnie was not ambivalent in the slightest. She professed loudly, often and at length her desire for children. Several of them. Bonnie was a sweetheart, and it was nice to see her so exuberant, but Sandy and I were both getting tired of hearing about what had lately become an obsession. She'd go on and on about how she and her husband timed their relations to hit the fertile days, how they would keep trying for a year and if nothing happened they would get tested, how they would try every medical procedure to address whatever problem the tests revealed. And how if all else failed they would adopt. "That's not bad, either" Bonnie would proclaim. "There are lots of happy families where the kids are adopted."

My aversion to the phrase "give me a break" notwithstanding, gimme a break. Sandy and I both believed that her desire to raise a family was genuine. Still, we were irked by the way Bonnie exploited the contrast: *See Daddy? Bonnie equals grandkids, Sandy equals no grandkids. Aren't you pleased with Bonnie?* And we were equally annoyed by the way Ken bought it wholesale. Bonnie had always been his darling; now she could do no wrong. Sandy, meanwhile, had become the recipient of Ken's sideways glances. On the other hand, we were amused by Bonnie's attempt to blur the difference between biological offspring and adopted babies. In this she had a point. To almost everyone in this day and age, there is no difference that matters. But Ken's retrograde prejudice was an exception, and Bonnie's self-serving campaign to move him beyond it was doomed to failure.

Bonnie was married now, of course. Not to the programmer, but to Ralph, a copier salesman who had made a call to her company. In retrospect, we know now that everyone in the family besides Bonnie could see from the first that Ralph Collins is a good-for-nothing sleazebag. Bonnie, however, was instantly infatuated and nothing could peel off her blinders. We understood that too. Ralph burst upon Bonnie's scene like a July 4 fireworks finale, sweeping her off her feet in a whirlwind of attention, flattery, gifts and tastes of life in the fast lane. If anyone could resist, it certainly wasn't Bonnie.

On the very first visit to Bonnie's company, Ralph told her that she looked sensational in her red sweater and asked her out for dinner. When she agreed, he told her that the place would be a nice surprise and she should dress up fancy. Right away, when she told them about her upcoming date, warning signals flashed in her parents' heads. The Legato family's style of eating out was more franchise casual than Four Seasons haute cuisine. So who was this guy trying to impress? And why?

But Ralph had his eye on a prize, and a sure instinct for how to claim it. True to his word, he brought Bonnie to the Bay Tower. It was perfect. Bay Tower, now dedicated to catered functions but then a public restaurant, is a spectacular room at the top of a downtown skyscraper. It has a magnificent view from fifty stories up, elegant décor, unctuous service, and very good food. On weekends back then there was dancing to a live combo. Ralph knew how to lead, Bonnie knew how to follow, and by ten o'clock there was full body contact during the slow tunes.

If Bonnie was enticed by her first taste of high living at the Bay Tower, the deal was sealed six months later when she went with Ralph on a week's vacation to Bermuda. The trip was an incentive reward provided by Ralph's company to the top ten salespeople in the Northeast region exceeding quota. Ralph had made the cut as number six, and he had hustled to earn it.

The trip was an unqualified success. The company wanted to pamper the stars of its sales organization, and its attitude was both generous and thoughtful. When the group first arrived, there was a fruit basket and champagne waiting in each room. Meals, bar tabs, and activities such as scuba diving and parasailing were all paid for. Tips were included. And the weather cooperated: the island was a glorious riot of flowers, the blue sky was brilliant, and the water sparkled in the sunshine.

Ralph was feeling good and treated Bonnie well. He taught her tennis. He took her shopping for clothing and souvenirs. He sent her to the spa for massages and beauty treatments. Bonnie confided to Sandy later that their sex had been "stupendous." Best of all, it seemed, he made Bonnie feel wonderful by the evident pleasure he exhibited in presenting her to his manager and company colleagues. Where she would have been content to have romantic dinners *á deux,* Ralph arranged to get together every evening with other couples in the group. "Kitten," he told her, "I'm so proud that you're here with me. I don't want to hide away in a corner. We'll have plenty of time for that. Now is my chance to show you off. I want everybody to know how lucky I am. I want people to jealous of me for once. Is that so horrible?"

It wasn't horrible at all. It was thrilling. As the group took a liking to Bonnie, Ralph felt increasingly validated in his perception of her and become even more expansive and affectionate. And to this day I believe it was for real. Bonnie was exactly what he was looking for. Made to order. Not only was she very beautiful, she was also utterly pliant to his wishes.

This was not an issue with Bonnie. Bonnie, too, knew exactly what she was looking for. She wanted to be taken care of. That was it, pure and simple. The insistence on independence, autonomy, equal standing in the domestic partnership—the qualities so central to the core of Sandy's being and part of the reason my respect for her runs so deep—all were lost on Bonnie. She cared nothing for any of that. Bonnie wanted a man to provide for her. She wanted material comfort and security. She wanted emotional support and loyalty. She wanted physical safety. She wanted good times in abundance. And she wanted her carnal appetites satisfied. If getting all this meant doing things the way her husband wanted, Bonnie considered that a fair deal. She saw nothing Faustian about the bargain. She wasn't selling her soul, she was being true to it.

In the face of Bonnie's obvious contentment with her chosen lot, the rest of us suppressed our misgivings. Over time, we were forced to concede the possibility that our early judgment may have been unduly harsh. Ralph had made district manager, and was pulling in large incentive commissions. They had the nicest house in the family, the spiffiest cars, the latest electronic gadgets. They went to upscale restaurants and far flung vacations. And it was perfectly clear that Bonnie had never been happier. This induced a collective suspension of disbelief, and we all succumbed to it.

All except Gladys, that is. Her refusal to give Ralph the benefit of the doubt was stubborn. Her reluctance traced back to a conversation she had with Bonnie upon her daughter's return from Bermuda. Bonnie had been gushing with enthusiasm over the trip, and Gladys had asked her, "So, what didn't you like?"

"What do you mean, didn't like?" Bonnie stalled.

Gladys was not to be deterred. "You know what I mean. No woman spends 168 hours straight in close quarters with a man without disliking something. Out with it."

"Moth-*er*," Bonnie tried out her put-upon exasperation gambit. "Ralph was wonderful the whole time. Don't be silly."

It didn't fly with Gladys. "Out with it."

"Well ... There was one thing ..."

"Out with it."

"OK ... One time, I came back to the room early. I was at the spa but I wanted to take a nap ..."

"And?"

"He had his laptop plugged in. He was on the internet. When I came in he closed the cover and shut it off, as if he were hiding something. I asked him what he was doing and he said he was checking his e-mail from work. I didn't really think so, though. He checks his e-mail all the time. If that's what he was doing he would have kept on doing it."

Gladys pressed on: "So what do you think he was doing?"

"I don't know, Ma." Bonnie wasn't too upset. She had thought this through, had made up her mind, and was comfortable with her decision. "I don't think he has somebody else—another woman, I mean—'cause he spends all his time with me. Anyway, I think a woman can tell. Don't you? So what else could he have been doing on the internet? I honestly don't know. A porn site, maybe? I don't see why. I shouldn't tell you this, I suppose, you're still my mother after all, but we were wonderful together."

Gladys smiled: "I'm shocked. Shocked!"

Bonnie grinned in spite of herself. "All right, Ma," she conceded, "You're a modern woman. Anyway, I also thought maybe he might be involved in something criminal. I guess that is possible. I just don't see any reason to think that. I have no evidence whatsoever. What do you think, Ma?"

"What do I think? I think secrets are a bad sign in a relationship."

"I know, Ma. That's true. But I have thought long and hard about this. We're not married. If there are certain things he wants to keep to himself, it is his right. I can't place blame on him for exercising his right, that's not fair."

"The one thing I'm sure of," Bonnie went on, "is that it doesn't have to do with me, or our relationship. Ma, you can tell when a man is happy, don't you think? He was—he is—happy with me. I know in my bones he is. So whatever he was doing, it was outside of our relationship. And therefore it doesn't concern me."

Gladys was like a terrier: she would not be shaken off easily. "Are you going to marry this guy?" she asked, getting down to the nub of the issue.

Bonnie was unwavering. "If he asks me, the answer is yes."

Gladys made her point: "Then everything is your business."

Not having a very good response for that, Bonnie shut down the discussion. "You said it yourself, Ma. No man is perfect. But Ralph is as near to that as I can imagine. More important, I feel great when I'm with him and I miss him when I'm not. It's my decision to make, and I've made it. You can either be glad for my happiness and share it with me, or you can sit in judgment and put a wet blanket on my life."

Gladys is blessed with uncommon wisdom. All of her instincts told her that Bonnie was making a mistake. But that was not the most important thing. She also knew that it was Bonnie's right as an adult human being to make her own mistakes, to suffer the consequences, and learn from them. Gladys understood too that it would not be doing Bonnie any favors to make her choose between her boyfriend and her mother. If problems did arise, as she expected, Bonnie would need her more than ever as a warm and comforting presence in her life, as an emotional hearth to come home to.

So Gladys said, "Sweetheart, if you're happy, then I'm very happy for you." She held out her arms. "Come here." And they hugged. Tightly.

Within two weeks, Ralph did ask, and Bonnie did say yes.

Bonnie and Ralph were much on our minds as we exited the Turnpike to 495 north. Their quest for parenthood had been the focus of the entire family's attention for several months. The subject was infinitely engrossing to Ken and Gladys, but Sandy and I were weary of it. We both wished she'd get pregnant already just to change the subject, even though we knew that this would launch a whole new and prolonged conversational fixation on obstetrics, pediatrics and child development.

We had been listening to the car radio without talking, so it was a function of our closeness that when Sandy grinned at me and said, "You taking bets?" I knew exactly what she meant.

"This is it," I said. "She's going to announce after grace."

"Why today?"

"Gut feel," I said. "Plus, the stars are in alignment. Mercury is ascending over Virgo."

Sandy laughed. "You're so full of shit. OK, you're on. I'll take the 'no'."

"Twenty minute back rub to the winner?" I proposed.

"Deal," she agreed. Actually, I wasn't risking much. I was always giving her back rubs anyway. Sandy was totally spoiled. But "making it interesting" boosted our spirits as we pulled up in front of the Legato house.

In general, we enjoyed and looked forward to family occasions with the Legatos. Aside from the tension with Ken over grandkids, relations throughout the family were easygoing and feelings warm. Even Ralph found acceptance, if not wholehearted trust.

Thanksgiving is a favorite occasion in particular, for exactly the same reasons that it appeals to just about everyone else: great food and no anxiety over gifts. But the Legatos have a singular tradition which adds to the pleasure of the day, and which I think especially sweet. After dinner is eaten and the clean up done, the family proceeds to the living room to trim the Christmas tree. This is an attempt—largely successful—to recapture the magic of the season remembered from the time when the "kids" were young. In those days, when everyone lived at home, this ritual took place in mid-December and was one of the recurring experiences that helped bond the family together. When Bonnie, the youngest, moved out, Ken and Gladys decorated the tree on their own but the joy was absent. Several years ago Jeff had the inspiration to revive the event but change the timing to Thanksgiving, when the whole family is together anyway. This plan proved to be a major success, necessitating only a switch from a natural to an artificial tree. Now firmly entrenched as an annual custom, Thanksgiving tree trimming is a treasured occasion for reliving fond memories. Each "remember when" in turn evokes more laughter than the last. Each "how could you ever buy me …?" evokes another round of affectionate teasing. If someone were to describe the Legatos as close knit, this would be Exhibit A.

In my early years with Sandy I sat in with the family and helped remove ornaments from the storage cartons. But with nothing to contribute and no frame of reference to appreciate the hilarity, I was less than comfortable. In due course Sandy recognized this and suggested that I retire instead to the den where I could watch football. Nobody would mind, she told me. "Make yourself an Irish coffee and enjoy," she said. Sandy is so great.

Despite the sluggish holiday traffic this year, we arrived in Westborough slightly ahead of schedule. Aside from Ken and Gladys, only Jim was there so far. "Sandykins!" he exclaimed as we walked in. "Jungle Jim!" Sandy replied as she raced into his waiting arms. Brother and sister hugged with obvious delight. Then Jim held her at arms length and said, "You're looking pretty good." Glancing at me, he continued: "This lug you married must be treating you OK." "This lug is the best thing that ever happened to me, and you know it," Sandy announced.

All of that was a script, played out exactly the same way every time they got together. These extended greeting rituals are another custom among the younger generation Legatos. It's corny but endearing. It sets a tone of warmth and belonging from the start of every gathering.

Jim and I shook hands and exchanged "Hi, how ya doin's." Improbably—a non-observant Jew and a Catholic Priest—we had become rather good friends over the years. This proved less difficult than I had imagined. For one thing, Jim was anxious to form a friendship. As I learned to my surprise, priests are often quite lonely. In part, this is a result of frenetic work schedules, forced upon them by an acute and growing shortage in their numbers. In part, it is a consequence of the way in which ordinary folks assign clergy to a status at once elevated and remote. Finally, of course, there is celibacy, the elephant in the parlor. Many priests who are committed to celibacy are skittish about forming a friendship with any woman they might find appealing, preferring to avoid temptation rather than wrestle it into submission. This reduces the pool of potential friends by a considerable percentage. For Jim and others, the problem with celibacy was not just the absence of sex. Perhaps the problem was not even *primarily* the absence of sex, but rather the barrier it presented to plain human intimacy. Jim was around other people all the time, but attending a church committee meeting is just not the same as sharing your innermost thoughts with someone you trust. And to meet that need, being married to God just doesn't cut it.

From my standpoint, what began as an attempt to please Sandy by relating to her brother morphed into a genuine attachment to the guy, fueled not only by enjoyment of his company but also an ever growing sense of respect, admiration and on occasion sheer jaw-dropping awe. His amalgam of warmth, kindness and clarity of thought was extraordinary, yet somehow he was able to display these qualities out and about in the world without the slightest hint of affectation. It was easy to see why he was much beloved among his parishioners and notably successful in filling both the pews and the collection plate.

At the same, Jim was very much a "regular guy." He kept up with the news, went to movies, watched TV when time permitted, was not averse to a spot of rye whiskey in his ginger ale or a cold brew in a frosted mug, and suffered the roller coaster fortunes of the Red Sox and Patriots along with all the rest of New England. Once, with some arm-twisting, I prevailed upon Howard to include Jim in one of his outings to Fenway Park. Thereafter Jim was re-invited on a regular basis. To my mild chagrin, he was re-invited more often than I was.

Early on we developed a custom of our own. After dinner at family get-togethers, we would take a walk in the neighborhood and we would both smoke cigars. That was a treat in itself. Beyond that, I'm a good listener. Jim found he could unburden himself to a sympathetic ear, knowing it wouldn't get back to his family. Most of his distress stemmed from his unhappiness with the policies and behavior of the Church hierarchy. He thought the rule against married clergy to be wrongheaded and destructive. He was offended by the hypocrisy of the Church in its attitude toward women, as it proclaimed the importance of just treatment while consigning them to second class status within its own ranks. And he was rendered desolate by the pedophile scandals, not just an abomination in its own right but an ever widening stain that revealed an institution more concerned with suppressing clerical scandal than with protecting the safety and well being of those who had entrusted their faith to its ministry.

During our walks, Jim explained to me how he could persevere in the face of such discouraging circumstances. He had a calling, he said, to serve God by following in the footsteps of Christ. Becoming a priest, being part of the Church, was the means that allowed him to do that. So he made what he called "a separate peace" with the Church. It was a deal that was strictly in his own mind, but it was his deal nonetheless. The Church, for its part, would provide a home base from which he could bring the peace of the Lord and the Catholic faith into the hearts of all that would accept it. And he would do it his way, in the light of right and wrong as he saw it. The deal did not include supine obeiscence to the dictates of clerical authority, never mind that he had pledged precisely that in his vows of ordination. He felt quite free to ignore whatever dictates from Rome that he considered inane or destructive. Thus he would freely discuss birth control with couples and often recommend it. His ministry was inclusive and embraced gays along with everyone else. Sometimes he supported divorce, in situations where relationships were abusive or beyond repair.

But in return for the privilege of doing God's work the way he believed God wanted it done, Jim kept his ministry quiet and private between himself and his parishioners. That was his end of the deal. He didn't make an issue of his differences with the Church, didn't publish articles in dissident journals, wouldn't present challenging papers at conferences, never complained about the Archbishop in public. In short, he refrained from making any stink that would embarrass his superiors in the organization.

One time I challenged him on this. I asked him if he weren't copping out on helping the Church fix what was wrong. Didn't he have a responsibility to not merely avoid being part of the problem but to be part of the solution? And didn't he feel that by staying silent about the things that troubled him he was helping to perpetuate those very failings?

It turned out that Jim was free of inner conflict on this score. First, he reminded me, there was much in controversial Catholic doctrine that he supported. The prohibition against abortion was an example, as was the position against capital punishment. In addition, he went on, there was much about the Church as an institution that he loved. It was, after all, the home and center of his faith. Beyond that were the many and great good works that it performed day in and day out all over the world. Think of the hospitals, charities, shelters for the homeless, safe houses for battered women, he told me; the list goes on and on and on. How can he not love the Church?

There's a practical side too, he said. Just as in any large organization, people who buck the system get ground down, chewed up and spit out. Such efforts accomplish little; they are suicidal attacks against impregnable fortifications, and in the end nothing changes. He knew there had to be people who could stand up and be counted in the face of that kind of adversity. He wasn't one of them.

But ultimately, he told me, all of that is secondary. The bedrock truth in his ministry, he told me, was the fact of his vocation. Catholics believe that a calling to the ministry is literally that: God actually calls on you personally, specifically, to serve Him by following in Christ's footsteps. How do you know when that happens? There's no diagnostic checklist. There's no indicator light that suddenly glows red. You just know.

Jim believes that God called him to His service knowing full well what kind of priest he would be. As Jim described it, "My place is on the retail end. It's my job to bring the revelation of God, through Christ, into the life of every person I come in contact with. One by one." To Jim, the retail end is performing the sacraments. It's delivering a homily every week. It's counseling couples through difficult times. It's comforting the afflicted in hospitals and nursing homes. It's sitting with the bereaved. It's going for a soda with a teenager after a basketball game to talk about whatever is troubling him.

"Barry," Jim said, "when I do these things I feel good. I feel right about the way I am doing God's work. I feel joy in being close to Him, in serving Him, in loving Him. Barry, I just don't believe if I were doing wrong his His eyes he would let me feel like I do. I just don't."

"And Barry," he added, "In the last analysis we all make our own choices and we all decide for ourselves how much is enough."

This last was a rebuke. It was mild, delivered in the diplomatic manner that was Jim's way, but a rebuke nevertheless. And I deserved it. What are *you* doing, Jim was saying, to help solve the problems of the world? He knew that Sandy and I both thought of ourselves as two of the good guys, even as we did precious little to make the world a better place. How did we justify going out to nice restaurants while people were starving in the Sudan? How did we justify cozy evenings snuggled in front of the TV while people were wandering homeless in the cold right here in Boston? How could we say we cared about the outcome of an election if we did nothing to influence the outcome except vote? All good questions without any good answers. So before you judge me, Jim was saying, look in the mirror.

When he's right, he's right. And that's most of the time.

This day I brought along a treat for both of us: expensive cigars, which I define as any that cost more than $3 apiece. I grabbed them from my coat pocket and held them up for his inspection. "Ah Laddy," he sighed, affecting a Scottish brogue, "If you think you can obtain God's grace by brdibin' a prdiest, you may just be rrright!"

I laughed and just then Jeff, Sharon and their kids walked in and the Thanksgiving event started in earnest. Ken and Gladys came down the stairs, everybody greeted everybody else, coats were hung in the closet, and we all were escorted into the kitchen where the island counter was laden with drinks and goodies.

Now if you love to eat and you've had Thanksgiving at Ken and Gladys', then you know what bliss is. The Legatos always put on a great feed but for Thanksgiving they pull out all the stops. The goodies on the counter are not just chips, dips, crackers and cheese. No. They are stuffed mushrooms, scallops wrapped in bacon, and a platter of shrimp with cocktail sauce. Plus chips, dips, crackers and three different kinds of cheese. Not to mention the Swedish meatballs. And it begins with Gladys' invocation of the impossible: "Enjoy but don't fill up."

In fact we try hard not to fill up because we know what is yet to come. The sit down part of the dinner is classic Americana, flawlessly rendered. Turkey, stuffing, cranberry sauce, gravy, mashed sweet potatoes, green beans in mushroom sauce with onion ring topping, the works, everything cooked to perfection. There is a line of thought in traditional philosophy, going back to Plato, which contends that the identity of any particular thing is determined by its underlying "form" or "ideal." The notion is that when you see a dog, even though it may be anything from a Chihuahua to Great Dane, you know it's a dog because they all incorporate the "ideal" of "dog." Well, all I can say is Gladys' holiday feast is the "ideal" of Thanksgiving brought to reality in its purest expression.

This, mind you, is not to take anything away from Thanksgiving with my own family. In alternate years Sandy and I have the holiday dinner with them, then Sandy drives her own car back to Westborough for the tree trimming. But many years ago my stepfather put his foot down: no more day of backbreaking drudgery in the kitchen for Mom. From then on, we would celebrate Thanksgiving with a good meal in a fine restaurant. My mother put up token resistance, but the protest was pro forma. As soon as Dad explained that it was not because her Thanksgivings were inadequate but quite the opposite—they were so good she got worn to a frazzle—she relented. Inwardly she was pleased. That incident was an example of why they have a good marriage. They understand each other, and act on that understanding with kind hearts. Indeed, their marriage is the model for mine. And Thanksgiving with them is definitely a treat. Still, the holiday at the Legatos is an experience straight out of Norman Rockwell, and to be honest it is even more of a treat.

Not long after we all moved to the kitchen Bonnie and Ralph showed up. I suppose it showed something about how I regarded Bonnie that my first thought was to wonder if she had timed their arrival to make a splashy entrance. Bonnie was charming and fun, but also something of the family peacock, prone to showing her feathers and strutting her stuff. In any event, there ensued another cycle of hugs and handshakes, with Bonnie and Ralph at the center of it all.

Pretty soon, though, we found ourselves back at the serious business of *hors d'oeuvres*, accompanied by the standard casual chitchat. It was all the usual stuff: work, health, TV, movies, gossip about friends and acquaintances. Ken was at the counter carving. Meanwhile, Bonnie and Ralph were conspicuously touchy feely. Observing this, Sandy and I made eye contact. I pantomimed a gesture feigning a pain in my back that needed massaging. She made sure no one was looking, grinned, and gave me the middle finger. I laughed out loud.

When Ken was ready, we were summoned to the dining room. This was another ritual. The dining room was off limits until this moment so that the setting would be pristine when we entered for the meal: the place settings just so, the cut glass stemware sparkling, the lace trimmed tablecloths gleaming white, the floral centerpiece a splash of vivid color. Entering the dining room was intended to be like viewing a stage set at the opening curtain. And like a good stage set, the table was to be appreciated as a creative work of art.

Presently we all were seated and looking to Ken to say grace. It didn't matter that a priest was sitting at the table. Ken was the head of the family and therefore he said grace. Jim approved of this. Jim felt close to God all the time. He didn't need a prayer to cement the relationship. If his dad wanted to reinforce his role as leader of the clan and in the process affirm his allegiance with the Holy Father, Jim considered this a plus from every angle.

"Lord, please bless our humble family with the wisdom to follow Christ and serve you with faith, charity and love. Please bless the bountiful meal that we enjoy on this day of Thanksgiving as we thank you for all the good things you have provided in the material world, and as we rededicate ourselves to helping those who find themselves in less fortunate circumstances than we do. And may everyone in your dominion enjoy the comfort and peace that can only come from accepting You and your son Jesus Christ into our hearts and minds. Amen."

"Amen" was repeated in a chorus. Then from Jim, "Dad, that was beautiful. I could not have done it better." And Ken beamed. As much as Ken prized his demeanor of authority and self-confidence, he equally respected technical expertise. And in the matter of God, Jim was the trained professional. Thus did Ken look for his approval in matters of piety. And Jim always, invariably, gave it.

Now the moment was here, and I turned instinctively toward Bonnie. In my peripheral vision I could see Sandy doing the same. We were not disappointed. Bonnie leaned forward and spoke up: "Mom, Dad. Ralph and I want to announce that we have something else to be thankful for today."

Everyone was quiet, sensing what was coming.

"Mom, Dad, everyone ... I ... am ... pregnant!"

Jubilation all around. Squeals, exclamations and applause from everyone. Then around the table it went.

Gladys: "Oh, honey, that's wonderful news."

Ken: "That's absolutely great. I'm very pleased."

Jim: "I'm thrilled for you, little sister. Ralph too."

Sharon: "Bonnie, this is awesome. Just know that I'm available any time you'd like to talk about any questions or problems."

Jeff: "I know how much you wanted this, and I'm very glad your dream is coming true. I love you very much, kiddo, and I just want you to be happy."

Sandy: "I just second everything everyone else already said, and double it."

Me: "Mazel Tov!"

That got a giggle from Sandy, a smile from Jim, and blank stares from everybody else. Sandy explained, "It means congratulations and best wishes in Hebrew." "Hear, Hear!" said Jim.

Ken raised is wine glass. "Time for a toast! Fill your glasses, everyone … First of all, Mazel Stuff." He looked at me. "Was that good?" "Close enough," I said. "You captured the spirit."

"Good. Here's to a new addition to our family. Here's to a new generation in the Legato family line. And here's to Bonnie and Ralph for making it happen. About *how* it happened, there's no need to tell me the details." Laughter. "Cheers."

Cheers around the table.

"When did you know?" asked Gladys.

Bonnie: "Tuesday."

Ken, annoyed: "Two days and you don't call us?"

Bonnie: "It was only two days. What I wanted … I just thought it would make for a festive occasion for everyone if I announced it to everybody at the same time while we're all here together as a family. Was I wrong?"

Characteristically, she stood her ground and we all waited for Ken's reaction. When none was forthcoming, Jim stepped in and said, "No, Bonnie, you weren't wrong." And that settled the matter and the awkward moment passed. Dinner proceeded in the usual manner, lively and festive, with an extra measure of buoyancy provided by the news from Bonnie.

Later on, while the Legatos trimmed the tree, Ralph and I watched the ball game. He had been drinking more than usual, I thought. He wasn't acting inebriated, but I sensed his guard might be down. So during a commercial, I asked him how he felt about the baby. After a few seconds had passed, he just shrugged.

"Whoah," I said, "Let's not get carried away with enthusiasm here."

He glared in my direction. "What do you want from me?"

"I'm sorry," I said, shifting into diplomatic mode. "I didn't expect to hit a nerve. I thought everyone was thrilled about this, including you."

"So why did you ask?"

"I was just trying to connect with you a little. I thought it was something good. I had no idea there was an issue."

"I'm in sales for a reason," he said. "It's a good fit."

"Meaning?"

"Meaning I can get you to think anything I choose."

"OK, Ralph," I said, "I didn't mean to pry."

We watched the game for a while. Then Ralph changed his mind. He picked up the remote, decremented the volume, and turned in my direction. "I know you mean well. Look, I'll tell you how I feel if you promise not to tell anybody else, including Sandy."

"OK," I lied, "Deal." I did this without guilt. Ralph was familiar with the relationship I had with Sandy, and had to know that the chance that I would withhold information from her that I got from Ralph was zero. So it wasn't a real deal. Consequently, I surmised that he intended whatever he had to say to get out to the family. He had decided to use me as a conduit. That was fine.

"I had a girlfriend in high school, long before Bonnie," he began. "Her mother had a baby during the time we were dating. My girlfriend had to help out all the time. I was old enough to see what it's like to care for an infant. I don't want any part of it. Right now our time is our own. We can make plans when we want to. We can be spontaneous when we feel like it. We have quality time together. We get enough sleep so that we can enjoy it. With a baby, all that goes out the window. Then there's the money. Just as I'm starting to make a good income and we're beginning to see some daylight on our bills, Bonnie is going to quit. So we lose her contribution, which isn't massive but it's not trivial either. At the same time, we add in a vast bottomless pit of new expenses. And all that for what?"

This wasn't a real question. Ralph was quite aware that I didn't want kids either, so his argument was pre-sold, so to speak. Hence when I answered, "So you can have the experience of loving, nurturing and taking pride in a new life that you and Bonnie bring into the world?" Ralph appreciated the irony in my tone. Even though what he said was, "Thank you for the testimony of a recognized expert in child rearing," he was not offended. Still, he had left the real question hanging out there. Deliberately. Begging to be asked. So I asked it: "If you feel this way, how come you're going along with the whole thing?"

He was ready, and as he launched into his answer I realized I was being used. I was hearing the story line that Ralph wanted to project to the family. The gospel according to Ralph. And who better to spread the word than Barry, the ultimate honest broker.

"The reason," said Ralph, "is that I love Bonnie so much. She wants a baby more than anything else. She's obsessed about it. And I can't find it in my heart to deny her. It's like Jim and his celibacy. You know how he says it's hard—torturous sometimes—but the very difficulty is what makes it an expression of his love for God? Well, it's like that with Bonnie and me. It is the sacrifice required by parenthood that makes this a meaningful gift from me to her, but a gift I want to give."

So there it was, and I had no real reason to disbelieve it. Just because it came from Ralph did not necessarily make it untrue. It seemed plausible. I wanted to believe it. Oh hell, let's be honest, I did believe him. The son of a bitch was right. He could make me believe anything he wanted.

3

Subsequent investigation by the police revealed that on Friday, the day after Thanksgiving, Ralph made a stop in Chelsea.

Chelsea is an industrial backwater adjacent to Boston. It is linked with the Charlestown section of Boston by the Tobin Bridge, which carries U.S. Route 1 north toward the upper reaches of the New England coast. But Charlestown, benefiting from its pre-industrial charm, its proximity to downtown, and the cachet of a Revolutionary past that includes Bunker Hill, has been gentrified to a fare-thee-well. It is, for example, the locale of the restaurant Olives, home base for the culinary empire of celebrity chef Todd English. Chelsea, meanwhile, is a sad sack of a town. A lonely wallflower, never invited to dance during the urban revitalization parties of recent decades which animated the rest of the Boston real estate scene, it was left with a housing stock, a central business district, and an economic base which are not merely old but tired. What we have here is the town that marketing forgot: a city of 35,000 souls bereft of even a single solitary Starbucks.

The dominant physical feature in Chelsea is the elevated Route 1 viaduct attached to the northern end of the bridge. The Tobin Bridge itself, as it crosses the Mystic River, is a picturesque assembly of steel girders and trusses perched on conical pilasters. Not especially when you're driving on it, but very much so when you're looking at it, the effect is airy and lacy and rather nice. Although built in 1950, the design has an aesthetic sensibility more reflective of the 19th century, a celebration of the age of steel manifest with admirable clarity of concept and refinement in execution. The half-mile viaduct, however, ripping through the heart of Chelsea, is one God-awful piece of crap. It is massive. It is gross. It is double decked and painted a bilious green. It is, in places, six stories high. It appears that at the time it was built, public works officials may have intended to do the City a favor by elevating the highway, thus preserving connectivity at street level between the two sides of town. If so, this is ironic. What they wrought was the road from hell, paved over with their good intentions.

But if the viaduct is a scar that disfigures the listless and dispirited face of Chelsea, the drama of ordinary human life still roils beneath the surface, anything but listless and dispirited. In that, Chelsea is no different from anywhere else.

And Ralph, as he exited the viaduct that Friday morning onto Chestnut St., was about to become a player in one of those dramas.

I'll tell you the story as best we can reconstruct it from what was uncovered during the investigation:

Descending to Chestnut and turning left on Second, Ralph heads to the parking lot at Mystic Mall. He's going to leave his car there, three blocks from his destination. No way is he about to allow his Lexus, less than a year old, to sit unattended on a street in Chelsea, even in daytime. The lot at the mall, teeming with activity and guarded by a security patrol, is a much better bet, he figures. So he has to walk a couple of blocks. No big deal.

Ralph has been summoned to a dry cleaning establishment. This one is in a great location. It's on a busy street, close to both apartments and businesses. It's within view of an on-ramp to the viaduct. It's a money-maker. It makes some sense, then, that the store has a prosperous appearance; it is clean, modern, and therefore looks quite out of place in Chelsea.

Ralph is not there to sell a copier. The store is a front for his bookie. This is a clever idea. It's open early, open late. There is heavy customer flow throughout the day. There are numerous cash transactions. Indeed, it's perfect.

Ralph takes a deep breath and goes in. The electronic sensor sets off the electronic bell. Marcel is behind the counter. Marcel doesn't look like a Marcel. He looks like a Rocco. People call him Rocco. He encourages that.

Though Ralph has been here often, this time there is no cordial greeting from Rocco. Instead, he gestures his head toward the back of the store and says, "The Chief is expecting you."

There's a section of the counter that's hinged to provide a pass-through. Ralph lifts it upright and heads toward the rear. Some of the space in back is used for dry cleaning equipment and operations. The remainder is occupied by one of those serpentine motorized racks that holds finished garments on hangars and moves them mechanically to the front when you push a button. The ranks of shirts, sweaters and slacks in glistening plastic bags obscure from sight a plain, unmarked door. Behind it is the Chief's office.

Ralph sweeps aside some shirts. He steps into the gap he's created and knocks on the door. He hears, "Yeah?" "It's Ralph," he says, "Ralph Collins." "Ah, yes," floats through the door, "Come in, Ralph Collins."

Ralph does just that. The Chief's office is generous, but not especially fancy. It has carpeting, but the indoor/outdoor type. There are no windows. The walls aren't blank, though. They are lined with floor to ceiling bookshelves, nearly filled, the way you might expect to see in the den of a college professor. The

Chief has read most of these books, too. He's an educated man who thinks about things.

The furniture is nondescript, except for his desk and chair. These are enormous, imposing, powerful. In contrast, the visitors' chairs are small and spindly. They won't collapse, but they seem as though they might. This is a ploy to nettle visitors and put them at a disadvantage.

Once you see the Chief in person, you don't forget what he looks like. His features are undistinguished, but he is tall—about six feet three—and exceedingly thin. Gaunt is how you would describe him, although he is not ill, he's just built that way. Sunken cheeks and a sharp nose accentuate a face that is already long and narrow. He is, in fact, just this side of concentration camp emaciated. He wears custom made suits because anything off the rack looks baggy. There is no expansion in his chest, no bulge to his stomach, no widening of his hips, no gluteus in his maximus. If you had a napkin ring that just fit the top of his shoulders, it would slide down to his feet.

The Chief is content with the way he looks. He knows that his odd appearance is magnetic, that it rivets people's attention on him. He also feels that it leads people to underestimate him. That may or may not be the case, but in any event those that would do so are likely to regret their miscalculation. It's not that the Chief is by nature a violent sort. True, his line of business can be a tad rough and tumble on occasion, and for that eventuality he has associates he can call on who are less fastidious than he. But as a rule, he prefers to achieve his objectives by getting other people to see things his way. As it turns out, the Chief finds the exercise of muscle rarely necessary. The background threat of it is usually quite sufficient. That, and the Chief's powers of logic and persuasion, which are more than a match for Ralph's. Overall, it is remarkable how often folks come to see things the Chief's way.

The Chief gestures to invite Ralph to take a seat in one of the spindly chairs. He dispenses with the usual social niceties. No *"so how was your Thanksgiving?"* No *"did you get in any golf before the weather closed in?"* Just, right away, all business: "So ... Ralph Collins ... how is life in the tony suburb of Newton?" Ralph and Bonnie bought a house in the tony suburb of Newton after Ralph made district manager. Ralph understands that the Chief's question is neither friendly nor disingenuous. It is an oblique reference to the fact that Ralph has a big mortgage now, leaving less cash available to pay off his gambling debt.

Ralph pretends to a sanguine nonchalance he doesn't feel, and in his anxiety he makes a mistake. "It's good," he says. "You know," he says, "one of the reasons we moved to Newton is the great school system. Now it looks like we did the right thing for the right reason. We just found out that Bonnie—my wife, Bonnie?—she's pregnant."

Never mind the cozy family photos on the credenza behind the desk. If Ralph is expecting a modicum of human warmth and collegiality from the Chief, he is disabused of that notion pronto. The Chief's eyes fix in on Ralph's. "A baby," he says, softly. "A kid." This is the curtain raiser, the overture to a tirade. The Chief will start quietly, then steadily ramp up the intensity and volume of his voice until it reaches a volcanic crescendo: "A kid, in your situation. Ralph Collins, do you have any idea how much a kid *costs*? Any clue? The slightest fragment of a scintilla of an idea? Have you fallen off the *precipice of sanity into the bottomless abyss of UNCONSTRAINED DEMENTIA? Ralph Collins! You. YOU! YOU are the world's PERFECT EMBODIMENT of an IDIOT! You, Ralph Collins, are the DEFINITIVE EXAMPLE of WORLD CLASS BRAINLESS TURD!!!*"

All this is just theatrics, an improv performance intended to put Ralph on the defensive. It does. Ralph shifts awkwardly in his spindly chair, then concentrates on regaining his composure. With all the calm he can muster, he offers his explanation. "I know a kid is expensive. I've looked into it. But I had no choice. Bonnie was driving me crazy over it. She was obsessed with wanting a kid. She never let up. I couldn't stand it any more. I couldn't say no any more. My sanity *was* at stake. Not to mention I had exhausted all my excuses."

The Chief strokes his chin. "Interesting you should put it that way. You've exhausted all of your excuses here too. And we also have the ability to put you, Ralph Collins, in a position where you can't say no. Interesting parallel."

Ralph: "I'm doing the best I can."

More chin stroking by the Chief. "I don't see it that way. For example, you're making payments on a Lexus. Not just any Lexus, mind you, but the expensive one. You could instead be making payments on a Camry or a Saturn or something, and paying me back the difference. It wouldn't be much, but it would be something. A token of your commitment to settling your account. How committed are you, Ralph Collins, to settling your account?"

"I'm committed. I'm very committed. But I need a nice car for business. In sales you need to look successful."

"You telling me you think someone who merely drives a late model Camry looks like a failure?"

"Well, I also got a fantastic deal. My brother in law's brother sells 'em, and he gave me a terrific price."

"Yeah, but they're killing you on the financing."

The volume on the alarm bells ringing in Ralph's brain takes a quantum leap upward. "How do you know about my financing?" he says.

The Chief allows himself a limited smile. "We'll get to that soon enough."

"OK. Well. It's the best I could get. My credit's a little shaky."

"Shaky? *Shaky?* You're over your head with your mortgage. Your credit cards are maxed out. You're making payments on a Lexus. That's merely what's on the books, the world according to Equifax. Off the books, you owe me roughly the national debt of a small African nation. Now you're having a baby. That's not *shaky,* that's Chernobyl."

Ralph has progressed by now from nervous to inklings of dread. "How do you know about my credit cards?"

The Chief shows his annoyance. "All right. All right, we'll get to that now *instead* of later. This is simple. This is even legal. When you first came on board with me, you signed a form for a charge account with the laundry here. That was a standard form where you give permission to a business creditor to obtain your credit report. That charge account is still open. I can get your credit reports any time I want, legitimately, just by asking for it and paying a small fee."

"Jesus," says Ralph, dismayed. He hadn't been aware of that.

"Let's get back to the subject of the car."

"Why?"

"Because it illustrates your self destructive combination of personal vanity and financial irresponsibility. Why didn't you lease it?"

Ralph is momentarily confused. "Huh?"

"The car. The fancy car you bought to keep up with you hoity-toity neighbors in tony Newton. Why didn't you lease it?"

For once, Ralph thinks he has a good answer. "Its cheaper to buy," he says with confidence, "over the long run."

The Chief shakes his head. No sale. "It's only better if you keep the car for a while. You never do that. You buy a new car every two or three years. For you there is no long term. For two or three years, for the term of a lease, the economics are equivalent. It's a trade off."

"No, Chief." Ralph thinks he has him this time. "A lease only covers 12,000 miles a year. I drive more than that."

But the Chief has known all along where he was taking this. "Ah, yes. But if your wife drove the Lexus, you could still show it off in your driveway in tony Newton, and she would run up less than 12,000 miles. Meanwhile, you could drive the new Impala the company gives you every other year, the one she's driving now, the one your company thinks is just fine for calling on customers."

Ralph isn't keeping up. "But why would I want to do that?"

The Chief now shifts his tone in order to sound as patronizing as possible, knowing this will provoke Ralph to anger. "Cash flow, Ralph Collins. I'm disappointed in you, Ralph Collins, you don't know the answer. The answer is cash flow. With a lease, you don't build up any equity, but in return you get the benefit of lower monthly payments. And that, Ralph Collins, that is what you *need*. You don't need to impress your customers with a car you can't afford. You *need* liquidity right now. *Lower monthly payments.* Ralph Collins, you made the wrong choice. Instead of making small payments on a Camry lease, you're making large payments on a Lexus financing. You know, Ralphie, the Jews have a terrific word for what you are: Putz. That's exactly what you are, Ralph Collins, you're a *putz!*"

As the Chief intended, Ralph is furious. There is nothing that galls him more than disrespect, and the Chief is rubbing his nose in it. But he can't do a thing about it. Ralph is in a precarious position and he has little leverage. So he grimaces and says nothing. The Chief, of course, cares nothing about the car. The whole routine is designed to humiliate Ralph as a means of dramatizing the power relationship between them.

The Chief picks up a manila file folder from the top of a pile on his desk. Opening it, he says, "OK, enough chit chat. Let's get down to business. Do you know how much you owe me?"

Ralph has a ballpark number in mind, but thinks it safer to play dumb. "Not really," he answers, "I guess it's quite a bit."

"Quite a bit, indeed." The Chief puts on his reading glasses and scans the top sheet of the file. "OK, here's a printout of your account. You've had a marker with me for four years now ... Time does fly, doesn't it? Are you having fun yet? Four years. On December 31st of the first year, you had accumulated net losses of $6,324 and accrued interest of $1,739, for a total of $8,063. Year two: you had additional net losses of $12,378, additional accrued interest of $9,578, leaving you with a debt of $28,280. In year three, you had additional net losses of $11,199, leaving total debt with interest at $53,678. Now it's almost December in year four, your net losses this year alone, including yesterday's games—yesterday was a bad day for you—are $12,409. Your total liability as of this morning is $83,468.

Ralph is stunned. This is not in the ballpark he had imagined. "Jesus," is all he can manage to say as the depth of his trouble begins to sink in.

The Chief nods his head. "Ah yes, the magic of compound interest!"

Ralph mumbles, "That's got to be a bitch of a rate."

The Chief is annoyed again. "Fifty five percent. You were fully aware of that when you first opened your account here. So don't give me any of this phony victim shit."

For once, Ralph says something honest. "I thought I was going to win."

His candor is not rewarded. "That just proves what I already told you. You, Ralph Collins, are a putz."

Ralph the putz is reduced to grasping at straws. "I admit I've been on a losing streak. The last few years have been rough for me. But that just shows that I'm due. My luck is bound to change. The odds are with me now. The laws of chance are in my favor."

The Chief leans back in his chair. "You know that's not true."

"I do?"

"You know that when you deal with a bookie, you have to factor in the vigorish. When you do that, the odds are never with the bettor."

"Yeah, yeah," Ralph says, waving his hand dismissively, "I mean besides that."

"Oh, well, besides that." The Chief leans forward, adjusting his glasses and gazing at the printout. "So here's what the journal for your account is telling us. That cumulative loss of $42,000 and change is a balance of roughly $39,000 in net winnings and $81,000 in losses. Those winnings are net of $4,300 in vigorish. So you're waving away $4,300 as if it were insignificant. Is that how you look at it? Petty cash?

Ralph backs off. "No. No, I don't mean that. It's just that in the overall scheme of things ..."

The Chief fixes his stare. "So you appreciate my point." Ralph is befuddled once again. The Chief is becoming exasperated. "My point being, your situation is so dire that $4,300 appears insignificant by comparison. Putz."

At this point, Ralph wants nothing more than to end the agony and escape from this room. "What do you want from me?" he pleads.

"Nothing, now." The Chief's tone has turned cold, as has his gaze.

Ralph says, "OK. Good. Great." His voice sounds relieved. "We'll work out a plan to pay you back." This betrays the fact that he hasn't yet internalized the seriousness of his trouble.

The Chief leans forward. "You don't understand, putz. I've lost all confidence that you *can* pay me back."

"No, Chief, no. Once I start winning again ..."

The Chief interrupts. "In 42 months you've been on my books, you've had 6 winning months and 32 losing months. With you, Ralph Collins, losing isn't a random proposition. It's a sure thing. There's a trend here. You don't have to be a PhD in statistics to see it."

"OK, OK," says Ralph. "I'll start paying off the loan."

"You can't," says the Chief.

"But I will," says Ralph.

The Chief raises his voice. "Ralph Collins! Putz! I just told you!" He calms down. "I just told you how much you owe. Even if you just pay the interest and nothing else, that's $3,655 per *month*. How you gonna' do that, putz? After the mortgage on your fancy house in your tony neighborhood, and the payments on your prestigious automobile, and the minimums on your maxed out credit cards, and your dinners out and your trips abroad and your high maintenance wife and your new kid, exactly how much is left to pay me, putz?"

"Man, I'll do everything I can to put things right."

"I don't think you get it. What we have here, Ralph Collins, is not random, not the roll of the dice, the luck of the draw. I have already told you, and evidently you were not paying attention. What we have here is a trend. Statistical proof, Ralph Collins, that you don't know shit from shinola about betting on sports. I cannot support you any more. I can't keep throwing good money after bad. I don't think I would ever begin to get my money back from you. Which is why, Ralph Collins, I have sold your account to a factor."

"A factor?"

"A factor. What the hell, Ralphie, did you flunk out of business school?"

"I majored in communications."

"Figures. You majored in putz. A factor, putz, buys accounts receivable for cash at a discount, and hopes to recover more than he paid. It's a common practice in business."

Ralph is getting very tired of this. "Are you finished insulting me?"

"I'm finished with you altogether," says the Chief. "You're Stanley's problem now."

"Who's Stanley?"

"He's the factor. People call him Cap. It isn't short for "captain." It's short for kneecap. He likes to break 'em as a way to focus people's attention."

"You're talking about a loan shark?"

The Chief is getting tired of Ralph, too. He makes a show of letting his breath out. "Yes, putz. Who did you think was going to be willing to buy your crappy debt, fuckin' J.P. Morgan Chase?"

Ralph is floored by this news. He knew that being called in to see the Chief could not be good, but he never expected anything so disastrous. He just stands there, speechless, trying to digest the whole business.

"He'll be in touch with you, I'm sure," says the Chief.

The needle on Ralph's tank of self confidence has come to rest at zero. "Chief, how can I possibly pay him? What does a loan shark charge, 100% or so? If I can't pay you 55%, how am I going to pay him 100%?"

The Chief has lost interest. "You'll figure something out."

Ralph begs. "Chief, please, don't do this. I'm one of your best customers!"

The Chief smiles just slightly and snorts, "Hah."

"What's funny?" asks Ralph, stupidly.

"You reminded me of that ancient business joke: we lose money on every item we sell, but we'll make it up in volume."

Ralph is back to begging. "Chief …"

The Chief is stone cold. "Don't humiliate yourself, Ralph Collins. This is already done."

Ralph's inner resources are exhausted by now. He feels just as defeated as he in fact is. Giving up, he says, "As long as I'm here, can I at least place some bets on this weekend's games?"

The Chief is flabbergasted. He leans back in his oversized chair and just stares at Ralph for a long time. "You still don't get it, do you?" he says, finally. "Your credit is cut off. You *can't* bet with me, unless you bring cash up front."

Ralph is stunned. The logic is inescapable, he just hadn't connected the dots before. All at once, his fear is no longer abstract, it's physical. He's feeling queasy, and he can feel the clammy dampness of sweat building under his armpits. What he says next, he says quietly, with utter sincerity and truth: "I can't not bet."

"Not my problem," says the Chief.

"I don't have cash. My credit cards are maxed …"

"Not my problem."

Ralph knows the meeting is over. He gets up from the spindly chair and heads to the door, no goodbyes, no handshake. Leaving the store, he avoids eye contact with Rocco. Dazed, he heads back toward his car. In the mall, there's a restaurant with table service and a bar. He wants to get plastered, but he won't. He has a sales call along with one of his field reps scheduled for two o'clock, and now more than ever he needs every sale he can get. Plus, it's one of his core beliefs that as a manager it is up to him to lead by example. Plus, he has an ironclad rule that he will never drive his Lexus with more than two drinks in his system.

So he orders one drink—a double—and while he's nursing it, he stews unproductively about his problems. When the food is served, he is startled. He has no recollection of having ordered, much less what he ordered. Oddly, the sight and smell of food makes his stomach feel better, and he realizes he is hungry. The next he's aware, his plate is clean and the check is in front of him. His thoughts are seething and churning all the while, with no productive output.

Then it is off to his meeting, where he helps make the sale. Later on, the sales rep who accompanied Ralph on the call, who had worked for him for nearly three years, will not remember Ralph exhibiting any unusual stress that day.

When Ralph arrives home that night, Bonnie tells him that there was a message on their home voice mail from somebody named Cap, who left the number for his cell phone. The next morning—Saturday—Ralph makes the call and they arrange to meet at 5:30 Monday afternoon at the Sheraton in Framingham. Cap has selected this location for its anonymity. It is a large business hotel near a Turnpike exit whose bar should be busy once the meetings taking place in its conference rooms have finished for the day. Cap's objective is to blend in with a crowd, neither noticed nor remembered.

On Monday, Ralph arrives on time. Cap has arrived early in order to make sure nobody who knows him is there, and at 5:30 is watching the door from a stool at the bar. They had described themselves to each other on the phone, so they make contact quickly. Since the room is crowded, they socialize for a while until a table opens up out of the way in the back along the wall.

Once seated, both order beers. It's a compromise. They both relish the calming benefit of hard liquor, but each wants to stay alert and in possession of all his faculties. Ralph doesn't know what to expect, and he knows better than to let too much alcohol dull his concentration.

It's Cap's show, and Ralph waits for him to begin. Irrationally, Ralph is comforted by the fact that Cap is smaller than he is, and doesn't look especially powerful. Think of, say, Kevin Spacey, the actor. Ralph would be less comfortable were he aware that one of Cap's goons is watching from the bar. Not that the danger is immediate. Cap just wants the goon to know what Ralph looks like for future reference.

Cap initiates the conversation before the beers arrive. "This situation," he says, "is like the saying about bankers. It goes: If you owe the bank $5,000 and can't pay, you've got a problem. If you owe the bank $5,000,000 and can't pay, *they've* got a problem. Well, in this case, I feel like the banker with the problem. The problem, of course, is you. You see what I mean?"

Cap pauses and appears to expect a response from Ralph. So Ralph says, "I do. I understand what you're saying. But I'm sure we can work something out."

Cap presses: "Do you have a plan?"

Ralph: "I've decided to quit gambling."

Cap is dubious. "Very admirable. You're a compulsive gambler. What makes you think you *can* do that?"

Ralph is dismayed by this turn in the conversation. He's not stupid, and the idea that he may be compulsive—what some people call addicted—has crossed his mind. But he has long kept the thought buried beneath a mountain of denial. Over the weekend, however, the protective topsoil of rationalization and excuses had been eroding quickly under the monsoon of adverse circumstances that presented themselves in Chelsea. Now his defenses are crumbling further under fresh assault from Cap. The pressure on Ralph's stress circuits is nearing overload, and he really doesn't want to pile on the burden of an acknowledged clinical compulsion.

Ralph says, "I can be pretty a determined guy."

Cap is unimpressed. He's seen this before. Often. "You still haven't given me an answer."

The beers arrive. Ralph takes a big gulp, then says, "To what?" He's stalling for time, but merely succeeds in irritating Cap.

"Do you have a plan to pay off your debt?" says Cap, with an edge.

"I thought we'd work something out right now."

"OK," Cap says. "Let's start with a fact. Right now your nut is $3,478 per month. That's pure interest."

Ralph is surprised. "That's less than I owed the Chief."

Cap lays it out: "That is because I bought your account from the Chief at half of the nominal value. I don't upcharge on the initial amount outstanding. But when you fail to pay the monthly interest in full, at 100% annual rate, it will mount up quickly. You can trust me on that."

Ralph chooses his words carefully. "I don't see how I can come up with $3,500 every month. When I was with the Chief, my plan was to win some bets." Then Ralph has a brainstorm. "Any chance that you can get me set up with someone else so that I can win enough to pay you back?"

Cap is bemused. "Forty five seconds? Fifty seconds?"

Ralph doesn't get it. He has a puzzled expression.

So Cap explains. "Fifty seconds ago you declared the end of your gambling. You were determined, you said. It sounded like a commitment. Now you want me to set you up. Some commitment. Your commitment had the half life of an exotic atomic particle."

Ralph is abashed. "Cap, I don't see what else I can do."

"Sell something. Or mortgage something."

"I don't have anything. The house is mortgaged to the hilt. I've already drawn down my 401K, what little I had in it. I had some stocks once, but they were dot coms, and they're all defunct or below water. My cards are maxed. I don't see what I can do."

Cap knows all this already. He's reviewed Ralph's situation in detail with the Chief. In business jargon, Cap has done his due diligence. He is just tightening the screws on Ralph gradually, step by step, to greatest effect. "Sell the car," he says.

"Sell the car?" Ralph responds in his dumb stalling mode.

Cap shows his impatience. "The Lexus, putz!" By this, Cap is deliberately telegraphing to Ralph that he is in close communication with the Chief, and knows everything. "You sell the Lexus. You lease a Kia. You drive the Impala from your company. She drives the Kia. You'll net more than twenty grand on the deal. You can't keep the money or you'll gamble it all away. So you'll hand it all to me. That will prepay about six months worth of interest. It'll buy you a chunk of time."

"Why wouldn't the twenty grand go to paying down the principal?"

"We can look at it that way. If we do, the interest goes down to about $1,800 a month. But you have to pick that up starting the very next month. Can you handle $1,800 a month any better than you can handle $3,500?"

Ralph can't. But now he says what's really on his mind. "There's a big problem with selling the car." Cap has pretty much guessed what's coming, so he listens intently. Ralph's psychology is key to Cap's plan. "If I sell the car," Ralph says, "Everybody will know my situation."

Gotcha! thinks Cap, jubilant. He is careful not to show it. "What do you mean?"

"Think about it," Ralph says. "Suddenly, for no apparent reason, I sell my beloved Lexus? And dump my wife into a friggin' Kia? And the money completely vanishes? How am I supposed to explain all that? What's my wife supposed to think? Her family? My family? The people at work? The questioning will be relentless. If the truth comes out, it will be a total catastrophe. And even if it doesn't, the rumors will be just as bad. I can't face that. I'll be destroyed."

"Do you have any choice?"

"I don't know. I hope so."

"What if you told the truth? Is that so terrible? Lance the boil, get it over with. It's a big embarrassment, sure, but then it's off your chest. You could get psychological help."

Ralph mulls this over for a while. He knows he shouldn't make any snap decisions. At length he says, "It's possible I could change my mind, but right now I don't see it. Maybe if I went through all that and it really solved the problem once and for all, it might be worth it. I could take my punishment and get over it. The pain would at least have a payback. But selling the car doesn't solve the problem. I'm humiliated, and all it gets me is a six month respite. Then I'm right back where I started. Minus the Lexus."

Exactly! Cap is thinking. Now we're getting somewhere. So he keeps it going. "How about a better job? Can you get a job that pays more?"

This hadn't occurred to Ralph. He is taken aback that he hadn't thought of it. "Gee," he says, "I don't know. But realistically, I doubt I can make that work. If I have to pay you $42,000 a year, that means I need a salary jump in the range of $70,000 before taxes to cover it. Can I find a job that pays that much more? Seems unlikely."

Good answer! thinks Cap. Cap is methodically leading Ralph through all the alternatives that won't work in order to pave the way for the one that will. He catches the waiter's eye and signals for another round. Then turning back to Ralph, he offers another suggestion: "How about a loan from somebody else? A relative? A friend?"

Ralph sees this for what it is: a proposal so lame that its sole purpose is to underscore the gravity of his predicament. No way is he about to reveal his problems to either side of his family. He merely moves his head side to side.

The waitress comes with the new beers. Ralph takes his directly from her hand and drains two thirds of it before setting the glass down on the table. Cap takes a sip from his, and decides it is time to let Ralph marinate in his apprehensions for a while. So he leans back and says nothing. Neither does Ralph. Silence.

The silence isn't that long, really. One ... two ... three ... *Cap is counting the seconds mentally* ... six ... seven ... eight ... nine ... *precisely ninety seconds* ... fourteen ... fifteen ... sixteen ... seventeen ... eighteen ... *but it is an unnerving experience for Ralph* ... twenty two ... twenty three ... *who doesn't know what to say* ... twenty seven ... twenty eight ... twenty nine ... thirty ... thirty one ... *and doesn't know what Cap is thinking* ... thirty four ... thirty five ... thirty six ... *and therefore imagines the worst* ... thirty nine ... forty ... *KNEECAPS! Oh My God!* ... forty three ... forty four ... *is that what he's going to do to me?* ... forty seven ... forty eight ... *Now? Today?* ... fifty one ... fifty two ... *he wants a plan*

... fifty five ... fifty six ... fifty seven ... fifty eight ... *Oh My God! A kneecap! ...* sixty one ... sixty two ... *Bonnie! Oh shit! What do I tell Bonnie?* ... sixty six ... sixty seven ... sixty eight ... sixty nine ... *run away? bolt out of here? escape? hide out?* ... seventy four ... seventy five ... *then what?* ... seventy seven ... *yeah, but with my bones intact* ... eighty ... eighty one ... *Jesus! Jesus Jesus Jesus!* ... eighty five ... eighty six ... *Jesus!* ... eighty seven ... eighty eight ... eighty nine ... ninety ...

"Insurance," Cap says.

Ralph just looks at him, wide eyed.

Cap's eyes bore into Ralph's. "You have to do something."

Ralph spreads his arms, palms up. "You tell me."

"I'm telling you that the current situation is untenable. I'm telling you that I've invested $40,000 in you, and I will not lose a penny."

Any remnant of composure that entered the room with Ralph flees now. "Cap, I'm trying! I'm thinking like mad. If you ... if you break my kneecap and I can't work, that doesn't help the situation."

Cap shakes his head. "Nah, we're a ways yet from the kneecap stage."

If that's supposed to give Ralph some reassurance, it fails. Quite the opposite. Ralph had been hoping that the kneecap thing was an exaggeration, an urban legend with more hype than truth. That hope had just rendezvoused with his composure.

"What do you mean by that?" he says.

Cap's tone is matter of fact. "I know better than you do, putz, that punishment doesn't help return my investment. At least not directly. That's why I only use it after I've abandoned all hope. At that point, with my investment already down the drain, it yields me a kind of salvage value. The salvage value is what you might call a motivational effect on my other clients."

"Motivational," Ralph murmers.

"Motivational," Cap repeats. "You are motivated, are you not?"

"Yes, I am motivated," says Ralph.

"Good," says Cap. "So think about insurance. Do you have any?"

"Just regular homeowner's."

"What else?"

"Health, from the company."

"What else? Life?"

"Yes, that's true, on me. It's part of the company benefit package. I forgot about that."

"Sometimes," Cap says, "people get a big windfall from insurance. You could use a big windfall right about now."

"No shit," says Ralph. Then it hits him. "Wait a minute. Are you talking about burning down the house for the insurance money?"

"Not exactly."

"Good. 'Cause that has the same problem as selling the car. How do I explain to Bonnie where all the money went?"

"Yep. That's a problem."

"Not to mention that I could end up in jail. So what are you thinking?"

"I am thinking more along the lines of life insurance."

"You mean my life insurance? Bonnie's the beneficiary. She gets the money."

"You could change the beneficiary. To me."

Ralph's outrage is for real. "Are you crazy? If I'm going to be dead anyway, why would I give you the money? Or the satisfaction? That's nuts!"

"Because, putz, we can make your life so miserable you would rather be dead. Dead might be better than crippled, out of work, panhandling on the street. Constant pain. Bonnie and the kid moved on. This could be a preferable alternative. A tragic accident. Over in a fraction of a second. Your reputation preserved. And you don't have to turn all the insurance over to me. Just what you owe me, plus the cost of arranging the accident, and a modest fee for brokering the deal. Depending on your coverage, there could be plenty left for Bonnie."

"God dammit to hell, you're talking about my death here is as if you were one of my friggin' prospects discussing the relative merits of alternate copier vendors! Forget it! I'm not ready to die. And I'm not ready to make Bonnie a grieving widow, and make our kid fatherless."

At this point, Cap puts his toe into speculative waters. He has no information on the subject, but he has a hunch. "You don't strike me as the kind of person that cares all that much about a kid. Especially one that you haven't met yet."

Ralph is irate. His tension and fear overwhelm his self-control. He explodes. "You arrogant asshole! What do you know about what I care about, you son of a bitch!"

Paydirt! thinks Cap. Cap, unlike the Chief, has no college degree. But like the Chief, he's a master at the psychology of everyday human behavior. And one of the patterns he's observed is that when people react badly to criticism, it is invariably because the criticism has hit its mark. People can, and almost always do, shrug off criticism when it's off base. They view the critic as stupid, the statement benign, and dismiss the incident as inconsequential. But criticism which finds its target in truth is threatening, and therefore provokes a defensive reaction. In this regard, Ralph's response is classic.

Cap continues to bear down even as he pretends to back off. "OK, OK. I didn't mean to offend you. We're just exploring here. I'm still looking for you to come up with a useful suggestion. So far, you're making me do all the work. It's getting me nervous."

"I'm trying."

"I don't see any heavy lifting. I don't see the effort. I bet you put more effort into selling a copier than you're putting right now into saving your ass."

"I'm an expert at selling copiers. At this," Ralph gestures in resignation, "I'm out of my league."

"That's not good enough," Cap says. "You may be out of your league, but you should be motivated. I don't imagine you want to be downgraded to one of my salvage value projects. Right?"

"No."

"It hurts like hell, Ralph. It never stops hurting. It only stops when you die. And you would want to die sooner rather than later. But you can't, if what you just told me is true."

Once again, Ralph is confused. "Huh?"

Cap, condescendingly, with exaggerated patience: "You just told me—not two minutes ago—that you don't want to leave Bonnie a widow and your kid fatherless. But if you *are* in such pain that you decide to end it all, that would be the outcome: widow and orphan. In addition, your life insurance will pay nothing on a suicide. You know that, don't you?"

Ralph stares morosely at his empty beer glass.

"What about Bonnie?" Cap says.

Ralph looks up.

"Is Bonnie insured?" Cap asks.

The word "alarmed" hardly begins to convey the sensation Ralph is experiencing just now. He continues to look up.

Cap repeats, "Is Bonnie insured? Yes or no?"

"No."

"OK. It's natural to take out insurance on the wife when she's pregnant. If a wife dies and the husband has to raise a kid alone, the additional expenses are devastating. Child care, housekeeping, food, doctors, clothing, it's major. The economic value of a wife and mother in a household is underappreciated but real. So mothers are insured all the time. But—hypothetically speaking, naturally—if

Bonnie were insured and something were to happen to her before the baby is born, then all your problems would disappear. Hypothetically speaking."

Ralph's reaction is immediate. "You are certifiably deranged!"

Cap is calm. "It's the only rational solution, Ralph. And don't forget: If you insure her for enough, there'll be plenty left over for you to have a very nice stake to start placing bets again. With cash. Another problem solved. It's a twofer, Ralph. And Ralph, you don't have to get your hands dirty. We take care of everything. For a fee, of course. All you have to do is arrange an alibi. Out of town at a business meeting is good."

At first, Ralph can hardly believe what he is hearing. But Cap is looking him straight in the eyes, and Ralph knows he has not misunderstood. This is unreal, he's thinking. This is the twilight zone. He's a putz, maybe, possibly, all right, if you say so. But a *criminal?* A *murderer?* His own *family?* All he can think to do is get up and storm out of the room. So he does that.

The goon shoots Cap a glance from his stool at the bar, wondering whether he should prevent Ralph from leaving. Cap raises his palm upright and shakes his head "no." Cap is more than satisfied. The seed has been planted.

4

The atmosphere had changed in the Legato family during the month following Thanksgiving. By the time the family celebrated Christmas, the euphoria had dampened, the mood had darkened.

Christmas at the Legato's is, in any event, less elaborate than Thanksgiving. The meal is invariably ham. No muss no fuss. Appetizers come from the freezer, desserts from the supermarket bakery. The gathering begins at about one thirty, late enough for Jim to fulfill his pastoral responsibilities and for Jeff to drive down from Portland, but early enough for the dishwasher to be loaded and the kitchen surfaces cleaned before dusk. This is by Gladys' decree. By nightfall on Christmas day, after hosting two mega-meals in less than thirty days, Gladys is pretty much familied out.

Even in its attenuated form, Christmas is a strenuous effort that taxes Gladys' flagging energies, and later on we learned that she was looking forward to the day when she could offload this celebration to her younger daughter. We found out that she had a plan in the works. The next year she was going to make a suggestion to Bonnie: "Rather than bundling up the baby for a trip to Westborough, and messing up his whole routine, why don't we all just come to your house. That way the baby can nap in his own room in familiar surroundings. And you don't have to bother will all the packing and unpacking."

Gladys recognized this argument for the transparent ruse it was, and fully expected that Bonnie would see through it. A four month old infant will sleep anywhere. And shlepping baby paraphernalia to Grandma's is never going to be more work than hosting nine guests for Christmas dinner. Gladys' real intention was to devise a gracious way of passing on the torch. By positioning the shift as something to make life easier for Bonnie, Gladys hoped divert her children's attention from the fact that she is growing older and more readily fatigued. The purpose of spinning it this way was not to paper over her own feelings, but rather to offer a fig leaf to help the transition go down more easily for the rest of the family. And she figured Bonnie would leap at the chance to become the center of attention on a major holiday, the attraction of that far outweighing the additional effort required. In its win-win elegance, the plan was classic Gladys.

As Sandy and I arrived in Westborough on this particular Christmas, we were somewhat prepared for the shift in atmosphere. We knew already that Jeff had been passed over for a promotion and was suffering a crisis of confidence. Jeff works for a small company that manufactures insert pads for shoes, similar to the Dr. Scholl's brand, but providing a low cost alternative. Joe, the Vice President of Marketing and Jeff's boss, had accepted a position with another company. As a product manager, Jeff was Joe's only assistant. Not unreasonably, he had expected to be promoted into the vacancy. Instead, the company was conducting a search to bring in somebody from the outside.

Jeff's problem was multilayered. On the surface, at the most elemental level, he was hurt and bewildered over being rejected for a job he was convinced he could do expertly. After all, he reasoned, he had apprenticed under the tutelage of a master. For seven years, Jeff had been learning from Joe the art, the techniques, and the conceptual underpinnings of the marketing trade. He had taken on assignments, responsibilities and projects covering every facet of the marketing craft. And Joe had recognized his growing skills with effusive praise in one performance review after another. Even more significant—from Jeff's perspective—was the fact that as a team they had contributed mightily to the company's bottom line. Wasn't *that* the bottom line, the acid test, the incontrovertible proof of his value to the company? Revenues had skyrocketed during his time there, climbing from less than $10 million to more than $30 million in the period he and Joe had worked together, an average annual growth rate of 17%. This was far above the industry average, signaling a whopping gain in market share. Profits, too, had soared. The marketing team had provided splendid results, and Jeff had his incentive bonuses in the bank to prove it. So, then, didn't it stand to reason that Joe should help him get the job? Well, then, why didn't that happen? Why didn't Joe persuade them to give him the promotion? Reasonably or unreasonably, hostility against Joe was starting to take root in Jeff, an emotional ulcer that was increasingly poisoning his normally placid disposition with the rancid bile of curdled resentment.

Jeff's unhappiness was compounded by the recognition that he was caught in the grip of his own corrosive and unproductive emotions. He was dismayed at how his feelings were running away with him. He knew very well that everyone suffers reversals in life, as often as not undeserved, and that there was no reason why he should be immune from the human condition. And he recognized full well that what happened to him might be demoralizing, but was not tragic. It wasn't the death of one of his girls, it wasn't even like Christopher Reeves falling off a horse. It was just a better job he didn't get. He should get over it. He should get a life. That's precisely what he would say if it happened to anybody else. And he knew very well that he *would*, in time, get over it. But none of that helped right now, none of that changed anything. His feelings of hurt and betrayal were *his feelings*, dammit, he was *entitled* to feel his feelings, so by God he was going to feel them.

Moreover, beneath the surface, underlying the immediate issue of his standing in the company, was a deeper discomfiture. Oddly, perhaps, it was related to the fact that Jeff doesn't really like living in Portland. To understand, you have to know how nice Portland actually is. It's the kind of city that writers of magazine articles call "livable." With a population of 62,000, Portland is holding its own as a regional economic center for southern Maine. It also attracts tourists. Indeed, Sandy and I enjoy one or two day trips there up every year; it's a two-hour drive. We arrive in time for lunch at a waterfront bar that serves great burgers and the local Shipyard beer. Then we spend the afternoon meandering around the Old Port district, an ancient commercial area brought back to life with boutiques, restaurants, art galleries and souvenir shops. It's small but charming, with a minimum of national retail chains and a maximum of quirky local entrepreneurs. If we arrive early enough in the morning we also take in the Art Museum, whose rotating shows are afflicted by an uncritical partiality to contemporary fads and fancies but whose permanent collection is very good: eclectic, sophisticated and grounded in quality. In the evening we usually join Jeff and Sharon for an early dinner, either at their house or at one of the many good restaurants in town. Typically, we're back in Boston by nine thirty or so.

So, it's not that Jeff dislikes Portland, exactly, he just hates living there. He yearns for life in the big city. He misses the excitement, the energy, the never-ending experience of discovery that you find only in a genuine metropolis. To him, small cities are just dull.

Jeff's move to Portland had been predicated on a rudimentary calculation: sacrifice living environment in the pursuit of career objectives. Now everything was complicated. Following Sharon's move to Portland to be with him, she had come to love it there. For her, the move to Portland had been a slam-dunk success. Not only had the relationship worked out, so had the city. Everything about it delights her. To Sharon, a small city is ideal. It means a living environment that offers everything anyone actually needs while remaining manageable, friendly and more or less hassle free. It means minimal traffic, minimal fear, and a public school system in which she has confidence. She doesn't identify at all with Jeff's complaint. She is baffled by it. "What can't we find here?" she asks him. "We have more restaurants than we can ever go to. We have movies, plays, music.

What exactly are we missing that you want to do?" Sharon points out that they can, and do, go to Boston any time they want. Ken and Gladys delight in taking care of the girls for a day or a weekend while she and Jeff cavort in the big city to their hearts' content. So as far as Jeff's problem is concerned, she likens it to Gertrude Stein's description of Los Angeles: "There is no there there."

Jeff can't explain. For Sharon, it is a matter of logic. For him, logic is beside the point; instead, it is all about how where you are governs how you feel. It's an intangible: it can't be measured but it is real nonetheless. Just as some people feel at home and at peace in the countryside, Jeff feels most alive and at home in the city. In a big city, what Jeff feels most is a sense of limitless possibilities. It's not, as Sharon would have it, about going to some place or other to hear music. The pulse of the city itself *is* the music. It's not about going to a theater to see a play. The city itself is an arena where the struggle, the sorrow, the triumph, the contest of everyday human striving *is* the play. In the great cities there is an aura of vitality, an electric charge of human intent and purpose which crackles and snaps; it energizes Jeff, brings him to life. But Portland … Portland just doesn't have any of this.

Thus the problem for Jeff is this: It is his way to look at and evaluate the facets of his life as a balance of plusses and minuses. One constellation in the overall balance is related to Portland. So long as his career was gaining lift and Sharon was happy, then despite his feelings about cities the debits and credits for Portland added up on the plus side, a net positive. But with the job soured, the balance was altered. As a result, some of his basic life choices were called into question. He had accepted the job in Portland *even though* it was in Portland on the premise that it would be a great career move. Now it seemed that this decision had been a massive screw-up. With his career derailed, his ability to get it back on track would be severely limited if restricted to local employment possibilities, yet now that Sharon was so attached to the area it would be hell to get her to move anyplace else. He felt trapped. Doomed.

And there was yet another factor in Jeff's distress, the worry that most characterized the episode as a crisis of confidence. Jeff was troubled—more than troubled: he was *haunted*—by his acknowledgement that the reason he was given for having been denied the promotion might be valid. The president of the company had told him that his marketing abilities were appreciated but his human relations skills were deficient. This didn't matter in his current job, he was told, because his role was self-contained. But they didn't consider him a candidate for upper management because in that capacity he would be supervising other people internally and representing the company externally. Such responsibilities placed a premium on interpersonal relationships. Jeff was lacking in this area, he was told.

When I heard about this from Sandy, who learned of it from Sharon, I couldn't say I was surprised. Jeff's personality *is* rather prickly, in marked contrast to the warmth and empathy which emanates from his brother Jim. Nor could he be described as communicative. Actually, the word I would use is word taciturn. When Jeff does say something, it is not infrequently something critical about the folly of somebody else. He's not without a sense of humor, but neither would he qualify as "fun loving." In this regard, Sandy once captured Jeff perfectly in a delicious turn of phrase when she referred to his "disdain for frivolity."

If you're wondering why a person like this pursues a career in marketing, you may be confusing marketing with sales. Marketing, as opposed to sales, is primarily a technical discipline; imagination is important but people skills are secondary. Marketing has to do with analysis of product functionality and design, packaging, pricing, advertising, and promotional activities. Sales, on the other hand, is driven by interaction with customers, and requires finely tuned sensitivities to their needs and motivations. Thus, for example, the marketing department develops a line of copiers, then Ralph goes out and sells them. But the requirements for success converge at the executive levels: good management in any business function requires people skills of the highest order. Jeff's company valued him as a savvy marketer but thought he'd make a lousy manager.

For Jeff, hearing this was a blow. He had never before considered any such thing, never imagined his personality would be a problem. He had always prided himself on his intelligence, his honesty, his integrity, his disavowal of the phoniness of office politics as a route to success, and more than anything else his forthright unwillingness to sugar coat the truth. Now he was being told that these very qualities, the ones he prized the most, were obstacles to his advancement because he wasn't "diplomatic" enough.

He was rocked. What if that were true? What if his career had peaked at thirty-four? Was he consigned to career purgatory, stuck at the junior management level for the remaining thirty years of his working life, forever implementing the decisions of others but never in charge? Or should he try to start over somewhere else? If so, what were his chances of landing a suitable opportunity in a hick burg like Portland, especially with the kind of lukewarm recommendations he'd be getting now? See, he was thinking, *what did I tell you*: no matter how you look at it, it keeps coming back to the fact that Portland is nothing but a small town. He hated being stuck there. Detested it. And he had no one to blame but himself.

My own reaction to Jeff's vexation was more accepting than Sharon's, Sandy's, and perhaps others in the family. As I share Jeff's sentiments about cities, I understood more than anybody else where he was coming from on that score. And equally could I relate to a career setback; I've had a few along the way. But also, in a manner of speaking—a manner not flattering to myself—I was grateful that a situation like this had arisen. This sounds terrible, I know. And it's not that I wished Jeff ill fortune, quite the contrary. But his difficulties had the beneficial effect of allowing me to have a more rounded view of him, more dimensional, less perfect, less—I must confess—intimidating.

In my admiration for Jeff, I wanted, indeed I still want now, the same kind of effortless rapport with him that I have with Jim. That still hasn't happened. But before Jeff's setback, I had always blamed myself. It was silly, I know, but I felt that if our interaction was less than easygoing and companionable, it was due to some inadequacy in me, or one that he perceived in me. As illogical and unfounded as it was, I couldn't help myself from feeling that Jeff was judging me, and finding me wanting somehow. It wasn't that he was hostile. He was usually gracious and never less than courteous. But he was never more than courteous, either. He would answer my questions but never inquire about my life and would never volunteer anything personal about himself. Whereas I would ask about his work, his experiences, his opinions, and he would respond, he almost never reciprocated by expressing an interest in mine. I long ago concluded that if he didn't express any interest it meant he didn't have any. It shouldn't matter, and it wasn't a huge deal. But it was disconcerting. What it boiled down to is that when we visited with them in Portland, it was Sharon I looked forward to seeing and enjoyed conversing with.

Sandy told me all along to just relax. "Don't worry about it," she would say, "It's not you. It's just the way my brother is." I believed her and yet for many years it didn't help. Because I held Jeff in such esteem, I always wanted him in particular to like me. Now, finally, I was able to remove him from the pedestal upon which I alone, unbidden, had placed him. It was a relief. In revealing his vulnerabilities, Jeff had lifted from me the self-imposed burden of revering him. And so, finally, I was able to do what Sandy recommended: relax.

Interestingly, Jeff and I do share one narrow interest where we connect with effortless fun and joy. We both love jazz. More than that, we both love the same kind of jazz. We discovered this quite by accident, not long after Sandy and I started dating. Jeff and I were watching the news in the Legato's den. Some blowhard politician was pontificating smugly on screen, and Jeff muttered, "Your mind is on vacation but your mouth is working overtime."

I looked at him, astonished. He had just quoted a line from a blues song, a song not part of general pop culture but known well enough among jazz aficionados. "Mose Allison," I said. That's the name of the singer on what is considered the definitive recording of the song. Equally surprised, Jeff looked back at me and said, "Yep." He nodded in appreciation of my expertise, with what I hoped was a new respect.

Though this incident didn't lead to us becoming pals, it did spark an ongoing game of playful one-upmanship. In the manner that men often challenge each other with sports disputes *(which was the better team, the 1970 Orioles or the 1927 Yankees?)* and sports trivia *(who was the latest National League player to hit a home run in his first major league at bat?)*, we would do the same with jazz. For example, he might say, "Who was the best be-bop trumpeter? Dizzy Gillespie?" Dizzy Gillespie was an all time great, and the challenge implicit in Jeff's question was for me to think of someone better. Louis Armstrong wouldn't work. Armstrong was surely an all time great, but not in the be-bop idiom. "Clifford Brown," would be my answer in this case. It is a worthy response and we would enjoy the next couple of minutes arguing the relative merits of Gillespie and Brown.

On occasion, our mutual interest led to instances of genuine warmth and bonding. Once, I remember, Sandy and I were at the movies with Jeff and Sharon. The film was "Kissing Jessica Stein." At the very beginning, underneath the title sequence, the music was a jazzy rendition of the show tune "Put on A Happy Face." Within seconds, Jeff and I turned toward each other and at exactly the same instant whispered, "Blossom Dearie," the name of the singer. Recognizing Blossom Dearie's voice, and knowing who she was, linked us together as members of a fairly exclusive club. It was a sweet moment.

But in my relationship with Jeff the jazz connection was the exception. Detachment was the rule. So Jeff was not about to open up about his troubles on Christmas day at the Legatos. My information was strictly through Sandy via Sharon. My perception, then, may have been colored by what I already knew. But it did seem to me that Jeff seemed even more subdued than usual. It was subtle. When I asked Sandy if she noticed it, she was dismissive. She said, sarcastically, "You mean my brother, that madcap *bon vivant*? How can you tell?" Yikes. Sandy can be tough sometimes, especially on her own family.

Still, we had forewarning about Jeff's mood of dejection. Discovering that all was not well with Bonnie and Ralph was a shock. It was more than obvious from the outset that something was wrong. There was none of their usual affectionate teasing between them. There was none of their usual billing and cooing. The body language was defensive and distant.

We had the chance to observe this right away during the gift opening phase. At the Legatos, the presents come first on Christmas day. Ken and Gladys see no benefit in making the kids wait any longer than necessary to open their gifts. They figure, what's the harm in making the kids happy. At that point, of course, the "kids" were only Sally and Heather, Sharon and Jeff's girls. Sweethearts they are, too. Despite my indifference to kids in general, these two have captured my heart.

Sally, who was eight—almost nine—at the time, is full of adventure and mischief, laughter and fun, with charm to spare. She loves it when I let her tickle me, and squeals in delight as she ignores my admonishments to stop. She also loves jokes. Now, I can't tell a joke to save my life, but I can read them. And so, as with Jim and the cigars, Sally and I also have a tradition. I read her jokes and riddles that I have found in books, magazines and on the net, and that I think she'll be able to understand. That's the hard part, calibrating to her level of understanding. But I do OK, I think. This day I had a couple of riddles for her. Question: How do you keep a noisy dog off the street? Answer: Put him in a barking lot. All right, it wasn't all *that* good. Hey, *you* try to find a joke that an eight year old will understand.

I did better with Heather. For her, I had this ancient chestnut that I first remember hearing from Rodney Dangerfield: The other day I went to the doctor. He told me I was very very sick. I said, "Doctor, I want a second opinion." He said, "OK, you're ugly, too!"

"Bada Boom!," went Jeff, who was listening.

But it did get a smile this time out of Heather, which was an achievement. Heather is two years older than Sally, and poles apart in personality. Where Sally is sunny, Heather is somber. Heather is serious about everything, all the time. She was the most grown up ten year old I have ever met. She cares deeply about other people and it is her mission to see to it that everyone is OK. As a result, she is always anxious. But she is also smart, incredibly so. Her level of understanding, her grasp on reality, is far beyond her years. It's unnerving, almost. It would be scary if behind it weren't so much sweetness, so much kindness, so much love. In any case, tickling is not the game I play with Heather. Chess is. She wins sometimes, legitimately. Granted, I'm hardly a Grand Master. But if my concentration wavers even briefly, I'm dead. Imagine, check mated by somebody less than eleven years old. When that happens, I'm slightly embarrassed but also impressed as all get out.

Sometimes it worries me that Heather acts so grown up. I fret that she is missing out on her childhood. Where is the silliness, the unselfconscious play, the merriment free of all burden of emotional freight that is supposed to define being a kid?

One time, I offered to Sandy an hypothesis as to the reason for Heather's preternatural maturity. I suggested that it might be traced to Sharon's divorce. Almost six at that time, Heather was just old enough to be aware of what was going on. Perhaps, I imagined, Sharon was devastated by the end of her marriage, and Heather felt it was up to her to bring her Mom come out of her depression. I envisioned Heather making peanut butter sandwiches for Sharon, sorting the laundry, playing with Sally, and doing everything else she could think of to help out. I imagined her initiating earnest conversations with Sharon in which she assured her mother that everything would work out and they would be happy again. And then, sure enough, it happened. Within six months of the day Heather's father kissed her good bye and left the marriage, Sharon met Jeff, and things did get better. Within a year after that they had moved north to Portland to live in Jeff's house. Nine months later Sharon and Jeff made it official, and Heather had a stepdad. Mother and daughters alike found themselves warm, secure and comfy in the embrace of Jeff's devotion. Things were not merely better, they were better than ever. It was not unreasonable, I surmised, for Heather in her own mind to take at least partial credit for the improvement. She had worked hard for it. And if she believed her efforts, her support, and her caring had made a difference, it was not unreasonable for the experience to be life shaping. She would, naturally, want to keep on making things better in the precise manner experience had taught her would work.

When I floated this theory to Sandy, she shrugged and said, "Could be." Sandy is not much into explaining people's behavior with simple insights that tie everything up in a neat package with a pretty bow. She thinks people are much too complicated for that, not to mention messy, inconsistent and even self-contradictory. I know that she is right, but I can't resist doing it anyway.

In any event, while Heather and Sally—and afterwards all the rest of us—were opening gifts, I was noticing trouble between Bonnie and Ralph. Sandy was too, I could tell. They were not the type of couple that routinely has tiffs. This figured to be a doozy.

The frost between Bonnie and Ralph persisted through dinner. I knew Sandy would tell me all about it on the way home. I assumed that mother, sister and sister-in-law would pry the story out of Bonnie as they gathered in the kitchen to clean up. I expected Bonnie to spill the beans with little resistance, her reticence to air dirty laundry no match against her yearning for understanding, sympathy and perhaps practical help.

To the charge that I enjoy not having to do dishes at the Legatos, I plead *nolo contendre*. The presence of men is not expected in the kitchen at any time, other than to carve a bird or a roast. This was a rule decreed by Ken early on in his marriage in an era when he could still get away with such a thing. Now the practice is so ingrained that nobody thinks that challenging it would be worth the battle. Even Sharon, a relative newcomer to the family who would never tolerate such a regressive anachronism at home, pitches in like the good sport she is and cuts Jeff some slack by not making an issue of it.

Hence, after everyone was stuffed with apple pie a la mode, and Heather and Sally had modeled to admiring ooh's and aah's the new party dresses from Grandma and Grandpa, it was time for my walk with Jim. The day was spectacular. The temperature was mild, mild for December in New England anyway, the sky deep blue and crystal clear. Five inches of pristine suburban snow on spacious Westborough lawns reflected a brilliant white in the sunshine. As we stopped at the end of the driveway to light our cigars, I enjoyed one of those elusive flushes of total well being, the rare sensation of tasting life at its sweetest. My health was good. So was Sandy's. My career was hitting on all cylinders. My family was fine. My marriage was great. And I wasn't all that concerned about the Legatos. I had every faith that Jeff would find a way to recover his equilibrium. And I assumed that whatever was bothering Bonnie and Ralph would blow over. Yeah, I was clueless.

First off, I asked Jim if he knew what was going on with Bonnie. He didn't. He said that today was the first inkling he had of any problem. I had pretty much anticipated that, since it was clear that Sandy too had been caught off guard. Sandy was a key node in the family communication network, and if she didn't know about something, it was likely that Jim was in the dark as well.

I was, however, a bit surprised to learn he was also unaware that Jeff was having a problem. Jim reminded me that the Legato communication infrastructure was actually composed of females, and since he didn't live with any of the family women he was often out of the loop. So I told him as much about Jeff as I knew.

This led to a second surprise for me. When I asked Jim if he thought Jeff might come to him for spiritual guidance to help him through his rough patch, Jim said, "I doubt it. He's an atheist."

"Really?" I said. "You've talked about it?"

Jim shrugged. "Somewhat. It's more that *he* talks about it. He thinks that because he's my brother, it gives him the right to show me the error of my ways. I mostly just listen. I don't argue."

I was fascinated. "What does he say?"

"He says that religion is illogical and irrational and he's not going to base his life on something that doesn't make sense."

"Ouch. And what do you say?"

"I say that Catholicism is not science. It's not mathematics. It's not subject to proof. It is a faith."

"Does it make you mad?"

"More sad than mad. Jeff is missing out on the peace of the Lord. And it's his own choice. He has closed the door on God. If God can't get in, He can't deliver on his promise of grace. It's like they say on the TV commercials: The offer is void where prohibited."

I had many additional questions, but I sensed that Jim was more bothered by this topic than he cared to let on. So I let the matter drop.

Riding home in the car with Sandy, we had lots to talk about.

"So?" I asked as we pulled away from the curb.

"Doesn't sound good," said Sandy. And then she related the story.

As you might expect, Gladys had not wasted a minute. She was all over Bonnie the instant the women hit the kitchen. Bonnie had been dreading this moment, but knew there was no escaping it.

"I honestly don't know that's going on," she began. "I honestly don't. But it's been going on since the weekend after Thanksgiving. He's moody, distant, nervous. He's a completely different person. All of a sudden I don't know my own husband."

Gladys honed in on the "all of a sudden." "That's the week you found out about the baby."

"Yes, Ma," Bonnie answered. "But I don't think that's it. He was fine the day the test results came back. He was great. When I called him at the office to let him know the outcome, he sounded excited. I told him I'd cook us a special dinner to celebrate, and when he came home he surprised me with a bottle of champagne. I had to tell him: no more alcohol for me in the next nine months. So you know what he did? He went right out to the store and came back with a bottle of non-alcoholic champagne. What could be sweeter than that? And then the rest of the week he was fine too. He was fine when we were here on Thanksgiving."

Sandy remembered what I told her about my conversation with Ralph that day, but thought it best not to bring it up.

Sharon asked what happened on the weekend.

Bonnie said, "It was Friday after work. I stopped at the supermarket. When I got home there was a message on our voice mail for Ralph, from a man named Cap. Ralph was quiet already when he got home that day. When I mentioned the message he shut down completely. Saturday and Sunday were a little better, but I couldn't get him to tell me what was wrong. Every time I asked, he said he was recovering from a bad day at work."

Bonnie got quiet. Gladys broke the silence: "Why don't you get to the point."

Bonnie looked at the floor, then stared out the window, unable to face her mother as she remembered their talk after the Bermuda trip. Then the dam burst. "My point is that he won't tell me what's wrong. He's closed up inside a shell. He won't come out and he won't let me in. All he says is it's not me and it's not the baby. He says not to worry, it'll pass. But I'm worried sick. He won't tell me *anything!* That's what driving me crazy. I can't stand it any more. I'm afraid, Ma. Our marriage is falling apart because he refuses to communicate, and I can't figure out what to do about it. I can't believe it, Ma. On Thanksgiving I am so happy I'm overflowing. Two days later everything turns to dust. And Ma, I'm not just scared, I'm angry too."

You're angry *because* you're scared, Sandy realized.

Bonnie wasn't finished. "I don't deserve this. I've been a perfect wife. Happily. Whenever we've had differences, we've always worked them out without much trouble. There's no reason for this. No reason, Ma, why he shouldn't tell me. I resent it, Ma. I resent that he won't trust me to be there for him. I love him. Until now he's been a great husband. Whatever it is, I'll support him. We'll see it through together. I resent it, Ma. Why won't he trust me, Ma, to be there for him? That's what hurts. He owes me that trust, I've earned it. I don't understand. When we talk at all now, it's just to argue about him telling me. Ma … Ma, please don't say it. You were right. I'll save you the trouble and beat you to it: You told me so."

At this last, Sandy and Sharon turned toward each other and exchanged *"what was that about?"* looks. But neither thought it a good idea to ask. So instead, Sandy said, "It sounds to me like Ralph is in some kind of serious trouble, and is pretty afraid himself. Maybe he thinks he's doing a good deed by protecting you from it."

Bonnie shot a scornful stare back at Sandy. "Well du-uh! The point is, whatever he's afraid of, he should give me the respect of believing in me enough to trust I can handle it, that we can face it together. I deserve that respect. Anyway, what is the worst it could be? Is he ill? If he's ill, he can't hide it forever. If he's in legal trouble, we'll get the best lawyer and fight it. If he ends up in jail, I won't abandon him, I'll visit him. With the baby. If he's in financial trouble, so what? I like the car, sure, but if we have to sell it, so what? I love the house, sure, but if we have to sell it and move into a little apartment, I can deal with that even. If he goes bankrupt, we just start over. The main thing is we'll still be a family. That's the most important thing. Anything is better than the way it is now. Anything."

The ensuing silence made everyone uncomfortable. At length, Bonnie spoke up. When she did, she didn't hide her irritation. "All right," she said, "I know just what you're thinking. You're thinking, *'Did I tell him all this? Does Ralph know how I feel?'* My God! How stupid do you all think I am? Of course I told him all this. He knows very well how I feel. I've told him many times. But it didn't change anything. Ma, what do I do?"

This time even Ma was at a loss. The best she could come up with was an invitation for Bonnie to move home for a while in order to get a break away from the situation. Maybe it would help Ralph get his bearings too.

Bonnie hated that idea. "No, Ma, I'm not doing that. First of all, this isn't my home. My home is in Newton, with Ralph. Second, it's completely the wrong message. My message is that I am with him no matter what. Staying here takes that message and tears it up into confetti. Thanks but no thanks, Ma."

And there the matter rested, unresolved.

As Sandy finished telling me about this in the car, I glanced in her direction and said, "You know what I'm thinking, don't you?"

"Sure," she answered. "Nobody has addressed the real problem. The real problem is not what's going on now between Bonnie and Ralph. The real problem is whatever the flaw is in Ralph's character that got him sucked into trouble in the first place."

"You got it," I said.

The rest of the ride home we were quiet. We listened to the Christmas carols on the CD and let our thoughts drift. The ecstasy of total well being was long gone, but it was replaced with something better: renewed appreciation for my immense good fortune in having met and married, now and forever, the woman sitting next to me.

5

On Wednesday of the week following New Year's, Ralph had a traffic accident that wasn't an accident. That, too, was in the police report. Filling in a few blanks, we think it went something like this:

Ralph's office is in Framingham, not far from the Sheraton where he met Cap. Framingham is a thickly settled suburb west of Boston, along the Turnpike. The geographic, business and population center of the area known locally as Metrowest, the town is a chaotic jumble of commercial strips, office parks, R&D labs, residential subdivisions, apartment complexes and shopping malls. It has a state college *and* a state prison. People tend to loathe it or love it. Detractors look down elitist noses at the 20 screen multiplex, the chain restaurants and the big box retailers, or merely think the place is an urban planner's nightmare of an unholy mess. I am fond of it, except for the traffic. To me it's jazz.

Ralph's office is near the old central business district. When Ralph heads home he drives about a mile through regular city streets before reaching the commercial strip and the Turnpike entrance. These streets have curbside parallel parking, traffic lights, crosswalks and all the other accoutrements of an urban grid. Ralph takes the same route every day. This day at 5:00 PM, the goon from the Sheraton bar is parked on one of those streets.

Another of Cap's goons is in a car in the parking lot connected to Ralph's building. He has a photo of Ralph in his hands, and he's concentrating on the flow of people exiting the building in order to match a face to the picture. Being January it's dark, but as a result of security lighting installed after 9/11, the doorway and parking area are brightly illuminated. Goon number two is a slight, wiry guy in his mid-twenties, a goon-in-training you might say. He admits to some anticipatory jitters about botching the job, but in fact it proves easy to recognize Ralph as he walks out the door. The ID is confirmed when Ralph gets into his Lexus.

Goon number two dials a number on his cell phone. Goon number one, parked on the street, answers on his: "Yeah?"

"It's Morty. Collins is pulling out of the parking lot now."

"K."

While Ralph was walking to his car, Morty had positioned his so that he will precede Ralph out of the lot. Thus begins a maneuver which is carefully choreographed. Rush hour traffic in Framingham center is a maddening crawl, and is unlikely to flow past goon number one at greater than fifteen miles an hour. But Morty's job now is to precede Ralph and make absolutely sure that he can go no faster than that even if the street should be unaccountably clear.

It isn't. Traffic conditions are normal, and Ralph is following Morty through the congestion with no idea that anything is going on. Goon number one glances at his watch occasionally but otherwise is focused on the scene in his side view mirror. Three minutes. Four minutes. There! He sees Morty's car approaching. Behind it is the silver Lexus. Good.

The stream of cars is gliding by slowly. Morty passes by. Then Ralph is there. Goon number one, already in gear with the wheels turned, stomps on the gas and swerves out. He smashes into the right rear door of the Lexus.

Ralph jams on the brakes. He can't believe it. "What in fucking hell?!?!" He turns around and stares at the driver. "Stupid asshole shithead!" he mutters.

Goon number one reverses back into his space. Morty, hearing the crash, lets out his breath with the relief of mission accomplished. He pulls to a stop a few yards ahead. Ralph storms out of the Lexus and starts shouting at the other driver: "You idiot! You stupid fuckin' idiot! How could you pull out into a continuous line of traffic without looking?" Ralph walks around to the right side of his car to inspect the damage. He is looking at the crumpled sheet metal and wondering if the frame is bent. It's going to be a hell of a lot more to fix than his $500 deductible. Meanwhile, goon number one has gotten out of the driver's side of his car and is standing just about three feet away. Ralph is repeating, "Oh my God. Oh my God. Oh my God." Then he looks at goon number one. Who is this imbecile, this reckless asshole who smashed the side of his car? He is trying to understand how anyone could do something so incomprehensible.

The man lets Ralph stew for a few seconds. Then he gives Ralph the middle finger and says, "Cap sends his regards." He turns, walks down to Morty's car, gets in the passenger side, and takes off with Morty. All the traffic is backed up behind Ralph, so the street ahead is clear. They are gone in a flash.

Ralph comprehends plenty now.

So what to do? Careful. Think it through. First thing is to get his car out of the way. OK. He gets back in, drives to the corner, and finds a parking spot on a residential side street. Now ... He has to report the incident. He has to, otherwise the insurance will not pay off on the collision damage. But he can't admit to the trouble he is in. After several minutes he has decided on his story, and calls the police on his cell phone.

Ralph waits by the goon's damaged car parked on the main street, and flags down the police cruiser when it arrives. He tells the cop that some idiot pulled out into traffic without looking and hit him on the side. Instead of waiting, the idiot ran down the sidewalk, turned the corner, and disappeared from sight. "He just ran away," says Ralph, "I thought of chasing him but I didn't think I could catch him."

Ralph shows the cop the damage on the goon's car. They walk to the Lexus, and view the damage there. The cruiser is still in the traffic lane next to the goon's car, blue lights flashing. They return there and the cop calls in the plate number on the other car. Both of them anticipate the news that comes back: the vehicle has been reported stolen.

Ralph gives a description of the man driving the stolen car. He describes me. Ralph is not trying to get me in trouble. He just thinks that his description will come off more convincingly if he has a real person in mind. He chooses me because I have no distinguishing features, and because I am unlikely to have a mug shot on file.

Back in his car, the police finished and gone, Ralph hyperventilates for a while. As the force of what has just happened penetrates, he is carried to the brink of panic. It's a good fifteen minutes before he calms down enough to begin marshalling a coherent thought process. After another fifteen minutes, he drives to Dunkin Donuts, near the Natick entrance to the Turnpike, where there's a pay phone. He dials Cap's number. Ralph is hugely relieved when the system puts him into voice mail. He leaves a message: "This is Collins. I received your greetings. I'd like to meet with you."

The ramming, as Ralph is beginning to call it, is the culmination of his month from hell. Ralph sits in his damaged Lexus in the Dunkin' Donuts parking area, rehearsing the whole of it in his mind.

The worst of it is how he messed up with Bonnie. He knows that his behavior with her was exactly the opposite of what it should have been. He should have been acting warm, loving and attentive. Instead he has walled himself off, and Bonnie has freaked out. What elset could he expect? So he can't blame her for being upset. He's been stupid. Suppose … just suppose … that he decides to go through with the … he can't bring himself to say the word yet … with Cap's … suggestion. Suppose. So look what he's done. What would happen? What would happen is that the cops would go and ask everybody in the family, "Did you notice anything unusual about Bonnie or Ralph recently?" Obviously they'd ask that. And obviously everybody will answer, "Yes. Right after Thanksgiving, Ralph suddenly started treating Bonnie like shit." Oh God. He's been so stupid. Stupid. Stupid. Stupid.

But then, he couldn't help himself. Can't help himself. If it were just the pressure from Cap, maybe he could deal with it. Maybe he could pretend to Bonnie that everything is hunky dory, buy some time to sort out his options. But he's cut off from betting right now, and it's driving him bonkers. Oh for the halcyon days—was it only four or five years ago?—when he could dial up a sports book on the internet, type in a credit card number, and be in on the action in an instant. He had a good life then. No longer. Those days are gone. The Chief turns off the spigot of credit, and bingo he is out of the action. There is nothing but cold turkey withdrawal. He is shut down. Locked out. Boxed in. He might as well have been mainlining heroin, the heebie-jeebies are so bad. He can't stand living in his own skin. He can't sleep, he can't watch TV, his work is suffering. He can't even get it up any more; he couldn't patch things up that way with Bonnie even if he wanted to.

But he doesn't want to. Dammit, no! Why should he? It's her fault, dammit, that all this trouble has happened. If she didn't spend so damn much money all the time, there would be enough cash to keep his account current with the Chief and none of this disaster would be happening. He certainly wouldn't have some palooka twisting his arm to have her killed. His car wouldn't look like it was in a God damned demolition derby.

And the way she spends, it's unbelievable. "Oh honey, it's so hot today, why can't we go out to eat tonight?" "Waddaya mean, hot? The house is air conditioned." "I know, honey, but we don't have anything good in the house for dinner and I didn't feel like stopping on the way home 'cause it's so hot." "I can't win, can I?" "No honey, not really, but you do get a reward. I'll put on that royal blue dress with the halter top you like so much." "There's another shoe to drop in this plan, isn't there?" "Well, you know, honey, that place downtown that everybody's talking about, Clio? Wouldn't that be great? You said yourself you wanted to try it." And she is indeed a vision of loveliness in that that blue halter top dress. But for the next three hours the meter is not just running, it is running amok: a dinner tab of $150, a tip of $30, $16 for parking, $3 in tolls. Two hundred bucks out the window 'cause it's a hot day. It's July for Chris' sakes, of course it's hot. Why couldn't he just have a steak from the freezer and a beer from the fridge. That's all he wanted, f'Chris' sakes.

Ralph is revisiting all his grievances. The house! He bought a fine home in an excellent neighborhood because it's a good investment. To her, this means that there is a bottomless pit of money for furnishing and decorating the damn thing. You think Bonnie would be content to fill it with stuff from Jordan's, Macy's, Bernie & Phyl's, places where normal people go? Not in your life. Not Bonnie. Specialty stores she needs. Custom cabinet makers. Creator showrooms. European design centers. Thaaaaaaat's Bonnie!

Clothing? Bonnie has stuffed the master bedroom closets and bureaus with so much crap that Ralph's things are displaced to a closet and bureau in a secondary bedroom. And vacations! Yeah, getting away is good. But what's wrong with the beach in North Carolina? Nothing is wrong with it. North Carolina has 250 miles of great beaches. So where does Bonnie have to go? Venice. Not Venice, California. Venice, *Italy*. The Euro is cheap, she says. What does she know? Yeah, it used to be cheap, but now it's in the stratosphere. You know how many God damn Euros it takes to buy a drink in friggin' Venice Italy? How many expensive dollars it takes to get to Venice, Italy. You know how she wants to get there? She wants to take the friggin' Orient Express all the way from friggin' Paris. A romantic adventure, she calls it.

On and on it goes. She's the reason there's no money any more to pay off Cap. Before she came along there was never any problem. If something happens now in a way it's her own fault. She's the one that's got him in this position. If it weren't for her he'd be fine.

She's the obstacle....

"*Wait a minute*," you must be thinking by now. This is crazy. It doesn't make any sense. *Bonnie* isn't the problem, Ralph is. Yes, that is true. But Ralph is an addict, and he is thinking like one. The logic of an addict is different from yours and mine.

So with the ramming, Cap has ratcheted up the pressure and as intended it has nudged Ralph across a divide. A seismic shift has taken place. A sea change has happened. Where previously Cap had been the problem, Ralph is just now beginning to see him as the solution. The seed that Cap planted is beginning to sprout.

Bonnie spends all the money.

She's the obstacle.

Ralph is not committed yet. But neither is it unthinkable any more.

He is still sitting in the car at the Dunkin' Donuts when Cap returns his call on the cell phone. Cap tells Ralph that he's out of town and won't be able to get together until Monday. This is a lie. Astutely, Cap is putting in place some time for Ralph to make the necessary psychological adjustment and come to emotional terms with what is going to happen. They agree to meet on Monday after work. Then Ralph calls Bonnie on his cell phone, telling her that he's been in a fender bender—he's fine but the car took a hit. That's why he's delayed, but he's starting for home right now.

Over the next several days, Bonnie is surprised and pleased to find that Ralph's disposition is noticeably improved. At first, mistakenly, she finds this cause for encouragement. He begins the new regime that very evening by keeping Bonnie company in the kitchen while she broils the lamb chops and tosses the salad, drinking his scotch at the kitchen table and telling her about the accident. Bonnie, of course, gets the sanitized police version. After dinner, they go out to the garage where he shows her the damage.

But then, Ralph still won't tell her what was bothering him all last month. And while otherwise he seems pretty much back to normal, there turns out to be a problem in bed. They make an attempt on Saturday afternoon, their first in more than a month, and Ralph can't perform. This in itself is not a big issue for Bonnie; she can be satisfied in ways other than by intercourse, and Ralph accommodates her. But Ralph's chagrin over his own failure is patently genuine. This is precisely what has Bonnie alarmed. There has never been a problem before. It occurs to Bonnie now, for the first time, that the entire episode may have had to do with cheating. Ralph's aberrant behavior may have been a manifestation of guilt, as might his inability to get hard now.

The thought puts Bonnie in a quandary. She desperately wants to know if her suspicions are correct. But they might just as well be unfounded; if that's the case, then confronting Ralph could make him angry and could re-ignite the problem of the previous month, whatever it was. At the same time, if she is correct, it would seem that the episode is over now. So that puts the ball in her court. She would have to decide what to do about it. Would she choose to send Ralph packing? After just one mess up, serious as it may be? No second chance? Leaving her alone with the baby that isn't even born yet? Or should she let it go? Let bygones by bygones? See if the relationship can still work? Try to reestablish her previous positive outlook? And never trust her husband again?

As we now know, Bonnie's anguish is justified but misdirected. Ralph is indeed suffering guilt, but not over any affair. Since the ramming, Ralph has not only turned a corner; he has also become aware that this is the case. Ralph may be sick but he is not a psychopath, so the realization does trigger some serious guilt. Yet the overpowering emotion, the controlling drive, the proximate trigger for the guilt, is relief. It's the relief that comes from making a decision, from offloading the crushing burden of an agonizing choice that is yet to be made. It's the relief of internal conflict resolved. It's the relief of shedding the debilitating tension of ambivalence and uncertainty over what he needs to do. Combined with the anticipatory relief of being in on the action again soon, the emotional pull is becoming irresistible. Guilt notwithstanding, an unstoppable tide is sweeping Ralph toward disaster, and with him the rest of the Legato family.

By Monday evening, Ralph is indeed emotionally ready. At the appointed time of 5:30, Ralph meets Cap in the parking lot of the Turnpike service area just west of the Natick exit. This meeting will take place in Cap's car while driving on the Turnpike so that absolute privacy is guaranteed. This is serious business now, and Cap is taking every precaution. For example, Cap is using his second car, the one that has no EZPass device. EZPass is the electronic toll payment system on the Turnpike, and using it creates a computer record with a date and time stamp recording your passage through a toll booth. This evening Cap will pay tolls in cash. No record.

Cap is waiting, and Ralph pulls into the adjoining parking space. He gets into Cap's car. Cap asks if Ralph wants something to eat before they take off. Ralph says no. He doesn't mention it, but he ate a high protein nutrition bar on the way over so he wouldn't be meeting on an empty stomach.

So Cap pulls out of the parking lot and merges into evening rush hour Turnpike traffic. He has relaxation mood music coming from the CD player. There is an interesting role reversal going on. For once, Ralph is the customer, and Cap is in the process of closing the sale on a really big ticket item.

Cap's initial approach is like that of a real estate broker selling a house. The first step is visualization: get the client to visualize himself living in the house, enjoying its pleasures, reaping its benefits. So Cap begins: "You mostly bet on sports, don't you?"

"Sports, yeah."

"So, who do you like in the Super Bowl?"

"I think Chicago and the Jets will make it this year. I would take Chicago plus six."

"That much better?"

"Definitely. The Chicago offensive line is key. They give Hammond time to find his receivers."

"It would be great if you could bet that game, wouldn't it?"

Ralph is irritated, thinking Cap is rubbing in his predicament. "C'mon, don't yank my chain."

"On the contrary. It's possible," says Cap, turning his head briefly in Ralph's direction to emphasize his point.

"How?" says Ralph, suddenly alert.

"If we make a deal—and that could be by the time I drop you off today—part of the deal will be to reestablish your line of credit with the Chief. I'll be your guarantor. I will guarantee your losses up to a reasonable amount. Then when the insurance pays up, part of the proceeds will go to me to settle up with the Chief. If we shake hands on an agreement today, you could be placing bets tomorrow on the playoffs."

"No shit?"

"Absolutely no shit. In the time it takes me to reach the Chief on the phone, you're in on the action again."

Now they drive a couple of miles without talking. Cap keeps quiet while Ralph absorbs this new information.

After a while, Ralph asks, "How much is reasonable?"

Cap answers, "Ten grand. That's about the amount you lose in an average year. I figure the insurance will pay off in less than a year, so I'm covering you for more than your average burn rate."

Wow, Ralph is thinking. This is incredible. He never expected this. A $10,000 line of credit with the Chief. Tomorrow! It's fantastic. Ralph is joyful. Elated. Momentarily forgetful of the gravity of his situation.

Cap lets him visualize for a while.

They pass by the exit for I-495. They are passing within the town limits of Westborough, and Ralph is reminded of the Legatos. This thought disturbs him less than he thinks it should, and that becomes a reassuring discovery.

After a few miles more, Cap figures visualization has run its course, and he shifts to building rapport. "This is the kind of deal I like best," he says.

Ralph looks at him. "What do you mean?"

"It's win-win," says Cap.

"How?"

Cap explains: "We're partners, you and me. Working together, I'm going to solve your problem, and you are going to pay me handsomely for my services. Better yet, both of us must succeed in our respective roles in order for either one of us to succeed. We have a complete commonality of interests."

"I guess we do," Ralph concedes. Ralph is ready to hold his nose and out of necessity enter a deal with Cap. He is not especially ready to join him at the hip and accept the implications of "partner." Nor is he prepared to take ownership of what he is participating in. He is participating *reluctantly,* out of *necessity.* He is, in effect, a *hostage.* This is not a *choice* he is making. No.

"Everybody benefits," says Cap, "even the Chief."

"La-di-dah," says Ralph, with as much sarcasm as he can muster. "Everybody but Bonnie," he observes. Despite the power of his addiction, Ralph is not without feelings for Bonnie.

In the jargon of the sales profession, this is called an objection. Cap has to find a way to overcome it, or to finesse it. He doesn't know yet whether the problem is a deal breaker, but it's better if he can neutralize it as soon as possible. So he steers the discussion in such a way as to scope out the nature of the issue. "That's gotta be hard for you, thinking about Bonnie."

"Of course it's hard! F'Chris' sakes, what the hell do you think?"

"Still in love with her?"

"Yeah, I still love her. You are one clueless son of a bitch."

"You're gonna miss her."

"Yeah."

"What's gonna be the worst?"

"I don't want to talk about it."

"It's better if you do. Let it out. Deal with the pain. It's important for you to be emotionally prepared. What's gonna be the worst?"

"The worst is that she doesn't deserve this. She's a good person, and she … *does … not …* deserve this."

"Well, it isn't something you're wishing on her. It's not some kind of cruel whim on your part. I don't see how you have any choice."

"You're damn straight about that," Ralph spits out. "Otherwise I damn sure wouldn't be here." The gears of self-justification are fully engaged right now.

Cap keeps pushing. "The circumstances are beyond your control. Otherwise you wouldn't be here. That's right."

"That's what I just said."

"So in the most basic terms, you're doing what you have to do. And if you're only doing what you have to do, you can't feel guilty about that, can you?"

"The thing is, she's a good person and she doesn't deserve it."

"Ralph, I'm going to ask you a question. I'd like a completely honest and candid answer. Will you do that for me?"

"Go ahead. Ask."

"OK. You say Bonnie doesn't deserve this. What I want to know is this: do you really, deep in your heart, believe that Bonnie is completely, 100 percent innocent in relation to your situation?"

The question amazes Ralph. It's as though Cap somehow knows what he's been thinking over the last month. How could that be?

Cap doesn't really know. It is a guess. But it is an educated guess. Cap has had a long career dealing with compulsive gamblers, and he has learned how addicts think. One of the basics is that they usually blame their problems on others. It has merely occurred to Cap that Bonnie would be a likely target for Ralph's displaced self contempt.

For Ralph the immediate question is whether or not he should give in to the temptation to be open with Cap, to share how upset he is with Bonnie over her spending. On the one hand, it is a balm to finally run into somebody who understands him. It's a rare pleasure to have the opportunity to talk honestly with a person who gets it, who will lend a sympathetic ear, who is not going to be judgmental. On the other hand, Ralph is aware that Cap is not a friend. He pretends he is but he's not. He's a business associate. More than that, he is nothing but business. Cap is a shark, a ruthless feeding machine. It just doesn't seem smart to put any trust at all in such an individual.

Ralph ponders all this for a while, taking comfort and finding distraction in watching the fluid, shimmering river of red taillights stretching out ahead in narrowing perspective. From Ralph's silence, Cap infers that he's hit pay dirt. Now it's just a matter of digging deep enough to expose the vein of Ralph's resentment.

Cap lets about five minutes go by. Then he says, "It's the money, isn't it?" To Ralph it appears that Cap is possessed of astonishing insight. In actuality, it merely stands to reason. If Ralph's problem is money, then it is money that is most likely to be his issue with Bonnie.

Warmed by Cap's apparent empathy, Ralph lets his guard down. "Yeah. She's a spender," he allows. "Big time."

Cap likes the direction this is taking. He tries to draw it out, get Ralph to focus on it. "What does she like to buy?"

Ralph knows that in saying anything to Cap on any topic at all, he is courting danger. The risk is high that the information will someday be used against him. But the urge to justify himself is too great to resist. "You name it," he says. "Clothes, furniture, kitchen gadgets. Art—not posters, mind you, but signed limited editions at $2,000 a pop. Restaurants, shows, trips. What doesn't she like to buy?"

At this point, it is Cap who takes a chance, venturing a question out of pure curiosity, aware that the query may backfire. But Ralph as an individual interests him, and he can't stop himself: "Why didn't you shut it down?"

Fortunately for Cap, the question intrigues rather than angers Ralph. No good answer comes to mind. Were Ralph minimally self aware, the answer would be obvious. The answer is, he likes to show off. Feeble protests notwithstanding, Ralph has never done anything to curb Bonnie's spending because her extravagance is proof of how good a provider he is. And through Bonnie, he is able to show off his earnings prowess to the Legatos, his neighbors, and the world at large. In truth, Bonnie never makes any significant expenditures without his approval; for her, the whole *point* of marriage is to make major decisions *together*. And Ralph never fails to provide his approval. Deep down, for the financial testosterone that it signifies, the material excess of their lifestyle is profoundly gratifying.

Ralph, oblivious to this dynamic in his relationship with Bonnie, dismisses Cap's question with a superficial male cliché: "It never seemed worth the argument. Besides, whenever I say OK to something major, we have the greatest sex afterwards. That's an area where I have no complaint whatsoever." Boasting is second nature to Ralph; his DNA requires it.

Cap sees that it's time to move things forward. "Is that what you're going to miss the most? The sex?"

"I don't know," Ralph says. "I'll miss the sex but it's not just that. Bonnie and I get along. At least, we did until Thanksgiving. Our relationship, normally, is comfortable. It's easy. I'll miss that."

"Are you afraid you'll have trouble attracting another woman?"

"No. I hardly think so."

"Then it won't be long until you have somebody else."

"Probably not."

"There are lots of great women, don't you think?"

"I guess."

"The sex can be just as good with somebody else. And new, too. And with a great new woman, things would be better than before."

"Why?"

"Well, for one thing, she won't spend money on things you can't afford. You'll make sure of that. For another, you'll have more money to play with."

"You mean the insurance?"

"Yes, but something else, too. I figure next time around you're going to marry a professional career woman."

"How is that?"

"Simple. No babies. You're not going to make that mistake again. And the woman that's willing to go along with that is most likely to be a dedicated career woman. Don't you think?"

"I guess so."

"So things will be better for you than they are now."

"Could be. But Bonnie still doesn't deserve it. She does spend all my money. But that doesn't mean it's a capital offense punishable by death."

"But you're going to do it anyway."

"As you said before, I have to do what I have to do. But I don't have to feel good about it."

Ralph is manifesting less enthusiasm than Cap was hoping for. He was aiming to get Ralph to embrace the project with zest as the door to a new and better life. He hadn't foreseen that Ralph would get sentimental about his old one. That's how Cap reads the situation: sentimentality. Although married, Cap himself has neither sentiments nor emotional attachments to other people; his marriage is another business deal contracted to obtain the convenience of readily available sex along with the appearance of respectability. Consequently, he fails to grasp that Ralph really does have genuine affection for Bonnie. But no matter. Ralph is indeed going to go ahead with it anyway. He doesn't care a whit about a new life, much less about a new wife. Ralph is driven by his need to start betting again. He is desperate. He is in the grip of the *compulsive* in compulsive gambler. Tomorrow isn't soon enough.

Ralph has reached his limit talking about the painful topic of Bonnie. He's ready to move on to the less agitating and somewhat interesting subject of logistics. "How does this work?" he asks.

Cap says, "Look. I need you to draw me a diagram of the house. We're just about in Worcester. Let me buy you dinner. You can draw me the diagram, and I'll lay out the whole deal."

Ralph agrees. Cap asks if he has to call his wife. Ralph tells Cap that he has already told her that he'd be meeting with a customer for dinner.

Cap leaves the Turnpike in Auburn, the exit for Worcester. He heads north on Rt. 12 a short distance and pulls into the lot for the Picadilly Pub. Picadilly is a small chain of casual eateries in Massachusetts. Cap likes their menu, which is varied; he always finds something that matches his mood.

As they get out of the car, Cap grabs a wirebound notebook from the back seat. After they are seated and the waitress has taken their orders, Cap opens the notebook in front of Ralph and tells him to draw floor plans of his house. He has previously driven by and examined the outside, but needs to know the interior layout. "Basement and both floors," he tells Ralph. "Show the windows."

Ralph is not expert but does a creditable job. Cap understands the layout from the sketches. He hands the notebook back and tells Ralph, "Show where the alarm box is and write down the codes."

Once Ralph is finished, Cap launches his description of the plan. "Here's how it's gonna be. There'll be two guys. Let's call them—I don't know, let's say Jake and ... whatever, I don't know ... Algernon ..."

"Algernon?" Ralph interjects.

"Don't be a smart ass. Just listen to me unless I ask questions. You'll be out of town, preferably with people who know you and can vouch for your whereabouts. It'll be the middle of the night. Say, 3:00 AM. Jake and Algernon will park in walking distance of your house, someplace where the car won't be noticed. Jake will walk to the house, let himself in with the key you are going to provide, and shut the alarm. You got a dog? A cat?"

Ralph shakes his head. "Just tropical fish."

Cap nods. "That's good. Otherwise the racket would wake Bonnie. It wouldn't stop us, but this way there's a sporting chance that she'll still be sleeping when Jake fires the gun. If so, she won't experience any fear, and death will be instantaneous. Jake will be as merciful as possible about it."

"Merciful. That's what you call it?" Ralph grumbles.

Cap is not offended. "I just want you to see that this will be handled professionally. Nothing gratuitous. No sexual assault. As quick and efficient as possible."

Ralph looks up. "How do you know that?"

Cap is quite sure of this. "I know that because that will be the specification of the assignment. And these guys are not junkies off the street. They do this for a living. If they play games, they'll never work again. It's not something you have to worry about.

"Anyway," Cap continues, "Jake will sneak upstairs and complete the assignment. Then he'll page Algernon, who'll drive to the house. Jake will let him in the garage. Your car will be at the airport, so a space will be empty. Next, the two of them will make it look like a burglary. They'll create a forced entry scene, probably cutting the glass from a window. They'll remove a few choice valuables—jewelry, electronics, whatever—you have time to make suggestions. They're going to keep that stuff; think of it as a tip for good service. What do you care? Your homeowner's covers it. They'll ransack the place just a little. Not wanton destruction, just open drawers and tossed garments like they're looking for stuff. I'm assuming you'll drive the Lexus to the airport so the Impala will be there. They're going to take that too. What do you care? The company's insured, they won't lose anything. They'll find Bonnie's purse and from it they'll take the Impala keys and her wallet. Don't forget afterwards to report the credit cards stolen. Then they'll load the goodies into their own car in the garage. Is there a TV in the bedroom?"

"Yes," says Ralph sardonically, "They want that too?"

Cap laughs. "No. They're going to turn it on, fairly loud. It provides an explanation why Bonnie didn't hear the guys enter the house during a (Cap gestures quotation marks with his fingers) "break in". If the police ask about the TV on, you're going to explain that Bonnie told you she does that all the time when you're gone. She misses you when you're out of town and having the TV on is a distraction that helps her get to sleep. Is there a phone in the room?"

"No," Ralph says. "We don't like to be woken up at night by wrong numbers. The upstairs phone is in a guest bedroom."

That's welcome news to Cap. "Good. If she hears an intruder downstairs, it's unlikely she'll leave the master bedroom. By the way, there's no lock on the bedroom door, is there?"

"No."

"Then the chances are that if Bonnie hears something she will lock herself in the bathroom and hope the burglars will take what they want and go away. Do your bathroom doors have locks?"

"No. In fact, we replaced the hardware when we moved in. We didn't want to risk being locked out if somebody has an accident in a bathroom. But what if she hears something and hides in there anyway?"

"That could get messy. Ideally, Jake would brandish his gun to coax her back into the bed. The whole point is to make it seem like a shooting incidental to a burglary. If he has to shoot her in the bathroom, that complicates the story. I'm not too worried, there's little chance of that. My guys know how to be quiet. It's part of their expertise. The odds are very high that she will still be asleep. That's why Jake can't cut the phone line—it would set off the alarm."

Ralph is very, very glad that the waitress arrives just now with his double scotch on the rocks. Cap is having a 7&7. A 7&7? Cripes, Ralph is thinking, how old is this guy? Ralph downs half his scotch in one gulp.

Cap takes a few sips from his glass and continues: "OK. After Bonnie is taken care of, they will load the loot into their car in the garage. How long will it take for the security system to verify the alarm and then for the cops to get there."

Ralph has no idea. He's never had murderers roaming around his house before. He tells Cap what he knows. "When I activated the system, the security people told me cops would arrive in five to six minutes. They would call the house first, then call the police when there is no answer."

"OK. That's why they can't take too much of your stuff. They have to make it look like they were in and out in five minutes. So after they put a few things in their car, Jake will reset the alarm and let it go off. They will leave immediately after that. Jake will drive home. Algernon will take the Impala to a chop shop. That's it."

Ralph doesn't know how Cap will react if he expresses his doubts, but decides to risk it. "I see some holes," he says.

Cap is calm. "Tell me."

Ralph pauses as the waitress shows up, sets down their appetizers, exchanges pleasantries, and moves on. "An awful lot," he begins, "is supposedly happening in those five minutes. The police are supposed to think that strangers, unfamiliar with the interior of the house, set off the alarm when they arrive, find things to steal, find my wife, kill her, find her purse, find her jewelry, disattach the DVD player or whatever electronics they take, find the Impala keys in the purse, find the inside door to the garage, find the garage door opener, use it, and escape."

Cap knows this. "The locations for everything you mentioned are pretty much standard. But in essence your point is well taken. The timing will arouse some suspicion. As will the whole idea of murder during a burglary; that's pretty rare. And why choose a house with an alarm and warning signs in the first place? Suspicion will deepen when they look into your finances. Worse yet, when the police find out about the new insurance policy, they will almost surely lock into you as the prime suspect in a case of first degree murder."

"But I'll have an alibi."

"Exactly. Airtight. So they'll know you didn't pull the trigger. They'll know it's a murder for hire, and that somehow you're behind it. But: they'll have to prove conspiracy. That's the key. The keystone of the whole deal, if you will: They will have no way of knowing who was in the house and no way of connecting them to you. Or me. Without that, they will have no case."

"How about the Chief?"

"What about the Chief?"

"Can they connect me to you through him?"

"Only if they can connect you to him first. How can they do that? Have you been discreet? Have you done anything stupid that might lead them in that direction?"

"Not that I can think of."

"Good. And even if they do, the Chief's own records are coded and secure. I don't see the police making the necessary connection."

Ralph is lost in thought as the steaks and baked potatoes are set on the table. He is reflecting on the contrast between the extraordinary, earth shattering conversation he is having and the prosaic setting in which it is taking place. The experience is surrealistic, dreamlike, disorienting. They should be someplace dark, remote, menacing. Instead, they are sitting in a brightly lit chain restaurant on a typical commercial strip just outside the sublimely nondescript city of Worcester, Massachusetts. The background murmur of restaurant conversation, punctuated by occasional peals of restaurant laughter, is so ordinary it's banal. The clatter of restaurant flatware on restaurant china, the tinkle of ice water poured into restaurant glasses, is trite. The booths, the walls, the uniforms on the waitresses, they are all so commonplace as to be iconic Americana. And yet … and yet … there is nothing ordinary in the slightest about the explosive dialogue he is having with a real honest to god criminal. Is this bizarre or what? It's like a bad movie. Actually, Ralph suddenly remembers, it's like a good movie; it's straight out of the opening sequence in *"Fargo."*

And then it comes to him. My God, this is actually going to happen. Incredible. A new shock: the realization flushes through his consciousness that in effect *it has already happened.* Ralph grasps at this moment that he has in fact already abandoned himself to his fate. It's like a ski jump, he thinks. He's never put on skis in his life, and yet somehow he has managed to wind up at the top of the world's biggest ski jump. And he has already pushed off from the starting gate. It's too late to stop. There is no turning back. He has placed himself in the hands of destiny, and all at once he understands that he's OK about that. In relinquishing control, he has also relieved himself of responsibility. He feels light, unburdened. By not fighting fate, by embracing it, he has reclaimed inner peace. If things turn out the way Cap portrays them, he will land at the bottom on his feet. He comes out a winner. If not, if he lands as a pile of shattered limbs and crushed vertebrae, he comes out a loser. What the fates have in store, so be it.

Either way, it's going to be one hell of a ride.

He looks straight at Cap. "You want to tell me what to do about the insurance?"

"Sure. First, we get the timing straight. When is your next trip out of town?"

"Third week in February. We have a sales managers' meeting in Atlanta."

"Good. Now. I figure six months for the insurance to pay off. So we're talking end of August. So by that time, here's what you'll owe me. You'll owe me the original $41,000. You'll owe me interest on that from last Thanksgiving through August, roughly 30 grand. And I'm assuming you'll owe the $10,000 that I'm staking you with the Chief, so that will be about 13 grand with interest. Then you'll owe 20 grand apiece for Jake and Algernon. And you'll owe my 40% fee for acquiring their services, another 16 grand. Figure 10 grand on miscellaneous expenses. Adding it up, you're going to owe me in the neighborhood of $150,000. So I'm thinking, how about insuring Bonnie for a quarter million? That's within a normal range, and will leave enough remaining for you to pay off your credit cards, pay off your car, and still have plenty left over to get back in business with the Chief. Sound good?"

The thought of all that money does sound good. Ralph starts to get excited. But then another worry pops into his head. "What about Bonnie? She's going to have a problem with this. She's going to think life insurance on her is a complete waste."

Cap has anticipated this. "Not a problem. Bonnie is not going to know about it. I have a doctor who owes me. He's going to fake the physical, based just on what you tell him about her. My write off on part of his debt is the miscellaneous 10 grand expense I mentioned before. I'm going to send you to my insurance agent. He's in Needham. You have any customers in Needham?"

"Norwood. That's close."

"Good. Visit one of them tomorrow. Then stop by my agent. Here's his card. I'll call him. He'll expect you. Tomorrow. You got that?"

"I got that."

They finish their meal without further talk. The waitress clears their plates. They order coffee. Cap decides it's time to pop the question. "Do we have a deal?"

Ralph is beyond the point where he can imagine backing out. "We have a deal."

"You are committed," Cap says. "I will call the Chief in the morning. Give it 'till noon, and your line of credit should be in place by then. Happy Super Bowl."

"Thanks."

"Don't thank me. This is not a favor. This is business."

On the drive back to the Natick rest area, they listen to the Celtics game on the radio. Ralph is exhilarated. He is on the cusp of getting his old life back. Or landing in jail. He has just placed the wager of a lifetime.

6

We'd been invited to dinner at the Legatos. It was the third Sunday in February. The date meant nothing to us at the time.

Ralph had left for his meeting in Atlanta the day before. That was unremarkable; the company routinely scheduled events over a weekend to take advantage of off-peak airfare and hotel deals. Gladys first thought of inviting Bonnie to visit so she wouldn't be lonely, and then had the idea on Sunday morning to call and invite everyone else. Jeff and Sharon had begged off; Jeff was weary from putting in overtime on a big project, and neither relished the idea of a long trip home with the kids late on a Sunday night. But Jim was there.

They say that life imitates art. I agree, sometimes it does. There is an artist named Thomas Kinkade. You may have heard of him; he's very popular, and a commercial success. He's made a lucrative career of painting scenes showing houses in the middle distance at dusk, a warm yellow glow shining through the windows from within. The houses appear ineffably cozy and welcoming. His work has a way of grabbing hold of your imagination. When you look at his pictures, they resonate with a peculiar but atavistic and irresistible fantasy of domestic tranquility. You can't help but muse about the lives of the people who might be so fortunate as to occupy these houses, and you envy them. You wish you could live there, and if not that then at least visit.

As we pulled up to the curb at six o'clock that evening in a Kinkade dusk, the Legato house beckoned with a Kinkade glow. Feeling another one of those flushes of well being, I impulsively gave Sandy a kiss. Her expression, head tilted and eyebrows raised, questioned: What was that about? "We are going to be *inside* a Kinkade painting," I said. Sandy knew what I meant. She said, "What a sap. Give me another kiss."

Bonnie's Impala was parked there already, so we knew she and Jim would be waiting for us inside.

"Sandykins!"

"Jungle Jim!"

The whole routine. That felt good too.

"OK, kids," said Gladys almost right away. "Ken, let's pour the drinks!"

Sandy and I exchanged looks in amusement. It was uncharacteristic of Gladys to betray impatience, but it wasn't hard to guess why she was in a hurry. With the holiday season a memory, we figured Gladys had embarked on her next project. She had been *shopping for the baby*. Drinks in hand, we retired to the living room. I was expecting to endure an hour of tedium. Surprisingly, I got sucked right into the general excitement.

In short order, Gladys came in with first one, then another, giant canvas laundry bags stuffed with packages. These were the spoils of her first expedition into the Grandma Zone, the fruits of her initial foray little into the land of infant paraphernalia. She'd been to the Framingham Mall, she'd surfed the Net. She had canvassed friends and acquaintances. She had reconnoitered the vast territory of baby stuff. She'd returned with spoils. She was, as she put it, "getting back in the game." She announced that this was a warm up exercise, not the main event. There was time later, said Gladys, to go shopping together with Bonnie for the major things—the crib, the high chair, the playpen. For now, she just wanted to get started with some "incidentals."

Some incidentals. The very first item out of the bag was a baby monitor with video. The product category had gone high tech. The transmission from the camera and microphone in the baby's room was wireless, so you could put the TV monitor anywhere in the house. You could move it around or set up multiple monitors in different rooms. The thing was definitely cool, but also it looked expensive. Just guessing, I figured at least $150. It occurred to me that Ken might not be all that happy about Gladys going out and spending so much, so I glanced in his direction. I detected nothing of the sort. On the contrary, Ken was positively beaming. I realized then that this kid would want for nothing.

Next out was a musical dinosaur doll. This was the merriest, friendliest, perkiest, most genial dinosaur I've ever seen. It was adorable. I wanted to be its friend. "We'll put it on your birthday list," said Ken, teasing me.

There was a crib mobile with interchangeable snap-on stimulation disks.

There was a feeding set, ergonomically shaped to help the parent grip the bowl in one hand while wielding the spoon in the other.

There were books. "Twenty Five Things Every Mother Should Know," was one. Another was "The Mother of All Pregnancy Books."

The next item seemed ridiculous to me, but Gladys took it quite seriously. It was called a Wombsong. With it, the mother-to-be could talk or sing into a headset microphone, or turn on a CD in a player in the pouch tied around her waist. The sound would be directed straight toward the fetus inside the womb. As Gladys explained, the idea is that by the third trimester a fetus is supposed to be calmed by relaxing music, mentally stimulated by speech, and bonded to the mother through her voice. According to the literature that came with it, the device "enhances brain development." A dubious proposition, I thought, but what the hell, I supposed it couldn't hurt, could it?

It turned out that I wasn't the only skeptic in the room. The Wombsong inspired a cavalcade of good natured teasing. "Enhances brain development?" Jim led off. "Dee-dee dee-dee, dee-dee dee-dee," he singsonged, mimicking the "Twilight Zone" TV theme.

"Uh-oh," chimed in Sandy, referring to Bonnie's notorious and oft remarked upon inability to carry a tune, "I hope that comes with a Surgeon General's warning: Any singing to a baby by Bonnie Collins can be hazardous to his health!"

"Maybe Jim could record some of his homilies," said Ken, still beaming. "Just to make sure the little tyke's enhanced brain starts off on the straight and narrow."

To which Jim replied, "If he's anything like my parishioners, that would just put the little tyke to sleep." Jim assumed his oratorical voice: "As the disciple Paul … wrote in his letter to the Corinthians …"

"Hey, I know …" said Bonnie. "Why don't I *really* mess the kid up? I'll sing him nothing but hymns all day. That way, he'll turn out to be a melancholy atheist just like Jeff."

Gladys threw up her hands in mock surrender. "All right, all right you guys. Scoff if you will. Just remember, when she—note, *she*—performs at Carnegie Hall, wins the Nobel Prize, and makes us all rich, you will change your tune."

"No problem, Mom," said Jim, "Just as long as we don't have to listen to Bonnie sing it."

"Oh hush," said Gladys, "Jimmy Durante couldn't carry a tune either."

And on that note of non sequitur nonpareil, Gladys had the last word. But everybody was smiling. Back and forth banter is another Legato family tradition. It reminded me of The Cosby Show in the '80's, where a deep and abiding love within the family was denoted by a leitmotiv of affectionate teasing. The writers on that program knew what they were doing.

There were more items in the bags, mostly crib toys, but they were anticlimactic after the Wombsong. Soon enough, we were seated at the dinner table. Ken, as was customary, said grace: "Thank you, Lord, for the bounty of the food that we are about to eat. Thank you for the blessing of a close and loving family. And we pray to you, Lord, that the child growing inside Bonnie will be born in health, strength and safety, and will come to know the peace of your grace in the footsteps of your beloved son Jesus. Amen."

Amens all around.

"Now," said Ken, "It's time for a little celebrating. Be right back." With that, he loped off into the kitchen and before any new conversation had a chance to get started, returned with a bottle of champagne in one hand and a non-alcololic substitute for Bonnie in the other. The champagne was not fancy or expensive; it was just a mass market brand no more costly than regular wine. But I thought the gesture hit precisely the right note. It was a terrific idea, and I said so.

"I agree," said Jim.

"This is a special time for your mother and me," Ken responded, addressing his children but knowing I would feel included. Happily, now that Bonnie was supplying a grandkid, the pressure was off for Sandy and me. Handing me one of the bottles, he asked, "Are you ready to do the honors?" I am acclaimed for my expertise in opening a champagne bottle without letting go of the cork and without allowing the contents to overflow. "I thought you'd never ask," said I.

I popped the corks, Gladys retrieved the stemware from the sideboard, Ken poured, and in a jiffy we were holding our glasses aloft. Ken went first: "Here's to a bright future for all the Collins household—Bonnie, Ralph and Junior alike."

"Hear, hear," said Sandy.

Bonnie, said, "Thank you, Daddy. That was really sweet."

"You know how much we love you, Cookie," said Ken. And at that, I winced.

Ken's remark had touched a sensitive nerve. He never made statements like that to Sandy. I felt for her. Sandy had recognized early in childhood that Bonnie was Ken's favorite and had long ago come to terms with this fact. She refused to compete with Bonnie for Ken's affection, knowing it was a losing proposition. To Sandy's credit, she had dealt with the situation and moved beyond it. But I felt protective on her behalf, and it troubled me. Despite Sandy's insistence that the whole business is a non-issue, the question continued to gnaw at my gut and I persisted in believing it rankled in hers. It just wasn't fair that it was Bonnie that had always captured Ken's adoration. After all, it was Sandy who got all A's in school. It was Sandy who helped Gladys around the house. Most mysteriously, it was Sandy who respected the family's rules and boundaries while it was Bonnie made a habit of testing them, yet Bonnie was more often rewarded than punished by Ken for her transgressions. Why, then, did Ken love Bonnie more? Sandy's answer? "Life isn't fair. If I can get over it, certainly you can."

I remember Sandy telling me about this when we were first getting acquainted. One of the stories she told me was about the toys. When she and Bonnie were children, Ken would take both girls from time to time on Saturday outings. This was their special day for Dad's undivided attention without the boys. The day would finish in late afternoon with a visit to the toy superstore along the Route 9 commercial strip in Westborough. Ken would set them both loose in the store with instructions for each to choose anything they wanted under, say, ten dollars. So Sandy would find something she liked for nine or ten dollars. Bonnie would choose something at twelve or fifteen dollars. "That's too much," Ken would say. But then, somehow, Bonnie would cajole Ken into buying it anyway. "I know," she might say, "but Daddy, this is sooooo much better than anything else that it's really reeeeally worth it. Buying something else would just be a waste of money, and you wouldn't want to do *that*, would you?" Or, other times, she might position the overage as an advance to be subtracted from her allowance the next time they visited the store. Whatever the ploy, it invariably worked. And it would no more occur to Ken to even things out by upping Sandy's limit than it would enter Sandy's head to exceed the ten dollar ceiling in the first place.

Nothing was simple, though. As conscious as Sandy was of Bonnie's special leverage with their father, she was also aware—even as a child—that it frequently worked to her own benefit. If Bonnie wangled one extra ride at the end of a day at the amusement park, she got to go too. If Bonnie sweet-talked Ken into an unplanned excursion to the ice cream shop, the whole family got to go. So the issue really wasn't who got how much of what. The issue was: Why did Ken treat Sandy and the boys alike with evenhanded fairness while awarding most-favored-offspring exceptions for Bonnie? When you pinned her down, even Sandy had to admit that the question still stuck in her craw just a little bit. Even into adulthood she could never make sense of it.

As Sandy was recounting this side of her upbringing, she made it clear to me that her consternation was directed at Ken, not Bonnie. In fact, she told me, her relationship with Bonnie was both close and loving. She was very fortunate, she said, to have Bonnie in her life. This was true back in their childhood, and was true now that they were grownups.

As you might imagine, my first reaction upon hearing this was to wonder whether Sandy might be protesting a bit too much. The bonds between sisters who are close in age are notoriously fraught with complications. Rarely are sibling relationships as straightforward as the one Sandy was describing. But as I got to know the family over time, as I came to understand the history behind their particular bond, and as I came to appreciate Bonnie's extraordinary qualities, my skepticism was eventually extinguished. The connection between Sandy and Bonnie was indeed both close and free of resentment. I also learned to appreciate the degree to which this happy outcome was the outgrowth of Gladys' deft interventions. Fortunately for all involved, Gladys had been sensitive to the situation between her daughters and Ken, and from early on took pains to compensate for Ken's bias by focusing extra attention in Sandy's direction. Then, as time progressed, Sandy found affirmation in abundance from friends, from teachers, from work, and most recently, of course, from me. So in the end, she was not especially scarred from the realization that Bonnie was Ken's favorite.

The other, and complementary, side of the story was that there was more to Bonnie than met the eye. What did meet the eye was a stunning blond. Think Britney Spears in the early pre-bizarro years: taller, perhaps, but softly rounded and perfect. And beyond her good looks, Bonnie was blessed with an abundance of friendliness and warmth. Unexpectedly, one discovered in Bonnie what can only be called an innate generosity of spirit. It was genuine, the real McCoy. It nourished all who knew her, Ralph included.

"Wait wait wait wait Wait!," I can hear you thinking. Who was this person, Mother Theresa in mufti? No, it wasn't like that. Bonnie wasn't a saint, far from it. And she certainly wasn't selfless. Call it a kind of *noblesse oblige.* The giving side to her nature was the yang to the ying of her calculated pursuit of self interest. In a way I've never seen before or since, there was a blithe unselfconsciousness to her generosity which was the exact counterpart to her unselfconsciously blithe sense of personal entitlement. Moreover, Bonnie was not competitive by nature. She cared little about what other people had or did. When she learned that she could get pretty much anything she wanted though non-combative methods, she also understood that she could afford to relax and pursue her yearning for connectedness with other people simply by being nice. To her, there was no contradiction. Because she was satisfied with and for herself, she didn't feel the urge to tear other people down. She had no need to pursue duplicitous agendas with her peers. On the contrary, the very same empathic instincts which accounted for her easy success in manipulating Ken, her teachers, her dates, her bosses and other authority figures—all except Gladys—accounted equally for the depth and duration of her felicitous relationships with friends, co-workers, and Sandy, Jim, Jeff, Sharon and me.

Circumstances and Gladys together had conspired to draw Sandy and Bonnie into a kinship that was especially close, even by the standards of sisters. When Bonnie was born, Sandy was two, Jeff was five, and Jim seven. The Westborough house has four bedrooms, so two of the kids had to share. At first, after Bonnie was born, that was the boys; Sandy and the baby were solo. When Bonnie was three, she was moved in with Sandy so the boys, now getting older, could have rooms of their own. That arrangement stayed in place for eight years until Jim went off to college in Rhode Island.

At first Sandy resented losing the convenience of private accommodations, and the status that went with it. Soon enough, however, Sandy began to enjoy her assigned role as Bonnie's mentor in the ways of the world. Gladys quite deliberately created for Sandy this niche in the family dynamic and coached her on how to fill it successfully. Emotionally, the axis of Sandy and Gladys neatly and symmetrically balanced that of Bonnie and Ken. In the process, Sandy gained proficiencies and self assurance in areas of competence that might otherwise never have emerged, or at least not until much later. And in becoming Bonnie's principal consultant on the realities of life, Sandy was provided a painless way of both differentiating and elevating her place in the family structure while simultaneously nurturing a "best friends" intimacy with her only sister. It was Gladys who quite deliberately promoted all of that.

It worked for Bonnie, too. Bonnie soon realized that she could turn to Sandy for practical advice, gaining instruction on how toys worked and how board and schoolyard games were played. It wasn't long before Sandy had learned to read, and was proud to take over the task of reading Bonnie her bedtime story; Bonnie loved the attention, and besides, Sandy drew on her experience to dispense with the boring stuff. Later on, it was Sandy who pointed Bonnie toward the coolest teen magazines, the hippest music. In junior high, Sandy decoded for her the mysteries of social mores and taboos, and the intricacies of pre-adolescent dress codes. In high school, Sandy taught her how to use the computer, and opened her eyes to the wonders of cyberspace.

For her part, Bonnie provided much of the fun. Most of the ideas for play came from Bonnie, who was a dynamo of inspiration. She created the scenarios when the girls played with dolls together. She invented variations on the game of tag when the children in the area played outside. She made up skits for the sisters to perform in the basement to an appreciative audience of Gladys and Ken.

The summer when Bonnie was eleven, she conceived and organized a neighborhood talent show with a dozen kids who lived nearby. Sandy, recruited to handle publicity, created a flyer on the home computer and distributed it door to door. Jim was the emcee. Bonnie herself belted out "Over the Rainbow." The tune was unrecognizable, but who cared, the girl had heart. About twenty of the performers' parents and siblings stood in the Legato's back yard to watch the show on a cloudy Sunday in August. Bonnie was more than pleased. She was pumped.

The success of that project inspired an encore the following year, but this time Bonnie had greater ambitions. She wanted to put on a real play. Ken suggested "Peter Pan." The idea was a good one. Bonnie cast Sandy as Wendy, Jim in the part of brother John, and herself in the title role. Bonnie's best friend from school was Tinkerbell, and other parts were recruited from the neighborhood. There was no shortage of nine year old boys who wanted to be pirates. The mother of two pirates, who was handy with a sewing machine, volunteered to make some costumes. Ken built the platform for a backyard stage and some rudimentary sets; he was more than pleased because it provided him the excuse he was looking for to purchase certain power tools he'd been eyeing at Sears. The Crocodile had an older brother who played guitar, and he became the orchestra. Gladys was in charge of props. Even Jeff got involved that year, taking over from Sandy as publicist. It was his idea to offset expenses by selling ads in a program book to local merchants. He contacted the parents of cast members and asked them to sell the ads to businesses where they were known personally as valued customers. At $5 for a page, $3 for a half page, and $2 for a quarter page, space in the sixteen page booklet was spoken for quickly. Ken bought a few reams of paper and reproduced the books on his office copier.

The performance was scheduled for the first Saturday afternoon following Labor Day (rain day Sunday) so as not to conflict with summer vacation schedules. It was a blowout success. Ken had rented one hundred folding chairs, and half again as many people were left standing, despite the fifty cent admission price imposed by Jeff. There were no wires, no liftoff during the flying sequences—the kids ran around with their arms stretched out and pretended—and everybody loved it anyway. The standing ovation at the end was well deserved, and after a summer of hard work Bonnie got the credit she had earned.

The experience was a high water mark for the family as a unit, and a milestone for each of the other Legatos individually as well. In the case of Jim, then entering his sophomore year at college, it was the last summer he would spend at home. For many years the recollection of this event would become a touchstone for the positive outlook that would carry him through the difficulties and sacrifices of his chosen career.

For Jeff, in contrast, it marked an unexpected departure in the direction of his life. Jeff was jolted by the discovery of a latent entrepreneurial bent in his personality. Then a high school senior, he had fancied himself a liberal political activist and anticipated a lifetime of service in the public or non-profit sector. But introspective and clear-eyed as always, he couldn't help but acknowledge the gusto with which had had taken hold of his marketing assignment. Jeff was also intrigued with the intellectual aspect of commercial strategy. For example, when the program pages sold out so quickly, he realized that his price was set too low. But, he wondered, how do you know in advance what the right price is? And while everyone else in the family supported his idea to charge admission, they argued that the price should only be a quarter so as not to drive potential customers away. Jeff, having never heard the term "price elasticity" but having a gut instinct for how it works, stood his ground at double that amount and was proven right. For Jeff, "Peter Pan" was the birth not only of a change in career direction, but also of a radically new perception of who he is as an individual.

And Sandy, excited and proud to be starting high school that September, discovered that she could stand aside without jealousy as the accolades rolled in for Bonnie. She could be genuinely happy for her sister's success. She was just then, in mid-adolescence, developing a sense of her own personality and character, and at that moment she was pretty happy with what she found.

Ken and Gladys, watching the show from the rear of the audience with their fingers intertwined, felt their cup of life overflow with good fortune. They knew they had gained a memory to share that was truly, as it says in the credit card commercials, priceless.

As Bonnie followed Sandy through the high school ranks, the connection between them grew stronger. One of the payoffs for Sandy from being Bonnie's designated mentor was that she also became Bonnie's principal confidante in affairs of the heart. It was a function that Sandy relished. Being at the time both shy and studious, Sandy's own social life in high school was disappointingly uneventful. Bonnie's, on the other had, careened between triumph and disaster like a soap opera on steroids. Sandy was glad to play a vital part in each of her sister's amorous adventures. Although for her the romance was vicarious, she savored the role of loyal campaign manager, the trusted inner circle *consigliere*, the *eminence gris* behind the scenes who mapped strategies, plotted tactics, debated options, celebrated victories, mourned defeats and propped her sister up to venture forth another day.

It was during this period, too, that Sandy was able to help Bonnie navigate successfully through two difficult episodes of upset in her life. The first was a conflict with Gladys and Ken over what she was going to do after high school graduation. Their parents were adamant that Bonnie should continue on to college. Bonnie, having no taste for academics and dreading the prospect of four more years confined to a classroom and shackled to homework, insisted that she was going to get a job. It was Sandy that conceived of, then mediated, the compromise that broke the impasse. Bonnie would enroll in a two-year community college. To their parents, Sandy argued that this route would have the effect of keeping Bonnie in the higher education game, and she could transfer later to a four-year institution with two years of credits and two years of additional maturity under her belt. *Plus*, she pointed out, community college would be cheaper. To Bonnie, she argued that community college wouldn't be all that bad since the particular one she had in mind wasn't all that demanding, and anyway their parents were right about how future opportunities were closed off without higher education. Bonnie only had to hang in for two more years, and then she could get a good job instead of a crummy one. *Plus*, it would be a fine place to meet a lot of new guys. She would have a blast. And thus was the crisis resolved. Kudos for Sandy all around.

The other episode occurred when Bonnie lost her virginity. This was in the summer between high school and community college. Bonnie was working as a hostess at a chain restaurant in town. On a warm Saturday morning in early July, she went with four co-workers on a trip to Nantasket Beach. The beach is on the south shore, about an hour and a half drive from Westborough. A couple in the group who were already dating sat in front. Bonnie sat with a bartender and a waiter in the back. The fit was snug and Sandy was sandwiched between them. She had on a tank top and shorts over her bikini; the guys were wearing T-shirts and shorts over their racing style trunks. There was no avoiding skin contact along the arms and legs. Bonnie had not the slightest desire to avoid it. The guys felt warm and smooth to the touch, and the sensation of feeling the bare skin of two men at the same time was deliciously arousing. The guys, of course, loved it too. Though nothing was said and everybody played it cool, the ride to the beach sizzled with suppressed sexuality. When they got there, the guys were sorry the ride was over and were already looking forward to the return trip. So, truth be told, was Bonnie.

Bonnie was attracted to Brian, the bartender. Brian was blond, beefy but muscular, and well spoken. Bonnie had already taken notice of him at work, especially when she found out he was home for the summer from Cornell. His pal, Russ, was cute too, but in a different way: his facial features were regular and well proportioned yet somehow sensuously full, while his olive complexion and dark, straight collar length hair added an intriguing dimension of mystery and depth. All that day at the beach, Bonnie flirted equally with them both. Though her sights were set on Brian, she thought the *frisson* of competition would make her seem a more desirable catch. At the same time, she ratcheted up the sexual tension by keeping the touching to a minimum. This was partly a deliberate tease, and partly a consequence of Bonnie's desire to preserve in an undiluted state the erotic stimulation she anticipated in the rear seat going home.

They returned to the car not long after lunch. Though a brief consultation in the men's room minutes before, the guys had already decided to approach the car wearing just their swim trunks. No t-shirts, no shorts. If Bonnie objected or covered up herself, then they could always put them on. Meanwhile, nothing ventured, nothing gained.

Bonnie did not cover up, did not object. Bonnie had been watching for a sign. Now she had one. She left her tank top and shorts where they were in her beach bag, which she stowed in the trunk. Then, wearing nothing but her bikini, she slid right in between the guys. They, of course, were thrilled. They looked at each other, hardly believing their luck. The couple in the front seat, Chuck and Betsy, looked at each other and did their best to stifle a laugh.

So now, for the long ride home, Bonnie would experience the titillation of cool, smooth, youthful skin touching and sliding against warm, smooth, youthful skin all the way from her shoulders down to her forearms, from her upper thighs to her calves, on both sides. Never before had Bonnie been so aroused. Well, that's not precisely correct. She had aroused herself, by herself, at night, with fantasies. But never before had she been stimulated like this in real life, with real boys. Up 'till now, though the feeling of touching boys had been pleasant; it had never traveled to her groin. Today her juices were flowing already and the car had barely left the parking lot. She couldn't resist glancing down at the guys' swim trunks, where she gleefully observed that they were standing at attention for her too.

By and by, Bonnie upped the ante. She found coquettish reasons to rub Brian's chest, to stroke Russ' leg, to massage both their naked shoulders. She leaned forward in the seat, holding both their bare legs, and invited both of them to give her a back rub at the same time. Just after they switched from Rt. 128 to the Turnpike, she had an idea. She unbuckled her seat belt and sat herself crosswise on Brian's lap. She stretched her legs across the top of Russ' thighs. "Brian," she said, "you can rub my head." To Russ she said, "You can massage my feet." To Betsy, she giggled and said, "You can turn around."

The feeling was unbelievable. Exquisite. It got even better, as she had hoped, when Brian—at first tentatively, then with increasing assurance—removed his hands from her scalp and started caressing her shoulders, her arms, her chest, her back, her stomach. He knew how to do it, too, not just with the palms of his hands but with his forearms also for maximum skin contact.

And then she realized exactly what she was doing. She became aware that today, for some reason, she was ready. Emotionally ready, that is. She understood, in an epiphany, that she had staged managed the entire scenario to make this the day. She had *decided* this would be the day. So this had not been her standard high school flirt, not her accomplished balancing act of keeping boys interested while not letting things get too far. Previously she had done many things many times with many boys, but intercourse had been off limits. Now, she realized that her patience had run out. She had had it up to here with being a kid. July 4 might be weeks away, but this was the day of her personal declaration of independence. She was keenly aware, too, that Brian and Russ weren't boys; maybe they were not quite men yet, but they were definitely not boys. She knew at this moment that given the opening she was going to go ahead and do it. She grasped that all through the day she had been setting the wheels in motion. Not consciously perhaps but purposefully nevertheless, she had steered events toward an inevitable conclusion. So now here they were, about five minutes from the moment of truth, and she knew the truth.

As they merged onto I-495 for the short hop to the Rt. 9 exit in Westborough, Chuck glanced in the mirror and asked, "OK, folks, where to?" Everyone understood that he was asking the trio in the back seat at whose house he should drop each of them off, and in what sequence. It was a loaded question. The moment of truth had arrived.

Brian looked at Bonnie, sitting on his lap, and chose his words carefully: "We have time before we have to get to work. Would you like to visit with me for a while?"

Bonnie, practical to the core regardless of the circumstances, said, "How would I get home to change?"

"I have a car," said Brian.

"OK," Bonnie said. Then she looked at Russ, but she had already decided about that as well. When in her life would she ever have another opportunity to match this one? She looked back at Brian. "Russ too?" she asked.

Brian was taken aback at first, not knowing how he felt about that. This was an unexpected curve ball. The idea of having sex with another guy present was a bit creepy. On the other hand, the last thing he wanted to do was cross Bonnie and blow the whole deal. Caution won out over squeamishness. "Russ too," he said, somewhat reluctantly. Then, louder, he said to Chuck, "We're all going to my place."

Brian knew that his house would be empty that afternoon. After offering soft drinks, which they declined, he led them up to his bedroom and closed the door behind them. Bonnie faced Brian and stated, "Nothing is going to happen unless you have condoms." Brian nodded yes. "Show me," Bonnie insisted. Brian retrieved a box of condoms from the back of his underwear drawer and placed it on top of the nightstand. "OK then," Bonnie said, "Now kiss me." Brian was a surprisingly good kisser, both gentle and passionate. After a while she parted lips long enough to say, "Hey, Russ, are you just an observer here?" So Russ embraced her from behind, and she was surrounded by taught warm male flesh. Russ was kissing the back of her neck and her ears. The combination of Brian in front and Russ in back got her juices gushing to the max. One thing led to another and before long they were on the bed and Brian, condom on, was inside her.

The first penetration hurt some but less than she was afraid of. Brian, though, youthful and aroused as he was, lasted all of about thirty seconds. Ditto for Russ. It wasn't enough. Bonnie, then, laid out her conditions. Her long experience in pulling strings, her mastery in the skills of getting her way with others, her self-confidence founded on years of manipulating peers and adults alike, paid off now. It allowed her to take charge effortlessly. "Listen up, guys," she said. "If you want this to happen again you're going to do what I tell you."

"Of course," said Brian. "Of course," echoed Russ. She instructed Brian on how to touch her and what he should do with his other hand. She guided Russ in what he should be doing with his hands. And within a few minutes she was satisfied too.

So what, you may ask, was the problem?

Think of it as residual Catholic guilt. This was the first time she had had intercourse, and the first time she had come to orgasm in the presence of anybody else. The thing was, Bonnie had drawn a line for herself early on. She had often approached the line, dallied near it, and even fudged the definition of it. But never before had she actually crossed it. Not only that, the deed was intentional. She couldn't pretend that she had been a victim somehow. She had actively made it happen.

A kind of buyers' remorse over her sinful behavior descended upon Bonnie during her shift at the restaurant that night, displacing the exhilaration she had felt just moments earlier and casting a pall on the events of the day. She had gone against everything her parents had taught her. She had gone against everything the Church had taught her. She had done wrong. It was nothing less than a mortal sin. What was the matter with her? What was she going to do now? She needed to talk to Sandy.

Sandy was living in Connecticut, where she was enrolled at Wesleyan and working at a summer job in Hartford. Bonnie called her on Sunday and they arranged to meet for lunch the next day. Over chicken Caesars and diet colas, Bonnie spilled out the whole story. Sandy's reaction, which she kept to herself, was this: I'm surprised it took you so long. What she said out loud was, "Did the guys use protection?"

Bonnie assured her that they did. All right, thought Sandy, relieved. Her assessment of her sister was intact. Bonnie might be hedonistic and impetuous but she wasn't stupid. Sandy also knew exactly what Bonnie needed from her. Bonnie needed reassurance that what she had done wasn't really bad. Bonnie needed Sandy's *permission*. She was perfectly willing to provide it. Sandy was experienced by then, too, and her personal views on the subject were quite matter of fact. Sandy asked, "Are you troubled in your own heart, or are you worried what God might think?"

"Both, and Mom and Dad too."

"Your own heart? Really?"

"I don't know," admitted Bonnie. "It was fantastic. But I keep thinking it was wrong for me to have enjoyed it so much."

That gave Sandy all the data she needed. She decided to cancel God out of the equation first. "Bonnie, let's look at it this way," she said. "How many Catholic women have sex before marriage in this day and age?"

"Lots of them, I guess."

"Most of them?"

"Probably."

"So," Sandy said, "Do you think they are all going to end up in hell?"

"I don't know, Sandy. It's a sin."

"So says the Church. But the Church defined it as a sin when that made sense. When there was no effective birth control and sex before marriage inevitably led to unwanted children. Now that's changed."

"But the Church speaks for God."

"Maybe," said Sandy, "Maybe not."

"Maybe *not?*"

"Let me tell you how I look at it," said Sandy, "And you can reach your own conclusion. This is what I believe. I believe that God sent Jesus to reveal His universal love for all of us. I also believe that God sent Jesus with a message, to remind us of what is really important to God. I believe what Jesus told us is that God wants us to love each other, to care for each other, to be just and merciful to each other, to help each other, to treat each other with good will and kindness. Jesus told us that living this way is how we express our love for God. I believe that Jesus took special pains to remind us especially not to let concerns over material things or worldly comforts get in the way of being kind and good. I believe that all the rest of it—repeat, *all* the rest of it, the Church and its rules included—is nothing more than men trying to figure out how to keep a church in business."

Bonnie, who had never before thought to question the specifics of Catholic dogma, was dumbfounded. Bonnie stared wide eyed at her older sister, digesting this amazing information. For all their closeness, the two had never had a conversation like this before. They hadn't avoided the topic. It just hadn't come up.

At length, Bonnie asked, "You don't think it's a sin?"

"No," Sandy answered. "I'm doing it myself. You know I have a boyfriend here. He doesn't just give me a peck on the cheek before going home. I'm telling you flat out, even though the Church defines it as a sin, I don't consider it sinful."

Sandy let Bonnie absorb this information for a time. She polished off the remainder of her salad. Then she switched gears to Bonnie's worry about their parents. "Let's talk about Mom and Dad," she said. "Do you know the phrase 'don't ask, don't tell'?"

"I've heard it," Bonnie answered.

"Yes, well, you were too young to be paying much attention to the news back then. Back in the early '90's, when Clinton was first elected President, he tried to get rid of the prohibition against gays being in the military. There was a big brouhaha over it. In the end there was a compromise which made no one happy but in practical terms worked reasonably well. It went this way: the military as an institution would no longer seek out gays in the ranks for the purpose of expelling them, and gays would remain both discrete and unofficial in their status. It all had very little to do with gays, and very much to do with the military brass being stuck in cultural time warp. They still imagined that the military was the domain of alpha males, and thought that acknowledging the presence of gays among them would diminish their own alpha-ness. There was no changing them. But the real deal was that by not asking, by not looking for gays, they could avoid seeing them and thus pretend they weren't there. The brass could maintain their cherished self-delusion that the military is exclusive preserve of men who are *men*. Meanwhile, the gays could continue doing their thing, as long as they didn't break ordinary military regulations. All the gays really gave up was the right to flaunt their lifestyle in the face of their superior officers."

Bonnie had a puzzled look: "Why are you telling me about gays?"

"Because it was only about gays on the surface," Sandy explained. "On a deeper, more important level it was about maintaining illusions. And that's exactly what you need to do with Mom and Dad, especially Dad. I'm saying that the military brass had an emotional need to maintain a certain illusion: that the Army is the exclusive preserve of Alpha males. And that's what I'm saying is the important thing about Mom and especially Dad. Dad has an illusion to maintain also: the illusion that you are chaste."

"Chaste?" Bonnie still didn't get it. "You think that's what Dad believes about me."

"I think that's what he *wants* to believe about you. I think you should let him. I think you should give him the gift of his illusions. There is no benefit to talking about what you're doing to either one of them. I'm telling you, Sis, if you don't tell he won't ask, and therefore nothing will upset him and nothing will change. This is the best way for everybody. Not saying anything to them is not bad, it is good. It is a kindness to them. It is best for everybody."

Not a thing Sandy had told her up until then was what Bonnie had anticipated. Bonnie was enormously relieved and very grateful. She was quick to express her appreciation. "I don't know how to thank you. I'm so glad I came here today. You're the *best!*"

Sandy wasn't looking for gratitude. She had another agenda. "Bonnie. I don't need thanks. I need you to listen to me. Will you do what I say?"

"What?"

"Two things. First, you can't have faith in condoms for birth control. They're not reliable. Right away—today, tomorrow at the latest—go to a family planning clinic and get a prescription for birth control pills. Start taking them in your next cycle. Do. Not. Trust. Condoms. Got that?"

"Got it. No problem. It's a good idea."

"Number two. I know how this works, so believe me on this too. Once you're taking the pills you're not going to want to bother with the condoms. And the guys hate condoms. Here's the thing. *It's very important.* Before you stop using condoms, you must—*must!*—get the guys to have tests for AIDS and other diseases. And you must—*must!*—have them show you the results on paper. The printed reports from the lab. And then they shouldn't be with anybody else. I'm not worried about God, Bonnie. God loves you. I'm worried about viruses."

You know what? Bonnie did what Sandy told her. She was nervous about asking the guys to be tested, but just as Sandy predicted they were so glad to get rid of the condoms that they complied gladly, even joyously. And then they proceeded to have as fine a summer as any eighteen year old and two twenty year olds have ever had. Bonnie was in love. Not with Brian. With *life!*

Anyway, back to dinner at the Legatos …

After the toasts, the meal was uneventful. That does not mean it was ordinary. The dinner was a memorable exhibition of how Gladys could put together a superb meal with minimal effort. Here's how you do that, Gladys style: start with fried mozzarella sticks and fried eggplant sticks. Don't make them from scratch; the ones that come frozen in packages are quite good. Serve a spinach salad, simple and refreshing, with fresh spinach leaves, chopped hard boiled egg, bacon bits, supermarket-sliced fresh mushrooms, and bottled honey Dijon dressing. For the main course, broil some swordfish. According to Gladys, there are two keys to swordfish: use only fresh, never frozen, and broil slowly on a low oven rack so as to come out fully cooked but still moist. Put a pat of butter on each portion and sprinkle with a little Old Bay seasoning, and let the natural intensity of its flavor burst through. Add some packaged rice pilaf and fresh asparagus, and you have a plate more satisfying than any you can find in the most splendiferous of restaurants. For dessert, visit the bakery department in the supermarket and pick up some éclairs. Have fresh brewed cinnamon hazelnut decaf ready as soon as the main course is done. Did I mention yet that Gladys is a wizard in the kitchen? That I adore that woman?

If great food and drink supplied the harmony and rhythm in the emotional music of that evening, the melody was a lively discussion about names. It was too soon to know the gender of the baby, so nothing was off limits. At first we tried to be serious, coming up with genuine suggestions: real names like Ed and Eric, like Alice and Amy. After a while, though, fueled perhaps by the champagne, we segued into a mirthful competition to see who could come up with the most outlandish inspiration. Ulysses jumped ahead at the gate, Aphrodite and Caleb were leading in the backstretch, and Zacharia, Euridice and Balthazar were neck and neck at the wire. Laughter and congratulations (Good one, Jim!) filled the room. So did good feelings. Then we moved on to a discussion about the connection between names and the characteristics of people attached to them. By the time this topic had run its course, the éclairs were history, memorialized by a plate of little empty oblong paper trays. At that point, Ken said something unexpected: "It's late. You kids run along home. I'll help your mother clean up."

That may have been unprecedented. It was Gladys who was beaming now.

"Way to go, Dad!" said Jim.

Ken laughed. "Don't get the wrong impression. I haven't turned into one of the good guys. I just feel like spending time with your mother today."

"Don't worry, Dad," said Sandy. "We know you have a reputation to protect." Hear that? As I was saying before, edgy comments like that one from time to time lead me to think that Sandy might not be so "over it" as she would like to think she is. For his part, Ken was in such a good mood that he shrugged it off without taking umbrage. And despite this little flicker, Sandy's mood was still good too.

We all hugged and kissed goodbye at the door. The Kinkade glow was not only illuminating the house, it was shining from inside each one of us as well. Gladys and Bonnie made arrangements to call the next day to make plans for a shopping expedition on Tuesday after work. And then we piled into the cars and were gone.

The next time any of us saw Bonnie, she was laid out in a casket.

7

Any of us except Gladys, that is.

Gladys calls Bonnie around dinnertime on Monday, as they had arranged, to pin down the details for getting together the next day. There is no answer. Gladys leaves a message. She calls again around eight. No answer. She leaves another message. She calls around nine. No answer. This time the message from Gladys is, "I'll call you at work in the morning."

Gladys goes to bed worried. If Bonnie had changed her plans and gone out for the evening, she would have called *her*. For all her free spirited spontaneity, Bonnie is not irresponsible. She would have in mind not to worry her mother. She would make a thirty second phone call.

Gladys sleeps fitfully that night. She hides her forebodings from Ken, not wanting to worry him and afraid of seeming foolish if nothing is wrong. Tuesday morning after Ken leaves, Gladys tries to distract herself with three cups of coffee and the Today show. The minutes crawl and crawl and crawl by until 9:15, when she dials Bonnie's extension at work.

An unfamiliar voice answers: "Bonnie Collins' phone."

Gladys: "Uh ... is Bonnie there, please?"

Voice: "I'm sorry, she isn't here right now. Can I help you?"

Gladys: "Uh ... I'm Bonnie's mother ..."

Voice: "Oh, hi! I'm Laura. I've worked with Bonnie for many years. I'm sorry, it's just that Bonnie talks about you so much I feel like I know you. She thinks you're very special. Her dad, too."

Gladys: "Uh ... Laura? ... I've been trying to reach Bonnie and I can't find her. Do you know where she is?"

Laura: "No. She wasn't in yesterday either, but I don't know where she is."

Gladys: "She was expected but she wasn't there?"

Laura: "As far as I know."

Gladys: "Is Mr. Benson there?" Mr. Benson is Bonnie's boss.

Laura: "He's in a meeting but I think he'll take your call when I tell him it's you."

Gladys: "Thank you. I appreciate that."

Gladys is on hold. Then, "Hello, this is Greg Benson."

"Hello, Mr. Benson. This is Gladys Legato, Bonnie's mother."

"Laura told me. Hello, Mrs. Legato, how can I help you?"

"Mr. Benson, I have to tell you I'm getting pretty worried. Bonnie was expecting me to call last night, but she didn't answer all night and she didn't call me. That's not like her. And she's not at work now and Laura tells me she was missing yesterday too."

"That's true, Mrs. Legato."

"Have you tried to reach her?"

"Yes, I have. When she didn't show up yesterday I called her home. I left a message. I was going to call her again today, but I was giving her a little more time."

"So you don't know where she might be?"

"I'm afraid not. I know she's pregnant. Maybe something medical came up."

"But then she would have called me. She wouldn't disappear. Something's not right. Well ... thanks for taking my call."

"No problem. I wish I could help. If there's anything I can do ..."

"I'll let you know. Thanks."

Consumed by apprehension, Gladys drives to Bonnie's house. From the outside things appear normal. But when she peeks through a window into the garage, she sees that both cars are gone. That doesn't make any sense. Where would Bonnie have gone, if not to work?

Gladys knows where the spare key is hidden. She lets herself in. At first nothing seems amiss. Then she notices the sound of what seems to be a TV coming from upstairs. But how can that be? Neither car is there.

"Bonnie?" she calls out. "Bonnie? Are you there?" No answer. She is unsure what to do. She thinks about calling 911. But what is she going say? That her daughter isn't home but the TV is on?

So, slowly, step by step, heart pounding, pulse racing, Gladys climbs the stairs. She follows the sound, remembering now that Bonnie and Ralph have a TV in their bedroom. Reaching the upstairs hallway, she stops and listens carefully. Aside from the TV, all she hears is an ominous quiet. Deathly quiet is the phrase that comes to her mind. Gladys has never been so frightened. She is fearful there may be danger in the house. But she is even more terrified of the scene that she imagines is awaiting her in the bedroom. By now, Gladys is fully expecting the worst. Her gut instincts have taken over. Her gut instincts rarely lead her astray.

It takes a maximum exercise of will to force her legs to move one step at a time toward the bedroom. It gets harder as the door gets closer. Then she is there. The door is open but the sightline from the hall doesn't take in the bed. "Bonnie?" she calls out. Nothing. The TV. She hears a woman telling a story in the animated style people use on TV. She hears the audience laughing in response. A thought flashes across Gladys' mind. She wishes she were in that audience. *Because then she wouldn't be here.*

She sees Bonnie's feet first. They are under the covers, but they're the right size and anyway who else could they belong to? The shape under the covers is immobile.

As Gladys moves further into the room, more of Bonnie becomes visible. Finally her face is in view, then her hair. Bonnie is lying on her back. She looks calm, peaceful. Gladys advances slowly, uncertainly. She is almost at the bedside before she notices the blood. There is a pool of dried blood on the opposite side of the pillow from where she is standing. Gladys slowly, gradually, steps back around the foot of the bed. A few steps up the other side she sees the bullet wound in Bonnie's head. It is surrounded by a splotch of clotted blood. Its nature is unmistakable.

Gladys' hands come up to her mouth. She turns away in horror. She fights back nausea, forcing herself not to vomit. This takes a very long time, several minutes. Afterwards she stands there, unable to move, unable to think, paralyzed. Again, several minutes. Then, when her mind begins to function again, she can only think one thing: how is she going to tell Ken?

Still not knowing how to tell Ken, Gladys goes down to the kitchen and dials 911. She gets the operator and somehow finds her voice. "I'm calling to report a murder."

"What is the address?"

"Two seven seven Rosedale Circle."

"Ma'am, are you in danger?"

"No, the murderer isn't here."

"Please hold, Ma'am, while I call for help." Then: "A squad car is on the way."

"Thank you."

Gladys has to get out of the house. She still has her coat on so she goes out the kitchen door. Waiting for the squad car, she paces back and forth, back and forth on the front walk between the house and the street. Pretty soon she is startled to see a police car pull to a stop at the end of the walk. She hadn't noticed it coming.

The blue lights are flashing. Two uniformed patrolmen get out of the car and approach her. "Did you call in a murder?" one of them asks.

"Yes."

"Tell us about it."

"I couldn't reach my daughter last night or this morning. She was absent from work yesterday and today. So I came here to see if something was wrong. I found her shot in bed."

"Where is that?"

"Upstairs, in their bedroom."

"Wait here while we take a look. Is the front door open?"

"You mean unlocked? No. I'll open it for you." Gladys reaches into her coat pocket to check for the key. It's there. She follows the patrolmen into the vestibule. One of them turns around and says, "We told you to wait outside. What are you doing?"

"I have to call my husband," Gladys says.

"Not in here," says the patrolman. "This is a crime scene."

A crime scene! "I have to call my husband," Gladys insists.

The patrolman reaches inside his jacket and pulls out a cell phone. "This is my personal phone. Use this. Outside."

They all go back outside and Gladys dials. The patrolmen wait. They want to hear what she says. Gladys doesn't notice this. She is consumed with figuring out what to say. Ken's phone is ringing in his office. Oh please, let him be there. The ringing stops. "Ken Legato here."

"Ken, it's me."

"Oh, hi honey."

"Ken, you have to meet me at Bonnie's house. Right now. Immediately."

"Why, honey? What's wrong?"

"I can't talk about it. You have to come here. It's an emergency."

"Is Bonnie all right?"

"No. I can't talk. Just come. Now. Please." Gladys can't handle any more. She turns the phone off.

The patrolman takes back his phone and tells her to wait in her car. She gets in and starts it up for the heat. Even when the engine warms up and the heat is pumping full blast, she can't stop shivering.

The patrolmen go inside, check out the bedroom, and call in to headquarters. Their job now is to secure the crime scene until the detectives, the forensic types, and the medical examiner can do their jobs.

In about twenty minutes, a detective in plain clothes shows up in an unmarked car. The detective is with the State Police; in Massachusetts, all murders outside of the City of Boston are investigated by the State Police. The patrolmen greet him, brief him, take him inside. When he comes back out, he heads for Gladys' car and gestures through the window to request that he be allowed to sit in the passenger seat. Gladys nods and unlocks the door. The detective folds himself into the car.

"I'm Detective Brisbane," he says. "Like the city. In Australia. I'm sorry for your loss."

Sorry? thinks Gladys. What does that mean? What am I supposed to say? Am I supposed to say thank you? Has he done anything for me? Has he helped me in any way? Does he deserve to be thanked for remembering to offer an insincere expression of counterfeit grief? *Has he lost a daughter?*

Gladys nods her head.

"You're Mrs ...?" he asks.

"Legato."

"Mrs. Legato, can you tell me what happened, as you know it, starting from the beginning?"

The beginning? thinks Gladys. What is the beginning? Is the beginning last night when Bonnie didn't answer the phone? Is it Sunday night at dinner, the last time I saw her? Is it when Bonnie met Ralph? Is it when Bonnie was born? Is it when she met Ken? What is the beginning? In the beginning God created the heavens and the earth.

"She was pregnant," says Gladys.

"Who, the deceased?

Deceased? Bonnie? "Yes."

"Any other children?"

"No."

"Can you tell me what happened, Mrs. Legato?"

And now she does, beginning with Sunday dinner. By the time she's finished, ending with the 911 call, there are half a dozen cruisers with blue lights flashing, three unmarked sedans, and a police ambulance clogging the driveway and spilling out into the street. Neighbors are beginning to gather on the lawn across the way.

This is when Ken rounds the corner and the last remnants of optimism are stomped out. He has been hoping against hope that Gladys was exaggerating, taking something manageable and blowing it out of proportion. The thought is farfetched, he knows. Gladys is not prone to hysteria. But it was not beyond possibility. It was something to hang on to. But look at this. Oh, shit.

Ken sees a man in the passenger seat next to Gladys and heads toward that side of the car. "That's my husband coming," Gladys says.

Brisbane lowers the window in anticipation. Ken leans down and looks across at Gladys: "What happened?" Gladys can't bear to say it. She looks with mute, helpless pleading at Brisbane. Brisbane turns to Ken and says, "Mr. Legato, your daughter was found murdered this morning."

"Was found? Waddaya mean, was found? Who found her?" Then it clicks and Ken gets it. He peers in the window at Gladys: "You?" Gladys nods yes. Ken can't believe this. Not only is his daughter murdered. Not only is his grandchild murdered. But his wife finds the body? How can anything possibly be worse? This can't be happening.

Suddenly Ken steps back from the car. "GODDAM SONOFABITCH! MOTHER FUCKING ASSHOLE COCKSUCKER!"

Brisbane turns toward Gladys, interested to see if she understands who Ken is yelling about. Gladys understands perfectly, though she's not ready to join her husband in leaping to conclusions.

Ken is still shouting. "IF THAT SLIMEY ROTTEN BASTARD HAD ANYTHING TO DO WITH THIS, I'LL WRING HIS SLIMEY ROTTEN BASTARD NECK PERSONALLY!"

Brisbane peers out the car window. "Mr. Legato, who is it that you're talking about?"

"Who wants to know?!?"

"That's right, Mr. Legato, we haven't been introduced. I'm Detective Brisbane, like the city. State Police. I've been assigned as lead investigator on the case."

"The *case*, Detective Brisbane, is my *daughter!* So you just go out and haul in that worthless son-in-law of mine and you can solve your *case* in time to make it home for dinner."

"I understand how you feel, Mr. Legato."

"No you don't! You can't!"

"No I don't. You're right. But Mr. Legato, be that as it may, I am not about to haul anyone in right now. I am an experienced criminal investigator. This means that my investigation will be orderly, methodical, and professionally thorough so that it results in a successful criminal prosecution. I am sure you wouldn't have it any other way, Mr. Legato."

Ken is quiet. Despite his outburst, it is true. An engineer to the quick, he really wouldn't have it any other way.

After a few seconds, Brisbane asks Ken, "Where can I reach the husband?"

"He's at a sales meeting with his company in Atlanta," says Ken.

"His name is Ralph Collins," says Gladys.

Ken has removed his PDA from his coat pocket. He taps with the stylus and reads out the number of Ken's company. Brisbane makes notes on a little spiral pad. "They'll know how to reach him," Ken adds.

Brisbane says, "I would like to be the one that calls him, if it's all right with you."

Gladys is relieved, grateful. She can't imagine having to tell a husband, any husband, even Ralph, that his wife has been shot. Ken understands that it is part of Brisbane's investigative technique. The detective wants to gauge Ralph's reaction when he presents the news. Ken is beginning to like this cop.

Brisbane asks the Legatos if they would be willing to come to headquarters the next day—say, 11:00 AM? Right now he will be occupied supervising the collection of evidence in the house. This evening and the earlier part of the next morning he will be reviewing the evidence and will start to develop a sense of what happened. If they come over late in the morning, he will have information by then to share with them. He will also know enough by then to ask them useful questions. It is agreed.

Brisbane spends half an hour making sure things are going properly inside and then calls Ralph's office. The receptionist tells him the number of the hotel in Atlanta. The front desk sends a bellhop to fetch Ralph from his meeting. He has a call. It's an emergency from home.

This is about 11:00 on Tuesday morning. Ralph is beside himself with anxiety. It's not about a call from the police. It's about the *absence* of a call. The fear has been building and swelling and pounding and tearing his insides to shreds. He has suffered 30 hours of the most excruciating hell, ever since the call didn't come on Monday morning. According to the plan described by Cap, the intruders were supposed to reset the alarm. It would go off and trigger a phone call from the security service to the home. When no one answered the call, the police would be summoned and the body would therefore be discovered early Monday morning, certainly by 4:00 or 5:00 AM. Consequently he should have heard from the police shortly thereafter. But he hasn't. He hears nothing Monday morning. Nothing Monday afternoon or evening. Nothing Tuesday morning. For 30 hours the panic proceeds to strengthen its grip. It's taking over. It's metastasizing. It's eating up his insides like an Ebola Virus.

All day Monday and thus far into Tuesday, Ralph does little but obsess about it. What happened? Did the contractors fail to show up? Did they fail to do their job? Did they rob the house and leave Bonnie alone? Did the alarm malfunction? *What the hell happened?* What if nothing happened? In that case, how's he going to square things with Cap? With the Chief? Will he have to go through this all over again? How's he going to arrange another alibi?

As the hours progress, new worries pile on top of the ones already in place. For one thing, his distress is attracting attention. Ralph is normally an active participant in meeting discussions, and he is known for his boisterous bonhomie in the off-hours socializing. But Sunday night, partying with his colleagues in the hotel bar, he is quiet and subdued, not his usual self. On Monday at the meetings he makes few contributions and appears distracted. At the group dinner on Monday evening he is so distant that colleagues start asking him what is wrong. Nothing, he says. A headache. He doesn't know if anybody is buying that story but it's the best he can do. He knows he should be acting normally, but he can't manage it. He is aware that his behavior is disastrous. He knows that when the police ask questions later, people will remember. This is just like when he screwed up with Bonnie after Thanksgiving.

And there's something else. On Monday night, after not hearing from the police all day, he's a wreck. So he downs five little bottles of liquor from the mini-bar in the room in order to make himself drunk enough to sleep. On Tuesday morning he realizes that this was a mistake. The minibar items will show up on his hotel bill. The cops will ask, why did he drink so much that particular night? Was he nervous about something? Why did he drink alone in his room instead of with the others at the bar?

Ralph is swept up in a whirlpool of terror, and he's spiraling out of control. So he is giddy with relief when he is called out of the meeting to take a phone call. *It HAPPENED!*

Trailing behind the bellhop Ralph keeps reminding himself: Act surprised. Act shocked. Act distraught. Ask questions. Ralph has rehearsed this call in his mind countless times over the past six weeks and he's prepared. The call goes well. He succeeds in acting surprised, shocked, distraught. He remembers to ask questions. He agrees to fly home immediately and drive directly to police head-quarters.

Ralph tells his boss that there's a family emergency and he has to go home. "No problem," his boss says. Ralph makes the 2:00 PM Delta, arriving in Boston at 4:31. By the time he makes his way through rush hour traffic and stops for din-ner, it's past 6:30 when he checks in with the desk sergeant at the State Police detective unit in Cambridge.

Stopping for dinner is Ralph's way of procrastinating in the hope that Bris-bane will have gone home for the day by then. That is understandable. Ralph is fatigued from his ordeal in Atlanta and he'd very much prefer to deal with the police tomorrow. In this, Ralph is being naive. Detective Brisbane is much more interested in meeting Ralph than he is in going home.

The desk sergeant punches Brisbane's extension, tells him Collins is here, and directs Ralph toward an interview room. Ralph waits there alone for five or six minutes. Brisbane figures it can't hurt to ratchet up Ralph's anxiety level a bit, and watches through a one way mirror. Ralph guesses he is being watched and forces himself to sit still so as not to betray signs of nervousness. That's a poor choice which has an effect opposite of the one Ralph intended. Brisbane, watching, is thinking that a normal husband who was told his wife had been shot would be agitated and frenetic, unable to sit still, crazed with the need to find out the details and to help the police catch the killer. Something's wrong with this guy, is what Brisbane is thinking.

He walks in and introduces himself. Then, before Ralph can open his mouth, Brisbane endeavors to throw him off balance: "It certainly took you long enough to get here."

"I'm here now," Ralph says, trying to sidestep the question.

Brisbane takes a seat across from Ralph. "I looked up the airline schedule on the internet, just trying to anticipate when you'd get here. I figure you caught the Delta two o'clock, arriving at 4:31."

"I did."

"It arrived on time. I checked."

"Yes."

"So it took you more than two hours to drive here from Logan. You must have stopped for dinner. A leisurely one at that."

Ralph says nothing.

"You were more interested in dinner than you were finding out what happened to your wife. Maybe you already know what happened to your wife."

Ralph searches for an answer. He finds one: "It's not that. I didn't have time to grab lunch, so I was famished. I thought we'd be here for a while and I wanted to be as helpful as I could without the distraction of being hungry, so I ate."

"Oh," says Brisbane, "Right. Why didn't I think of that?" He leans back in his chair. "I just want to make it clear," he continues. "There are no suspects yet. This is just an interview for the purpose of obtaining information to aid the investigation."

Ralph attempts to seize the initiative. "How about giving me some information, then. What did you find out today?"

"All right, Mr. Collins, here's what we found out today since I called you." Brisbane consults his little wirebound. "We found out that your wife died sometime between 9:00 PM Sunday and about 9:00 AM Monday. We know that from the temperature of the body and the stage of rigor mortis. We will probably have a more precise fix on the time when we do the autopsy and check the contents of the stomach. We understand she ate dinner at your in-laws Sunday night. Meanwhile we know she was absent from work on Monday, so that tends to corroborate the timing of late Sunday night or early Monday morning."

Ralph interjects: "On the phone you said something about intruders?"

"No. What I said is that we found evidence of a breaking and entering."

"Well, then there had to be intruders."

"Really," says Brisbane in full sarcasm mode. "How do we know there wasn't a break in sometime previously? Or afterwards? How do we know the break in wasn't staged? Mr. Collins, do you know something about this that we don't?"

"No, I just thought ..."

"Leave the thinking to us, Mr. Collins."

Ralph nods his head to show his assent.

Brisbane continues. "The other interesting fact is that the security system was turned off. No alarm signal was sent to the security company. Therefore nobody called or came over to check things out. There was no notification to the police. Yet when we had the company come over this afternoon, they demonstrated that the equipment was working perfectly. How do you account for that, Mr. Collins?"

Ralph thinks a while. "I can't," he says.

"Do you think your wife would have turned off the alarm?"

"I suppose it's possible."

"With you out of town?"

"Like I said, I can't account for it."

Brisbane presses on. "Here's the problem, Mr. Collins. If you didn't shut off the alarm, and your wife didn't shut off the alarm, then I have to believe the killer did. That means he knew the code. How do you account for that, Mr. Collins?"

"I don't know. Lucky for me I can leave the thinking to you."

If Ralph weren't so tired, he wouldn't be so smartmouthed. It's damaging. Ralph's wisecrack is not in itself incriminating. But it does serve to fix in Brisbane's mind the impression that this guy Collins is not exactly acting like a stunned, devastated widower.

Brisbane keeps up the pressure. "Mr. Collins, this doesn't smell like a random occurrence."

"Why not?" Ralph asks.

"The alarm, of course. But also, it's unusual for a burglar to select a house where somebody's home."

"Maybe they thought the house was empty."

Brisbane pounces: "They? How do you know it was more than one?"

"I don't."

"A slip of the tongue?"

"They, he, she, whatever."

"All right. One or more people entered while the car was there. Even more significant, the TV was on in the bedroom. Would a random burglar enter that house?"

"Maybe the TV wasn't on. Maybe the killer turned on the TV afterwards."

"He shoots your wife and then hangs around to catch the Letterman monologue?"

"I guess that doesn't make much sense."

"No, Mr. Collins, it does not. So you see my issue, don't you? Why would a burglar enter a house that has a sign outside from the security company, where a car is present, and where a bedroom is illuminated with the light from a TV screen? And if he did enter the house anyway, why would he go upstairs when he could hear the TV sound coming from up there?"

"Don't know."

"Uh huh. And there's something else. We'll know more when the forensic analysis is completed, but it appears to me that your wife was shot a close range, execution style. That is not typical for burglars who are taken by surprise and shoot in panic. Also, there is no evidence that your wife was armed. Therefore there appears to be no reason why a burglar should shoot her. Mr. Collins, this smells to me like a murder that was planned."

Ralph remembers to put on his act. "Oh my God. Oh my *God*. That's horrible."

"Yes, horrible. Mr. Collins, can you think of anybody who might have wanted to see you wife dead?"

Ralph pretends to consider the question. "… No … no … not that I can think of."

"Think hard, Mr. Collins. If you know anything, now is the time to tell us. We're going to find it out eventually, and if there's something you should have told us that you didn't, it will put you in a less than favorable light."

"There's no one I can think of. Bonnie was well liked. Everybody loved her, including me."

Brisbane pauses for a little while. "All right, Mr. Collins. That's all for now. You can go. We'll keep in touch."

"That's it?"

"That's it for now, Mr. Collins. But you can't go in the house. It's still a crime scene."

"When can I go back?"

"Probably Thursday evening. Do you have anyone you can stay with until then?"

"I'll check into the Marriott," Ralph says. There is a Marriott in Newton just off Rt. 128.

"If you need to pick up some personal belongings, a patrolman will let you in the house and accompany you for that purpose. One thing, though. If you go home, be prepared to meet the press. They're staked out on your lawn waiting for you to show up."

The press. Ralph hadn't thought about that. Damn. More traps. More chances to screw up. And the whole world is going to know. He's going to have to cope with people offering their condolences. Bonnie's friends will send over casseroles. He doesn't even like casseroles. Well, macaroni and beef isn't so bad.

He's in a room at the Marriott by 8:30. An hour later he goes downstairs to have some drinks at the bar until 11:00, then returns to his room to watch the news by himself.

This is what he sees:

The station logo, the news logo, the music.

The Anchor reads the opening teaser:

The wife of a sales executive is shot to death in Newton. Labor troubles shut down a manufacturing plant. And the Celtics mix it up with the Nets.

Close up of Anchor:

The wife of a sales executive was found dead in her Newton home today with a single gunshot wound to the head. WBST reporter Honor McCorkle is live at the scene. Honor?

McCorkle on screen, live remote:

Brad, the peace of this quiet neighborhood of luxurious homes in Newton was shattered when numerous police vehicles converged upon this house on Rosedale Circle. They arrived in response to a 911 call from the victim's mother.

Film of body in closed body bag being removed from house and put into ambulance, McCorkle voiceover:

It's quiet now, but earlier today the residence was swarming with police as they searched for clues to solve the mystery of who shot Bonnie Collins, wife of sales executive Ralph Collins. Neighbors were at a loss to understand why anyone would want to kill Mrs. Collins, who was described as warm and friendly.

McCorkle on screen:

Earlier this afternoon, we talked with State Police Detective Arthur Brisbane, who's leading the investigative team.

Film of McCorkle interviewing Brisbane in front of house, in daylight:

McCorkle:	Detective Brisbane, do the police know the story of what happened here?
Brisbane:	No. That is what the investigation is going to reveal. We are just getting started.
McCorkle:	Are there any suspects at all?
Brisbane:	It is still too early. We are just getting started.
McCorkle:	Have you talked with the husband yet?
Brisbane:	Yes, on the phone. He's out of town at a business meeting. He is on his way back now.
McCorkle:	Detective, was this a random break in, a spontaneous act of rage, or a pre-meditated murder?
Brisbane:	We don't know yet. The evidence so far is contradictory.
McCorkle:	Thank you, Detective Brisbane.

McCorkle, live:

Brad, officials are tight lipped about the course of their investigation as of now, but we have been told that the husband's alibi that he was out of town on business has been confirmed, so this does not appear to be a case of domestic violence.

Anchor, in studio:

Thank you, Honor. Meanwhile, WBST sources close to the investigation confirmed this evening that police are now leaning towards the theory that this was a targeted murder, rather than a random burglary gone bad. That's all they are willing to reveal at this time.

After these messages, a strike at Savannah Manufacturing Company in Stoneham ...

Ralph thinks, "That wasn't so bad."

Gladys and Ken are watching the same broadcast. "I knew it!" says Ken. Gladys bursts into tears.

8

Tuesday evening we were all …

Scratch that. Definitely not all.

Tuesday evening the family came together at the Legatos. This was no Kinkade moment.

Heather and Sally were sent off to the den with a video, while the adults gathered in the living room. There, Ken did something unusual: he put some wine and liquor bottles, and mixers, and ice, on an end table. He knew people would want refills. He knew people wouldn't want to leave the room to get them. It was a subtle gesture that reminded me of something I was prone to forget: Ken is quite capable of nuanced understanding. It's a trait that is often obscured by his commanding physical presence, his avuncular style. He even has the capacity to be empathic and sensitive, although, I hasten to add, that side of him erupts sporadically and unpredictably. But that night Ken was great.

So it was that as Gladys told us her story, Ken sat quietly and held her hand. He was tuned in to her need to talk about it, and thereby connect with the rest of her family. He sensed that talking about it would help her take the first step toward making sense of the inexplicable, toward beginning to bring reason to insanity, toward starting the process of imposing order upon chaos.

Gladys began at the beginning, unsparing with the details: the unanswered calls, Laura, Mr. Benson, the TV, the blood …

After their conversation in the car, Detective Brisbane had urged them to leave. "Pretty soon," he said, "this place will be crawling with reporters. They'll descend like locusts. You don't want to be here." The Legatos knew this was good advice, but they were in no condition to act on it. All they could do was sit in Gladys' car. They didn't talk, they just sat. Only when a TV remote broadcast van pull up nearby, a bright electric lime colored obscenity sprouting rooftop transmitters and satellite dishes, with beautiful people in the cab joking insouciantly and heedlessly with one another, were the Legatos provoked to mobilize. "Follow me," said Ken as he heaved himself out the door on the passenger side.

Gladys did that. As she put the car in drive, she knew instinctively that their destination would be Jim's parish church. The church is in Waltham, a town adjacent to Newton. Regular city streets connect the two communities, traversing the town line. Gladys followed Ken along some of those streets and soon they were parked side by side in the lot at the church.

Amy's cheerful greeting proved to be a source of excruciating pain. Amy is the parish secretary. "Hello Mr. and Mrs. Legato. What a pleasure to see you," was all she said. Amy, brimming as always with the good cheer that is born of good will, was a person still engaged in ordinary life, and ordinary life was now a parallel universe. She had no idea. The world was collapsing and she had no idea. The universe at hand was disintegrating and she had no idea. For everybody but Gladys and Ken, ordinary life was still happening. For Gladys and Ken, ordinary life was finished. The reminder unwittingly delivered by Amy's greeting, bringing home the breadth and depth of the chasm that separated the Legatos not only from other people but also from their own lives as they had known it before this morning, was unbearable. The burden was heavy, crushing.

Ken composed himself. Amy was blameless and there was no call to take out his fury on her. "Nice to see you too. Is Jim here?"

Jim wasn't. Amy offered to page him, and that's what happened.

Jim was disturbed enough after he called in and Amy told him his parents were waiting. When he drove up and saw both cars in the lot he got ready for serious trouble. "Come on in," he said to Ken and Gladys as he passed through the waiting area on his way to his office.

The ritual of removing and hanging up the winter coats, arranging the chairs, settling down, bought them some time. But all too soon the inevitable silence descended. One of them, Ken or Gladys, would have to fill the vacuum.

Ken felt it was his responsibility. "It's about Bonnie."

Jim waited for more.

"She's dead. She was murdered."

When Jim had been thinking trouble, he never imagined trouble anywhere near as terrible as this. Somebody sick, maybe. A divorce. An accident. A fire. He was ready for that kind trouble. But not this. He needed to regroup. "What happened?"

Gladys and Ken told the story together, in tandem.

When they finished Jim asked, "What do the police think happened?"

Ken shook his head. "They don't know. It's too soon. It's been less than three hours for them."

"Dad, what do you think?"

Ken hurled his thunderbolt. "I think that no good scumbag of a husband was behind it. I think that somehow some way he arranged for it to happen."

Jim felt the sensation of being sucked helplessly into a swirling vortex. "What? Dad, what are you saying? Ralph? *Ralph?* Why would you think a thing like that?"

"Because. Because *just* when he happens to be out of town, *that's* when an intruder comes? Not just any intruder, but a murderous one? I don't think so. It's too coincidental. It's too convenient. And Bonnie wasn't armed. She has no gun. She would never resist. There was no reason why a burglar would shoot her." For Ken, the logic was airtight. The conclusion was inescapable. The more he put it into words, the more he could see that it had to be true.

Jim was floored. Because he understood what his father was saying, he couldn't dismiss it. But if his father's suspicions turned out to be correct, the ramifications were staggering. Jim's protest was less a function of disbelief than of unwillingness to imagine the consequences: "But Dad, think of what you're saying. Ralph is part of our family. Bonnie loved him. You're making him out to be a monster. You're saying that Bonnie loved and married a murderer. But why? I mean, why would he do that? What would be his motive?"

Ken's anger bubbled up to the surface. "I don't know his motive, dammit! But I always knew he was a piece of shit! … It's only a small step to being a monster."

Even for Jim, who is accustomed to dealing with emotional traumas, this was a lot to absorb all at once. He couldn't imagine what to think, much less what to say. Gladys, however, had her mind on something else. "Ken," she said, "I didn't know you felt that way."

"I never told you," said Ken.

"But why not?"

Ken found this difficult to explain. He wasn't all that clear about it himself. He knew he had avoided making issue with Bonnie over her choice of a husband, and had justified this on the grounds that doing so would upset Bonnie without accomplishing anything constructive. Since he hadn't told Bonnie how he felt, he couldn't very well tell Gladys. Ken also knew that Gladys had made Bonnie a promise to extend to Ralph a warm welcome into the family, in spite of her misgivings. He was therefore able to tell himself that it would be harder for Gladys to keep that promise if she were aware that Ken shared her doubts. At the same time, keeping his own distrust of Ralph secret from his wife helped Ken keep his feelings hidden from Bonnie as well.

With Jim listening in astonishment, Ken offered these convoluted and circular explanations. If his disclosure was an admission of sorts, it fell far short of a full confession. It was reality refracted through the prism of Ken's need to justify past behavior that in hindsight appeared less than admirable. And if his argument strikes you as a peculiarly disingenuous rationalization, which is how Jim saw it, that's because it was. Had Ken had been more candid about his motives, he would have had to admit to a purpose much less noble than that of maintaining Bonnie's untroubled state of mind. The truth was both less complicated than Ken's self-delusion and less flattering: simply put, he was loath to risk alienating his favorite daughter by confronting her with his views on her poor selection of a spouse. Just as surely as he knew he could not dissuade Bonnie from marrying whomever she wanted, he also knew deep down that he should give it a try anyway, as Gladys had, if for no other reason than to maintain his self respect. But he had not. In the tug of war between Ken's unslakable thirst for Bonnie's unwavering devotion and his responsibility to act like a parent, the exigency of his quest for Bonnie's unalloyed affections prevailed. The bottom line was that he had wimped out.

On the other hand, for the moment, then and there in Jim's office, some credit was due. While Ken's spin on the matter was incomplete and self serving, it nevertheless required a modicum of courage for him to disclose anything at all, because he was owning up to at least some degree of complicity in Bonnie's fate: If he had known Ralph was no good and had said nothing, some blame was attached to him for the outcome. And he also showed some courage as he apologized to Gladys for keeping his assessment of Ralph a secret for so long. He expected her to be sore in the extreme about that.

She would have been more than sore, she would have been irate, had she not been flooded with relief at the revelation that she wasn't alone. For all these years, Gladys had struggled with the feeling that she was the sole dissenter in the matter of Ralph, that she was out of step with everyone else in the family. She had second-guessed and suppressed in her mind the intuitive doubts about Ralph that stubbornly refused to subside in her gut. She had begun to doubt her judgment. She fretted that there was something wrong with her. She fretted equally that there was something wrong with everybody else. It wasn't the biggest pressure in her life, but the questions plagued her insistently, like mosquitoes in the countryside at dusk. Now in an instant, her thoughts, her feelings, her very being had all been validated. The mosquitoes were gone. It made her flush with tenderness for Ken. It made her unable to summon the anger that she knew was justified. So she told Ken she wasn't mad. "Thank you," Ken said.

Jim looked at his mother. "You never liked Ralph either?"

"No"

"Bonnie knew that?"

"She knew I didn't trust him."

He asked the logical next question: "Mom, does this mean that you agree with Dad? Agree that Ralph is responsible?"

"No," Gladys said. Her voice was quiet and firm. "But it's not impossible, either. I'll have to be shown some actual evidence before I agree with your father. But I can't disagree. It's too early. We'll see what the police turn up. Meantime, I'm keeping my mind open."

They all were quiet for a while. The phone broke the silence. He had forgotten to tell Amy to hold his calls. Jim picked it up. He listened, then said, "I'll have to call you back later." It wasn't about Bonnie and it was nothing that couldn't wait. As he replaced the phone on the cradle, he asked Gladys, "How are you holding up, Mom?"

"All right so far. Thanks for asking. It doesn't seem real yet. I guess it hasn't sunk in."

With this descent into superficial palaver, Ken decided that the visit had run its course. "Son, we'd like you to do something for us."

"Sure, Dad."

"We'd like you to call the rest of the family. We just don't have the strength to do that."

"Sure, Dad. No problem." It was not "no problem." But Jim understood why Ken would make the request and thought it was reasonable. As his dad always said, he was the professional. That didn't make it any easier, though.

"And son," Ken continued, "Everybody is going to want to come over. Tell them not to arrive before dinnertime. Tell them not to call. Tell them we're going to take the phone off the hook. Gladys and I need the afternoon to be alone together. Just the two of us. We need a few hours by ourselves and they can come at dinnertime. Will you do that?"

"Of course, Dad."

Gladys thought: that was good. She looked at her husband and gave his hand a squeeze. Sometimes Ken was a man of superb instincts. It reminded her of why she married him.

And then they went home.

They hit the kitchen first, Ken taking a detour along the way to grab some wine and some bourbon from the dining room sideboard. Once in the kitchen, he took the phone off the hook, then filled a tumbler with wine for Gladys and another with bourbon and ice for himself. Anesthesia was the objective of the moment. The idea was to overpower the anguish through brute force of alcohol. Already it seemed like the day was never ending, like they'd been on the go for 48 hours straight. It wasn't even noon yet.

Outside the sun was shining and the whole world seemed to sparkle under a cloudless azure sky. This seemed to Gladys like a direct slap in the face from God. What had she done to deserve such punishment? *Where had she failed?*

Ken and Gladys sat at the table in quiet communion. They were waiting for the onset of a liquor-induced stupor sufficient to buffer the shock and wall off the nightmare. Neither one could figure out another way to get through the next few hours. Neither could think of any other way to stave off the question that was beginning to assault them both with escalating force: *What could they have done to prevent this?*

They gulped down the alcohol quickly, greedy for escape, waiting impatiently for it to dull their senses. Finally, after half an hour or so, they began to feel woozy and lightheaded, and decided to go upstairs and lie down. As they stretched out on the bed together, arms touching, Gladys said, "Ken?"

"Yes?"

"Jim had a good question. If you are right about Ralph, what was the reason?"

This was the missing link for Ken, too. "I don't know that, honey. If I did, I'd tell you. I'm pinning my hopes on Brisbane. I'm hoping the guy is good enough to figure it out."

And with that, the alcohol took control and they slept.

Ken awakened around three. As he got up to go to the bathroom, the motion woke Gladys. When he returned, Gladys asked him if he wanted to accompany her to the supermarket. Puzzled at first, he suggested that they bring in pizza or Chinese. Why should she cook? "Because," she answered, "If I don't do something to keep myself busy, I'll go crazy." No argument there. He went with her. In the end, she made stuffed cabbage with raisin sauce accompanied by home made spaetzle. Comfort food, but labor intensive.

That evening in the living room, when Gladys finished telling her story and Ken had made his case for the prosecution, Jeff was the first to react: "You know I got that son of a bitch his promotion?"

Jeff had the floor. "Yeah. I got him in the door at Impulse Communications." That was Jeff's previous employer. "He sold them three big copiers and that clinched the manager's job for him. I feel like an idiot."

Jim led a chorus of protestations to the effect that no one could possibly have known what was going to happen, and what he had done was a good thing intended to benefit Bonnie. Gladys added a reminder that Ralph's culpability was nothing more than a theory at this point.

"Yeah? Well, gravity is nothing more than a theory, too," said Ken.

"Do you know," Jeff went on, wiping his eyes, "that Bonnie was the only one in this family who ever cared enough to challenge my religious beliefs? I know what you're thinking, my lack of beliefs. OK. Still, she didn't just dismiss them as some kind of youthful episode that I'll get over soon. She didn't write them off as the embarrassing rantings of the family's black sheep. She took them seriously. She cared about them. She cared about *me!* She wouldn't let up. *Isn't life empty if there is no meaning in it beyond yourself? Isn't it hard to endure the difficult times in life if you can't turn for support to a higher power who loves you? Isn't it unlikely that the universe came together in such an amazing way merely by accident? How can you stand the existence of so much injustice and hurt and evil in the world if you don't see it all as part of a larger plan for good?* The thing is, I never convinced her to see anything my way, and she never changed my mind either. But that didn't matter because she came to understand and respect what I had to say, and, though you may not believe it, I came to understand and respect her point of view too. The faith she had was a genuine faith, a faith that came from her bedrock need to believe that life has meaning. Her faith was unshakable, and I absolutely positively loved her for it. And what did it get her?"

Jim answered softly. "It got her a life graced with the comfort and companionship of a loving God."

"Really? And where was God on Monday morning?" Jeff snapped. "Maybe he was distracted by his cell phone while somebody came in and blew her brains out."

"Enough!" said Ken.

Jeff started talking again. I had never before seen him with so much to say and such an urgency to say it. "Do you know that if it weren't for Bonnie, Sharon and I might not be together now?" He turned to Sharon. "Mind if I tell?"

Sharon shrugged and patted his knee affectionately. "If you want to remind everyone how you almost screwed up major big time, by all means be my guest." Sharon reminds me more than anyone else of Jane Pauley, observant and unflappable as she takes in the folly of the human circus, floating slightly above it all in mellow and good natured bemusement.

But of course, that evening wasn't about Jeff, it was about Bonnie, so Jeff was unabashed. The story of Jeff and Sharon is embedded in the family lore. They met at a Saturday night dinner party hosted by mutual friends. For once, the matchmaking worked. The instant he first laid eyes on her as he entered the room he whispered a single word: Wow! More importantly, he drove home that night thinking he had found what he hadn't even been aware he was looking for. Sharon was different: She was smart, she was not only honest but candid, and she was direct, without pretense or artifice. Jeff was powerfully attracted to those qualities. He was excited by them. In fact, she took his breath away. He pretty much knew by the time their salads were finished that he was going to want to marry this woman, kids and all. The only question remaining was whether she was going to have any interest whatsoever in him.

He needn't have worried. Sharon was coming off a failed marriage to her college heartthrob, who was gorgeous and sexy but also vain, inflexible and controlling. The relationship had begun deteriorating within months after the wedding, and grew progressively more frustrating and empty for both of them. The children made it harder, not better. In the end, he had an affair, she kicked him out, and he never looked back. Sharon learned a lesson from her mistake—there's more to marriage than bagging a hunk—and was not about to repeat it. Yet the experience also taught her that she enjoyed the intimacy of marriage. She found deep satisfaction in the bonding of two individuals into a couple. Far from turning her sour on the institution of marriage, the episode taught her that she deserved a good one.

Jeff was planning to call Sharon to ask her out. She beat him to it, taking the initiative to call him the very next day. From her perspective, the guy seated next to her at the dinner party may not have been 100% perfect: he could use an extra dose of self-confidence. But she was drawn to his gentle sweetness. There was sensitivity and civility in this man. She could tell that Jeff was suffused with the sort of fundamental decency encountered less and less often in a culture more characterized by jostling elbows than by helping hands. At the dinner she was aware of the good chemistry between them. And upon reflection afterwards, she recognized that his amalgam of character traits were exactly the ones she was yearning for in a lifetime partner. They were also the ones she was praying to find in a father for her children. If she had possessed the vocabulary, she would have told herself that she had come across that scarcest of rare commodities: a real *mensch*.

Jeff liked the fact that Sharon would do something as ballsy as break the rules and call him first. He liked the fact that she intuited he wouldn't get hung up over the role reversal. He liked the fact that she was interested enough in him to go ahead and do such a bold thing. So he made the suggestion that rather than meet for a conventional dinner date, perhaps they might go somewhere during the day that next Saturday and include her kids—the Children's Museum, maybe, or possibly the Aquarium. Sharon liked *that* idea very very much.

And the relationship moved forward from there. They learned that the qualities they had observed in each other at the dinner party were both genuine and reliable. They discovered that they communicated easily and well, so much so

that it was only later and with surprise that Sharon became aware of the diffidence with which Jeff related to almost everybody else. They found the same
things amusing. Their views on right and wrong were congruent. And to the
amazement of Jeff and Sharon both, he connected effortlessly with Heather and
Sally; as a result, when they went out they were more likely to dine at Chuck E
Cheese than at Chez Henri.

All of the Legatos adored Sharon from the outset and she quickly became a
fixture at family get-togethers. Thus when Jeff showed up alone one night about
eight months into their romance, her absence was cause for alarm. Jeff offered the
excuse that Sharon had "something else she hadda do." No one was satisfied with
that explanation, but everyone other than Bonnie thought it best not to pry.
Fearless as always, Bonnie thought otherwise. After the meal was over, she
grabbed Jeff's hand and literally dragged him into the den.

That much was witnessed by the family. Now, for the first time, Jeff related
what had happened there.

The den has a couch and they sat on it side by side. Bonnie wasted no time:
"Are you going to tell me what's going on?"

Jeff managed a grin. "Do I have a choice?"

On this day after Bonnie's death, as Jeff began to recall that conversation on
the couch from years ago, the memory of his sister made his eyes well up with
tears. This was another story about how much Bonnie cared about him. Another
story about the time when she was still a living, breathing human being. Another
story about when she was still a vibrant presence that lit up any room she entered.
About why he cared so much about her. About why he was hurting so much.

"No choice," Bonnie had said, back then on the couch.

Jeff made the decision at that point to level with her, as if it were possible for
him to do anything else. He had bared his soul to her on previous occasions and
had never regretted doing so. That night, sitting with her in the den, he was more
grateful than ever that Bonnie was there for him. It didn't matter that he was the
older of the two. Although still in her dating years, she was the one that brought
to their relationship the wisdom of life experience. He could never figure out
where that came from, yet it was undeniable. Sandy had that quality too, but
Bonnie was the one who somehow always managed to put things in just the right
perspective.

Jeff had said, "You know how I've been spending weekends down here with
Sharon?"

Bonnie nodded.

"From time to time, she comes up to Portland for the weekend?"

Bonnie nodded.

"Well all that traveling back and forth was getting old, for both of us."

"So?"

"So a few weeks ago she told me that her lease runs out in a couple of months and the landlord asked if she planned to renew it."

"And you told her?"

"I told her that it would make me the happiest man alive if she would tell him no and move to Portland and live with me."

"And?"

"And she told him no."

"But you're not the happiest man alive ..."

"No. I'm the worriedest man alive."

Bonnie couldn't help giggling. "Worriedest?"

Jeff smiled and gave her a playful tap on the shoulder. "You know what I mean. Most worried. Bonnie, I'm 27 years old and Sharon is my first serious relationship ever. Moving in together is a huge step. I don't know if I can handle it. I don't know if I can be there for her in the ways she will need me over the long haul. I don't know if I'm really the man she thinks I am. I don't know if I'm the man I think I am. And it changes everything with the kids. Right now I'm just their friend. If they moved in, I would be their de facto father. What kind of a father could I make?"

"I don't know," Bonnie said.

"Don't know what?"

"All of the above. The answers to any of your questions. Did you tell her this?"

"Yes. She got angry. She said if I'm thinking about throwing away what we have together I'm an idiot. I said I don't want to throw anything away, I just want to take things more slowly. She said I can take it as slowly as I please all by myself, and I should give her a call when I figure it out."

"Want to hear what I think?"

Jeff's face had a rueful expression. "Sure. I can only imagine."

"She's right. You're an idiot."

"I appreciate your tact," said Jeff.

"Look," Bonnie went on, "for somebody who's always so concerned with logic, I'm amazed you don't see where the logic of what you've been saying will lead to."

"Where?"

"It will lead to you going to your grave a lonely old bachelor."

"No."

"Yes. Jeff, none of the questions or doubts you talked about can be resolved in any way by taking things slowly. The passage of time by itself won't provide—can't provide—any answer about whether you will make a good husband or father. Long distance dating will never provide those answers. The only way you can ever find out is if you try it. You have to do it and see what happens. If you put off trying it until you think you already know the outcome, that moment can logically never ever arrive."

Jeff stared at Bonnie. He hadn't thought of it that way. He considered logic to be his specialty, and here was Bonnie running rings around him in the logic department.

She wasn't finished. "You love her, don't you?"

The question caught her brother off guard. "Uh. Yeah. Sure. Definitely. Very much."

"Why?"

"Why do I love her? Because she's terrific."

"Oh? Do you think that every guy that's ever known her loves her the same way you do?"

"No, that doesn't seem likely."

"Why not? Isn't she the same terrific person when she's with other men?"

"I would think so."

"Then logically they should all love her like you do. But they don't. Some people are terrific but it doesn't mean everybody else falls in love with them." Bonnie broke into a wide grin. "Hey, I'm terrific. Not everybody falls in love with me ..."

"Yes they do."

"Jeffrey, be serious. Most people are not terrific, so most people fall in love with other people who are definitely not terrific. Jeff, listen up: love has nothing to do with one or the other or both people being terrific."

"It doesn't?"

"No. Jeff. Love is not about what each person is like. It's about how the two people involved connect with each other. That's why what you think is a problem is not in fact a problem at all. I'll tell you what you think: You think that Sharon's terrific and you are not. You think if you live together she'll discover how unterrific you are. You'll be exposed as a fraud—*oh my God, this bozo Jeff is not as terrific as I thought*—and therefore she won't love you any more. How'm I doing so far?"

"Oh, Bonnie, I don't know ..."

"I'm doin' good, so keep listening. The only real problem is that you don't understand why she loves you. So understand this: whether she loves you is not about how terrific you are. It's about how you make her feel. So let's turn the question around. What about *her* makes *you* feel good?"

"I don't know … I guess, that she understands me."

"Good answer. Do you understand her?"

"Yeah. Pretty well."

"You think she likes that?"

"Yeah."

"Is that going to stop if she moves in?"

"No …"

"OK. Now we're getting somewhere. Who understands her better than you do?"

"Nobody, I think."

"OK then. What about Sharon would you change?"

"Not a thing. She's perfect."

"Then that's all there is to it. Jeff, listen to what I'm telling you: Sharon doesn't love you because she thinks you're perfect. She loves you because you understand her better than anybody else in the world, and because you love her and accept her just the way she is. That makes her feel wonderful. Is there anybody else on the planet that could do that better than you? Is that going to change if she moves in?"

"But, that's easy."

"Yes," said Bonnie. "If it comes naturally, then it's easy."

"Sis," said Jeff, "when did you get to be so smart? Did you ever think about becoming a lawyer?"

"God forbid," said Bonnie.

"You'd be good. Big bucks, too," said Jeff.

"Becoming a lawyer takes too much school," said Bonnie. "It's a whole lot easier to marry one."

Jeff had thought overnight about what Bonnie said, and had called Sharon the following morning.

The next recollection of the evening about Bonnie came from Jim. Jim had been crying as the memories came flooding back. Now he was ready to speak. "If it weren't for Bonnie," he said, "I wouldn't be a priest." This was a story we all knew, and Jim knew that we knew it, but his need to express his love for Bonnie was too insistent to suppress.

At the time he was referring to, Jim was about to graduate from college with a degree in sociology and had no idea what he was going to do with it. Week after week the Boston Globe was stuffed with employment classifieds, and not a single one had a heading that said: "Sociologist Wanted." Jim was aware that many sociologists have academic careers, but this did not appeal to him. He saw little point in teaching undergraduates a discipline that would deposit them in the same situation that he was in right then. Nor did he fancy the idea of using teaching as a perch upon which to roost while he built a career in research. He wasn't interested in deconstructing what other people did. He wanted to be out and about doing things himself.

On Easter in the spring of his senior year, Jim's employment prospects were topic number one at the Legato's dining room table. The subject had been exhausted and they had moved on to other things when Bonnie piped up over dessert: "The Peace Corps. What about the Peace Corps?"

Just about everybody stared at Bonnie as though she were daft. Sandy put into words what almost everyone else was thinking. "How is that going to help him find a job?"

Jeff was the exception. He understood. "It's not about finding a job. It's about finding himself."

Ken was derisive. He couldn't restrain himself, even though the idea had come from Bonnie. "Find himself? When did he lose himself? Was himself misplaced? Was it misplaced in Tanzania or some broken down place like that? What if he goes off to Tanzania to find himself, and it turns out himself is sitting there waiting to be found in Zimbabwe? Or what if himself is in Zimbabwe while his career is waiting to be found right here in graduate school?"

"OK, forget it," Bonnie said.

But she didn't forget it. She cornered Jim alone after dinner was finished. She asked him, "Will you at least think about it?"

"I don't know," he said. "I'm not the kind of person that joins the Peace Corps."

Bonnie was ready for that one. "What kind of person is that?"

"You know, a ... what's the word ... do gooder."

"You don't want to do good?"

"Sure, but in Tanzania?"

"Why not? Look. What's the most exciting thing you've ever done?"

"Well ... I don't know if I should say this ... I had sex a couple of times."

Bonnie waved her hand dismissively. "You and maybe seven billion other people. I don't mean that. I mean, what have you done that's unusual, that's a little different, where you test yourself, where you see what you're made of?"

"I don't know. Never, I guess."

"Right. And when do you plan to do something like that in the future?"

"I don't know. I haven't thought about it."

"Right. So now is the perfect time to think about it. You're young, you're single, you have no responsibilities. Why not have an adventure? Why not think of the Peace Corps that way, as an adventure? And not only that, the government pays for it. An adventure for free. Think! If you never do anything like it again, it will be the adventure of a lifetime. You'll treasure the memory. You'll look back on it and say to yourself, "Holy cow, I actually did that?" And if it changes everything and you end up with a life full of adventure, then it will be a life altering experience. Jimmy, all I'm saying is for you to check it out. Look at their web site. Read their literature. Talk to people. Then decide."

Jim said he would but didn't mean it. He thought he had brushed aside the whole silly notion, little knowing that Bonnie's crazy idea had stealthily entered his bloodstream and in due course would infect his brain. Over the next few weeks, despite himself, he began more and more to visualize what it would feel like to have an adventure, or more precisely, what it would feel like to come home after having had an adventure. He began to realize that somebody like him, who never had adventures, was precisely the kind of person who needed one most. Almost furtively, he found himself looking at the Peace Corps web site. He stole glances at the literature. He submitted an application, just for a lark, nothing more than that. And in June, the week before graduation, he received an invitation to join a group of volunteers going to Peru. His acceptance went out by return mail.

He was sent to the town of Huancayo, a regional center of trade and provincial government nestled on a plateau high in the Andes. His assignment was to help the local priest, a Catholic missionary from Great Britain, set up and run a community health center. It was indeed a life altering experience. He loved the work but at the same time became envious of the priest. Father Timothy had something he didn't: a life that was settled. He had more than that. His life had focus, it had purpose. It was embedded in a community, it was connected to other people.

Jim shared this observation with Father Timothy one evening over dinner in the rectory. "Perhaps all that is true," said Father Timothy, "but the main thing is, my life is embedded in a community of faith. It is connected to God."

It wasn't that night, or even that week, but several months later that it dawned on Jim. He was lying in bed but unable to sleep because he was thinking of home. Then it came upon him like rays of sunshine bursting forth from behind a cloud. It was like tumblers in the lock had fallen into place and the door to the safe had swung open. *There was no need to envy Father Timothy. He could be like Father Timothy!* Yes! Of course! It was so obvious! That was why he was here! It was no accident. The Peace Corps had made the travel arrangements but God had planned the trip. He was here, three thousand miles from home and eleven thousand feet above sea level in the middle of the Andes mountains, for the purpose of meeting Father Tomothy. He was here for the purpose of getting up close and personal with the rest of his life. He was here to meet his destiny.

So this is how you know. When God calls you to your vocation, this is how you know. You just know.

Thank you, God!

The following morning before the clinic opened, unable to contain his excitement, Jim sought out Father Timothy and described the awakening of his calling the previous night. Father Timothy's response was the best it possibly could have been. "Jim," he said, "I've been waiting." The remaining year and a half of Jim's Peace Corps term sped by in a fog of frenzied activity on the outside, inner peace and contentment within. Jim tended to his duties at the clinic by day and was tutored in the ways of the Catholic ministry by night. Before returning to the States, Jim applied to and was accepted by one of the finest seminaries. That was easy to accomplish. He had a glowing letter of recommendation from Father Timothy.

Jim's call to the ministry was a family legend. Years later, as he retold the story in the Legato's living room, everyone knew the sequence of events but was eager to hear it again anyway. This time, however, Jim finished the story by bringing it back to Bonnie. "Without Bonnie," he said, "I would never have gone to Peru, never have met Father Timothy, never have attended the seminary. Sure, Bonnie was being Bonnie, but she was also doing God's work. If that isn't the very definition of an angel, I don't know what is."

"Amen," said Ken.

And the stories poured out. Everybody in the family took turns remembering how Bonnie had touched their souls, had changed their lives for the better. They recalled the Christmas tree decorating parties. The brouhaha over college. The high school romantic intrigues, conquests, and disappointments. Peter Pan. Around and around it went, with remembrances to fill the night and recollections to last a lifetime.

And so it was, in the living room over white zinfandel and bourbon, at the dining table over stuffed cabbage and spaetzle and homemade carrot cake with homemade cream cheese icing, that the communal family memory of Bonnie Legato—not Bonnie Collins—was collectively sculpted, molded, cast, cooled, burnished, unveiled and consecrated by Gladys, Ken, Jim, Jeff, Sandy, Sharon and me.

9

It is almost eight o'clock when Ralph wakes up on Thursday, late for him. He opens his eyes in a hotel room in the town where he lives and he is neither disoriented nor confused.

The problem has been plaguing him: how should he handle making contact with the Legatos? What he truly wants is to avoid them entirely. But in the real world that is out of the question. There will be a wake, a Mass, a burial, a criminal investigation. Avoidance is not an option.

Ralph is thinking about this as he showers and shaves. His plan had been to act the shocked, distraught widower for a week and then discretely drop off their radar screen. That won't work now. That detective has already made it clear that he is under suspicion. No surprise there; Cap had anticipated that. But the fact that this has come up so soon complicates his dealings with the Legatos. It is more likely than not that Brisbane has shared his suspicions with the family. It is possible, too, that the family has developed suspicions on their own, especially with the memory of the month after Thanksgiving still fresh in their minds. The absence of any attempt at contact from the Legatos looms as significant. There has been no call on his cell, no message left at home, nothing on his office voice mail. Clearly, nobody on that side of the family is concerned about how the grieving widower is holding up.

On the other hand, he hasn't called them either. To begin with, he doesn't know what to say. Should he be consoling them for losing their daughter? Shouldn't they be consoling him for losing his wife? OK, both. So, who goes first? Secondly, he has little appetite for coming to grips with the likelihood that if the Legatos are suspicious, they will be hostile as well.

And it's not as if his relationship with the Legato family has ever been all that warm and fuzzy. They're cold, that crew. Bonnie was the exception. Bonnie was not only intelligent and gorgeous, she was hot hot hot. But the rest of them, what a zoo. Take the sister, Sandy. She's cute enough, sure, more than cute in fact, but she's also sarcastic and a ball buster. Who could stand being married to her? The brother up in Maine? What a negative, gloomy loser. Although ... he did all right with Sharon. Sharon's quite a looker, and she has this quality of ... I don't know ... of inner peace, you might say, a serenity almost. She must need that, being married to the loser. What she sees in Jeff is a mystery. The priest? What a waste. Here's a guy who understands people and gets along with everybody, and what does he do? He spends his life driving around in a minivan visiting sick people. Hell, with his brand of blarney he could easily have made VP of sales somewhere and raked in moolah by the truckload. What a waste, too, to give up sex for life, when he could have had his pick. Any babe he wants. Seriously, forget about babes, he could make a great husband for some woman. That's not just a waste, that's a shame. And Barry, the poor schnook who has to put up with Sandy? He's decent enough, but dull dull dull. Ken is the hardest to deal with. He hates me 'cause I made off with his precious daughter, but hell, nobody would be good enough for his precious daughter. Besides which, what the guy is, is your basic garden variety prick. Gladys, though, she is OK. She has a good head on her shoulders and a lot of common sense. And damn, can she cook.

Ralph is aware that his general lack of good feeling toward the Legatos is reciprocated, especially by Gladys and Ken. He has always felt marginally accepted by Bonnie's siblings and their partners, reluctantly tolerated by the parents, but embraced by no one. So now his attitude is: screw'em. Except that he can't. He has to position himself carefully. If he acts the grief stricken victim, the Legatos may not buy the act. If they think he was involved, that would stir up even more antagonism and suspicion, which is the last thing he needs. On the other hand, if he doesn't act that way, he will be handing the police and prosecutors a treasure trove of weirdness that they'll surely use against him.

What he has to do is figure out how to appear sufficiently natural not to trigger any reaction at all from either the Legatos or the police. This is easier said than done, of course, but as he dresses and then as he breakfasts in the Marriott coffee shop, a concept starts to take shape and crystallize. It is this: He will get in touch with Ken and Gladys immediately, but it will be all about practical matters. As the husband, the body will be released to him, not them. With complete sincerity, with no phoniness, he can extend an olive branch to the Legatos by offering to cater to their preferences in arrangements for the wake, the Funeral Mass, and the burial. This costs him nothing. This he can do. It will tide him over this week with the expedient fiction that he is an integral part of the family. After that, it doesn't matter anyway, since he never has to see them again.

He makes a quick visit back to his room to call the medical examiner's office, and then he's off to Westborough. He rings the bell. Ken opens the door. "What do you want?"

"To coordinate. On practical matters."

"What matters?"

"First, I want to say: I know you don't like me. I know you don't trust me. I know Brisbane has suspicions about me, so maybe you do too. So first, I want to tell you I had nothing whatsoever to do with Bonnie's death. Nothing. I loved her. More than you can imagine. Whether you believe it or not doesn't change it. But what you think of me is irrelevant. Water under the bridge. We can still reach an amicable agreement about arrangements."

"What arrangements?"

"I just called the medical examiner's office. They said the body will be released tomorrow afternoon. That means released to me." Ken reacts to this with a grimace. In truth, it hadn't occurred to him that Ralph would have custody of Bonnie's body, but of course as the husband he would. Ralph notices Ken's discomfort with satisfaction. He continues, "Well, I would like to accommodate your wishes. You choose the funeral home. You choose the church, Jim's I assume. You choose the cemetery. Whatever."

"OK," says Ken. "Good. Thank you. I'll let you know what we decide. Can I reach you at home?"

"No. That's still a crime scene. I'm staying at the Marriott."

"Is that all for now?"

"Unless you think of anything else ..."

"I'll be in touch."

Brrrr, cold, thinks Ralph, forgetting for the moment his role in creating the current atmospheric conditions. He has nothing else to do the rest of the day. The office is empty, as his colleagues are scheduled to fly back from Atlanta later that afternoon. He has no appointments with customers scheduled, since he was supposed to be at the meeting. His paperwork is caught up. So first he goes home to pick up some clothing. To his relief, Brisbane isn't there and he only has to deal with a pair of uniformed Newton patrolmen guarding the scene. Then he returns to the hotel and spends the rest of the day dividing his time between watching junk on TV and logging on to the internet with his laptop to study the point spreads on the upcoming weekend basketball games.

Basically, he is putting off until evening the chore he has been dreading the most. He will have to call his parents. They still live in the house where he grew up in Overland Park, Kansas, an affluent suburb across the Mississippi River from Kansas City, Missouri. His father is a federal bureaucrat, a senior contract administrator with the Kansas City district of the U. S. Army Corps of Engineers. His mother is a homemaker with a part time job at the Overland Park public library. There is also an older brother, Chuck, with whom Ralph has nothing in common. Chuck became a podiatrist, stayed in Kansas City, and married a boisterous woman with a plain face but a body that's buff and sexy in a muscular, athletic way, like many of the women who play professional tennis. They have a baby boy, so Ralph is an uncle.

Ralph is comfortable with the distance between Boston and Kansas City. He enjoys visiting his family on occasion, but time and cost make these special events when Maureen, his mom, pampers and fusses over him. Stuart, his dad, is emotionally and conversationally constipated—Ralph has never known him any other way—but at least they share an interest in sports. His parents have been to Boston twice. One time was for the wedding. The second was a layover on route to a vacation in Greece, when Ralph suggested that they stop in town for a day so they could see his new house in Newton. It was Ralph's way of showing them what a success he'd become. But that was an exception. Generally, Ralph reveals the minimum about himself to them. He doesn't want them to participate in his life, and he has no desire to participate in theirs. Nor does he want them looking over his shoulder at his behavior or the choices he makes. He doesn't want their advice, and he certainly doesn't want them to render judgments. The distance between Boston and Kansas City is as much emotional as geographic.

That is why the prospect of calling them is so loathsome. The news of Bonnie's death is only the tip. The iceberg is all of the information about his life that will come out if he is arrested and brought to trial. His parents will learn about the financial hole he and Bonnie dug for themselves, and they will want to know how such a thing could have happened, what with his grandiose earnings and all. At best, they will look down on him with scorn for his financial irresponsibility. At worst, the police will discover his association with the Chief, and his gambling will be exposed, and they'll be shocked. And if he's charged with a crime, who knows how they will take it? Oh, sure, they will profess their love and stand by their son, but there's no telling what they'll think after they hear about the alarm system and the TV and the month after Thanksgiving and God knows what else the cops will come up with. Like the ramming, for instance. His parents, they'll want explanations. Worse, they'll want to help. They'll want to *be there for him.* It'll be awful. Damn Bonnie and her spending. Damn damn *damn* her.

And it's going to start right away, this plague of them being there for him. At the wake, at the funeral, they'll be all over him. Oh, sure, they may even come through with some actual help, like money for a lawyer. But in that case, they'll think they *deserve* explanations. They'll be *suffocating* him with support. Yeah, their intentions will be good but they will want to know: Have there been other break-ins in the neighborhood? Do the police have any leads? Why do the Legatos seem so distant? *Why didn't you phone us right away?*

Ralph has to call his parents tonight. He can't put it off any more. Tonight, which means they'll come here tomorrow, which means they'll be here three days through Sunday. How is he going to stand it all the way through Sunday?

His dad was especially fond of Bonnie, which makes it extra hard to tell them. At first, the man was as closed up and battened down with Bonnie as he is with everybody else. But Bonnie was not deterred. You know Bonnie: she saw that as a challenge. She experimented with various stratagems for connecting with his dad until at length she found one that did the trick: blatant, shameless over the top flirting. Bonnie took to giving him big, theatrical hugs. She entwined her arm through his as they went from one room to another in the house. She sidled up close to him when they sat on the couch. She massaged his shoulders as he sat in his reclining chair. She complimented his taste in clothing. She lavished praised on his selection of wine when he took them all out for a meal. She hung on every word he said, affirmed the acuity of each of his observations and the sagacity of all his opinions. She told him that it wasn't until Ralph first brought her to Kansas City that she understood why her husband is so devastatingly attractive: he inherited his good looks from his dad.

Stuart lapped it up. Proper, sober, humorless ol' gray flannel Stuart. Who would'a thunk it? The guy couldn't get enough of Bonnie's fawning over him. Although Maureen saw clearly what was going on, she wasn't especially upset with Bonnie about it. She was, however, conflicted. On one level she saw it as benign. Through harmless sexual fantasy, Bonnie had found a way to inject some juice of life into the waning years of Stuart's colorless and dreary existence. So what? Maureen had long since abandoned hope that she could ever do that herself. She was a realist. She had never, in her prime, been a match for Bonnie in looks and charm. Now, what her marriage lacked in passion it made up for in comfort, convenience and familiarity. She was willing to settle, and Bonnie wasn't a threat.

But along side her tolerance was her dismay over the way her husband was making a fool of himself. Maureen could not understand why Stuart didn't see through Bonnie's theatrical and obviously contrived performance. She regarded her husband's reaction to it as nothing short of pathetic, and that was a circumstance she didn't care for one bit. So, inevitably, some of this negative emotion did spill over in Bonnie's direction, and the relationship between the two of them was not quite as close as it otherwise might have been. It wasn't bad, though. Bonnie's behavior toward Maureen herself was beyond reproach, and Maureen gave her daughter-in-law credit for making Ralph happy. She enjoyed Bonnie's vivacious manner and positive outlook. Most of all, right now she was thrilled about the baby. With Chuck's little boy a delight to Maureen, she was ecstatic over the prospect of a second grandchild on the way. And Bonnie was most gracious. She had already told them that they were more than welcome to visit in Boston whenever they wanted to spend time with the baby.

Shit, shit, shit! Ralph is thinking, he is going to be telling them that their grandchild is dead too. *What a fucking mess.*

Ralph fritters away the afternoon alone in his room until five o'clock, which he considers a respectable time to hit the bar. He is leaving his room with his hand on the door handle when he remembers. Damn! Brisbane. He should check in with Brisbane and ask how the investigation is progressing. He'd rather not know how the investigation is progressing, but he knows he should ask.

He makes the call from his room. Brisbane is in and tells him that little progress has been achieved so far. Physical evidence is meager. The autopsy will be conducted the next morning and they will recover the bullet, but it won't do any good unless they recover a matching gun. Since the gun was not found at the scene, locating the weapon appears unlikely. There is the transparent tape that was used to replace the window pane that was removed with a glass cutter and suction cup in an effort to fake a break in. There are unidentified fibers here and there on the carpet. But unless the tape can be traced to a store or the fibers can be positively identified, such evidence is useless. "However, we're not giving up," Brisbane assures him.

"Good," Ralph says

Brisbane is poised to spring a little surprise. *Ready:* "Just to be thorough, we have to check you out too."

Ralph tenses up. "Why? I was in Atlanta."

Aim: "Yes, but we don't think this was random. It could be a conspiracy. Like I said, we have to cover all the bases."

Ralph reverts to wisecrack mode. "Yeah. You certainly wouldn't want to leave a base without a cover."

Fire: "That means we will need to examine all of your financial records. That includes six months of statements for every bank account, every brokerage account, every credit card. It includes every insurance policy. It also includes your phone records, home and cell. You can make it easy and provide all that voluntarily, or we can get court orders and subpoenas."

Ralph acts pissed off to hide his anxiety. "Hey, how can I get all this to you when I'm barred from my house?"

"We'll be done in your house by four tomorrow afternoon. You're free to return after that. And let me give you some good advice," Brisbane adds. "Don't hold out on us. If we discover anything later that you have failed to provide us, it will make you look very bad."

"You'll get everything," Ralph assures him and hangs up. Now he absolutely can't wait to get down to the bar. Once there, sipping his scotch, he observes the other customers. Like the Sheraton in Framingham, this is another hotel geared to business travel. The people in the bar all look like central casting for a Cadillac commercial: prosperous, well educated, white collar, sophisticated, and relaxed. They all appear successful and in control of their lives. Ralph thinks: that has got to be an illusion. Some of these people must have jobs that are hanging by a thread. Some of them must have unhappy marriages. Some must be juggling extra-marital affairs, like maybe those two in the booth over there. Some must have rebellious kids, or kids who take drugs or shoplift. Some must be enduring chronic back pain, or fighting cancer, or caring for a parent with Alzheimer's. Whatever it is, for some of these people, for most perhaps, the look of self assured contentment has got to be a mask. After all, if any of these people noticed him, all they would see is a guy in his prime, making strides in his career. They might even envy him, but that's only because they would have no idea how his life has gotten totally fucked up. Everybody wears a mask.

This isn't working, Ralph decides. This bar is making him morose. He's got to go out for dinner somewhere away from this building. He decides on a Mexican place he's familiar with in downtown Waltham. His reasoning is that it won't remind him of Bonnie, since they never went there together; Bonnie never cared much for Mexican food. So he buys an Esquire magazine in the hotel gift shop and drives to Waltham. This tactic doesn't work either. As he downs his Margarita, as he polishes off his steak fajita, as he makes quick work of his flan, the magazine lies unopened on the table. All he can do is think of Bonnie. He didn't *want* to do this. He *had* to.

The previous day, Ken and Gladys had kept their 11:00 AM appointment with Detective Brisbane at the office of the State Police detective squad in Cambridge. Brisbane has an agenda but eases into the conversation gently. The plan is to schmooze a while first to try to build rapport. "How are you two holding up?"

"We've been better," says Ken.

"Yes," says Brisbane, "this is pure tragedy. There is no silver lining here."

"No," Ken agrees, impatient with small talk.

Brisbane can see that Ken and Gladys are not receptive to schmoozing, so he shifts gears and he begins to circle in on his objective for the meeting, which is to gain their cooperation with his investigation into the family. "Mrs. Legato, I hate to say this, but my instincts are leading me in the same direction as your husband's."

Gladys nods her head. "What do you have?"

"Not much, really," Brisbane admits. "It's just my feeling at this point." He goes on to describe his interview with Ralph the previous evening, including the stop for dinner, the execution style gunshot wound, and the conundrum of the shut off alarm system. As he's talking, a thought occurs to him. "Mrs. Legato, did Ralph try to reach you at any time between Sunday night and Tuesday morning?"

"No, why?"

"I was just thinking, most young couples, especially in the early years of marriage, talk by phone every day when one of them is traveling. Besides that, Bonnie was pregnant. So I would think—wouldn't you?—that Ralph would have expected to hear from Bonnie sometime Monday evening, or would have tried to place a call to her. Does that sound right?"

"Knowing Bonnie, yes."

"So if he tried to reach Bonnie Monday night and couldn't, what would he think? What would he do?"

Gladys hesitates before answering. "I'm not sure. I guess he would leave messages."

"Sound logical. That's what I think, too, except that we didn't find any messages from him on their answering machine. Mrs. Legato, did you check their messages when you were in the house before the patrolmen arrived?"

"Oh, no. I never thought of doing that."

"Right. So you didn't erase any messages. All day and all night Monday there's no contact from Bonnie and no messages. Now it's Tuesday morning. Does he call you to see if you know where Bonnie is?"

"No."

"Right. Does he call her office? Not as of 9:15, when you called. Later, maybe? Perhaps. We'll check and find out."

Ken is following Brisbane's reasoning with intense interest. "That cocksucker," he says.

Brisbane continues. "It's no smoking gun, Mr. Legato, but it could be part of the picture. At the very least, it would suggest that your son-in-law was little concerned with the unaccounted absence of his pregnant wife. At worst, it could indicate that Ralph already knew what happened to his wife."

"Wait a minute," says Ken. "There's something I don't understand. Ralph isn't stupid. Why wouldn't he leave some messages just to put them on the record?"

"I have to admit, Mr. Legato, I don't have the answer to that." Brisbane is quiet for a while, then continues. "I have a hunch about it, but it's very speculative. It leads to more questions than answers. My hunch is that it has something to do with the alarm being turned off. I think he was rattled by that. I don't think that was supposed to happen because it doesn't make any sense. It's the evidence that puzzles me the most. It flashes out in big neon lights that the killers were not random intruders. They knew the code. Yet they also staged evidence of a break in. Why bother with that and then leave the alarm off?"

Ken thinks the answer to this is obvious. "The killers—by the way, why do you say killers instead of killer?"

"They took the Impala."

It takes about two beats, but Ken catches up. He slaps his forehead, grinning widely, and says, "Of course! One person to drive the Impala away and a second to drive the car they came in."

Brisbane smiles. "You got it."

Ken is anxious to return to his original point. "The killers are probably not candidates for Mensa, are they?"

Brisbane. "No."

"Then I suggest that in the excitement of the moment, they simply forgot to reset the alarm."

"I suppose that's possible," Brisbane concedes.

"Sure it is. People in responsible positions make bonehead mistakes all the time. CEO's. Politicians. Doctors. Why should criminals be any different?"

"Another possibility," says Brisbane, "the one I was thinking of, is that the killers intended to implicate Ralph."

Ken asks, "Do you think that's as likely as the forgetting scenario?"

Brisbane mulls it over. "I guess not. But either way, there's a subject I have to bring up to you now that may be sensitive."

"Go ahead," Ken says.

"There's good news and bad news in the situation we have here. The good is that we have a strong candidate for a suspect. We don't have to root around blindly looking for clues to identify a random burglar. The bad is that everything leading us to Ralph's complicity is circumstantial. There is nothing physical, no forensic evidence of any kind, that links Ralph to the crime. Nor is there any evidence that leads us to the shooters. Mr. and Mrs. Legato, at this point I don't think we are going to find any. As a result, our only hope is to back into a solution by putting Ralph's entire life under a microscope."

"That's good. I like that," says Ken.

"Maybe yes, maybe no. Hear me out. The key to solving this crime is motive. If we figure out the why, that may lead us to the how and the who. Without motive, we are literally clueless. This wasn't a crime of passion. There was a reason for it. The reason may be money. It may be a romantic entanglement. It may be something else. But the reason may involve Bonnie. After all, she was the target, so we have to find out why. Mr. and Mrs. Legato, we may have to investigate Bonnie as thoroughly as we investigate Ralph. The investigation will start with Ralph, but it may not end there."

Gladys knows her daughter. She says, "You go right ahead, Detective Brisbane." Ken knows his daughter too. He is less comfortable with this development than Gladys, but he's not about to say so.

Brisbane is pleased and relieved. The investigation would proceed regardless, but it will be easier with the Legatos in a supportive mode. He takes advantage of Gladys' permission immediately. "We can get things moving quickly if you'd care to start helping now. The place to begin is for you to tell me everything you can about Ralph, and his relationship with Bonnie." Begin at the beginning, Gladys thinks.

Ken and Gladys talk for an hour. The Bay Tower. Bermuda. The courtship. The wedding. The promotion. The house. The pregnancy. The mysterious moody month after Thanksgiving. The curious news related by Bonnie of how Ralph had suffered fender bender in Framingham and had returned to his normal pre-Thanksgiving disposition on the same day. Their doubts about Ralph's character from the outset, and their inability to put their fingers on why they felt that way.

Brisbane takes it all in, jotting notes. When they finish, he thanks them, tells them they were very helpful, and promises to keep in touch. Ken and Gladys are putting on their coats when Ken remembers. He looks at his wife. "You forgot to tell him about the computer."

Gladys is mortified that she hasn't thought of this herself, not because of Ken, just because she can't believe it slipped her mind. She turns to Brisbane. "After Bonnie came home from Bermuda, she was all aglow about how wonderful everything was. So I asked her to tell me anything that bothered her. I simply figured that no woman could spend a whole week in close quarters with a man, especially in a new relationship, without being bothered by *something*. At first she insisted there was nothing, but when I kept pressing she told me about the computer. It seems that one time she returned to the room unexpectedly early and found Ralph on the internet with his laptop. He logged off and shut the computer down quickly, as if he were hiding what he was doing. She asked and he told her he was doing e-mail, but she didn't believe him because he checked his e-mail all the time with her in the room. To this day, we don't know what he was doing. Do you think this is significant?"

In fact, Gladys' story has brought Brisbane to full alert. It has triggered another hunch. "Mrs. Legato, that may be the most significant thing I've heard all morning."

Ken asks, "Why is that?"

"Because it suggests something to me that may lead us to a motive. Suppose Ralph was on the internet doing something that millions of people do every day, but that he would be ashamed for Bonnie to know about?"

"Porn?" asks Ken.

"Could be," says Brisbane, "but I don't see the path to a motive in that. How about if he was gambling?"

The Legatos are thunderstruck. The thought had never entered their minds. Yet now, hearing it from Brisbane, it seems painfully obvious. It is so fitting with Ralph's personality. "How does this lead to a motive," Gladys asks.

"Money," says Brisbane. "Suppose, just for the sake of argument, that Ralph is a compulsive gambler. In that case, internet gambling would only be a temporary phase, lasting until his credit cards max out. Then he would have to find a bookie who would give him credit. Let's say he loses consistently and exhausts his line of credit with the bookie. But he's tapped out. His legitimate credit was gone before he ever went to a bookie. He can't pay. Now he's in serious trouble. He wouldn't be the first husband who killed for the insurance money."

Ken stands in awe of Brisbane and his theory of the case. It not only fits the circumstantial facts in evidence, it also sounds exactly like Ralph. And: it absolves Bonnie of any contributory guilt in the matter. It is more than brilliant, it is elegant.

Brisbane senses Ken's reaction and promptly does his best to put a damper on it. "Please, folks, don't make more of this idea than it deserves. It is not evidence. It is not a case. It is not an answer. It is only a starting point. An initial hypothesis. A place to begin looking for the answer. That's all."

"Nevertheless," says Ken, "it is a very good start. I'm impressed. Thank you."

"Don't thank me yet," Brisbane cautions as he rises to shake their hands. "When we get a conviction in court, that will be the time to thank me."

Outside on the sidewalk, Ken says, "We are very lucky."

Gladys knows what he means. "Brisbane is good, isn't he?"

"Yeah, he's good," says Ken.

Gladys chuckles. She can't help it. "What?" Ken asks.

"You," says Gladys, still chortling. "The detective mentions the internet and what's the first thing that pops into your mind? Porn!"

Ken can't resist chuckling himself, and takes her hand as they walk to the car. Perversely, his touching Gladys' hand triggers an avalanche of thoughts about Bonnie. Mostly, he is desperately hoping that she was sleeping and didn't see it coming.

On Thursday, Ralph returns from his dinner in Waltham to be greeted in the hotel lobby by two uniformed officers of the State Police. They thrust a piece of paper in front of his face and tell him it's a court order to seize his laptop computer and his PDA as evidence in the murder of his wife.

Ralph is incensed and frightened in equal measure. This is getting serious much sooner than he anticipated. "Wait a minute. Wait a minute. All my work is on my laptop. All my business contacts, my customer phone numbers, appointment schedule, everything like that is on my PDA. How can I work if I don't have them?" His resistance is half hearted since he knows it's futile.

This feeble protest is easily deflected by one of the officers. "You won't be working the rest of the week. You're in mourning, or did you forget that little detail? If these items provide no evidence, you'll get them back before next Monday. If they do provide evidence, you've got problems a lot bigger than not being able to look up phone numbers on your electronic gizmo."

This last remark is chilling. Until now, the legal peril facing Ralph has not been front and center. He had merely been thinking that if his work tools were seized, his boss would become aware that he is under suspicion. Now he is experiencing the leading edge of panic as the realization dawns that his exposure to criminal prosecution is acute. His stomach churns as it sinks in that he'd better get a lawyer. Right away.

Just what I need, Ralph is thinking, another problem: how do I find a good lawyer? The only times Ralph has ever seen a lawyer are when he and Bonnie chose a hack from the Yellow Pages to write their wills, and when they bought the house. How the hell is he going to find a lawyer who knows what he's doing in a murder case? "They'll never prove anything," Cap had told him. Asshole. What the hell does Cap know? He also said they would turn the alarm back on. Fuckin' asshole.

Wait a minute! The Chief! He'll know a lawyer! Better yet, Cap himself.

The cops accompany Ralph to his room and leave with his laptop and PDA. Ralph follows them out and heads down to the bar. It is not quite yet the last minute before he has to make that call to his parents.

10

The wake was scheduled for Friday evening at a funeral home in Westborough. Unexpectedly, dinner beforehand at the Legatos turned into an impromptu family meeting. The sole item on the agenda was how to treat Ralph.

It was notable that the meal that night was Chinese take-out. Already, for Gladys, the protective armor of shock was dissipating and the piercing agony of loss was beginning to make itself felt. There was little energy left for cooking. Nor was there much of a drive to take care of the house. At one point during the afternoon Sandy went upstairs to sit alone in the bedroom that was Bonnie's for all those years. She told me later that as she passed by her parents' room she noticed that the bed was unmade. We both thought this was a telling detail. It sticks in my mind even now.

Still, Gladys led the side of the debate that argued in favor of civility toward Ralph. For her, she said, the presumption of innocence was paramount. As awful as Bonnie's death was, nothing could be worse than the horror of accusing Ralph falsely. Gladys understood full well where Brisbane was heading with the investigation but in her mind there was plenty of time to hate Ralph later after theory was proven to be fact. To act as judge and jury before all of the evidence was in simply wasn't right. To do so would only compound the tragedy if Ralph were not guilty, and meanwhile would do nothing to help bring him to justice if he were. So Gladys counseled, if not a cease fire, then at least a cooling off period to forestall the premature commencement of overt hostilities.

Surprisingly, the leader of the hawks in the family was Jeff. Filled with rage, Jeff professed an uncompromising conviction as to the certainty of Ralph's guilt, and was therefore unwilling to allow him any slack. "Honestly," he said, "is there one single person at this table who actually has a reasonable doubt that Ralph is behind this? Is there anybody whose gut isn't screaming at them, *This is Ralph's doing*? Whose mind can conceive of any other plausible scenario?" Nobody could contradict him. "So who are we kidding?" he went on. "Why are we protecting the feelings of this vicious psychopath? Why does anyone care about his feelings?"

"Because," said Jim, "we might be wrong. Because time after time we see how people who are actually convicted of a crime and spend years in jail turn out to be innocent. This is in spite of testimony by witnesses who are adamant in their identification of the suspect, in spite of district attorneys who believe with passion in the justice of their prosecution, in spite of careful deliberation by juries who sincerely believe that they are without reasonable doubt. In spite of all that, everyone turns out to be wrong. I know very well what a vile and unspeakable crime has been committed against our family. I know how strongly we all believe that Ralph is responsible for it. Nevertheless, the strength with which a belief is held is not a measure of its validity. Think about suicide bombers. Think about how strong their beliefs are and how at the same time how wrong their beliefs are. Look, Jeff, I'm not saying that we can never reach the point where it is justified to blame Ralph. I'm just saying it's too soon and we're not there yet."

Sandy spoke up last. She sided with Jeff. "Mom. Jim. What you say is true in principle. But it's not real for me. Reality for me is total revulsion. I can't stand that creep. I can't stand even the thought of looking at him, much less talking to him. I hate him. I detest him. I loathe him. If that's not fair, it's too bad. If it turns out I'm wrong, I'll have to live with that."

The debate went back and forth for a while until Jeff's gaze settled on his father and everyone realized that Ken had not yet said anything. So, cued by Jeff, we all turned his way. Ken spoke softly, in despair. "If there is any revulsion, it should be directed at me. I knew he was no good. I did nothing to stop the marriage. Your mother, bless her heart, tried to warn her. It did no good, but she tried. While I did nothing. I said nothing. A *am* nothing."

This was a bombshell. It wasn't at all like Ken, who rarely shared his feelings and never expressed self doubt. For him to display his vulnerability this way was to expose the convulsive force of the guilt that was tearing him apart. Gladys welled with compassion for her husband. She rose from her seat, kneeled down beside Ken's, took his hand, looked up into his eyes, and said, "Nobody blames you, dear."

Ken looked toward her upturned face and said, "Thank you. But I still have to answer to myself for what I did. And for what I didn't do."

No one spoke up to contest the sentiment behind Ken's statement. It wasn't that any of us agreed with him. It was because we understood that none of us could provide the forgiveness he needed. Only Ken could provide that to himself. Eventually.

We still were anxious to hear what Ken had to say about the matter on the table. He realized this and picked up the thread of the conversation. "As for the subject under discussion, here's what I think: I don't see a need for us to have a unified approach on how to treat Ralph. I think that those of us who feel angry should feel free to express it. I think those of us who feel that restraint and civility are in order for now should act accordingly. And here's what I think is most important. I think it is absolutely critical that each and every one of us in this room honors and respects the differences among us. We cannot—*I will not*—allow this catastrophe to create divisiveness and rancor within the family. Do I make myself clear? Jeff?"

"Yes, Dad. I agree. Wholeheartedly," said Jeff.

"Jim?"

"Of course," said Jim.

"Sandy?"

"Definitely," said Sandy.

And that's how it was settled. And throughout, nobody had asked for my opinion, nor Sharon's for hers. And that was good. I was greatly relieved. I have no idea what I would have said.

Later that night, as events unfolded at the funeral home, Ralph's worst fears for the occasion were realized. The Legatos were frosty, and he was forced to come semi-clean with his parents. Yet that wasn't all bad for him. It took a bit of weight off his mind. Not much, but some.

Ralph picked up Maureen and Stuart late in the afternoon at the airport, then took them to a Legal Sea Food near the Turnpike exit in Natick for an early dinner. His choice of a restaurant was carefully calibrated: Legal is a moderately fine dining establishment sufficiently upscale to demonstrate to his parents his high standards and good taste, yet not so upscale as to impart any suggestion of a celebratory atmosphere. After dinner, he pretended to lose his way en route to the funeral home. This was to minimize the chance of a potentially embarrassing moment. If he got there before the Legatos and had to greet them as they arrived, things could get awkward.

On that score, he needn't have worried. The Legatos were there a half hour early by prearrangement with the funeral home. This was to have some private time to bid Bonnie goodbye. It also provided an opportunity for Ken to meet with three private security guards he had hired to keep the press at bay. He didn't know what to expect, but reporters had been flooding his voice mail both at home and at work so he wasn't taking any chances. He had selected this particular funeral home because there was both adequate parking on the premises and rear access to the building from the lot. No one would have to fend off reporters on the public sidewalks. This plan worked well. Reporters went back to their studios lacking juicy quotes and nothing showed up on the news that night.

Ralph's delayed arrival plan also worked well for a while. By the time he and his folks showed up, the wake was densely populated, and the mourners included a considerable number from his side. That is, among the crowd were a sizable group from his office, a sprinkling of customers, and some buddies from college. Most of his and Bonnie's joint friends and neighbors, aware from TV news that he had been in Atlanta that night but not privy to police suspicions, were friendly and supportive. Ralph circulated among these people, accepting their condolences and commiserations and introducing them to his Mom and Dad. This consumed a sizable block of time.

Brisbane showed up too, and for a while this also worked to Ralph's advantage. Brisbane was there to acquaint himself with the cast of characters in Ralph and Bonnie's life. Quickly, Ken was by his side, introducing him to one and all as the talented police detective who was going to crack the case and nail the perpetrator. Every time Ken said that, Brisbane was careful to append a disclaimer: "Well, we'll certainly do our best." Brisbane also managed to detach himself from Ken in order to have a chat with Maureen and Stuart. He asked them if they knew any reason why Bonnie might have been in danger, and gave them his business card in the event that they should remember anything later. At no point did Brisbane as much as hint at what he was really thinking, and Ralph began to relax a bit, feeling he had dodged a bullet.

Ralph's time and luck ran out, however, when Maureen decided that the moment was past due to pay her respects to the Legato family. "I've got to say something to Gladys," she told Ralph. How could he object? So, Stuart in tow and Ralph trailing reluctantly, Maureen approached her daughter-in-law's mother. They stood waiting just outside the circle where Gladys was engaged in conversation.

Gladys didn't exactly recognize the mature looking couple who had walked over with Ralph—she had only seen them years ago when they came for the wedding—but she inferred from the situation who they must be. Gladys' principles and good intentions evaporated as soon as she saw Ralph coming toward her. She knew she would be cordial to Maureen and Stuart, but she was shocked to realize that she would be incapable of saying a single kind word to Ralph. She was indeed sitting in judgment. What was the word Sandy used? Revulsion. Gladys glanced at Maureen, lifting her hand and raising her index finger to acknowledge their presence, then continued for a minute or so in the conversation she was already having. She needed the time to shift mental gears. But in due course she excused herself from her friends and made eye contact with Ralph's mother.

"Maureen? Stuart?"

Maureen nodded and answered, "I have no idea what to say. Nothing I can think of seems adequate to your pain. I'm so sorry."

A chill flashed through Gladys' bones. Sorry? Does she know about Ralph? But Gladys rejected the idea immediately. There was no way that Ralph would have confessed to them. Maureen's "sorry" had to be referring to the loss, not the crime. "Thank you," she replied. On impulse she added, "It's your loss too."

"Oh, yes!" gushed Maureen. "That's really what I wanted to tell you. About how wonderful Bonnie was. Not that you don't know that, of course. What I mean is, with us, how wonderful she was. It was only a few years we knew her. A handful of visits. But in that short time, not very long really, we came to love her very much. Already we loved her and felt she was a regular part of our family too. And she made Ralph very happy."

And that was the instant, right then, exactly at that second, when the dam ruptured and the full tidal wave of grief swept over Gladys and engulfed her, swept her out to sea, dragged her under, drowned her. What triggered it now was something entirely unexpected: the unveiling of a whole new dimension to this calamity. For Gladys realized in a flash of clarity that the impact of the disaster was not confined to the Legatos in their loss of Bonnie. It was also about to wallop the bejesus out of the Collins family as well. *They were about to lose their son.* Soon, she realized, Maureen would find out that the child she'd birthed and suckled and raised and nurtured and taught how to tie his shoes and helped with his junior high science projects and sent off to college with satisfaction and pride—the son they thought they knew so well—did not in fact exist. That person was an imposter. That person was not even a memory, it was a chimera. The real Ralph Collins is a cruel and vile murderer. A *premeditated* murderer. Can there be any worse horror for a parent than to discover that her child is a murderer?

As a profound compassion for Maureen and Stuart swept through Gladys, any remnant of regard for Ralph was flushed out. Gladys would later remember thinking at the time, "I'm not being a very good Christian." She would remember realizing that she didn't care. Tears welled up and flowed as she was overcome by the all-encompassing enormity of the catastrophe.

At this point, Jeff came over and said to Gladys, "Sandy needs to talk to you." Gladys withdrew gracefully and went with Jeff. Sandy didn't need anything. She had thought her mother might be trapped talking with Ralph and his family, and had sent Jeff on a rescue mission. Gladys felt appreciative that her children were looking out for her and were sensitive to the stress she was feeling, but was also a not a little irked that they thought she was so fragile and debilitated that she couldn't fend for herself. "Where have I given them reason to think that?" she wondered. "Why am I being patronized by my own family?" On balance, Sandy's maneuver was not helpful.

Meanwhile, as Gladys moved away toward her children, Stuart narrowed his eyes and said to Ralph, "All right, what's going on?"

"What do you mean?" said Ralph, taking cover behind his befuddled innocence act, as he had months earlier with the Chief. His success was no greater this time. "Cut the crap," said Stuart.

Ralph was not being smart. Nobody was more familiar with Ralph's dumb innocence routine than his father, and it merely served to ratchet up Stuart's aggravation and concern. "You think we're stupid? You think we're doddering old fools, just 'cause we're your parents? You think we haven't noticed that not a single person from the Legato side of the family has said a goddamn word to you all evening? You think that's not going to strike us a peculiar? It's not natural, Ralphie. *What the hell is going on?*"

Resigned to his fate, Ralph sighed. "OK, let's find someplace where we can talk in private." Their search yielded an alcove on the second floor with several chairs and no other people.

Maureen and Stuart waited patiently for Ralph to explain, but for a long while nothing came out. Ralph was afraid. He was reliving an experience from his childhood. He was six years old and his parents were demanding to know what happened to his brother's frog. What happened was that Ralph had flushed it down the toilet, just to spite his brother. The consequence was that this was one of the few times he had ever been spanked. He had confessed, but Ralph's take-away from the incident was not what his parents had intended. The spanking was an extreme and unusual measure intended to impress upon Ralph the supreme importance of reverence for life. Unfortunately, the lesson he took from it was that confession is good neither for the soul nor for certain body parts. Moreover, the worst consequence wasn't the blows but the fear that he had lost his parents' love. This fear, which persisted for weeks, was engendered by the uncharacteristically intemperate nature of the punishment. Thus for Ralph, remembering this experience, confession did not present itself as an opportunity for cleansing and redemption, but rather as a bad bet with no upside potential.

Yet now he could see no alternative. So Ralph being Ralph, he decided on confession lite. He said, at length, "OK, here it is. Here's the reason. The reason is ... they think I had something to do with this."

There was a long silence while Stuart and Maureen processed this news. Finally Stuart asked, "Why"

"I don't know. They never liked me. I'm not good enough for their princess of a daughter."

Maureen was puzzled. "That isn't the impression I got at the wedding. They seemed happy that Bonnie was happy, and they were perfectly nice to us."

Ralph's tone was dismissive. "Ma, they were putting on a show. They didn't want to spoil Bonnie's special day."

Stuart wasn't buying what Ralph was selling. "Ralphie, cut the crap. There has to be something more. What is it?"

"All right. OK. Well, there was an anomaly that came out in the investigation."

Stuart was growing increasingly impatient. "Anomaly? What the hell does that mean? Stop talking in goddamn riddles."

"The alarm system was turned off." Ralph put that out there as if it were self-explanatory, in the futile hope that he wouldn't be asked to explain.

This ploy flew completely over Maureen's head. "So?"

Ralph was forced to explain. "So they think the killer knew the code in the security system. They think that means it wasn't a random intruder."

Stuart bored in this. "Who's they? The Legatos? They think that? Did they tell that to the police?"

In a spasm of candor he regretted immediately, Ralph confided: "I think the police told them."

Maureen was far behind her husband in grasping the implications of what their son was telling them. "Oh, sweetheart," she said, "They think that somebody you know murdered Bonnie? How terrible."

Stuart, rolling his eyes at Maureen, wanted to hear Ralph's version. "What do you think really happened?"

"I don't know. It's truly a mystery."

"You must have some notion."

"I'm thinking somebody from the alarm company was involved."

Stuart wasn't buying this either. His tone was sarcastic. "Somebody from the alarm company had a grudge against Bonnie?"

"No, they wanted to rob the place."

"Why your place in particular? Why that night in particular? If Bonnie was sleeping in her room, why kill her at all?"

"I tell you I don't know. I only know I loved her and had nothing to do with her death."

Stuart was no longer interested in the Legatos. He could see where the police might be going with their case and it wasn't a pretty sight. "Ralph," he said, "you need a lawyer."

Ralph's response startled his parents. "I already have one."

"You need a specialist in criminal defense."

"I know. He is. He was recommended by a friend. I'm seeing him Monday."

From this, Stuart knew that Ralph understood he was in serious trouble. And this had to mean that Ralph was the focus of the police investigation. True, the police would be guided by statistical probabilities, so it didn't necessarily mean he was guilty. And it's not uncommon for police to leap quickly to erroneous conclusions. Nevertheless, his son's behavior this evening did not inspire confidence. Stuart could feel a headache coming on. Maureen usually carried Advil in her purse. He hoped she had some now.

Ralph had already followed through on his idea to find a lawyer through Cap. The morning after his computer and PDA were seized, he got a message through to his loan shark. Ralph was under strict instructions never to contact Cap directly, so he had called the Chief from a pay phone in the Marriott lobby. The Chief told him he would relay the message. By early afternoon, Ralph had received a call from a lawyer. The lawyer told Ralph to stop talking to the cops and to call him immediately if they wanted to ask any more questions. They made an appointment to get together at the lawyer's office on Monday. Meanwhile, no statements to the press, either.

Stuart asked, "Do you have enough money to hire a good lawyer?"

The answer to that was no, but Ralph being Ralph he had an angle. He was banking on his assumption that Cap would finance his legal defense, on the theory that Cap's payday from the whole deal was at risk. If Ralph were to be found guilty of murder for hire, the insurance wouldn't pay off and Cap would be left with nothing. It seemed unlikely that Cap would trust his $150,000 jackpot to just any unknown wet behind the ears court appointed neophyte legal bumpkin. Cap would want somebody really good in there to protect his own interests. Cap would want to be in control. On that assumption, Ralph told his father, "I think so."

Maureen and Stuart were left stunned by the revelations of the evening, while Ralph was embarrassed, so they all sat in the alcove for quite some time without anyone saying a thing. None of them had the stomach for any more mingling with other mourners. None of them wanted any further encounter with the Legatos. All of them were brooding about tomorrow, which promised to be the most miserable day of their entire lives. The Funeral Mass was scheduled for 10:00 am.

◆   ◆   ◆

As we waited uncomfortably on a hard wooden pew in Jim's church on Saturday morning, I had time to let my mind wander. In particular, I was contemplating how the unfairness of life presents itself with such a brazen, in your face insolence. I was thinking about how bad behavior not merely goes unpunished but is often rewarded. How good behavior not merely goes unrewarded but is often unrecognized. How a tornado destroys one house and leaves its neighbor unscathed. How an innocent child develops a fatal disease while a scoundrel lives hearty and hale into his dotage. How a well-known gangster wins the state lottery while hardworking folks never get out of debt. How a beloved family member is senselessly murdered, and the perpetrator may or may not be brought to justice.

Thoughts such as these were familiar territory. Somewhere along the road I had come to think that religious faith is at bottom a mechanism to allow people to cope with the fact that life is unfair. Sure, I know, this may seem obvious on some level. But if you really take it to heart, if you take it as the touchstone, the starting point, your perspective is altered and radically so. For example, you stop worrying about which religion is true. You cease to wonder how somebody of a different faith, who is perfectly intelligent and reasonable in all other respects, can adhere to the tenets of the religion he grew up with when these beliefs are so radically at odds with the logical and reasonable tenets that you yourself hold so dear and that are so obviously correct.

None of that matters any more. For me, the insight that faith is about fairness was accompanied by a great sense of a burden having been lifted. This was because the differences among religions used to trouble me. I used to think that the main job of a religion was to explain the *why* behind the *what* and the *how* of science—that is, to answer questions not amenable to the experimental method—and I thought as well that the most important requirement for a religion was to get it right. I thought if a religion didn't get it right, didn't accurately capture the cosmic truth, then it was faulty and not doing its job. But of course the flaw in that line of thought is that there are many religions, all different. They couldn't all capture the cosmic truth. If one was right, didn't that make the others false? And how could one tell? Was it by numbers? Was Christianity more true than Judaism because there are more Christians than Jews? But less than 40% of the world's population, a bare plurality, is Christian. Does that mean that 60% of the world is deluded? Was that what God intended? Did that make sense? So, what did make sense? Was it logical to think that God had revealed his love for mankind by sacrificing his only son to a grisly, gruesome and protracted death, only to wind up with a 40% share? And that share itself rent with divisions, schisms and controversy?

As I said, these things used to trouble me.

Not now. No longer do I see the job of religion as defining cosmic truth. Now I see its job as providing a much needed balm to those afflicted by the unfairness of life. It is doing its job, I think now, when it succeeds in providing believers with an alternate reality—a meta-reality if you will—in which kindness, good will and above all justice prevail, and the wrongs of corporeal life are redressed. A religion, I now think, doesn't have to be "true" in the objective sense to accomplish this purpose. Rather, it has to be deeply and profoundly believed. That is, it has to inspire faith.

All of this was much on my mind as we took our seats in Jim's church for Bonnie's Rite of Christian Burial because I was alarmed by the effect this tragedy was having on Sandy. Surely, I was thinking, nothing can test one's faith so much as the shocking murder of a sibling by another family member, especially by an inner circle brother-in-law who turns out to be a soul-less psychopath, motivated—if Detective Brisbane's theory pans out—by gambling debts. How could anything be more unfair. This, I was thinking, is exactly the kind of situation in which faith is supposed to help. This, I was thinking, should be what faith is for.

Beyond that, one of the things I admired about Sandy, one of the things that attracted me to her, was the depth of her faith. It wasn't because I shared it. On the contrary, the Christian premise—that God's truth is revealed in Christ and we know it's the truth because Christ revealed it—is too circular for my mind to find congenial. But the fact that Sandy's faith defies my own sense of logic doesn't mean I think she's illogical. It means instead that her craving, her need, her *requirement* for fairness, for justice, for transcendent moral order trumps her need for logic. It is more important than logic. How can anyone not love that?

What had me alarmed was that Sandy's faith wasn't helping her. At least it wasn't helping her the way I thought it would. She was by turns inconsolable and enraged. One minute she was weeping and then next she was plotting her revenge on Ralph. Four days had passed. I kept expecting her faith to kick in and provide her some measure of comfort, if not peace. But I'd seen no evidence of that yet. Nor had I seen her pray. Maybe, I thought, I didn't understand how it works. Maybe it was still too soon. Is there supposed to be a delay in the process? Is the delay built in, something like the time it takes for an office copy machine to warm up? Nah, that didn't make any sense. I was afraid to ask her about it, though. Her moods were on a hair trigger, and I didn't want her to interpret my questions as a challenge.

I did ask her whether she thought her pain was intensified by her role in mentoring Bonnie as they were growing up. The question might sound naïve but I had a purpose. I figured that if perhaps in that mentoring role Sandy thought it was part of her responsibility to protect Bonnie from harm, then she might be feeling a special sense of failure. I thought that if that were the case, I might be able to help Sandy at least understand that she was blameless in Bonnie's death, that there was no way she could have foreseen or prevented it, and that grief was normal but there was no reason to deepen the sorrow with undeserved guilt. Sandy's response was that I might or might not be right but in any case she couldn't change how she was feeling.

So for the most part I just worried about her, and wished there was something I could do to help her. I felt, in other words, totally ineffectual. And then Jim began his homily, and by the end of it I was starting to worry about him too.

The Catholic funeral Mass does not include a eulogy as such. Midway through, the priest delivers a homily. The purpose of the homily is not to look back on the life of the deceased, not to celebrate the story of the life that was ended, but rather to remind those who remain and are entering the period of mourning that comfort and consolation is offered to all through faith and through the community of the Church. Still, when the priest has had a close relationship with the deceased, it is not uncommon for him to work in some personal comments in memorium.

And that's what Jim did. This was his homily:

"The gospels of Matthew and Luke tell us that as Jesus was dying on the cross, he cried out, "My God, my God, why hast thou forsaken me?" Has there ever been heard a more heart rending, gut wrenching cry of pain than that? I think not.

"This passage comes to mind because I too am in pain right now. Our family, the Legato family, is in great pain, as are Bonnie's many friends and colleagues. And the Collins family is as well. Right now, for us—as for many other people who experience devastating events such as this—just when the need is greatest to feel that God is close at hand, that is when God seems hardest to find. We have so many questions: Why has God allowed this to happen? Why didn't God protect the innocent, the victims? Why, at the very least, doesn't God help me to understand what happened and why? We ask these questions and we don't get answers. So it is only natural to move on to the next set of questions: God, we want to know, where are you hiding? God, do you hear me? My God ... my God ... why hast thou forsaken me?

"And yes, it may seem to us as though he has indeed forsaken us. As it seemed to Jesus. His cry to God mimics our own, and in so doing it resonates in our hearts and reaches into our souls. As Jesus connects with us with his cry of pain, that connection simultaneously calls us back to a place of comfort and peace. It brings us back to this place by helping us remember that in his moment of extreme despair Jesus was both reciting and manifesting the prophesy of the 22nd Psalm of David. It is a signpost pointing us in exactly the direction that we need to go at precisely this time.

"And this is where, from the depths of his despair and ours, we find the beauty of the Holy Scripture. The brilliance of it. For the word of the Lord, through Jesus, speaks directly to us in this our time of need. Let us remember the nature of the anguish of Jesus on the cross. Yes, he was in a world of physical hurt. Yes, the people were taunting and mocking him. But none of that was the pain that caused Jesus to cry out. The worst torment, the most excruciating anguish, was that Jesus felt separated from God. He thought, for a while, that God had forsaken him. So if the last few days have left you wondering where God is hiding, you're in good company. When Jesus could not see the face of God, it was more than he could bear. So he recalled the 22nd Psalm. A prophesy.

"I've been talking about how the 22nd Psalm begins. Let us now remember how it continues and how it ends. As revealed in the prophesy of the Psalm, we hear Jesus pleading with God. He cajoles and implores to be returned to the Lord's good graces. But never does Jesus lose faith. "But be Thou not far from me, Oh Lord," he says. His faith is invincible. And we see how his faith is rewarded. Jesus has not been abandoned. God has turned away momentarily, but has not forsaken him.

"Jesus understands this suddenly, abruptly, without an intervening event or communication. In Verse 21 Jesus is still pleading: "Save me from the Lion's mouth." In Verse 22 it is, "I will declare thy name unto my brethren." Jesus is still nailed to the cross. The multitudes are still jeering at him. Yet in a flash, Jesus is at peace. All is calm. Faith has conquered doubt. But how? There has been no missive. No outward sign. Jesus has many questions, and just as it is with us today as we cope with the loss of Bonnie, none of these questions is answered. So what has happened? Here's what has happened: Faith has conquered doubt from within.

"What a sterling example Jesus gives us. What a lesson is there for us as we grieve the death of Bonnie Collins. We grieve over the loss of a beloved member of our family, a beloved member of our community. We grieve over the cruel, senseless, untimely and undeniably evil manner of her death. We grieve equally over the death of her unborn child: over the possibilities that were extinguished, over the potentials that are never to be realized, over the love that will be imagined but never fully cherished. We feel the pain, and the anger too. Anger at the perpetrators, of course, but also perhaps at God.

How could he let this happen? And so it may come to pass that, as happened to Jesus in his final hours, we begin to wonder if God has forsaken us.

"If that does happen, remember the lesson of the 22nd Psalm. For in the end, God does not spurn or disdain Jesus in his misery, but hears him. And so Jesus rejoices, and in his elation proclaims, "For the kingdom is the Lord's."

"How does Jesus know that God hears him? Does Jesus stop hurting? Does God smite the people who are tormenting him? Is there a sign of any kind at all? Not so anyone can tell. Psalm 22, which is so expressive and poetic about so much else, is silent on this question. Exactly. Exactly, because the knowledge comes from inside Jesus himself. It is all internal. It comes from his faith.

"So it is with us gathered here today to mourn the passing from earth of Bonnie Collins to a better place. Each of us will grieve the loss. That is natural. Some of us may slide into hate and rage against the perpetrators. That, too, is natural but ultimately counterproductive, because it leads us further away from God instead of closer to him. And finally, in our pain, some of us may wonder if God has simply abandoned us. If you feel that way, if you are tempted to feel that way, that is natural also. Jesus felt that way. But only for a little while. Jesus returned quickly to his faith and then knew that God had heard him. That is the lesson of the 22nd Psalm. God is always close. Bonnie and her baby are with him now. And he is with us, too, so long as our faith is there to connect us.

"For it is only within the comfort of our faith that we can maintain the memory of Bonnie is a way that honors her own life of faith. Have you ever seen anyone more kind, more giving, more generous than Bonnie? Add to that her intelligence, her wit, and, yes, her physical beauty. And top it off with her love, her laughter, her fun, her unparalleled zest for life. She loved God and was happy because she was secure in God's love. It is a blessing to us to have been part of her life. Let us not allow hurt or anger or doubt about God to curdle the memory. Let our faith keep the blessing alive and well in our hearts."

That, I thought, was a terrific homily.

So why did it make me uncomfortable, so ill at ease? I paid little attention to the rest of the Mass. My mind kept circling back around and over and through Jim's homily, examining it from every standpoint so I could try to understand my visceral reaction. Gradually it came to me. This was an oration. It was a closely reasoned, superbly crafted, finely honed exegesis of scriptural text. But—and it's a huge but—that was totally out of character for Jim. Jim's homilies are always folksy and homespun. They always illustrate the meaning of a scriptural passage with an anecdote from his personal experience of the previous week. The anecdote will be prosaic. It might be something about a small gesture of kindness that he witnessed on the street, or about the joy that he saw in the eyes of a mother caring for a handicapped child. As often as not the logic is strained, the story not precisely on point in relation to the scripture at hand. But that never matters. You always understand what Jim is trying to say. This homily, on the other hand, was close to a scholarly treatise. It was like a philosophical manifesto. What the hell was that about?

Maybe, I thought, it was an argument directed toward someone who needed more than a down home anecdote to be persuaded. Maybe that someone could be Jim, if he were struggling with an issue of importance. An issue, say, such as whether God had abandoned him. Or whether he might be tempted to abandon God. Uh oh, I thought.

11

Brisbane catches a lucky break.

Over the next several days he has thought the situation through. He sees that crime scene evidence will lead nowhere, so he formulates a new plan. He decides that his only hope is to trace Ralph's recent comings and goings and see if he can find any connection to a contract killer.

What he ought to do, Brisbane decides, is construct a detailed time line of Ralph's activities since Thanksgiving. This will be a major undertaking, he knows. The effort will be *brobdingnagian*. Brisbane savors the word, stops to enjoy the sound of it in his mind. Brisbane is attuned to words, cognizant of how they serve as containers for thought. This one he's relished ever since he saw it in Time magazine and looked it up.

Politically, the making of a time line will pose a problem. His boss, the Chief of Detectives, will not be happy to have him spending so much time on one case. The State Police squad in the Middlesex district has only a few detectives, and since they are understaffed, each individual is assigned a variety of crimes simultaneously. Brisbane knows he will have to fend off pressure to spend more time on other cases. It will become a contest with his boss, a tug of war whose outcome is preordained: overtime. Lots and lots of unpaid overtime. This in turn will make his wife unhappy. Oh Lord. But he can't just let it go, either. Every once in a while a case gets under his skin, and this is one of them. Collins pisses him off. The guy is a slime bucket. Brisbane doesn't want to let him get away with it.

Brisbane is glad now that he's learned how to use the computer. He's not an expert, but he is sufficiently adept that he can make productive use of the tools that come loaded with the machine. One of these is a database program. He is especially fond of this one because if he enters his notes and other data in the right format, he can slice and dice and collate the information any way he chooses. Seeing the same facts from a variety of perspectives stimulates useful insights. And, if he sorts and prints the data in chronological order, he has the makings of a time line.

Inputting the data into the computer is the time consuming part. Some people would regard this stage of the process as a tedious chore, but not Brisbane. In fact, he enjoys it. Whether it's interview notes, telephone records, financial statements, whatever it is, the very process of typing stuff into the computer prompts him to give every individual bit of data some thought, assessing how each might fit into the larger picture. This preliminary exercise is often just as fruitful as examination of the finished reports that print out afterwards. The task of sifting through a mountain of data to find nuggets of information that become useful clues is profoundly gratifying to Brisbane.

During the early part of the week following the murder, while he's waiting for the subpoenaed bank, telephone and credit card records to arrive, Brisbane fills in the time by conducting interviews. These are necessary but pro forma: his expectations are low that they will yield anything of value. He talks to people at the copier company and asks if anybody was aware of a problem with Ralph's work, or in their personal lives. Nobody was. He talks to a sampling of Ralph's customers. Same story. Uniformed patrolmen have already canvassed Ralph's neighbors to ask if they heard or saw anything suspicious that night. Now Brisbane revisits the neighbors to ask more probing questions about Ralph and Bonnie as a couple. Nothing new comes from that, either.

By Thursday the interviews are completed and enough subpoenaed records are on hand to make it worthwhile to begin building the database. Brisbane is thinking this way: begin with the credit card statements and correlate the transaction locations with the locations on the customer register for Ralph's sales district. At the very least, poring through the postings on these statements will be a good way to get inside Ralph's skin. It will lead him to understand his quarry's habits and proclivities, to start getting a feel for the man behind the mask. Surely Ralph's overweening self confidence, his oily glibness, has got to be a mask. And who knows? It's possible that buried in the records something truly interesting may turn up.

In fact, something interesting does turn up.

Brisbane flips through the American Express statements to find the one from November, since the trouble seems to have started around then. Locating that one, he flattens it on his desk and makes the first entries in his database. Two hours later comes the break. There is a charge for $18.74 from someplace called Gordon Paley Enterprises in Chelsea. Chelsea? That's a long way from Ralph's sales district, which encompasses all five states of New England but excludes the part of Massachusetts along and inside of the Route 128 beltway around Boston.

Brisbane logs on to the internet, goes to a yellow pages web site, and does a search for "Gordon Paley Enterprises." An address and phone number appear on the screen and he dials the number. A young woman answers: "Gordon Paley Enterprises. How may I help you?"

"I'm Detective Arthur Brisbane from the State Police," Brisbane says. "We ran across your phone number in the course of an investigation, and I wonder if you can tell me what type of business you are in."

"We own a restaurant, sir. This is the business office."

"What is the name of the restaurant?"

"Gordon's Grill, sir."

"Where is it located?"

"In the Mystic Mall. Maybe I should connect you to Mr. Paley."

"That won't be necessary," Brisbane says. "I'm all set. We're investigating the activities of one of your customers. I don't see any reason for you or Mr. Paley to be alarmed. You've been most helpful." Brisbane hangs up, logs on to a mapping site, and prints out a street map showing the location of the Mystic Mall.

Now the detective's mind is fully engaged with this new development. The charge is a business credit card, he is thinking, so if Ralph expected his expense reimbursement to clear he would most likely have gone to this restaurant on a weekday. The charge is posted to Ralph's account on the last Monday in November. That means he would have eaten there the previous Friday, or perhaps Wednesday. Not Thursday, that was Thanksgiving. The charge was $18.74, too little for dinner. It had to be lunch. By himself. What is he doing there having lunch by himself? In Chelsea?

His bookie, maybe? Could his bookie be in Chelsea? Could a visit to his bookie have set in motion a chain of events leading to murder? Don't get too excited, Brisbane reminds himself. That is a big leap. The compulsive gambling scenario is nothing more than vapor at this point. There is no hard evidence yet.

So maybe we can get some.

Brisbane doesn't know any cops in Chelsea, but he has contacts in Boston, and he calls one of them. The receiver is picked up: "Dunhill here."

Brisbane launches the "shtick" that he's developed with Dunhill over the years. "Who's that? Dunghill, you say?"

The laugh Brisbane was expecting shoots back across the wire. "Well, if it isn't old Wizbang himself. Hey, Wizbang, what's this I see on TV about a murder in Newton? I thought you guys were supposed to keep the citizens safe out there in the boondocks."

"The citizens in Newton are still safe. This was a murder for hire. We think the husband arranged it."

"No shit."

"No shit, peabrain, which you would have already known if you had been listening to what that broad McCorkle was saying on the tube instead of lusting after her and creaming in your pants."

"OK, Wizbang, I'll take your word for it since you're the expert on creaming in your pants. But you never call me just to give me compliments. What'cha lookin' for?"

"I'm working the murder. I have a lead on the husband that takes me to Chelsea, and I don't know anyone on the Job over there. I need a connection, someone who can take me around and introduce me to the local bookies."

"I'll work on it. I should be able to get back to you tomorrow. By the way, how are Barb and the kids?"

"They're good. Give my love to Gail. And can we try to get this thing moving?"

Dunhill answers, "You got it, pal," and hangs up. Brisbane is smiling broadly. Avery Dunhill: it's a name that defies all expectations for a cop, as does the person it belongs to. Dunhill looks rough hewn like the actor Nick Nolte, but in fact he is the scion of a distinguished family of Boston Brahmins. Avery wasn't so foolish as to refuse the trust fund, but he did reject the career as an attorney or banker that comes as standard equipment with his patriarchy. Instead he chose to be an officer of the law, and he also chose to make his way up through the ranks on his own merits. Wisely he had been assigned to the police district that includes Back Bay. There he is able to exercise to best advantage one of his principal merits: knowing how to deal tactfully with the lawyers, bankers, media moguls, entrepreneurs, socialites and other self-entitled prima donnas who lend the neighborhood its unique flavor. Yet he is just as comfortable downing some brews at a corner bar out in Southie or lunching on crab cakes and arugula salad at some precious but undiscovered bistro in Jamaica Plain. Brisbane is smiling because he enjoys his friendship with Dunhill, a relationship at once familiar and undemanding, and also because he can tell from his friend's tone that he's going to get the help he is looking for.

Dunhill does call the next day, Tuesday, with the name and number of a Patrolman Ted Schrader in Chelsea. Brisbane leaves a message and hears back at the end of the day shift. They agree to meet Wednesday at 1:00 PM in front of Gordon's Grill.

Brisbane treats himself to lunch on Wednesday at Gordon's just to see what it's like and to visualize where Ralph spent part of the day after Thanksgiving. He is waiting outside afterwards when Schrader glides his cruiser into a parking space, gets out, and shakes Brisbane's hand. They walk several blocks together as

Schrader leads them to the Chief's dry cleaning store. Rocco is not surprised to see them enter. Schrader has called ahead to give the Chief a heads up about their impending visit, and the two of them have achieved a basic meeting of the minds on what is going to happen. Patrolman Schrader may not care to upset any profitable apple carts, but neither is he inclined to ignore a murder.

Rocco gestures his head toward the back of the store and Schrader leads Brisbane through the garment conveyer to the Chief's office door. Schrader knocks, the Chief calls them in. He pretends to be absorbed with paperwork as the two policemen seat themselves on the spindly chairs. The experience brings the Chief down a notch in Brisbane's estimation. If authority is based on genuine power, you shouldn't need to play games with furniture to flim flam visitors into submission. On the other hand, he can imagine Collins sitting in this exact chair and feeling intimidated, so may the idea isn't so bad after all.

The Chief looks up and leans back in his executive chair. "Gentlemen?"

Schrader speaks. "This is Detective Brisbane of the State Police. Detective, meet the Chief."

The Chief gestures palms up with his hands. "How can I help you?"

Brisbane sees no point in being coy, as Collins is already aware of his status as prime suspect. "The woman who was murdered last week in Newton? We have reason to believe it was a murder for hire arranged by the husband. That would be one Ralph Collins." Brisbane pauses to see if there is any reaction from the Chief. None is apparent. "We also have reason to believe that Collins has a gambling problem. We know that he had lunch at Gordons's Grill the day after Thanksgiving. Chelsea is far outside his sales district. We think he may have been here to see his bookie. We think that would be you. Was he here?"

The Chief is calm and controlled. "I have no knowledge of any murder in Newton."

Brisbane looks at Schrader. Schrader is motionless, his expression blank, his face impassive.

From these responses, Brisbane sees the whole picture. He has confirmation that his hunch is right: Collins is a compulsive gambler and he was here on that Friday. That much is good On the other hand, he has also learned that neither the Chief nor Schrader will help him delve any deeper to find the killers. He settles quickly on a working hypothesis: the Chief's statement may be literally and technically true, but there is more to the story and he's not going to get it out of either one of them. The net result is that Brisbane feels deflated, cheated out of the breakthrough he thought was coming. He's pissed at Schrader, too. The

Chelsea police had better not ever want the State Police to go out of their way to help *them*, is what he is thinking.

On his way back to his office, Brisbane decides on his next step. He is pretty sure now that his guess about the financial motive is a good one. The obvious source of financial benefit to Ralph from Bonnie's death would be an insurance policy on Bonnie's life. However, none were included among the documents that Ralph provided. Back in the office he scans Ralph's bank statements and sees no record of life insurance premium payments. So if a policy on Bonnie exists, how is he going to find it?

OK. Think. If a policy exists it must be paid for. If so, there must be another bank account that Ralph is hiding. The next step, then, is to get whatever court orders are necessary to force every bank and insurance company that does business in Massachusetts to reveal any dealings they've ever had with Ralph Collins, murderer. Brisbane dials the number of Anita Banks, the prosecutor in the District Attorney's office assigned to the case.

Anita sees to it that the necessary warrants are issued. The process takes several weeks to play out, with dozens of frustrating hours invested in making fruitless phone calls, but eventually Brisbane hits pay dirt once again. He uncovers the information that Ralph has a recently opened an account at a small credit union in a North Shore suburb, far from Newton and outside of his sales district. There are only three checks written against the account, one in January, one in February, one in March, each for the same amount. Unfortunately, the bank statement does not indicate the payee. It is time to pay Mr. Collins a little visit.

Early the next morning, Brisbane is sitting in a marked police cruiser in the parking lot of Ralph's office waiting for him to show up for work. He has gone back and forth in his mind at length about how to handle this confrontation: with discretion, or in a flamboyant manner calculated for maximum dramatic effect. After mulling it over the previous evening, he has come down on the side of drama. He can see no difference between the two choices from the standpoint of advancing the case. The preference, in the end, comes down to emotional satisfaction. Brisbane's emotional satisfaction. The delicious pleasure of seeing Ralph squirm.

So the detective sits in the cruiser sipping coffee and listening to "Morning Edition" on his portable radio, watching for Ralph. Ironically, though he is unaware of it, his vantage point is similar to that of goon number two the evening of the ramming back in January. Right before eight, amidst a stream of other arriving workers, Ralph pulls into the lot and notices the police car. Without actually seeing his face, Ralph assumes the figure inside it behind the wheel is Brisbane.

Brisbane can't help grinning as Ralph saunters with a nonchalant air towards the building entrance. He intuits what Ralph must be thinking: "Hell, I'm not going give that son of a bitch cop the satisfaction of going to him. Let the bastard come to me." Brisbane, in turn, is thinking: What a jerk. An innocent man would have raced over here full tilt to find out the latest news. So Collins wants me to come to him, does he? Very well, Ralph my friend, you're going to get exactly what you wished for. Here's the plan, Mr. Collins. First I'm going to sit here for half an hour, just to let you stew in your own juices for a while. Then I'm going to go in and announce myself loudly to your receptionist so that everyone in the office will know that something is going on. Then we will have our chat. Then I will escort you out, conspicuously passing by the receptionist, on our way to your house where we will pick up the cancelled checks. Then you will come back here and spend the rest of the day trying to get everybody to believe whatever bogus explanation you concoct for the events of the morning. You dumb jerk. If you had simply come over to me in the parking lot, all that would have been avoided. Ralph Collins, you are not an ordinary jerk. You are a world class champion jerk.

Brisbane would have savored the word *putz* if he had known it.

Thirty minutes later, Brisbane has the receptionist summon Ralph, and shortly thereafter he emerges through a door into the reception area. Instantly, for the benefit of the receptionist, Brisbane erases any hint of warmth or friendliness from his tone. "We're going to have a conversation in your office, Mr. Collins," he says, and strides toward the door. "Lead the way, Mr. Collins. Now."

Ralph sits behind his desk in his office, waiting, while Brisbane's eyes make a sweep of the room. There he notices nothing remarkable. There is a picture of Bonnie on the credenza by the window but no other evidence of a personal life. That is not unusual, though. Ralph is still in his thirties, and Brisbane has observed that guys don't usually get sentimental until after their mid-life crises.

Brisbane settles into the visitor's chair. "Good news."

"Really?" says Ralph, surprised, thinking *what the hell?*

"We uncovered some new evidence."

"Oh?"

"Yeah. I think it's going to break the case wide open."

"Really?"

"Really. Guess what we found."

"How would I know?"

"Well, only because it's something of yours.

The high pitch in Ralph's voice betrays his anxiety. *"Mine?"*

"Yours. You don't want to guess?"

"I have no idea."

"It's a bank account, Mr. Collins."

Ralph feels himself starting to tremble and grabs on to the arms of his chair, hoping Brisbane hasn't noticed. *Oh shit. It can't be that bank account. I'm fucked if it's that one.*

"It's your account with East Pines Credit Union. The rinky-dink credit union with two rinky-dink offices up in Beverly. The account has your name on it, Mr. Collins. Your address."

Ralph can't think of anything to say.

"Mr. Collins, you tried to hide this from me."

"No. No. Not at all. I just forgot."

"Let me get this straight. You opened the account just this past January. You went out of your way to seek out a rinky dink bank in a small town far away from Newton and way outside your sales district. You remembered to write a check for $117.36 every month since then. You remembered to make deposits just suffi-cient to cover those checks. And now you want me to believe that you simply for-got to include it with the rest of your financial documents?"

"Yeah."

"That's your story and you're sticking to it. Right? Never mind, then. We'll go to your house now and pick up your cancelled checks from that account."

"I think I ought to call my lawyer."

Brisbane is unfazed. "By all means. Be my guest. He will just tell you that if you don't turn the checks over voluntarily we will get a court order and you will have to do it anyway. But think about it. My guess is that your lawyer doesn't know you lied to us by trying to hide a bank account. What is he going to think of you when he finds out? How is he going to feel about the fact that you height-ened our suspicions by holding out on us? Is he going to think you are smart, or very, very stupid? Whereas, if you don't call him there'll be no subpoena and we can all just pretend that the statements were included in the original package that you gave us. He might never know. The choice is yours, of course."

This gives Ralph something to think about. Brisbane is patient and makes no effort to hurry him. Eventually Ralph makes up his mind. "OK, let's go." The deciding factor is not fear of his lawyer's reaction, but of Cap's.

So that's how Brisbane gets the name of the insurance company, and by the end of the day he has succeeded in getting them to fax over the entire file, including the policy, the application forms, and the medical report on Bonnie. Ahead lie interviews with the insurance agent in Dedham who sold the policy and the doctor who authored the fraudulent report. But in effect, he now has the motive nailed. Unfortunately, that is the least important part of the picture. It is evidence, but useful only in support of other evidence. Motive is valuable to help a jury understand the story of a crime, to help them put the other evidence into a comprehensible narrative context. But right now, Brisbane is quite aware, he has absolutely nothing that ties Ralph to the murder itself. Nor does he see anything out there on the horizon.

Time for a conference with the DA's office.

Brisbane is happy with the staff prosecutor assigned to the case. She is trim, pert, peppery and smart, reminding him of the actress Holly Hunter. He has worked with her before and likes her style: direct, efficient and focused. He appreciates her effectiveness in the courtroom, and equally the depth of preparation that makes that effectiveness possible.

In addition, Brisbane is attracted to her, and is curious about her personal life, but to no avail. She is all business all the time. She doesn't do small talk; there is no casual banter. He has no idea whether or not she is married, straight, in a relationship, a parent. He doesn't know where she lives or where she grew up or where she went to law school. On the few occasions when he's made cautious, tentative attempts to socialize a bit, like colleagues normally do at work, she has politely but firmly rebuffed him by changing the subject. "Let's go over the arrest report," she would say, or, "When do you expect the blood analysis from the lab to be ready?" And it's not personal with him. He has witnessed her behaving the same way with others. Yet Brisbane doesn't read any of this as coldness. Her compassion for victims is patently genuine, her prosecutorial methods never vengeful or vindictive. On the basis of nothing but wishful thinking, Brisbane is convinced: there just has to be a ton of pain bottled up and stored away inside that walnut shell of hers.

Anita Bank's office is in the same building as Brisbane's: 40 Thorndike Street, the Edwin J. Sullivan Courthouse in Cambridge, just across the Charles River from Boston. This used to be the Middlesex County Courthouse. In 1997, however, the state began a three year process of eliminating the governmental functions of seven of the fourteen the counties in the Commonwealth, including Middlesex, while assuming responsibility for their operations directly. In the process, the state inherited the Courthouse. Forty Thorndike Street, the Courthouse, is a beached whale of a building, an 18 story concrete behemoth plunked down in a neighborhood of frame houses and mom and pop businesses. Designed in an architectural style known as New Brutalism, this gross and heedless edifice lords over its puny neighbors like King Kong towering over a meadow.

Brisbane calls Anita for an appointment to discuss whether it is time to make an arrest. It is now five weeks after the murder and press coverage, while less intense, is more pointed: "Detective Brisbane, if it wasn't a break in, can you tell is the motive"? "Detective Brisbane, do you have a suspect yet"? "Detective Brisbane, when can we expect an arrest to be made?" The reporters' instincts are right. It's time to make something happen.

They get together later that week in the prosecutor's office. True to form, they get down to business quickly and within a few minutes have listed the pros and cons in dry erase marker on a white board. It looks like this:

Pro	Con
1. **Abundant evidence of motive**	1. **Collins alibi airtight; identity of killers unknown**
• **Massive debt**	
• **New insurance policy**	2. **Connection between Collins and shooters unknown**
• **Pregnant wife**	
• **Bookie in Chelsea**	• **How did he first make contact with them?**
2. **Persuasive evidence that murder was not random break in**	• **How did he communicate with them (directly? Through a go between?)**
• **Alarm turned off**	• **What was the deal?**
• **Execution style shooting**	
• **House unlikely choice for burglary**	3. **No evidence tying Collins to shooting**
3. **Consciousness of guilt**	• **No witnesses**
• **No call home from Atlanta**	• **No usable forensic evidence**
• **Hidden bank account**	• **No leads**
• **Trouble in marriage after Thanksgiving**	

By the time the list is completed, Brisbane and Banks know that an arrest would be premature. They agree on what to do next: update the Legatos. And so it is that early in the next week, Arthur Brisbane and Anita Banks are sitting with

Ken and Gladys Legato in a conference room on the second floor of 40 Thorndike Street.

This is the first meeting between the Legatos and the prosecutor. Brisbane does the introductions, after which Ken speaks up quickly: "Miss Banks ... uh, is that Miss or Mrs.?"

"I'd prefer Ms., if that's OK?"

"Of course. Ms. Banks, I just want to tell you how grateful we are for the vigor with which you and Detective Brisbane are working on this case. He has been phenomenal in getting to the bottom of things, and now we're very much looking forward to working with you as well."

Anita nods her head slightly. "Thank you. Yes, I've worked with Detective Brisbane on several previous cases. He's one of the best. You are fortunate to have him as lead investigator. You could hardly have done better."

Brisbane could hardly have been more thrilled. He is concentrating on trying not to show it. Until now, he has had no idea at all what Anita thinks of him. He sensed, he thought, a basic level of respect. But "one of the best?" Fortunate to have him? Wow. But, does she actually believe that? Or is she just saying it to butter up the Legatos? Oh, damn. *Damn.* He feels the warmth flowing into his cheeks. He's starting to blush. *Damn! Damn!* God, don't let her notice. *Please.*

In fact, he'll never know whether or not she notices. She just goes on addressing the Legatos. "I want to make sure at the outset that you're clear about the role of the prosecutor in a case like this. As a policy of this office, as a policy of prosecutors' offices throughout the nation, and as a matter of my personal inclination, we welcome involvement by victims and their families. We encourage their input and participation. We solicit their opinions. That being said, however, it is necessary for you to understand that we are not representing you. You are not actually a party to the case. Our client is the Commonwealth of Massachusetts. Our duty is to represent the people as a whole, and to pursue justice and public safety on their behalf. What you think and what you want will be important considerations as we make decisions along the way, but the determining factor will always be our responsibility to the public. I don't want to sound unfeeling, Mr. and Mrs. Legato, but I have to make sure we're starting off on the same page."

Ken is miffed. This is not what he expected to hear. Gladys understands, however. It makes sense to her. She can see that Ken is disgruntled, so she speaks up for both of them. "It was a good idea to clarify things, Ms. Banks."

Anita then reviews the evidence, using the white board—which she has moved to the conference room from her office—as an outline. Ken listens attentively and patiently to Anita's presentation, but he has immediately grasped the problem with his first glance at the board. "The case is thin, isn't it?"

"Yes, Mr. Legato," Anita confirms. "Perhaps worse than thin. Maybe emaciated."

"What are the chances of beefing it up?" Ken asks.

The question falls into Brisbane's bailiwick, and he takes over. "We can get more if we go to a grand jury, but even then I doubt we're ever going to have enough evidence to secure a first degree murder conviction. The bottom line, Mr. Legato, is that we have nothing right now that connects your son in law to the actual killers. I think that is unlikely to change."

Ken is aghast at the next thought that comes to mind. "Are you telling me that Ralph Collins is going to get away with murder?"

Anita steps in. "No, Mr. Legato. We're saying precisely what Detective Brisbane said: that it would be difficult to obtain a conviction on a charge of murder in the first degree. As things stand now, there is too much room for a competent defense attorney to establish reasonable doubt."

Gladys tilts her head at an angle. "Ms. Banks, exactly what it is that you are trying to tell us?"

Anita breathes in and squares her shoulders. "Mrs. Legato, Mr. Legato, this is hard to say because I know how you feel about Mr. Collins. But Detective Brisbane and I are both experienced in these matters and we both agree. We both believe the time will come when I will have to make a decision. The choice will be, on the one hand, to bring Mr. Collins to trial on murder one and lesser included charges, with a significant chance of losing on everything, or, on the other hand, to allow Mr. Collins to plead out on a lesser charge with a guarantee that he will serve time in jail. This won't be an easy decision, and it doesn't have to be decided now. The investigation is ongoing. But I thought it was only fair to inform you honestly about how this case is shaping up so far. We wanted to give you time to absorb this information and sort out your feelings."

"My feelings? I'll tell you my feelings. I feel like I want to vomit!" Ken spits it out.

Gladys glares in his direction. "Ken!"

Anita's voice is soothing. "We understand, Mr. Legato."

Gladys touches Ken's arm tenderly. "Let's go."

Ken looks up. "How can you stand it?"

"It's out of our hands."

"Yeah. Sure." Ken's posture is downcast, his visage bleak. "Maybe Jeff is right."

"*KEN!*" Gladys is genuinely shocked. In forty one years as a couple, she has never before seen his faith waver.

"Yeah, you're right. Let's go."

After mutual assurances about keeping in touch, the Legatos are gone. The detective and the prosecutor review briefly what comes next in the case, and then their business is concluded. But before he leaves, Brisbane cannot resist asking. He has to know. *He has to.* "Uh … maybe you'll think I'm foolish to ask … but I'm going to anyway … Did you mean it? What you said before? About me?"

He thinks he sees a shadow of a smile flash across Anita's face, but it's gone before he can be sure. He is sure, though, of what he hears her say: "Yes."

One of the best. They're lucky to have him.

That's *something*.

12

Sandy hit me with it after dinner on Easter Sunday. I never saw it coming.

The meal that afternoon in Westborough was the first time the family had gathered together since the funeral two months earlier. This was just a few days after the meeting in the District Attorney's office. There was lots to talk about.

Gladys had set a place for Bonnie in her customary location at the table. On the dinner plate, a votive candle was burning in her memory.

Ken's grace reflected the rawness of the wound: "On this day, especially, Oh Lord, we thank you for the sacrifice of your only son so that mankind could be given the gift of salvation. Thank you, too, for the bounty of the feast we have before us. But Lord, we beseech you, help us to understand the terrible tragedy that has befallen our good and faithful family. We know that Jesus instructed us to forgive those who would trespass against us, but it's hard. Lord, help us to find a way to follow Jesus and do that. Help us, please, to heal. And Lord, I mean no disrespect, I truly don't, but the police could use some help too. Amen."

This was not quite the way Jim would have put things. Nevertheless, neither could he bring himself to find fault with his father; as I was later to discover, Ken's feelings resonated with his own. Gladys too, while she did think Ken's prayer bordered on the profane, was similarly willing to make allowances.

In fact, Gladys' tolerance derived from a larger apprehension which eclipsed any concern over the saying of grace. Ever before the master of disciplined strength and self control, Ken seemed to be—well, for lack of a better word—losing it. This was frightening on a variety of fronts, not the least of which being that coping with her own bereavement was taxing every resource she had. There was little strength to spare for dealing with an emotional meltdown by her husband. She had been prepared for his breast-beating proclamations of culpability and guilt, his unremitting self-flagellation, his sullen withdrawal from marital intimacy, his skyrocketing consumption of alcohol. The unexpected, scary part was that he was allowing the unraveling of his psyche to show itself at work.

This was cause for alarm because Gladys knew that Ken's success in his career went to the very core of his sense of worth as a man. Ken was proud, of course, of his proficiency in the roles of husband and father, pleased that his children had turned out well, content that he had conducted his life in an ethical, morally upright fashion, satisfied that his material comforts had been earned and his self respect deserved. But that, he thought, was the easy part. Anybody could do that. All right, if not anybody, lots of people then. What made him different, what set him apart and ahead of the pack, was that above and beyond all the good personal and family virtues he was both a first rate engineer and an excellent manager in business. Face it, there aren't many who can justifiably make a claim like that.

There was only one sore spot. Ken's career had benefited from fortuitous timing and he was sensitive to any appearances in this fact that might devalue his achievements. He had graduated from engineering college during the Nixon administration and had found employment immediately courtesy of the Water Pollution Control Act of 1972. This law provided federal funding for construction of sewage treatment plants, thereby providing simultaneously for the cleaning up of the nation's rivers and for the full employment of civil engineers. So Ken found himself designing sewage treatment plants, and serendipitously discovered that he was good at it. By the time the effects of the Reagan administration's funding cutbacks were felt fifteen years later, Ken had risen to a position of senior responsibility in the engineering firm where he was employed, and was immune to the attendant layoffs. Thereafter, when someone might remark on his ascendant trajectory of success, Ken would respond with the airy dismissal that he was "just in the right place at the right time." Ken would say this in full awareness of its truth, but it was phrased and uttered in a disarming, self-deprecating offhand manner calculated to denote it's diametric opposite. It was a rare display of defensiveness for Ken. It was disingenuous, a word not normally used in describing him.

Appearances aside, Ken was not troubled by the role that luck had played in his career. He felt, rather, that he had played the hand that was dealt him, and done it well. Others had entered his profession at the same time as he, but few had risen quite so high in companies quite so large and prestigious. And he never harbored the slightest doubt that what made him a success was a combination of hard work, engineering acumen, and a knack for supervising people.

Gladys never doubted this either. It was the concordance of the clues, large and small, that spoke volumes to her about Ken's character and led her to infer that he was superb at his job. Most people, for example, would be excited at being recognized and praised by political dignitaries during the dedication ceremony of a treatment plant that they had designed. They would welcome as a treat the rare moment in the limelight. Not Ken, though. For him, ceremonies were nothing more than a public relations chore that he would stoically endure for the benefit of his company. The thrill for Ken would come several weeks earlier, when they tested the equipment in the plant and the laboratory tests came back showing that the process was working to specifications. She knew, too, that people liked working for her husband. They would come up to her and tell her this at company functions and social occasions. He engendered a loyalty among his staff that was both spontaneous and abiding. He set high standards, but he set them by example rather than fiat. He expected drive and dedication, but never greater than his own. He led his teams toward challenging objectives, but they were set by mutual agreement, not intimidation. Ken gave credit to others joyously whenever it was due. And he liked nothing better than to treat his entire design team to a blowout steak celebration dinner at Morton's when a job was completed and sent out to bid.

Gladys knew that yes, her husband loved and took great satisfaction in his family. But his *energies*—which were formidable indeed—were devoted to his job. That is why the call from Chet Townsend left her so shaken.

"Hello, Gladys," he said. "This is Chet," he added superfluously. Gladys knew the voice. Chet was a founding partner in the company. He had first hired Ken during those Nixon years, and had been his boss ever since.

Socially, her relationship with Chet and his wife was warm but not especially close. A call from Chet during business hours could not be good news.

"Gladys," he said, "How are you holding up?"

"All right. It's hard, Chet."

"You know ... if there's anything we can do ..."

"Thank you. We just have to work our way through it."

"OK, just so you know we're here for you." Now came the uncomfortable pause ...

... "Why are you calling, Chet?"

"We're worried about Ken."

"Tell me."

"... He's not doing his job."

"What do you mean?"

"Oh, Gladys ... He spends most of the day just sitting at his desk and staring into space. He's letting his calls go into voice mail and not returning them. He's not even opening his e-mail. He's stopped leading. When his team comes to him for decisions or advice, he tells them to do whatever they think is best. At staff meetings he has nothing to contribute. I don't dare take him with me on new business calls."

"What are you getting at, Chet?"

"You know how much we love Ken. He's family. So are you. That's why I'm calling you first."

"First before what, Chet? Just spit it out, please."

"The business is suffering. As much as we love him, I can't allow that to happen."

"Just what are you getting at?

"I think Ken ought to go on a sabbatical. A paid sabbatical. Medical leave, if you'd like to look at it that way. But the point is, I need to reassign his responsibilities to other people. So the work gets done. Temporarily. Until he recovers."

"And you're calling me because …"

"Because … well, several reasons. One is that I wanted you to understand. To know why we have to do this. To tell you in advance so you're not taken by surprise. We didn't want you to have to deal with the news unexpectedly, at the same time Ken hears about it. We wanted you to be prepared so you could help him deal with it, help him come to terms with the necessity for it.

"And one other thing. Gladys? I thought maybe you could help me find the right tone. Figure out how to position this so it isn't so hard for him to swallow."

Gladys was too numb to give it any thought right then. "When are you planning to do this?"

"Next Monday, right after Easter. No point in ruining Easter."

You mean, ruining it for Ken, Gladys was thinking. How about ruining it for me, she was thinking. Why is that OK? She said, "I'll call you before the end of the week."

"That's great. Thank you, Gladys."

Gladys agonized all evening over what to tell Chet. Ken didn't notice. Later in the week she did talk to Chet and told him that if things were as he described, Ken would want to do the right thing for the business too. It would help, she added, if his duties could be parceled out to a variety of individuals rather than have one person actually replace him. That way, he wouldn't have to face the idea that he could be replaced so quickly and easily."

In the end, Gladys was only partially right in her advice to Chet. As she thought, Ken was accepting of the sabbatical, a little grateful in fact for the opportunity to shed responsibilities that he was clearly not fulfilling. He reacted badly, though, to the idea of spreading those responsibilities around. To Ken, this signified that not only was he interchangeable with others as individuals, but also that his entire function—his very job itself—was dispensable. If his job could successfully be sprayed around to others, then it showed that the company didn't need a Managing Director of Design Operations at all.

Chet didn't argue with Ken. They sorted things out amicably, like the long term friends and people of good will that they were, and one of Ken's project managers—Ken's choice—was appointed to replace him on an interim basis.

But on Easter Sunday, Gladys knew what Chet was planning for Monday and Ken did not. And she didn't know how Ken would take it. And more than anything, she hated keeping secrets from her husband. She would never even plan a surprise party for him. Keeping this secret was nothing short of torture.

In an effort to steer life back toward a semblance of normality, Gladys had prepared the traditional Legato Easter meal: homemade pea soup, honey glazed ham, potatoes au gratin, fresh asparagus, and coconut custard pie. This time she cut a corner. The pie was store bought. This was comfort food at a moment when everyone very much needed comfort.

Topic A, the criminal investigation, was avoided during the meal because Heather and Sally were at the table. Jeff and Sharon, however, were upset with Ken's version of grace, not for religious reasons but because the girls had not been told how Bonnie had died. They knew that Aunt Bonnie was dead and had gone to heaven, but had been told that it was due to an accident. They were told Aunt Bonnie had been hit by a car. As parents, Jeff and Sharon agreed that neither of their daughters was ready to process the fact that their aunt was the victim of a violent murder by gunfire, much less that such an abomination had been perpetrated by someone they knew. So, now, there went Ken talking about the police right in front of the girls. They knew instinctively that Heather would pick up on that.

Ken was not unaware of how his son and daughter in law felt, but it didn't inhibit him. He thought it stupid to lie to the kids about an "accident." Ken believes that truth is always best, even if it has to be filtered and simplified so that young minds can come to grips with it. Jeff and Sharon were aware of Ken's feeling on this and respected it, but felt in turn that their own point of view should be respected equally, and that as the parents their decision should prevail. That Ken should use grace to sabotage their policy on this matter was a source of immediate and deep chagrin.

Jeff and Sharon knew their daughters. No sooner had Gladys finished serving the soup than Heather piped up. "Grandpa? Why does God need to help the police?"

That put the kibosh on conversation for a while. Nobody knew what to say.

At length, Sandy decided to brave a response. "Sweetheart, all Grandpa meant … Sweetheart, the police investigate every accident to make sure that it really was an accident, and to make sure the person who caused the accident didn't break any laws. All Grandpa meant was that if the man who caused Aunt Bonnie's accident broke any laws, he should be arrested and punished."

I admired Sandy's willingness to fill the void, but she herself didn't feel good about it afterwards. It was evident that Heather was dubious about that explanation and was accepting it only because it's source was Aunt Sandy, a person of heretofore-impeccable credibility. Sandy, who fundamentally agreed with her father, felt that she had betrayed that credibility for an end that didn't justify the means. Her impulse had been an act of generosity toward her brother and sister-in-law. Later she regretted it.

So already, Gladys was uptight about Ken's work, Ken was defiant about Heather, Jeff and Sharon were annoyed at Ken, Sandy was disappointed in herself, and the soup wasn't even cooled down yet.

During the rest of the dinner, things managed to stay on an even keel more or less. Everyone navigated the conversation through safe and well marked topical channels.

Jeff was asked about life with his new boss. After New Year's, he and Sharon had negotiated a deal: If he still wanted to leave the company after getting to know the incoming VP, he would invest six months in making a good faith effort to find a new position within commuting range. Failing that, Sharon would agree to move providing the job opportunity was better than anything available locally. Just the knowledge the he had a way out, an escape route, helped Jeff to relax and take the measure of his new boss with a degree of calm objectivity. What he found was that he liked what he saw. As a result, he reported, his search for a better career situation had lost its urgency. He was content now to see if something enticing came up in the Portland area, but to keep in abeyance any plan to uproot Sharon and the kids.

Heather and Sally were asked about school. Sally was pumped up about some new friends she had made during this year, and was excited about a pajama party they'd invited her to over the upcoming weekend. Heather was both looking forward to and nervous about the Spring Concert coming up in May, her second as a member of her elementary school band. With no particularly musical background on either side of the family, nor in the family of the children's father, it came as a pleasant surprise to her parents when Heather decided on her own to take up the clarinet at school. Their delight was not so much with the thought that she would master an instrument; they could tell quickly that her native musical talent was modest. Rather, they foresaw that in the process of learning to play, she would take away an understanding and appreciation of how to listen to music, a benefit that could yield her satisfaction and joy for the rest of her life. At the same time, this development became the source of another sore spot between Jeff and Ken. They avoided broaching the subject this time, but Jeff never failed to marvel over his father's lack of consistency. In one breath Ken would laud the musical accomplishments of his granddaughter, and in the next he would rant about the waste of taxpayer money spent on "superfluous extras" such as music, art and drama in the public schools, and he could never be made to see the contradiction. On this occasion, Jeff kept his irritation to himself.

In due time the girls were ushered out, plates of coconut pie in hand, to watch videos in the den so the adults could talk. Everyone was eager to know about the meeting with Brisbane and Anita Banks. Ken and Gladys told the story in their characteristic tandem fashion. Since the details of progress in the investigation were new to everyone else at the table, the family sat in rapt attention.

Sandy was comfortable with the tenor of the meeting with the prosecutor as described by her parents, as was I. Ken remained disgruntled. Thus began another ... well, let's not call it an argument. Let's just say it was a spirited discussion.

Sandy started it. "Dad," she said, "I don't see the problem. Wouldn't the worst thing be to go through a whole trial and then have it come out not guilty?"

Ken, already out of sorts from the contretemps over Heather, sat stonefaced.

Gladys tried to paper things over. "Honey," she said, addressing Sandy, "It's very upsetting for your father to think that if there's a deal, Ralph could resume his normal life in just a few years, as if nothing had ever happened."

Ken looked at Gladys and shook his head back and forth. His tone was querulous. "That is *not* why I am upset. I am upset to think that if the option of a plea is out there on the table, then the prosecutors will be predisposed to slack off. Their motivation to apply their best effort will be destroyed. They'll have an easy out, where it won't be necessary to invest the sweat and blood necessary to obtain a genuine, honest to God conviction the old fashioned way: in a trial where they nail the bastard."

Sandy wouldn't let go. "But Dad. These are seasoned professionals. They are simply telling you that in their expert judgment, there may never be enough evidence to make a case that would win before a jury. They're just being realistic. You wouldn't want them to sugar coat reality, would you."

Ken glared at Sandy. "You are so idealistic. You are so *naive*. You want realistic? OK, I'll give you realistic. Realistic is all about the numbers. Statistics. The clearance rate. That's the holy grail for bureaucrats like them. The percentage of cases that are brought to a successful conclusion. You have to see where they're coming from. For them, what is a successful conclusion? One: OK, so a conviction in court is a success. But two: a plea bargain is also a success. And here's the a difference. A conviction is hard to obtain. A plea is easier to obtain. If you're a bureaucrat looking to make the numbers, I ask you, what's the point of doing it the hard way when there's an easy way? I am not attacking Mr. Brisbane or Ms. Banks personally. I am saying, it is the system. The way the system is structured drives even good people to do certain things certain ways. The path of least resistance. Instead of following the road to justice, we are being taken down the path of least resistance. That is why I'm upset."

About then it occurred to me that it was time to show Sandy some support. "Ken, aren't plea bargains necessary to make the whole system work in this country?" This was bold for me; usually I steered clear of spirited discussions with Ken. "Most cases are pled out, if I'm not mistaken. Only a small minority are brought to trial."

I was rewarded with a look of scorn. Suddenly it was my feet dancing on the hot griddle. "Your point," he said, "is both correct and irrelevant."

But I sensed in my peripheral vision that Sandy approved of my intervention, so I was encouraged to keep going. "But Ken, you were criticizing the system. The relevance of plea bargaining is that it *is* the system. It's the system we have because it is the only way to keep the cost of the machinery of criminal justice from overwhelming us all. The overriding reason we have the system we do, with all its faults, is because it's the maximum the American public is willing to pay taxes to support. You hate taxes as much as anyone I know. Even with the system as it is, there aren't enough courts and judges to handle the load; that's why people have to wait three years in this state for a civil case to come to trial. Isn't that realistic too? Surely you wouldn't want to pay the taxes on what it would cost if every suspect were brought to trial. Anyway, isn't the real issue something else: isn't the question not a debate over the merits of the plea bargaining process in general, but rather whether or not Brisbane and Banks are correct in this particular instance when they say it is impossible to marshal sufficient evidence?"

Ken glowered at me. "So tell me then: How the hell am I supposed to have any confidence in their determination on that precise question if I think their motivation tainted by the temptation to cut a deal?"

Actually, I didn't have a good answer for that. When I failed to respond, Ken waved the back of his hand dismissively in my direction as his eyes made a sweep of the rest of the family in a kind of ocular victory lap. It didn't matter, though. Sandy rested her hand on my arm affectionately, so all was right with the world.

"Jim, what do you think about it?" That was Jeff asking.

Jim took a while to respond. Everyone waited.

"He shall wash every tear from their eyes, and there shall be no more death or mourning, crying out or pain, for the former world has passed away."

Nobody said anything. Nobody understood what he was talking about.

"Revelations," he added. "Chapter 4, Verse 21."

That clarified nothing. A classic non sequitur. Nobody, still, knew what to say. Eventually, Gladys stood up, planted a kiss on the top of Ken's head, and said to Sandy, "Let's start clearing the table."

Sandy got up, planted a kiss on the top of my head, and began to help her mother. Sandy's kiss should have been a flag that something was cooking. She is sensual and playful in private but rarely demonstrative in public. But I missed the signal. My attention was focused on drawing Jim outside to take our walk. I wanted to ask him what was behind the Revelations quote. I got his attention across the table by waving an imaginary cigar between my fingers, Groucho Marx style, and he nodded OK.

We lit up the smokes outside and walked through the neighborhood in silence for about a quarter mile. I was debating with myself over whether to ask him what was on his mind. I didn't want to intrude where I wasn't welcome, but neither did I want him to imagine that I was indifferent to his suffering. Finally I said simply, "Would you like to tell me what the Revelations quote was about?"

Jim continued walking in silence for a while before answering dejectedly, "I'm not sure I can explain."

"Maybe if you try, it will help you figure it out for yourself."

The pause was shorter this time. "The Scripture promises that God will wipe away the tears and ease the pain. I'm not sure that's going to happen."

Jim? Questioning Scripture? Doubting God? And besides, I was baffled. Isn't the *Book of Revelation* about the apocalypse and the second coming? What did that have to do with feeling better now? "Jim," I said, "Isn't it too soon for wiping away tears? Doesn't healing take time? Aren't you supposed to give it time?"

Jim was pensive but started walking faster, as though there were some release to be found in sheer physical activity. "I suppose … But I don't feel right with myself just now. I feel like I don't know who I am any more. I don't know where God is any more. I'm being tested, and I'm flunking the test. My grade is an "F." As in failure. As in fraud. Barry, that's what it is coming down to. I am a fraud."

As gratified as I was that he would open up to me like this, I was dismayed over the import of what he was saying. I could think of no response adequate to the gravity of the situation. I heard myself say, "I know you enough to say that I can't believe that … that you're a fraud. It must be that you are being unnecessarily hard on yourself." It sounded awkward and stupid as it was coming out of my mouth, but it was the best I could do. I wanted to keep the conversation going because now I felt it important to understand very clearly what it was he was telling me.

"It's complicated."

"Sandy says I'm a good listener. There's no time limit."

He remained quiet, so I tried another tack. "Damn it, who the hell else are you going to talk to about it?"

This worked. He even managed a brief smile. After a pause, he stopped and turned toward me. "It's about forgiveness. Uh ... I'm going to have to explain some things to you about the Christian faith. Do you really want to hear this?"

"Absolutely," I said.

"All right," he went on, starting to walk again. "In the Christian faith, there are three kinds of forgiveness. The first is God's forgiveness of mankind's original sin. This forgiveness was made available to all by the sacrifice of Jesus on the cross, and is obtained by Christians through the sacrament of baptism.

"The second kind is God's forgiveness of one's own sinful acts as an individual. This, too, is relatively simple to obtain if you are a Christian: you ask God for it. But there is a precondition. In order for God to forgive a sinful act a Christian must both confess—that is, acknowledge responsibility—and repent. Repentance is not about being sorry. It is forward looking. It is about a change in one's mind and heart so that one is resolved not to repeat the sin in the future. As an ordained priest, I am a vessel in which God's forgiveness is delivered to repentant sinners.

"The third kind is where my problem lies: our own forgiveness of other people who have sinned against us. In other words, this is where it comes down to Ralph and me. Ralph ... and me.

"You may be surprised," he continued, "that forgiveness between Christians is a matter of some controversy within the Church. There are some who say we should follow God's example and only extend personal forgiveness to those who repent. This is based somewhat on *a priori* logic in inferring what God would want of people based on the conditions He set for himself, but it also has some scriptural foundation in Luke 17:3, which goes something like, 'Be on your guard. If your brother does wrong, correct him; if he repents, forgive him.' Notice the contingency there: *if he repents.*

"Others argue that forgiveness between people must be unconditional. This is based on the premise that it is not up to you to judge. God will do that. As a matter of fact, Scripture says that if you do not forgive others their sins, God will not forgive you yours. This view is based on several passages in Scripture. For example, Mark 11:25: 'When you stand to pray, forgive anyone against you whom you have a grievance so that your heavenly Father may in turn forgive you your faults.'

"Is this making any sense to you?"

Luckily I had been paying attention. "I think so," I said. "Ralph is not about to repent. So if forgiveness is conditional, then it is not an option for you. If it's unconditional, I don't think you want to forgive Ralph. But either way, whether you *can't* forgive or whether you *won't* forgive, you may be cutting yourself off from God's forgiveness of you. You're in a bind."

In Jim's agitation, he was striding so fast I could barely keep pace. "It's worse than that. There's more to it. It goes back to the absolute cornerstone of Christ's message, which is Christian love.... I don't know if I can explain it all. I have to go pedantic on you. You don't want to hear all this."

"I do want to hear all this. You're doing great so far. Keep going. Please. Anyway, you're cute when you're pedantic."

Jim grinned and gave me a shove on my upper arm, the way kids do. In its guileless intimacy, it was wonderful and welcome gesture. "All right," he said, "OK. You asked for it. Christianity 101. Here goes. Christian love has two aspects, which are conjoined and inseparable. The first is love of God, and the second is love of thy neighbor as thyself. Now, you must also understand the Christian conception of sin. Sin is not the breaking of a rule. It's not a verdict on bad behavior. Sin is alienation from God. Separation from God. Refusal to be part of God's family. But—here's the thing—God never stops loving the sinner. He hates the sin but never stops loving the sinner. That means that God wants everyone to be close to him, wants nobody alienated from him. God wants sinners to come back to him, to be reconciled with him. And how can that happen? If the sinner repents, that's how that can happen. So if you're a Christian and you follow the most basic teaching of Jesus, which is to love God, what does that require? If you love God, it requires that you help him with what he wants most, which is reconciliation with the sinner. He wants it not because reconciliation between sinner and God is best for God, but because it is best for the sinner. And how do you help do that? The Scriptures tell you how. It is right in Matthew 18:15: 'If your brother should commit some wrong against you, go and point out his fault.' Remember what I said a little while ago about Luke? 'If your brother does wrong, correct him." It's the same thing. And that's the New American Version. The old Saint James Version doesn't say correct him, it says rebuke him. It's stronger yet. Barry, it boils down to this: I am *required* by the Scriptures to confront Ralph, to rebuke him, to try to get him to repent so that he can be reconciled with God. That is what it means to love both God and your neighbor.

"Barry, I don't want to do that. I don't want Ralph reconciled with God. I hate the rotten bastard. I want him alienated from God. I don't want forgiveness for him, I want retribution. I want him to rot in hell. Not just in jail, in hell. For eternity.

"That's why I'm a fraud. I wear a collar. I'm supposed to love God. Loving God is my vocation. And I'm not doing it. I can't hate Ralph and love God at the same time. I'm not who people think I am. I'm not who I thought I was. I'm phony. I'm a sham, a fake, a dissembler, a hypocrite. I'm a mock Christian. A clergyman who's masquerading as a Christian. *What am I going to do?*"

Whoa!

Whoa.

It was another quarter mile before I could collect my thoughts enough just to say, "If there's anybody who's the genuine article, Jim, it's you. It takes some time. But the day will come when you will be ready to do what your faith requires. It's only eight weeks now. It's not time yet. But the time will come. I know it will." I knew nothing of the sort. I had no idea. But what else could I tell him?

We were almost back to the Legato house. It was visible in the middle distance. The cigars were long since finished, extinguished, and disposed of down a storm drain. The late afternoon shadows were long across the landscape. A breeze was picking up and a chill was settling in. It seemed much colder that it really was, and I was more than ready to go back inside.

"Thanks for listening," Jim said as we approached the driveway.

"Glad to, Jim," I said, "But I don't think I've helped you much." I meant what I said. It was backed by a feeling of frustration that was becoming all too familiar. Sandy was still deeply despondent and I hadn't figured out how to help her either.

Jim tried to reassure me. "It's not something you can solve. You're helping just by listening. I need that too, and I'm grateful for it."

As we came in the front door, Sandy came out of the kitchen and told me, "Don't take off your jacket. We're on our way." Within minutes we were in the car and heading for home. I knew now, of course, that something was up. Her mood seemed better, though, so I wasn't worried. I assumed she would let me know when she was ready.

She was ready after we merged into traffic on the Turnpike. There were no preliminaries, there was no preamble. There was just a declarative sentence: "I want to have a baby."

I didn't want to say the wrong thing, so I didn't say anything. I was in shock and my mind was reeling. I was thinking of filthy stinky diapers. Crying fits. Food on the floor. Crayons on the walls. Unreasonable demands. Tests of wills. Tantrums over broken toys. Endless worries. Sleepless nights. Our lives no longer our own. We'd need a bigger place. A house. Weekends dissolving into an endless treadmill of chores around the house. Money. The cost of bringing up a kid. The cost of the house. Was she going to stay home and take care of a kid? How could we afford that?

I couldn't believe it.

Where did this come from? I wondered.

Then I wondered, where *did* this come from?

And all of a sudden the light bulb went on: This is a replacement for Bonnie's baby!

Oh my God. She's pinch hitting. No, not exactly that. More like, this is how Sandy thinks she will be able to take Bonnie's place in her father's affections. Yeah, like that.

Oh my God, I thought. That can't be a good reason to have a baby.

Can it?

My mind was on total overload. I had no concept of what to say or do. We were approaching the Weston tolls before I could even manage to ask her, "Do we have to discuss this right now? Can you give me some time to sort out my feelings?"

"No problem," she chirped. Her voice was cheerful, buoyant, for the first time since Bonnie was murdered.

No sooner did we get in the door of our condo than she made a beeline for the bedroom. Curious, I followed her, just getting a glimpse of her back as she disappeared into the walk-in closet there. I stretched out on the bed, waiting so see what would happen.

What happened was that she slinked out of the closet wearing her sexiest summer outfit: white short shorts and a red tank top, the one with the low cut V-neck and straps cut way back at the shoulders.

Sandy has the most gorgeous shoulders, and shoulders are my favorite, most erotic part on a woman. Hers are broad, square and perfectly rounded at the arms, and combined with her velvety, flawless skin, they drive me wild. This outfit shows off her shoulders to best advantage, and does she ever know it.

Sandy is expert at firing up my libido, and she can do it any time she wants. Any time at all. It doesn't matter if I'm tired, stressed, irritable, whatever. Whenever she chooses to use it, her power over my loin is complete and irresistible. I am utterly helpless before it.

This time she knelt by the side of the bed, shoulder within touching range. She opened my belt and undid my zipper, and then her warm silky hands were caressing my parts.

Baby, schmaby. I was a goner.

It was like the old days.

An hour later, while we were snuggling and enjoying the afterglow, it occurred to me: could she have stopped taking the pill already? The question of a baby, yes or no: could she have just rendered it moot?

She wouldn't do that.

Would she?

13

Brisbane spends the days following the meeting with Anita and the Legatos poring over the case file to see what he has missed.

This time one of the items which catches his attention is the police folder on the accident in Framingham. Early in the investigation, as a matter of routine, Brisbane had initiated a search for any civil or criminal records concerning Ralph or Bonnie Collins. He had made document requests of the State Police, of the Massachusetts court system, and of the local police in Newton and Framingham, the towns where Ralph lived and worked. The folder on the accident is the only fruit of these searches, and at first glance it had not appeared to be of value. Now, grasping at straws, Brisbane decides to give it a second look.

According to these documents, which include an accident report by the Framingham patrolman and an investigative report by a Boston police detective, the stolen car involved in the accident is owned by one Manuel Yuyali. Mr. Yuyali lives in Lexington and is employed as technology manager by a software firm in Woburn. On the day before Ralph's accident, he had driven to downtown Boston to have dinner with some business associates who had just arrived from Chicago. They were staying at the Westin and Mr. Yuyali was to meet them for dinner at The Palm at 7:30. Mr. Yuyali arrived on time and was prepared to pay for parking in a garage but serendipitously found an empty space on Stuart Street. When dinner was concluded at 9:30, Mr. Yuyali returned to the space and found that his car was missing. He reported the theft using his cell phone.

Focusing now on the details of the report, Brisbane notices for the first time that a fingerprint had been found in the car interior. The car had been towed to Boston for investigation by police because that was the jurisdiction where the theft had taken place. The Boston police, using ninhydrin spray and ultraviolet light (crime scenes aren't "dusted" any more), had located a latent partial from a right hand index finger on the ash tray cover in the passenger side door panel. The print had been photographed, scanned into the computer, and transmitted to the State Police Automatic Fingerprint Identification System for a match. The system had responded with a possible identification: Daryl Gustafson, with a residential address in Mission Hill and a record of several youthful arrests for burglaries and fencing of stolen goods. The Boston detective assigned to the case went to Mission Hill to investigate, but was told by neighbors that Gustafson had moved. Nobody knew where he went. He was not listed in any telephone directory in eastern Massachusetts; there were two entries for D. Gustafson but neither turned out to be Daryl. The trail ends at this point. Apparently the Boston detective put the file in his stack of unsolved cases and went on to other, more pressing matters. Brisbane understands. To begin with, the identification was far from conclusive. It was a six point match, enough to justify further investigation but not enough to pass muster in court. More importantly, from the perspective of the Boston Police, the car had been successfully recovered and released to a body shop where Mr. Yuyali's insurance would underwrite the repairs, and thus the victim would soon be whole again. There was simply little urgency to justify spending time on this case at the expense of work on other cases that demanded resolution with a higher priority.

Reflecting on it now, the accident strikes Brisbane as peculiar. What are the chances, he wonders, that a car would be stolen in Boston one night and crash into his murder suspect the next? Logically, he knows that if the accident were truly random, then the chance that it happened to Ralph must be identical to the chance of it happening to anybody else. But in the Boston area there are four million anybody elses. That makes the chance of a random occurrence about as small as the probability that O.J. Simpson was innocent. More than that, this thing simply doesn't smell random. It doesn't even smell like an accident. The driver of the stolen car pulled out suddenly into a continuous line of traffic, an extraordinarily heedless maneuver. Yet wouldn't the driver of a stolen car be extra careful to avoid attracting the attention of law enforcement? And if not that, careful to avoid reducing the resale value of his stolen property? And besides, what the hell was the car doing in Framingham anyway? Why wasn't it handed off to a fence or a chop shop right there in Boston earlier that day?

As the questions pile up, the juices of Brisbane's investigative instincts begin to flow. Let's look at this, he thinks, from another angle. OK. Ralph didn't materialize on that street from out of nowhere. He was driving home from work along his customary route at his customary time. It would have been easy for anybody to tail him for a few days and pin down his commuting habits. So what if this accident was not random? What if Ralph was a target? OK, that's possible. But a target of what? Revenge? Maybe. On the other hand, maybe not. Maybe not because the whole thing cost Ralph a $500 deductible and a little bit of hassle. That's a very small payoff in revenge for the substantial effort involved in stealing a car in Boston, tailing Ralph's movements, and staging a crash. The payoff relative to the effort expended doesn't add up. So if it's not revenge, what else? Brisbane's mind is cooking now. A warning? OK, a warning about what? The gambling debts, maybe? A warning from that bookie of his, the skinny guy in Chelsea? From a loan shark? A warning with a message: "You are not safe, Ralph. We can find you anywhere, Ralph. Any time. When you least expect it. You are going to pay up, Ralph." Something like that, perhaps?

It would help, Brisbane concludes, if we could find the guy who was driving the stolen car. As a first step, Brisbane calls Mr. Yuyali at his office. Yuyali answers and Brisbane identifies himself.

"How can I help you?" Yuyali offers.

"We believe your car may have been stolen in connection with another crime. You are not implicated, but you may be able to help us with some evidence. I just have two questions. First, was there anything in the car when you got it back that wasn't there when you parked it on Stuart St.?"

"Holy Moly. You mean something left there by the thief?"

"Yes."

"Holy Moly. No, I didn't see anything."

"OK. Then the other question: Do you by any chance know how many miles the car was driven between the time you parked it and the time you got it back?"

"As a matter of fact I do."

"You do?"

"Yes. It's nothing strange. I keep a mileage log so that I can get reimbursed when I use my car for business travel, which I do often. Which, in fact, I was doing that night. That's what caused me to notice. The car was only driven about a dozen miles. I don't understand. Why would they steal it for just a dozen miles?'

"We think it wasn't a joyride. We think they had a specific purpose in mind."

"Holy Moly. What was it?"

"We'd rather not say right now. If you have that log, I'd like to send a trooper over to pick it up. The original, that is."

"Sure. Not a problem."

"Thank you. You've been most kind."

Next is a call to the Boston Police Department, Back Bay district.

The phone is picked up. "Lieutenant Dunhill."

"Bloody hell," says Brisbane, "I was looking for a real cop."

After half a second, Dunhill recognizes the voice. "Wizbang! Two calls in two months. That's unprecedented. You must be getting lonely in your declining years."

"What can I say? I miss the warmth of your smile. The sunshine of your personality. The lilt of your voice. Tell me again how you *pahked* the *cah*."

"Wizbang, you're lucky I don't *pahk* my *cah* up your rear end, seeing that I have an SUV. OK, I can tell this isn't a social call. You're too old to get by on your charm. You're after something. What's up, Wizbang?"

"You got me, I'm busted. Super sleuth hits the nail on the head. I do need your help. I'm looking for somebody, and I think he's one of your Boston scumbags."

"Take your pick. We've got'em by the trainload."

"This one's named Daryl Gustafson. There's a wrinkle in the Newton murder. I think Gustafson may be involved."

"Trigger man?"

"Probably not. But I think I can use him for leverage against some of the more central characters in the plot. He's not at any of his known addresses, so I need your help with your snitches to track him down. His priors have him in Mission Hill and Dorchester. I doubt I'll find him hanging out in Weston or Wellesley. Do you think you can get a line on him?"

"I can try. I'll talk to some people. I'll call in some markers. What's the name again?"

"Gustafson. Daryl Gustafson. Thanks. You're a good friend. I'll pay you back somehow. OK, Dunghill, send my love to your wife. Tell her if she ever gets tired of you, I'll divorce Barb and marry her in a minute."

"Dream on, Wizbang. Yesterday she made me Chinese spareribs for dinner. Is that true love or what?"

"Dream on, yourself. I'll bet you they were takeout she brought home from Chopsticks 'R' Us. Take care, Dunghill."

"Take care, Wizbang. Regards to Barb."

And so it is that a week later Brisbane finds himself sitting alone at a table in a bar on Huntington Avenue in Mission Hill. He is nursing a beer—officially he's off duty—and watching the door, hoping that Daryl Gustafson will make an appearance. Dunhill wasn't able to find out where he lives, but according to the CI's, his confidential informants, this is where the man hangs out.

It takes three nights and six beers. Brisbane is not impatient. The bar stocks Shipyard lager, and the people watching makes good entertainment. Observing twenty-somethings trying to hook up is a hoot. It doesn't make him wish he were young again. To the contrary, it makes him glad that—idle fantasies about Anita Banks notwithstanding—his life is settled and comfortable with Barb, and that he has much to be thankful for in his "declining years," all things considered.

Finally, on night three, Gustafson comes through the door. He takes a stool at the bar between two other guys, just ordinary guys. Brisbane recognizes his face immediately from the mug shot, but his overall appearance is not at all what the detective expected. Far from looking like a petty street hoodlum, Gustafson turns out to be a dark skinned black man with a lithe body and attractive features, trim and handsome in the manner of the young Sidney Poitier in "Guess Who's Coming For Dinner." He is dressed in neatly pressed khaki slacks and a light blue button down dress shirt. He could waltz into your office posing as an IBM computer salesman and you wouldn't bat an eye.

Leaving his beer on the table, Brisbane walks over to the guy on the stool to the left of Gustafson. Putting his hand on the man's shoulder, Brisbane says, "How about moving to another stool? I have matters to discuss with Gus here."

The guy on the bar stool makes an attempt to stand up for himself. "Screw you. I was here first. Go and talk somewhere else."

Brisbane assumes a tone of exaggerated reasonableness. "I don't think you quite understand. This gentleman here—his name is Gus, by the way—this gentleman here is a repeat felon. In fact, his file in the computer is so big that the system crashes every time you call it up. Just printing it consumes so much paper it denudes a forest. Now, you two sittin' here cozy like, who knows what kind of criminal enterprises you both might be cookin' up?"

"Criminal enterprises? You're crazy! He just walked in. We never said a word to each other."

This dimwit, Brisbane thinks, is a few noodles short of a casserole. "Maybe the meeting was prearranged. The point is, if you piss me off you'll regret it." Brisbane squares his shoulders and stands as tall as he can. He grabs the front of the guy's shirt in each of his hands. "GET THE FUCK OUT OF HERE!"

That works. The guy slinks to the other end of the bar. Gus looks up and meets Brisbane's gaze. "Yes, sir! I'm impressed as hell. You're one tough dude. So, waddaya want from me?"

"You messed up big time."

Gus doesn't react. This is a cool customer, Brisbane thinks. It's Brisbane who's impressed. He continues but takes a calmer, more conciliatory tack: "Seriously. You're in trouble. Your print was found in the car you stole back in early January. The Infinity you boosted on Stuart St."

"I didn't boost anything."

"Your print was in the car."

"This is bullshit. I repeat: I didn't boost anything. Even if I *was* in this car you're talking about, it doesn't prove I stole it. All it proves is sometime later, I was in it."

Were in the car, Brisbane thinks. Not *was*. Even if I *were* in the car. Sloppy use of language is one of his pet peeves. It drives him nuts. He sees it as a sign of sloppy thinking. It is part of society's losing battle against entropy—the tendency of all systems to degenerate into chaos. But Gus is correct about one thing. His print in the car doesn't prove he stole it. A partial print, at that. And it was on the passenger side. Brisbane presses on anyway. "There's something you don't know. The car you were *in* is connected to a murder. The fingerprint connects *you* to a murder. I'm a Statie. Homicide."

For the first time, Gus' eye's betray some anxiety. His earlier show of bravado was little more than a front, and the façade is fragile. "Waddaya want," he says again, but this time his tone is less cocksure.

"Somebody hired you to steal that car. We want to know who."

"I didn't steal it."

"Then you know who did."

"Look. Suppose I did know something. I'm not saying I do, just suppose, then I couldn't say anything anyway."

"Dead man walking?"

"You got that right."

Brisbane thinks it over for a while. "You could be dead anyway if we let it out on the street that we're talking to you."

"You wouldn't do that."

"Sure I would. This is a murder. I want to solve it. You're in a position to help me. Why wouldn't I? I could start by arresting your ass right now."

"You can't arrest me from just that fingerprint."

"I can hold you on suspicion for two days. Forty eight hours. I have forty eight hours before I have to press charges or let you go. By that time a lot of people will know where you are and who you've been talking to."

"All right, all right. Waddaya want?"

"I want to know who ordered the car stolen, who received it after you stole it, and where you dropped off the merchandise."

"If I knew all that, I say *if*, what good would it do me?"

"I'd forget I ever found you, and you'd have time to get the hell out of town before one of your buddies comes looking to clean out your bowels with a Roto Rooter. Look, pal, I know leaving town is a bit of an inconvenience, no doubt about it, but the fact is, you had the rotten luck to get caught up in something that's bigger than you are, and your options are severely limited."

"I don't have any money. I can't afford to leave town."

"Seems to me you can't afford not to."

Gus is beginning to form a realistic view of the situation. "Shit, piss and corruption," he murmurs.

Brisbane lets Gus stew for a little bit, then stands up and says, "Let's go to my table." He catches the eye of the bartender and signals for another round.

Back at the table, the fresh beers drained half way down in their glasses, he senses it is time to push. "So?"

Gus is still conflicted. "How do I know if I can trust you?"

"I'll give you the names of three references you can call. Would that be satisfactory?"

Gus appreciates the sarcasm and smiles in spite of himself. Then the smile fades, his shoulders slump, and defeat is acknowledged. "Ah, what the fuck," he says. "I'm screwed no matter what, aren't I?"

Brisbane knows that his quest has made it over the hump and allows himself to relax a little. "I'm afraid so, Gus. You seem like a swell guy and I'm enjoying your company. But this isn't a social occasion. I'm here on business."

"All right, Detective … what's your name, anyway?"

Brisbane takes his ID from his jacket pocket and holds it up.

"Brisbane. All right, Detective Brisbane. First of all, I don't know shit about any murder."

Brisbane's tone is reassuring. "I understand that."

"All right, the heist wasn't my gig. I just went along for the ride."

"Went along with who?"

"A friend of mine."

"You're ratting on a friend?"

"Shit, piss and corruption, Brisbane! You're the one that told me I have no choice!"

"OK, Gus. Calm down. I shouldn't have said that. I wasn't trying to insult you. I was just meditating on the fact that crime doesn't pay and the Lord works in mysterious ways to punish the wicked."

"There you go again!" Gus' umbrage is quite genuine. Brisbane is mystified and his expression shows it, so Gus keeps going. "*I am not wicked!* I may be impulsive. My parole officer told me once I have trouble with delayed gratification, whatever the hell that means. But I am not wicked."

This time it is Brisbane's turn to smile. "Officer Krupke."

"Who's that?" says Gus.

Brisbane has to explain. "It's not a who. It's song. A song in a show. *West Side Story*. The song is about some juvenile delinquents who insist they aren't bad, just misunderstood."

"Yeah, that's me. I'm misunderstood."

"Who's your friend?"

Gus hesitates. "... What you said? About ratting on a friend? How about if I tell you what my friend said, without telling you who he is?"

"Tell me what he said and I'll see."

"He said he had a commission—that's the word he used, commission—to steal a car. He was hired by somebody named Cap. Cap must be a nickname but he never told me a real name. He did say that Cap is a loan shark. He said the fee was two grand."

"How did he collect?"

"We took the car to my friend's house and hid it in the back. The next day, around lunch time, we took the car to Brighton. We went to a bar on Washington St. I forget the name of the bar but I remember where it is. There's a hospital right near there so we parked the car in the hospital garage. Then we walked to the bar and met Cap and there was this other guy, I don't know his name either, but he was big with muscles like a wrestler or a bouncer. Cap and my friend went into the john. My friend handed over the keys and the parking garage ticket, Cap gave him the money, and that was it, we left. We hadda hike three quarters of a mile over to Commonwealth to pick up the 'T' there. Froze our asses off."

Brisbane mulls this over. Then he says, "Here's the deal. If it works, you won't have to rat on your friend. We're going to try to track down this Cap through that bar."

At this, Gus' eyes shoot wide open. "Whaddya mean, '*we*?'"

"You're the only one that can smoke him out. You're going to go in the bar and ask for him. You're going to pretend you need a loan. You're asking for him because you want to do business. You're looking for him *there* because there is where you met him before. And your friend can vouch for you. He doesn't have to know what's really going on."

Gus' stomach is churning. "I don't know about that. I don't think I can do it. This plan sounds like it should come with a warning from the Surgeon General. It may be extremely hazardous to my health. Anyway, how do you know that somebody in the bar can hook me up with Cap?"

"I don't *know.* But people are creatures of habit. If he met with your friend in that bar, it's probably because he is comfortable there. And that would mean he feels safe there among people he knows. It's just a guess, but an educated one."

"Some plan. I lure a murderous gangster with a bodyguard the size of Attila the Hun into a trap, and when the trap is sprung the muscle-bound mangler hunts me down and gets even. Dandy for you, but from my perspective the plan is seriously flawed."

Brisbane is tickled. He likes Gus. "Nothing like that is going to happen. Now, you make inquiries at the bar and leave your cell number ... you have a cell phone?"

Gus gives Brisbane a *what planet have you been living on* look.

"Sorry," Brisbane concedes. "All right, so when he makes contact, you make an appointment to meet. When you go to the appointment, I'll be there with backup and we'll nab him. Then you're going to hightail it out of town right then and there. Immediately."

Gus' face lights up. "Can I keep the money?"

Brisbane's expression is blank. Gus presses: "The money I'm supposed to be borrowing. If I'm going into hiding out of town anyway, why don't you let him give me the money before you arrest him? That way I'll have some money to buy a new identity and start a new life."

Brisbane gets it now, of course. What he is hearing pleases him even though he recognizes that it is unlikely to happen. Cap will have to be arrested as soon as possible so as not to risk his escaping. If they let Gus abscond with the money in the process, that will make them all look bad and will muddy the eventual prosecution of the case in court. But Brisbane doesn't reveal what he's thinking. It is better if Gus believes he's going to get some money; it will make him more likely to cooperate in the plan and show up when it's time to meet Cap.

But the plan, as Gus would say, is flawed.

The preliminaries, nevertheless, go well enough. Gus visits the bar and asks for Cap. He has a cock and bull story ready about needing $10,000 to buy a stock on an insider tip from his brother in law. He's going to score big with it, can't miss. The bartender takes it all in without expression and tells Gus to leave his number and Cap will get in touch with him.

Cap does call the following morning and they set up a meeting at the bar for 7:30 that evening. Then Gus pages Brisbane, who tells him to come in to head-quarters at three in the afternoon. They'll review the plan, go out to dinner, and then go to meet Cap.

Brisbane has a surprise in store when Gus arrives at Thorndike Street. "You," he says, "are going to wear a wire."

"No!" says Gus. "No, no, no, no, no! Never. I can't do that. You never told me this was going to be a Kamikaze mission. It's not fair."

"Maybe not," admits Brisbane. "But I've got a murder victim on my hands. A twenty eight year old girl. Three months pregnant. A family grieving and angry. You're the only link I have to the people responsible for it all. What is fair for the victims?"

"I don't care about no victims! Shit, piss and corruption, Brisbane! My skin only works properly when it's attached to the rest of my body. That's all I care about."

Brisbane assumes a placating tone. "Gus, look. You don't have to worry. I'll be in the bar and I'll have backup out on the street. You'll be safe. And don't forget, it's the difference between facing a car theft beef on one hand and running away with Cap's money on the other. Think of it as an experience, a thrill. A great story to tell your friends, your girlfriends especially, your kids eventually. Here's the wire. It's just this little gizmo, no big deal. We're going to try it on and test it out."

As they work with the equipment, which is a miniaturized microphone and transmitter that straps around Gus' midsection, Brisbane is at pains to coach him in the art of not arousing suspicion. Don't talk too much. Answer questions but don't offer more information than is necessary. Don't talk too little. Don't make up stuff. Whenever possible tell the truth. Make eye contact but don't stare anyone down. Don't ask any questions that are not relevant to the transaction at hand. Not much different, Brisbane thinks, from the instructions one would give a witness before testifying at a trial. Also, he tells Gus, talk in a natural tone of voice, not slowly or with emphasis. The mike is plenty sensitive to pick up normal conversation. And Cap's ears will be plenty sensitive to pick up unnatural speech patterns.

Later, Brisbane treats Gus to dinner at the Stockyard, a popular middle market steak house in Brighton about a mile from the bar. There is a slight risk in this. It is conceivable that Cap could be eating there that night as well, then recognize them afterwards in the bar and get curious. But Brisbane assesses the possibility as remote, and decides not to worry about it.

Brisbane uses some of the time at dinner to forge male bonds with Gus, and the rest of mealtime to pump up his confidence. His approach is mostly flattery, a play on Gus' vanity. Brisbane tells Gus how lucky he, Brisbane, is to have found in Gus someone who has the ability to pull off a stunt like this. Ninety nine percent of the people he encounters on the street, Brisbane tells him, are riff raff, losers, low lifes who would never have the brains to handle such a delicate task. "Gus," he says, "you're in the top one percent, the elite ninety ninth percentile. Otherwise, I wouldn't trust you with the job. Gus," he says, "listen: if I'm wrong about you, tell me now. If I'm reading you wrong, if you're not head and shoulders above ninety nine percent of the blokes whose fingerprints are found a stolen car, now is the time to let me know, 'cause if I'm wrong about you, if you're not as smart and as smooth as I think you are, then I don't want to go through with it either. The last thing I need is a bumbler who's going to screw it up. So listen, here's the deal: tell me you're not the man I think you are, tell me you're as much of a screw up as everyone else, and we'll walk out of this place in opposite directions. No Cap, no car theft, no charges, no wire, no money, no nothing except me wondering what the hell ever happened to my ability to size people up. How 'bout it?"

Dessert is on the table by this time. Both work on their strawberry shortcakes as Brisbane allows time for Gus' competing emotions to battle it out. The fear factor is a powerful deterrent; Gus is not physically brave. At the same time, he likes Brisbane quite a bit and is loath to disappoint him. Gus is surprised to realize how much he craves the admiration and respect of this crazy cop. In the end, the balance is tipped by something Brisbane had said almost in passing. "Gus," he had said, "it boils down to how you're going to feel about yourself afterwards. You're going to have to look back on how you were faced with a challenge and you slunk away with your tail between your legs. If you back out now, how are you going to feel about yourself later? What is going to happen to your pride? What's the damage to your self respect and how much damage can it absorb? Answer these questions honestly and you'll know what to do."

This is a novel approach for Gus, and when he thinks about it in that manner it does give him the answer. "We're a go," he tells Brisbane. "Final answer."

They arrive for the appointment precisely on time. They enter separately and find stools at opposite ends of the bar, Gus near the back and Brisbane near the door as prearranged. And that's the moment when the plan begins to go awry. No sooner have they ordered their beers than two men come through the door. Neither, however, is Cap. Instead, they are Cap's goon number one from the Sheraton and the ramming, and Mort, the goon in training, also from the ramming. Gus recognizes goon one as the beefy hulk who was with Cap on the day he came out here with his friend to deliver the car. Mort, however, he's never seen.

Goon one casts a glance at the bartender, who flicks his head toward Gus. The two goons approach Gus and, one on each side, escort him into the bathroom. Mort slides the trash can in front of the door to barricade against other customers coming in. Goon one demands to see Gus' driver's license. He compares the address, age and social security number against the information on Daryl Gustafson he has obtained from an internet background check. Gus, meanwhile, is shitting bricks. He realizes that Brisbane has never seen Cap. He is confident that Brisbane will understand that the beefy hulk is the guy with muscles whom he described as Cap's bodyguard. What worries Gus is that Brisbane has no way of knowing that the other guy, the young bozo with the garbage can, is *not* Cap. For sure, Brisbane will assume that it *is* Cap. What else could he assume? How does that change things? How does that affect the plan? Gus doesn't know. It's too complicated to figure out. But it's unexpected, and unexpected cannot equal good.

Goon number one starts the grilling. The questioning begins as standard operating procedure, just a normal screening process they always do to get a reading on anybody they haven't previously lent money to. Due diligence, Cap calls it. Cap's a straight up guy, goon one thinks, but sometimes he uses words that nobody knows what the hell he means. He does notice that Gus seems nervous, but that's not unusual in situations like this; making people nervous is part a of goon's job description.

"Why ten grand?" goon one wants to know.

"I told Cap on the phone," Gus says. "I have a stock tip from my brother in law. Inside information."

"Sure thing?"

"Absolutely. A dead lock."

"Then why," asks goon one, "only ten grand. Why not twenty grand? Why not a hundred?"

Gus remembers Brisbane's advice about telling the truth. "I didn't think of it. Ten thousand dollars seemed like a big number to me. I'm not in high finance like you. If you want to give me a hundred, I'll take it."

Goon one is unimpressed. He keeps prodding. "Why come to us? Ten grand isn't much. Why not take out a loan from a consumer finance company at a hell of a lot lower interest rate?"

This question brings Gus up short. It's something else he didn't think of. Brisbane never brought it up; apparently he hadn't thought of it either. Gus scrambles for an answer. He could mention that his credit sucks, but that doesn't seem like the right topic to bring up just now. He racks his brain for something else.

The only reason can he dredge up from his increasingly panicky brain is not very good: "It takes too long. The news on this company could break any day. Any hour. I couldn't afford to wait for all the paperwork to process."

For goon one, Gus' answer fails to pass the smell test. Nowadays, banks and loan companies take applications for personal loans over the internet and offer approvals within 24 hours. This joker here took more time than that merely to track Cap down and arrange for the meet that's going on now. Naw, something doesn't smell right about this.

A turning point has come and gone. Gus is in trouble.

"What is the name of the company?" goon one wants to know.

Gus can't remember! Of course, there really is no company. But Brisbane had spent hours doing research on line to identify a suitable answer to this question. He needed a company that is small but publicly traded, where it is plausible that an announcement of a new product or government approval would vault the stock price skyward. He had found such a company and described it to Gus that afternoon. In his agitation, Gus has forgotten the name of this company.

Gus says, "I was sworn to secrecy."

"Who's more dangerous, me or your brother in law?"

"No, really," Gus insists, "my brother in law told me it has to do with the government. They watch for stuff like this and pounce when they detect anything out of the ordinary. That's how Martha Stewart got in trouble, he told me."

Goon one waves this away. "I'll take my chances."

"No, he meant that *he* might get into trouble himself."

"I'll take *his* chances."

Cornered, Gus tries a Hail Mary desperation pass. Remembering the wire and knowing the cops are listening somewhere, he is hoping, by simultaneously alerting them to the absence of Cap and signaling the mounting peril of his predicament, to trigger a rescue. So he says, "It could put Cap at risk. Speaking of which, where is Cap, anyway? I thought he'd be here."

With that, Gus has blown his last chance to recover his footing. There is one thing he could have said that might have made sense to goon one. He could have said that he was keeping the company secret for his own protection. He didn't want to give Cap so much leverage over him. Insider trading is illegal and if Cap knew enough about it he could blackmail him, Gus, with that information. He would be beholden to Cap for the rest of his life.

That is a story goon one would have understood. As it is, however, goon one can only recoil in amazement at the stupidity of what Gus actually said. *Worried about getting Cap in trouble?* What is that all about? It's ridiculous. Cap is a career criminal. Cap makes his *living* breaking the law. And this twerp is concerned about putting Cap at risk over a stock transaction? Who is this idiot?

The pivotal question comes now to goon one, unbidden, as a mere catch-phrase, as a meaningless expression, as a banal cliché: *is this guy for real?* But the answer to that question occurs to the goon in a jolt, as a clarifying shock: *maybe not. Not* would explain a great deal, goon one realizes. So now the vague disquietude that has been nagging at goon one can no longer be ignored. What had earlier presented itself as a formless mist of uneasy suspicion instantly precipitates into a deluge of bedevilment, a soaking downpour of doubt that extinguishes any and all possibility of a deal.

He turns his head to look at Mort and says, "Frisk him."

Gus is quaking. He desperately wants to run but the trashcan is preventing his rapid escape. He can only think to shout, "Wait a minute! Wait a minute!"

Goon one and Mort freeze as if in suspended animation.

Gus didn't know what he was going to say after "wait a minute" but thankfully something comes out of his mouth that seems OK. He says, "Look. I came here to do business. That's all. Business. As a customer. Nothing else. But you guys seem to think I'm up to no good. OK. You don't have to take me on as a customer if you don't trust me. I can go to the bank like you said. So let's just shake hands and walk out of here and go our separate ways. Waddaya say?"

Mort and the goon look at one another. Each knows what the other is thinking. In less than a split second, goon one is barking, "Frisk'm!," while Mort is simultaneously lunging at Gus.

Mort is lightning quick and, to Gus, unexpectedly muscular. In no time Mort has Gus' left arm twisted behind his back in a painful hammerlock and his body turned around so his chest and face are pinned against the rest room wall. The hurt Gus experiences is significant but is greatly intensified by his mortal trepidation. In truth, the level of pain inflicted on Gus by Mort is deliberately measured, sufficient to ensure that Gus is kept under control but not egregiously excessive. Compassion this is not. Rather, goon one and Mort both instinctively grasp that it would not be beneficial to attract the attention of other customers in the bar.

Goon one strolls over and starts patting Gus down. Half way through he feels something under Gus' shirt. He yanks the shirt up and exposes the transmitter attached to the strap. Reflexively Mort bends Gus' arm further up. "OW!" Gus yelps.

"Shut up," growls Mort.

Please God. Please God. Please God. Pleeeeeeease, God, Gus is praying, *send in Brisbane now!* Unfortunately for Gus, that is not to be. But Mort and the goon are in a predicament too, albeit one less severe than Gus'. They know that Cap will want to interrogate Gus to uncover the story behind the wire. That means they have to get him out of the bar alive and drive him to Cap's house in Brookline. The problem is that with Gus wearing a wire it is likely that the cops are listening nearby and keeping the bar under surveillance. That narrows their options. Goon one lifts up his pant leg and removes a pistol from a shin strap holster. His goal for the time being is modest. He simply wants to stabilize the situation until he can figure out what to do. He moves near the wall where Gus can see him. "Don't move, he says.

Don't move? thinks Gus. He can barely manage to keep himself upright. His legs are quivering uncontrollably from terror. Any second now he's going to collapse like a marionette whose strings have been severed. His eyelids are helplessly trapped in a spastic nonstop flutter. The second he stops concentrating, he'll pee in his pants. *Don't move? What a joke! Brisbane,* Gus pleads in anguished silence, *where the hell are you?*

Meanwhile, goon one is formulating a plan. It's not a great plan but it's the best he can do on short notice. There is an alley behind the bar, for deliveries to all of the businesses on the block. Using hand gestures so as not to reveal the plan over Gus' wire, he communicates to Mort: leave the back way through the kitchen, get the car, and pick them up in the alley at the kitchen door. The concept is that if the cops are out front, maybe they can slip away unnoticed from the rear. No, it's not a great plan but he can't think of anything better. It's better than no plan.

Goon one replaces the trash can after Mort leaves. The car is parked not far away, and goon one estimates that it will take about four minutes for Mort to retrieve it and pull up to the kitchen door. As the wait begins, the goon is nearly as tense as Gus. This is because he can't figure out what is going on. If the police are listening in through the wire on Gus, they know the device has been discovered and that their operation—whatever it is—has imploded. Why, then, haven't they barged in and rescued their man? And what were they after in the first place? And what is it that they're still waiting to hear before they launch the rescue? And what can he possibly say to keep them listening for four more minutes while disguising the fact that Mort is absent?

At first, he contemplates destroying the wire. He is afraid, though, that this would bring in the cops immediately, having removed any incentive for them to hold off. Then he has a better idea. Here's what he does: He jabs the hand holding the pistol forward to get Gus' attention. He says, "No moving. No talking." He steps back to put some distance between the two of them. With his left hand, he reaches into his pants pocket and pulls out his cell phone. Holding it in his left hand, he uses the middle finger of his right hand, which is still holding the gun, to dial a number in the 617 area code. He doesn't care whose number it is. He doesn't care if it is traced eventually. He is making the number up at random. It rings, a woman picks up the receiver, says, "Hello?" Goon one says, "Cap. It's me. Yeah." The woman says, "You have the wrong number," and hangs up. Goon one says into the dead phone, "Yeah, we're at the bar. We have a problem. You have to come here … I wouldn't call you if it wasn't necessary … Ten minutes? Good. We'll be waiting in the john." He hopes the microphone on Gus' belly is still working. He puts the phone back in his pocket.

Now comes the tricky part. The hallway between the bathroom and the kitchen is short, but it has an opening to the main bar area. Goon one has two worries: (A) Gus could bolt through the opening into the bar, and (B) cops could be watching the opening and waiting for them to appear. He wishes he had told Mort to come back inside after bringing the car around. He monitors his watch for four minutes and is about to start moving out with Gus when the trash can screeches along the floor and the bathroom door opens a few inches. He braces for trouble but instead Mort's head appears through the crack. When Gus and the goon failed to meet him out back as he drove up with the car, he thought there might be trouble. Still, Mort isn't sure whether he's done the right thing by leaving the car and coming back in. Hesitantly, he opens his mouth to ask but goon one shuts him down by signaling quiet with a finger against his lips.

Goon one leads Mort into the hallway, where they can whisper out of range of the wire. This leaves Gus by himself in the john momentarily, but it doesn't matter. There is nothing he can say into the wire that the cops don't already know. He uses the opportunity to plead in an urgent stage whisper: "Brisbane. Where the hell are you? Get in here now!" Gus frets that the goons will overhear him, but he's desperate.

In the hallway, goon one takes care to put Mort at ease: "You done good," he says. He instructs Mort to block the opening to the barroom until he and Gus pass by, then follow them through the kitchen out to the car. Then he thinks to ask, "Are there cops out back?" Mort swivels his head in the negative. The goon is puzzled. He can't understand why the alley isn't swarming with them.

Gus has the same expectation. He, too, thinks that the police should have the place surrounded by now. And, of course, he is not privy to the status update from Mort. So when goon one comes back in and motions for him to go out in the hallway, Gus is relieved. Although it bothers him that he can't figure out what the goon thinks is going to happen, the reassuring scene that he imagines is about to unfold comes straight out of *"Dog Day Afternoon"* and a hundred other movies: A battalion of tactical forces is arrayed in all the upstairs windows, rifles cocked. Sharpshooters line the rooftops, crosshairs fixed on the kitchen door. Uniformed officers are crouching behind their squad cars, pistols gripped in both hands. A middle aged captain in suit and tie, hair crew cut and firm jaw jutting, stands poised to negotiate with his amplified bullhorn. The kitchen door swings open and the showdown begins. Hostage negotiations ensue, as the air crackles with tense demands from goon one while the crew cut captain parries with supple cajoleries. The goon brandishes the gun at Gus' head. Some stupid cop gets jumpy and fires his weapon; he is reprimanded harshly and sent back to the precinct. Finally, somebody smart, who no one would pay attention to at first, figures it out and a deal is struck. Things end well, in the movies.

In real life, goon one, Gus and Mort emerge from the kitchen door, and the alley, aside from Mort's car, is completely empty.

Gus is in shock. He is stunned. *How can this be? I've been set up! Brisbane! I'll be there with backup,' you said. 'We'll nab him,' you said. 'Don't worry,' you said. 'You'll be safe', you said. Brisbane, how could you do this to me? WHY did you do this to me? I was straight with you 100%. I trusted you! And now I'm going to fucking die. WHY?*

Oh God, I don't deserve to die. I DON'T DESERVE IT! I didn't kill anybody. I didn't even know that pregnant broad. No, I'm not perfect, I know that. But God, I never killed anybody. I don't even have a gun. I never pushed drugs. I never hit my girlfriends. I never threatened anybody. I didn't ever, ever do anything to deserve this. And now, thanks to you, Brisbane, I'm going to fucking DIE. Today!

Oh my God, he's corrupt! That has to be it, he's corrupt. What else could it be? He's dishonest, that's already been proven. Somebody must be paying him off to have me killed. But who? But why? Cap! Cap must be paying him off. Brisbane, I trusted you!

Oh, God, what are they gonna do to me? Please just shoot me. I'll tell you everything you want to know if you just have mercy and shoot me quick. Shoot me clean and surgical, that's all I ask. Please God, don't torture me. Don't make me suffer, please. Oh God, don't pull out my fingernails. Oohhhhhh! My bones. They could break my bones. Burn me with cigarettes. Oooohhhhhhhh!! Oh my God, a root canal without Novocain. Oh God, Brisbane, why? ...

By the time Gus pops out of his panicky reverie and takes notice, they are on the Turnpike Extension heading outbound toward Route 128. The direct drive on city streets from Brighton to Brookline takes less than fifteen minutes at this time of night, but Mort is driving a circuitous route that will take much longer.

He needs to make sure that they aren't being followed. By taking the Pike out to 128, heading south, and doubling back to Brookline on Route 9, Mort hopes to discern whether they are being tailed. To this end, he checks the mirror constantly.

By the time they are heading back east through Newton on Rt. 9, Mort feels confident enough to report that he believes there is no tail. Goon one, sitting in back with Gus, still can't understand it. "You sure?" he asks. "I'm almost positive," Mort responds, "I'm doing the best I can." Goon one is still dubious, but also willing to cut Mort some slack. He is cognizant of the difficulties in doing this kind of thing at night. All Mort can actually see in the mirror are headlights. He is working the mirror as hard as he can, and at the same time, he is making abrupt lane changes and similar evasive maneuvers to try to induce a tail, if there is one, to become more conspicuous. But none of this changes the fact that the mirror is filled with nothing but headlights. Goon one, for his part, takes comfort in the thought that if they are being followed, it is no less dark outside for the cops; all they have to go by are taillights.

Mort is right. Nobody is tracking their taillights. Gus, listening to the dialog between Mort and goon one, has given up. There are no cops. There is no rescue. There is no hope. There is no God. He is going to die. Tonight. Shit, piss and corruption.

Not too much later, they pull into the driveway of a tidy Tudor style home on Blake Road. It's before nine o'clock; the lights are on inside. Mort rings the doorbell as goon one waits in the car keeping guard on Gus. A teenage boy answers, listens, disappears inside, and presently Cap is standing in the doorway. He hears what Mort has to say and motions goon one to come inside. In single file they troop through the foyer and down the stairs to the basement: first Mort, then Gus, then goon one, and finally Cap. As the pass by the living room, Gus can't help noticing a very attractive blond on the couch watching TV. That's gotta be his wife, Gus figures. *Look at this house!* he is thinking. *Look at that wife.* Who says crime doesn't pay. And all I get is prematurely dead.

Cap has an office in the basement. The walls are paneled with real oak. The floor is plush carpeted. There is a sleek desk with a modern computer and a flat liquid plasma monitor. There is a printer/fax/copier combo, a multiline phone, a shredder, the works. Gus feels like he's gotten a reprieve, although he knows it's temporary. He doesn't think they'll torture or kill him here, not with all this expensive stuff in the room, not with his wife and kid a few feet above them.

Cap says, "I've seen you before. Where have I seen you before?"

Gus reasons that there is no benefit in being evasive or cute. "At the bar when my friend Arnie delivered the Infinity back in January." He believes his best shot is to be cooperative and communicative so as not to provoke Cap's anger.

Cap turns to goon one and says, "I get it now. This has to do with the Collins job." As soon as it comes out of his mouth, he realizes he's made a mistake and it is too late to fix it. In the tumult occasioned by the goons' unexpected arrival, he has neglected to ask whether the wire has been disabled and if it hasn't, to disable it himself. He looks at his goons and asks belatedly: "Did you silence the wire?" Goon one's face flushes red; he should have done that while still in the car. He shakes his head 'no.'

Cap is less angry than he would like to be, acknowledging to himself that he was guilty of the same offense. Goon one now unstraps the wire, then exits through a door on the other side of the office. In short order, the sound of hammering and splintering plastic fills the space. For Gus, this is a reminder of the jeopardy he finds himself in. His legs start quivering again. His pulse starts racing. *I'm gonna die. There's no way I can survive this: I know where he lives. Please God, let it be quick ...*

BANG. BANG. BANG!

A *pounding.* Everybody's head snaps to attention. This is not goon one with his hammer. *What the hell?*

Cap knows. It's the sound of pounding on his front door. Cap *knows.* It's over. Damn it to hell.

"IT'S THE POLICE! THE HOUSE IS SURROUNDED! OPEN THE DOOR!"

On the word "police," Cap's wife is leaping off the couch and racing toward the entry. No way is she about to let the cops destroy her beloved house by bashing the door in. She swings the door open and Brisbane plus six men from the Special Tactics and Operations unit swoop in past her. Only once they're all inside do they stop short, bunch up together, turn around, and look back at her. It would be comical, Keystone Kops style, if it weren't so fraught with consequences. Cap's wife points toward the basement stairs.

Gus is ecstatic. His heart is pumping wildly with relief. As the troops hurtle down the stairs, he is laughing uncontrollably in excitement and exultation.

Cap and the goons offer no resistance. They know it's futile. They are put under arrest for assault and kidnapping against Gus, and conspiracy in the murder of Bonnie Collins. They are cuffed and their rights are read.

When all of that is finished, Gus pulls Brisbane aside. "Where the hell were you? You said you would nab him. You said I wouldn't be in danger. No danger?

I could'a died from heart failure. They could'a built a whole city with the bricks I was shitting. I thought I was history for sure. Why did you make me go through all this?"

"Yeah," Brisbane says, "sorry about that. But we got your message that Cap wasn't there."

"That was to tell you I needed to be rescued!"

"But the whole point was to get Cap.

"But they were going to kill me!"

"Naaawwww. We knew exactly where you were all the time. Your wire had a GPS transmitter in it."

Gus is unaware. "A GP what?"

Brisbane explains. "GPS. Global Positioning System. The transmitter in your wire sent out a signal to a space satellite. The satellite sent back a signal to our receiver pinpointing your location anywhere on earth within three feet. We never lost track of your whereabouts."

Despite this news, Gus is still put out by the fright he has just endured. "You are one crazy dude. I hope to God I never meet another cop as crazy as you."

Brisbane grins with amusement and affection. "I hope so too."

Something else occurs to Gus. "Hey, wait a minute. That GP thing. What if Cap lived in a big tall apartment block, you know, like the Brook House or something? How could you tell from that GP thing what floor I was on?"

The smile disappears from Brisbane's lips. He has no answer for that.

14

It was four weeks after the arrests. At half past seven in the morning, when the Legatos left the house in Westborough, the sky was overcast, the humidity oppressive. They were enveloped in a steady drizzle as they stopped to pick up Jim at the rectory in Waltham. By the time they reached Thorndike Street the rain was torrential. Ken steered the car cautiously through a monsoon that defeated the wipers and sent sheets of water cascading across the pavement. Throughout Cambridge, the water was backed up hubcap deep on the streets before storm drains hopelessly inadequate to their hydraulic mission.

Ken braked to a stop in front of the Courthouse, where his wife and son made a dash for the entrance, before he proceeded to the nearby parking structure. Walking back under his umbrella, he dwelled on his distemper of despair. He was annoyed with himself over this. There is no rational reason, he chided himself, why gloomy weather should portend bad news. Stop being ridiculous, he told himself. Good things happen all the time when the weather is bad. People win the lottery. People get job offers. They get promotions. Healthy babies are born. Test results come out clean. So knock it off, he scolded. Go in with a positive attitude.

No dice. No amount of logical analysis could dispel his premonition that this was going to be a very bad day.

Back in the lobby, he found that Sandy and Jeff had already arrived and were waiting with Gladys and Jim. Both had put in for vacation days in order to be present when the pivotal decisions would be made in determining the prosecution strategy; this might be their one and only chance to influence those decisions. Ken hugged his younger son and daughter warmly and then everyone passed through the security screen. They were quiet as the elevator carried them to the District Attorney's suite, and as they were ushered into the conference room. Waiting on the table was a tray of coffee, orange juice and pastries. Goodies, thought Ken, is how you soften people up before delivering bad news.

It wasn't long before Brisbane and Anita Banks made their appearance. Jim, Jeff and Sandy were new faces to Anita, so Ken made the introductions.

Abruptly, it was time for business. This was Anita's show. "Thank you all for coming," she began. "Don't be shy about helping yourself to refreshments any time." Brisbane helped himself to coffee. Nobody else moved. Nobody else felt like accepting Anita's hospitality until they heard what she had to say. They didn't yet know if she was friend or foe.

"Let me bring you up to speed," she continued. "You are aware, I believe, that as a result of a rather creative sting devised by Detective Brisbane, we arrested Stanley Mulvaney and two of his accomplices. We have established that Mr. Mulvaney, who is also known by the nickname Cap, makes his living as a loan shark. You may be surprised to hear that Mr. Collins is currently in debt to Mr. Mulvaney in the neighborhood of $50,000."

This last bit of information was indeed news. The Legatos exchanged looks, the kind of palms up, eyebrows raised eye contact that conveys the message, "I had no idea, did you?"

Anita registered their reaction and moved on: "We believe that in an attempt to discharge the debt, Mr. Collins entered into a conspiracy with Mr. Mulvaney to have his wife killed for the purpose of obtaining the proceeds from a large life insurance policy that Mr. Collins took out on your daughter during January, about six weeks before the murder. In other words, we have developed substantial evidence which tends to support Detective Brisbane's original theory of the case."

Gladys had stopped listening. She couldn't get past the part about the $50,000. She interrupted Anita's presentation. "Wait. I can't understand this! $50,000? That's *all*? That's *crazy!* We would have given them $50,000 to save Bonnie's life. Wouldn't we? Ken, am I right?" Ken agreed and shook his head vigorously to show it. Gladys finished the thought. "So if they had just come to us, the loan shark would have been paid, the problem would have been solved, and Bonnie would be alive today. Our grandchild would be alive. None of this would have happened. How crazy is this, that we lost Bonnie over $50,000?"

It seemed crazy to Anita, too, so she couldn't think of anything helpful to say. Sensing this, Brisbane decided to step up. He had been living with the case day and night for four months, and felt he had a pretty solid handle on the psychology of one Ralph Collins, heretofore solid citizen and now reigning scumbag of Newton, Massachusetts.

"Mrs. Legato," he said, "It is definitely crazy. And I don't want you to think that what I'm about to say is justification in any way for what Ralph did. But I can make a suggestion as to why I think Ralph didn't come to you for help."

Gladys wanted to hear. "Please do," she said.

"I've spent a lot of time trying to get inside Ralph's head. Some things about him are obvious. His preening narcissism, I think you'll agree, is a front, nothing but a façade. It is a cover for his fundamental insecurity and feeling of inadequacy. A feeling of inadequacy that is richly deserved, I might add. I think this front is his way of suppressing his demons and papering them over with outward signs of achievement and success. This much, I imagine, you already know. Pop psychology 101, you might call it.

"OK, but here's how I think it goes deeper. Until now, you see, this façade of his worked for him. Under normal circumstance, it was functional enough. It was, however, useless when the time came for him to cope with a genuine crisis. At that point, he was rudderless. He had no core of decency to protect, no inner moral gyroscope to steer him, no fundamental integrity to maintain. So instead, as always with Ralph, it became all about the symbols that propped up his facade: his upper management job, his house, his car, his clothes, his trips, and—tragically—Bonnie. His sense of self was entirely contingent on these external symbols. It was all he ever had."

"You're telling us that Bonnie was one of his symbols? Oh, I see," said Ken, quickly getting the point. "You're telling us that Bonnie was a trophy."

"Yeah. I think that's a good word for it." Brisbane was relieved. He had been hesitant to share his assessment of Ralph with Bonnie's family for fear that they would get angry with him, mad at him for devaluing their daughter's marriage. He knew how they felt about Ralph but had been reluctant to say anything that might be interpreted as cheapening the memory of Bonnie. He realized now that he needn't have worried. Across the board, the Legatos regarded the murder as prima facie proof that Ralph never loved Bonnie, and therefore that the marriage was a sham from the outset.

But Brisbane hadn't answered Gladys' question: *how crazy was this?* Jim voiced what the others were thinking. "How is being accused of murder good for his—how did you put it—sense of self?"

"It isn't good, exactly," Brisbane replied, "but the alternatives were worse, most especially asking Ken and Gladys for money. Then he would have had to tell them why he needed it. I don't think he ever seriously considered doing that."

Jeff was aghast. "You're telling us he killed Bonnie to avoid *embarrassment?*"

"In my opinion, that's what it boils down to. To him, asking the family—either side, yours or his own—would have been humiliating to a degree he could not endure. Try to see it from his perspective, not to justify it but merely to understand it. Remember that he got into this mess because he is a compulsive gambler. So to come to you would have required him to admit that he is damaged goods, unworthy of your daughter. In other words, he would have to admit that your family was right about him all along. Worse yet, he would have had to admit to Bonnie that he was liar and a phony. Far from supporting their opulent lifestyle, which—you must admit—Bonnie reveled in, he would have had to reveal that he was diverting their income to feed his addiction while they teetered on the edge of bankruptcy. Her reaction to that was unpredictable. He risked losing his trophy."

Jeff burst in. "But he lost it *anyway!*"

"The issue was *how* he lost it," Brisbane answered. "Remember that the cover story was a shooting during a break-in. This allowed Ralph to save face with the positioning that his beloved wife was taken away from him, rather than that he lost her due to his own inadequacies."

Jeff was still struggling to understand. "Wait! He had to expect the police to look into his finances and as soon as they did, that his gambling would be exposed and he would become the prime suspect. How is that good for his 'positioning'?"

"Jeff's right," added Jim. "Why would he prefer that we hate him for killing Bonnie than for his gambling away their money?"

Hate? thought Ken and Gladys simultaneously. *Jim?*

The picture made sense to Brisbane. He did his best to explain it. "Consider his choices. The question is, which choice incurs a greater wound to his pride, which is all Ralph really has. On the one hand, in confessing the truth to the family, he reveals himself as weak, as sick, as a liar, as a fraud. His pretenses are shattered. Don't forget, his entire structure of self esteem is built on a foundation of pretense anyway: on the illusion of success, on the illusion of prosperity, on the illusion of competence, on the illusion of control. Fessing up means destroying all that. And—this is key—because these illusions are critical to him, he projects that they would be equally critical to Bonnie. He projects that if he reveals his true self, Bonnie will reject him. That's only logical, because if *he* doesn't like his true self, why should Bonnie? It doesn't matter whether this assessment is correct; it only matters that Ralph believes it. And Bonnie's love is the one thing Ralph has that is real and true. He doesn't love her in return, we know he's not capable of that, but he *believes* that he does. In truth, what he loves really is the fact that she loves him, that he has her, he has his trophy. To Ralph, that's the same thing. He's oblivious to the difference. Since losing her is too big a risk for him to take, he can't ask for help with the money."

Jeff interrupts. "But he *did* lose her!"

"That's true," answered Brisbane. "In the end, with his vicious loan shark tightening the screws, Ralph only has two alternatives, and neither one is any good. For him, both require losing Bonnie. This, then, is how he sees it: On the one hand, the fessing up to the family option means losing her in combination with humiliation and shame. On the other hand, the murder option means losing her with his public persona intact, his debts paid off, lots of extra cash in the bank, and the possibility of replacing Bonnie with another trophy later on. If you are Ralph, which hand do you choose? Assuming, of course, as he does, that you will get away with murder and can continue thereafter to proclaim your innocence, OJ style."

Sandy, alert as always, was first to cut to the chase. "Well, is his assumption correct?"

The question fell in Anita's bailiwick, and all eyes turned expectantly in her direction. This was the moment Anita had been dreading. "I cannot say no with a high degree of confidence."

Jeff barked out loud what the rest of the family was thinking, although the others would have expressed it in a more diplomatic tone: "Can you translate that gobbledygook into English?" Then, recognizing that it wasn't a good idea to alienate the prosecutor, he added more gently, "Please."

Jeff's outburst fell short of the maximum reaction Anita could have expected, and she was encouraged to go on. "The first thing you need to understand is that murders for hire are almost never solved by means of conventional "Law and Order" type detective work. Almost always, such cases are solved or prevented from happening only because somebody who knows about the scheme comes forward and rats it out to the police. And when that happens, it is almost always true that the principals involved in the plot are amateurs. That is not the situation we have here. Forgive me if my language is insensitive, but Bonnie's murder was a professional hit. The shooters were professionals hired by other professionals. There are no horrified civilian witnesses running to the cops with stories to tell. As a result, we don't know who the shooters are.

"At the same time, we have no crime scene evidence that links anybody to the murder. We have no fingerprints, no gun. We never found the Impala, nor any of the other stolen goods. Nor do we have any evidence of any payments to any shooters."

Bad day, Ken was thinking, *I knew it*. He said, "You think these are holes through which a competent defense lawyer could drive a truckload of reasonable doubt."

Time to be candid, thought Anita. "In a word, yes. All the evidence we have on Ralph is circumstantial. Circumstantial evidence is not in itself bad. If it's strong, it can be damning. If, for example, we had proof that Ralph flew home from Atlanta that night and returned early the next morning, that would be damning. But we have nothing like that. We have behavioral stuff, consciousness of guilt stuff. We have motive, with the gambling and the insurance. We have opportunity, with Mulvaney. However, we still have nothing which specifically links Ralph to the crime of murder. The problem is, none of the suspects is talking. They are all betting that the case is borderline, so they're denying everything. They're taking that stance because the case is in fact borderline."

Sandy spoke up. "Don't you have any leverage? Can't you make a deal with Mulvaney to nail Ralph?"

"I don't see how. My strong hunch is that Mulvaney is paying for Ralph's lawyer. I can't be sure about that, but we know Ralph doesn't have the money. It has to come from somewhere. It's not like Ralph to go to his parents for it. At the same time, Mulvaney has a strong reason to pay for Ralph's lawyer; that way he can control the nature of Ralph's defense. It is in Mulvaney's interest for Ralph to stand pat. If they all stand pat, it will be hard to convict anybody. So yes, we've been looking for points of leverage, but we have little to offer Mulvaney in exchange for his giving up Ralph. All we can do for him is take murder off the table. Unfortunately, with Ralph silenced, it is already off the table. By way of contrast, we do have something to offer Ralph: a lighter punishment. We can do that by charging him with conspiracy instead of murder. Five years instead of life, in return for testifying against Mulvaney."

Interestingly, surprisingly, Ken found himself closely following the thread of Anita's exposition. His engineering mind was processing all the variables and he grasped the rationale she was developing. Meanwhile, it occurred to him that he should be furious over the mere suggestion of a deal with Ralph, and yet, somehow, he wasn't. That puzzled him. Instead, it was Jim who couldn't contain his emotions. "You can't be serious!" he blurted out. "That is outrageous! Ralph gets off with five years? That's not justice, that's a monstrous perversion of justice."

Ken was moved to act the diplomat. "Let's hear her out. Then we can react on the basis of all the information available." Even Gladys was surprised. She gave him a curious glance.

Anita leaped at the opportunity to resume her analysis. "OK, then, what would a deal with Ralph gain us? It would get us a guaranteed conviction under a plea agreement as opposed to a very possible verdict of not guilty in a jury trial. At the same time, we would nail Mulvaney as well, who after all was the instigator and manager of the whole crime, and paymaster for the shooters, and who is in every way an all around bad actor."

Jeff was very unhappy. "That's all well and good for you. You chalk up two convictions. Your numbers go up, your statistics look great. What do we get? We get *bupkis*."

Jeff's comment irritated Brisbane. "If that's bupkis, how would you describe a verdict of not guilty?"

For the first time that morning, Gladys had something to say. "Jeff. Please. I want to think some more about what is right here and what is wrong. Ms. Banks has given me a lot to consider. I don't mean about evidence and reasonable doubt. I'm talking about what is fundamentally right and fundamentally wrong. The way it appears to me, if they try Ralph for murder he therefore has no incentive to testify against this Mulvaney person. As a result, Mr. Mulvaney gets clean away with his part in the whole thing. That doesn't seem right to me."

"What do you mean, Ma?" asked Jeff.

"Jeff, a terrible deed has been done, that we know. And all along, we've been totally focused on Ralph's responsibility in it. That's understandable. We've suffered not only our loss of Bonnie, but also Ralph's betrayal. Now Ms. Banks is trying to show us that Ralph is only part of a larger picture of crime and punishment. This man Mulvaney, who it appears to me is a real beast, he has at least as much moral responsibility, not to mention legal ... what's the word you lawyers use?"

"Culpability," suggested Anita.

"Yes, culpability, as much culpability as Ralph does. Am I on the right track?"

Anita was glowing with satisfaction and relief. "You're doing beautifully, Mrs. Legato."

Gladys finished the thought. "Here is how I see the picture Ms. Banks is painting for us. She has two choices. Neither one is ideal. Isn't it odd how we seem to be talking so much about choices this morning, first Ralph's, now Ms. Banks?"

"It's not odd, Ma," said Jim. "It's in the parable of the sower and the seed, Matthew 13. God has given us free will, and moral choices are embedded in every minute of our lives."

"Yes, Jim, I believe that." Gladys' thoughts were crystallizing even as she gave voice to them. "For Ms. Banks, choice number one is to prosecute Ralph fully for the crime of murder, in which case neither he nor Mulvaney cooperate in any way. As a result, punishment for Ralph is possible but not likely. And for this Mulvaney character, there is essentially no chance of punishment for the murder. That's aside from the loan sharking, the kidnapping, those are separate, I would think?"

"That's right, Mrs. Legato," Anita said.

"And the Feds will probably get him on tax evasion," Brisbane added.

"Good, but Mr. Mulvaney gets away with murder for sure. Then there's choice number two: make a deal with Ralph. In that case, punishment for Ralph is not what it should be, I understand that. But the punishment, inadequate as it is, is guaranteed. In addition, punishment for Mulvaney is almost certain because Ralph will have to testify. I think Ms. Banks is trying to show us that when you balance these two choices overall on the scales of justice, the second choice has a lot more weight."

Anita was blown away by the insight shown by the victim's mother. She hadn't expected it. "That was beautifully put," Anita said. "Thank you."

Then Brisbane had something to add. "Even though Ralph's punishment would not be the maximum, you should realize that it would still be harsh. Five years in a state penitentiary, even medium security prison, is no picnic. Besides, he will lose his job immediately, and with no income he will lose his house and car. The house is mortgaged to the hilt, so he has little equity, and what there is, Mulvaney or his friends will go after. When he gets out, he will be broke and will have to start a new life as a convicted felon. My guess is that he will wind up slinking back home to Kansas City, tail between his legs."

Jim, Jeff and Sandy were waiting for their father to push back. The notion of a prosecution deal with Ralph was anathema to all three. It was Ken, after all, who had brought them around to that view in the first place. They waited in expectantly, and in vain. Ken was silent. The meeting was over.

Ken realized that his attitude had been transformed during the last hour. He knew that now that both his opinion and his feelings had moved into alignment with those of Gladys, although for different reasons. At the same time, he recognized that both of them were ahead of their children with respect to this issue. No matter how compelling the rational argument in favor of a deal, the kids weren't ready to hear it yet. They might be persuaded on the merits, but to grasp it cognitively was a far cry from accepting it emotionally. He needed time to bring the kids around. He queried Anita, "Do we have to respond on this now? Can we have a few days?"

"Of course," Anita said. "Not a problem at all."

It was not quite ten o'clock. The Legatos had expected to be there until lunch. So, in their customary fashion, they had a family powwow about what to do with the extra time. They decided to keep it simple and adjourn to the cafeteria inside the Courthouse building, several flights down the stairs. There, amidst all the cozy ambience and alluring charm that only an institutional food service facility in a government building has to offer, they sat around a Formica table sipping coffee from Styrofoam cups and nibbling on bagels with cream cheese served on plastic plates.

In short order, the younger generation made known their frustration. Jeff led the charge. "Dad! I don't get it. It was you who insisted *no deals*. It was you who said that a deal is the lazy way out, a bureaucratic abomination. How can you even think of turning around 180 degrees and going along with this?"

It was a good question. The answer was that within a span of sixty minutes Ken had undergone not merely an alteration in his point of view but a seismic, indeed tectonic, shift in his entire perspective. Both the rain outside and the gloom inside had vanished. The discourse between Anita Banks and Gladys had led him to see everything in a fundamentally different way. He had, in a wholly unexpected and amazing fashion, found the solution to his anguish. The sensation was so new that he didn't yet trust it. It might not clear the hurdle of logical analysis. It might not stand the test of time. It might not work at all. Accordingly, he wasn't ready to share it with his family yet. Still, right now it was providing a welcome beacon of hope that he had, finally, at last, rounded the corner and was on the road recovery.

The sick leave had been helpful for Ken. Unburdened of the worries attendant upon letting down his colleagues in the office, he had been set free to focus on the task of grieving. This was fortunate, since the mourning process, as Ken experienced it, had not been going well.

Ken felt immobilized, mired in his grief without forward motion through it. Once on leave, he had developed the habit of spending his days taking long walks, using the hours to try to understand how it came to pass that such excruciating pain had been visited upon him and his loved ones. He hiked mile upon mile along the wooded trails in nearby state parks. He ambled all morning long on the walkway that follows the Charles River from Watertown to Mass General, and then consumed the afternoon making his way back. He traversed on foot the length of the rail trail from Arlington to Bedford, then returned on foot to Arlington. Over and over and over and over, and over and over and over again, on every walk, his mind kept grappling with the age-old question: why do bad things happen to good people? Or—the same question—how does one account for the existence of evil in the dominion of a supreme and loving God?

In his technocratic way, Ken hadn't just agonized over the question, he had researched it. He had scoured the Religion shelves at Borders and Barnes & Noble's, purchasing not just Christian interpretations but Jewish ones too. He had indulged himself in some especially hopeful moments when he had run across and brought home a copy of Harold Kushner's book, *"When Bad Things*

Happen to Good People," since the title seemed so apt to his dilemma. But it didn't pan out. He discovered that the "When" in the title neatly conveyed Rabbi Kushner's central point, which was that no one carries immunity to bad things; there is no vaccine to be derived from good character or innoculation to be extracted from righteous behavior.

Ken had picked up the book in the first place because he had failed to find solace where he had originally expected to locate some: in the Christian teachings. For him, the notion that tragedies are part of God's plan, and therefore occur in the service of some greater—albeit unknown—good, provided no relief. It begged rather than answered the central question: Why him? Why did God's plan single him out for calamity, rather than somebody else? Worse yet, why would God's plan target Bonnie's unborn baby? Ken took note, too, that Rabbi Kushner's title did not promise more than the book could deliver. It was *when*, not *why*.

And surely, he was convinced, the answer could not possibly be that God's plan was predicated on meting out some form of justice. True, he had little doubt that he himself could be found wanting in the eyes of the Lord; at the very least, he had failed miserably in protecting his daughter from that piece of shit she'd married. Bonnie, too, was not perfect. She was good of heart but Ken recognized now that she was also materialistic and hedonistic. Granted, then, in those respects she was not exactly a model follower of Jesus. Even so, did his neglect and his daughter's delight in worldly pleasures amount to transgressions so severe as to warrant punishment as drastic as this? And even if they did, what about Gladys? If anyone is a exemplar of Christian virtues, it has to be Gladys. Why should she be picked on to suffer in such extreme measure? And the baby. What about the wholly innocent baby?

If this is how God shows his love, Ken could do without it. If this is God's plan, it stinks.

In all his research, Ken came upon only one strain of Christian thought on the subject of evil that did make sense to him. Interestingly, it was a point of view shared by Rabbi Kushner. This was the understanding of evil as a necessary concomitant to free will. The concept goes like this: If God had made man in His image, then of necessity mankind must be imbued with free will. Free will, in turn, implies the reality of moral choice. The *possibility* of real moral choice is necessary but not sufficient. For moral choice to be a reality, it is required that immoral choice—that is, the choice to do evil—must sometimes be made in actuality. If human beings were always to choose good, always to avoid evil, then the choice would not truly be free and the putative endowment of free will would therefore be spurious. In that event, human beings would be little more than automatons, little different from animals whose behavior is guided by mere instinct. The existence of evil is therefore the logically necessary price that humans must pay for having been created in the image of God.

OK, Ken thought time and again on his endless walks, that idea is good as far as it goes. As a solution, however, it comes up short in a head on collision with the blessing of prayer. If the evils of nature—storms, volcanoes, disease and the like—are governed by natural laws and processes that God himself created and set in motion, and if God is hands-off when it comes to the evils of man as ordained in the doctrine of free will, then what is the use of prayer? Where, between the laws of nature and the preserve of free will, is there room for God to answer prayer and intervene? Does God suspend natural laws just for the asking? Does he override the exercise of free will just because we implore him to keep our loved ones safe?

Ken knew full well that many Christians would answer "yes." He understood that this is the very definition of a miracle. When we petition God to intervene in order to arrange a favorable outcome that would not otherwise occur, we are literally asking for a miracle. But that just brought Ken back to the original question: Who gets a miracle and who does not? Most do not. Why then, the question remained, do bad things happen to good people? Including him. And Gladys. And Bonnie. And the baby. And Jim. And Sandy. And his mother Alma, Bonnie's grandmother. And Gladys' parents, Dave and Paula, who of course were Bonnie's grandparents too.

Then he had heard what Gladys and Ms. Banks had said that morning. Something inside had told him to listen and pay attention. And as he listened, the answer hit him like a thunderbolt. Everything seemed to fall into place, magically, amazingly. It was as though a brilliant white beam from a spotlight, as in a darkened theater, had landed on God's plan, illuminating it, directing his rapt attention and allowing him to see it with perfect clarity. And what he saw was that Bonnie's death was not the triumph of senseless chaos and mayhem as he had previously thought. What he saw was that a greater good was going to come of it. There was a *reason for it*. There was a *purpose to it*. As a result of her sacrifice, a major league criminal had been taken down. The criminal would be punished. Regardless of the outcome of the murder case, his criminal enterprise had been destroyed and there would be no more victims in the future. Meanwhile, Bonnie and the baby were at peace in the presence of their maker. Their lives had been brief, but important and significant. *Their lives were consequential. They had made the world a better place.*

Ken felt exhilarated, ebullient, as the weight of senseless futility lifted from his shoulders. He had sensed, this morning, the presence of God in that conference room. It was a glorious moment of indescribable elation. But how could he explain this to his kids? God, in his wondrous but often unexpected ways, had been speaking to him through Miss Banks and through Gladys. It was as though God's plan had been right in front of his eyes the whole time but he had been unable to decipher the print. It had all been an unintelligible blur. Then that morning, God had handed him a pair of celestial reading glasses, and all at once the print in God's plan was in perfect focus, the meaning crystal clear.

Still, it was all new, just an hour old, and Ken was still unsure of himself. He wanted to share it with Gladys, to bounce it off her faith and common sense, before he tried to explain it to his children. So his answer to Jeff did not reveal much. That could come later, when he was more settled with it himself. For now, all he wanted to say was, "Yes, I know I've changed my mind since the night we discussed all this over dinner. I'm only saying we should be open to considering all options in the light of additional information that we currently have that we didn't have back then. For one thing, we didn't know about Mulvaney back then."

Sandy was as confused as Jeff by her father's radical turnabout. "I don't understand, Dad. You neither, Ma. I get it, all right, that some good to society is accomplished by putting Mulvaney away. But I don't see why it should matter to us all that much. Yes, Mulvaney organized the logistics. But how can we ignore the fact that it was Ralph who set everything in motion by running up those gambling debts. Fifty thousand dollars, for God's sake! Even worse, as you said yourself, Ma, he could have solved everything simply by asking you for the money. Or his own family! But he didn't. He *wouldn't*. He *chose* not to. I don't see any way around the fact that the primary responsibility for what happened belongs to Ralph. So how can it be OK to let him off with only five years? That's *nothing!*"

Gladys was too weary to answer. She wasn't upset that the kids were challenging her but she was too exhausted to hassle with them. She wanted Ken to say something. Anything. Whatever was happing with Ken that morning, it seemed good. So she hoped he had the energy to deal with the kids on her behalf. She desperately wanted to go home. She was focused on one thing and one thing only: getting into bed and taking a nap.

Gladys had been sleeping little. She was hardly eating. Where Ken was angry, Gladys felt ground down by an overwhelming sadness. Bereavement was a constant pressure in her chest, making it an effort to breathe.

Gladys had returned to the gift shop part time after several weeks, feeling a responsibility to the owner and the business, and hoping that the work would provide a distraction. She needed to get out of the house, for when she was home she spent all of her time poring over the traces of their life through the years, dwelling on the connectivity to Bonnie these keepsakes aroused but also wallowing in the rich, dense, deeply gratifying saga of the Legato's thirty-four year adventure as a family. She was astounded to discover how many remnants of this history were there to be found in the form of domestic artifacts. There were, for instance, photo albums, a dozen big thick ones. There were stacks of home videos. In the attic, she found a carton filled with reels of 8mm home movie film, dating from before the era of the video camera. She searched unsuccessfully for their old home movie projector, but Ken was a dear and took the films to a place where the film images were transferred onto DVD. In a closet there was a filing cabinet for personal papers. One drawer was stuffed with family memorabilia, which included: programs from school events; party invitations; diplomas; artwork by the kids; school assignments; report cards; letters from camp; awards and certificates, valentines to Mommy and Daddy; Jim's letters from the Peace Corps.

Every item, every sequence of video, opened the floodgates and let loose a torrent of tears. Even when it didn't involve Bonnie directly, it was still all about the family. Her family. Her family that was mutilated now, a gaping hole where Bonnie should have been. The memories were sharp and vivid. She remembered where she and Ken went with the kids went, what they wore, where they sat, what they ate. Every recollection was sweet and wonderful. Every one gored another gaping, bloody wound in her eviscerated heart.

Oh, Lord, look at that. There, on one of the DVD's transferred from film, was Peter Pan.

The best—the worst—were the wedding videos. Sandy's first. Jim's church. Outside. Inside. The flowers. Ken escorting her down the aisle. Barry watching them, beaming. Jim officiating. The best man, Howard, their friend from the restaurant downtown. There was Bonnie, the maid of honor. *Oh, Bonnie, do you know how I hurt, how I ache?* The receiving line, both families. Departing church for the reception. *Gladys had to smile as she watched that part: no fancy schmancy limosine, no horse and buggy folderol for Sandy and Barry. Jeff and Sharon drove them in their van, with the girls. That was so much like those two kids, God bless them. It was a perfect Sandy and Barry moment.* There they are arriving at the reception. That's the entrance to Howard's restaurant. *Howard was very generous, Gladys was reminded. As a wedding gift, he had not only closed his place for their private party, he had also donated an open bar for wine and beer.* There's Howard, behind the bar, clinking glasses of beer with Barry's brother. Now the toasts: Jim, Jeff, Barry's brother. Barry's friend. Bonnie! *That's right, I remember now, Bonnie gave a toast.* "Why should men have all the fun," *she said.* Now the dancing. Sandy and Barry. Sandy and Ken. Barry and herself. Barry and his mom. Bonnie and her date, pre-Ralph. Everybody dancing, the floor crowded. What's that? Oh, right, they're doing "YMCA." *Even Jeff!* The cake. *No smooshing it each other's faces, not these two, no way.* Kissing. Sandy looking radiant. Thanking Howard, hugging him. Leaving for the airport in the van with Jeff and his family.

If watching Sandy's video was tough, watching Bonnie's was torture. Ralph was in that one. The poignancy of the scene ripped Gladys apart. It felt like surgery with no anesthesia.

The splendor of Bonnie's wedding was all that a bride could desire. Four maids of honor, Sandy and three friends, in matching pastel gowns. Ralph and his best man in tuxes. A limo. Reception at the Boston Harbor Hotel, overlooking the waterfront. Champagne toasts. Wedding cake from Konditor Meister. *The whole kit'n'kaboodle, her father Dave had said.*

Bonnie had planned the wedding for months on end, obsessive about every detail, devouring suggestions from magazines and web sites, able to talk about little else. She consulted *ad nauseum* with her mother, her sister, Ralph. By and by Gladys and Sandy hit a wall of fatigue on the subject and couldn't wait for the whole thing to be over, but Ralph was attentive and supportive throughout. He was amused by it all, and found Bonnie's effervescent enthusiasm adorable. If he couldn't quite bring himself to care what shade of pink the napkin rings were going to be, he nevertheless was happy she was happy, and the conspicuous display of consumption suited his personality just fine. And why shouldn't he be happy, Gladys thought at the time. He wasn't paying for it.

The cost became a serious point of contention between Gladys and Ken. Gladys didn't reject the tradition that the bride's family funds a wedding. At issue was the exorbitant cost of this one in particular. As month followed upon month and decision after decision clicked into place, Gladys watched with ever growing discomfort as the tab climbed to outlandish proportions. She thought it more than extravagant, she found it grotesque. Just imagine, she often pondered, what Jesus would think if he happened to stop by the Boston Harbor Hotel on a certain Saturday afternoon. Suppose, attracted by the music, the Son of God were to peek into the ballroom and take in their shameless spectacle of unrestrained excess. "Please," our Savior would say, "Would somebody kindly bring me a barf bag?"

Ken, however, was impervious to his wife's blandishments that he put a lid on the spending. Ken's attitude was that a wedding is not a one-day event; it is the making of a lifetime memory. Bonnie had the memory she wanted fixed in her heart, and nothing was going to persuade him to deny it to her. Not even the argument she thought most likely to work with Ken—that it was all a racket designed to scam them with inflated prices, and he was allowing himself to be duped by the rapacious, unprincipled wedding industry—could make him budge.

As Gladys watched the video in the weeks after the murder, all of this was brought to mind. But she also recalled that on the day itself, the tug of Bonnie's joyful exuberance had been irresistible. Her ire about the unbridled intemperance of the affair and her rancor with Ken over it melted away as she surrendered her misgivings and "went with the flow." Bonnie was such a stunning bride. Ralph was a handsome, cheerful groom. Improbably, all the complex arrangements were executed by the obsequious, overpaid vendors per expectations and to Bonnie's satisfaction, with neither crisis nor calamity crashing the party. By the last half hour of the reception, when Bonnie shed her veil, kicked off her shoes, and started swing dancing with first Ralph and then his dad, it appeared as though their daughter would indeed have her perfect memory. For that day, at least, Gladys had capitulated to wishful thinking. Maybe, she said to herself as she and Ken left the ballroom hand in hand, everything will be all right.

No matter how many times she replayed the video now, Gladys could not discern anything that should have made her think otherwise. Why then, she wondered, was she so consumed by her obsession with the past, especially when it hurt so much? "Easy," said Ken, bless his heart. "It is your way of keeping Bonnie alive."

Ken, in fact, had been supportive of Gladys throughout the ordeal, and as a result she never loved him more than she did now. True, he had been morose and withdrawn. True, he had drunk himself to sleep every night, causing her no little anxiety over the condition of his liver. And true, when he went on his daily walks, she was glad to get him out of the house. But at the same time, he was insightful as to her trajectory of grief and solicitous of her needs in getting through it. When her housekeeping standards hit a nadir, he never complained. He came back from his walks laden with takeout for dinner, knowing she didn't feel like cooking. And as they sat at the dinner table with the paper sacks and Styrofoam platters, he scarfing the food down with an appetite made ravenous by exercise and she barely picking at it, he listened, he really listened, while she described the mementoes she had looked at during the day and rehearsed the feelings these had evoked. On most days he did more than listen; he engaged with her, joining in her reminiscences and contributing recollections of his own. Gladys was well aware that her husband would rather have been watching the news on TV, and appreciated in full measure his kindness in providing her the companionship she craved in exactly the way that she craved it.

It was also helpful that Ken empathized with her aversion to the stock expressions of condolence and her impatience with the well-meaning people who offered them. Ken took them in stride, but for Gladys her irritation with the clumsy attempts at comfort from friends and acquaintances was as troubling as it was unexpected. The formulation that ticked her off most was "God never asks more of us than we can endure." It made her cringe. First of all, it was patently untrue, as the suicide rate attests. More importantly, she found the very idea was nonsensical. It was no more acceptable than an employer who would lay off a woman instead of a lesser-performing man because, as the woman was not the sole support of a family, she could better endure unemployment. Gladys vehemently rejected the idea that God allocated pain on the basis of a cruel joke: *Your faith gives you strength? The laugh's on you!* Gladys understood her friends' intended message of encouragement behind the words: that however bleak things seemed now, they were confident she would find her way through it and out the other side. Why didn't they just say that and leave God out of it?

Best of all, Ken left Gladys to mourn in her own way, without criticism or scoffing or telling her what to do. Just as he expected to take his walks and down his bourbon without interference from her, so equally did he respect her right to find her own path to recovery. Gladys would remain forever grateful for that. And when she fretted that her obsession with the past was unhealthy, Ken's words were reassuring. "Don't worry about it," he told her. "Healing takes time. There's no right way or wrong way. You're doing it your way."

Gladys snapped back to the present. Her daughter was staring at her, expecting an answer about how she could justify a deal with Ralph. Ken was silent, not helping her. Everyone sat mute for a while. They self-consciously sipped coffee and nibbled on the bagels, alarmed that a serious rift might be developing within the family. At length, Jim turned to his sister, because she was by nature a problem solver. "Sandy, what do you think we should do?"

"Nothing," Sandy said.

This got people's attention.

"What I mean is that there is no point in getting into a family spat over this because the question is moot. The issue isn't decided by Anita Banks, it is decided by Mulvaney. Mulvaney is paying for Ralph's lawyer, and no way is he going to let Ralph cop a plea. Let Ms. Banks make her offer to Ralph. It doesn't matter. It will be rejected. Dead on arrival. End of story."

As is so often the case, Sandy had seen her way to the heart of the matter. And so it came to pass: the offer was made and rejected, just as Sandy had predicted.

15

The trip from Anita Banks' office to 12-G is short: 10 floors up in the elevator.

Twelve-G is a courtroom of moderate size, laid out in the conventional geography familiar to viewers of movie and TV dramas. The décor is contemporary, spare but not unpleasant. Wood veneer surfaces lend a degree of warmth to the boxy, well lit space, while a double high ceiling connotes both the dignity of the immediate proceedings and the overarching majesty of the law itself. Jurors sit in comfort on individual cushioned chairs. Tables and seating for both prosecution and defense are spacious and well positioned. Only the spectator accommodations are Spartan—a bare four rows of hard wooden benches—but no matter; a media circus is not expected in the case of Commonwealth of Massachusetts vs. Ralph Walter Collins. With no sex, celebrities, abused children or gruesome torture to prime the ratings, the cameras have long since turned their attention elsewhere.

It is now fifteen months since the murder. The prosecution is ready for trial.

As ready, Anita keeps reassuring herself, as she'll ever be. This is no slam dunk. As she and Brisbane told the Legatos a year earlier, the case against Ralph is "iffy" and the outcome is a tossup. And Ralph has a good lawyer.

Opposing counsel is Blyer Noche (pronounced *NO*-chay), an experienced hand of the old school and a crafty trial tactician. He is a personage known widely throughout the city and state, and not only among fellow members of the bar; he is equally familiar to plutocrats and panhandlers, pols and prisoners, potentates and parking attendants. His reputation for personal integrity combined with courtroom creativity has been earned. Meanwhile, his unpretentious, slightly rumpled, highly ordinary appearance belies an uncommonly calculating intelligence. His Rolodex is crammed with the names of satisfied clients.

That's right, his Rolodex. Blyer does not embrace modernity; rather, he yields to it grudgingly and selectively. The man has no PDA, hence the Rolodex. He has no cell phone. His office has no voice mail, just an old fashioned answering machine with a cassette tape. There is a fax in the anteroom but no computer on his desk. His administrative assistant has a computer for word processing but it is not connected to the internet. Therefore, no e-mail.

Blyer Noche practices solo. Eschewing any whiff of the entrepreneurial mentality, he has neither partners nor associates. This is a blissful self-indulgence. In return for foregoing the opportunity to generate significantly greater income, he savors the luxury of absolute independence. He is free to do exactly what he wants, when he wants, how he wants, with no one to second guess his choices or, for that matter, gainsay his mistakes.

It also leaves him free of pressure to straighten up his office, the condition of which seems to define the very concept of entropy. His desk, the table, the couch, the chairs, the windowsills and the floor are crammed in inchoate immoderation with unruly stacks of files, folders, transcripts, and miscellaneous papers and pleadings. It looks chaotic but don't be fooled: the pervasive dishevelment of his workspace notwithstanding, he can locate anything, always, immediately. It is not that Blyer prefers disarray. It is simply that at any particular time, there is always something for him to do with a higher priority at that moment than cleaning up.

Having crossed swords with Blyer in the bargaining over Cap's plea agreement, and again in his successful battle to obtain Ralph's release on bail, Anita is acquainted with his style. As expected, Ralph has stood fast and has never implicated Cap in the murder. Blyer's negotiations on Cap's behalf over usury, extortion and assault charges were lengthy and arduous, but finally culminated in allocutions leading to a minimum time served of twelve years. The kidnapping charge for snatching Gus is still pending under federal jurisdiction. It is, in all, an outcome Anita wouldn't celebrate but could live with.

Anita arrives in court an hour early on the first day of testimony and sits alone at the prosecution table. She is not there to catch up on her work. The preparation of her case is complete. She has rehearsed and polished her opening statement a dozen times. Rather, she is priming herself psychologically for upcoming contest. She is girding her mindset for the battle that lies ahead. She is collecting her mental focus and distilling her concentration.

It is a relief to Anita that jury selection is behind her. In a way, she finds that initial stage of a trial the most harrowing of all, because the illusion of control is so tantalizing yet so very misbegotten. In fact, the process of jury selection is sufficiently mysterious and difficult that it has spawned an entire industry of erstwhile consultants, hired by lawyers, who become part of the team and whose job it is, in effect, to shoulder the blame when things go wrong.

It is all about the challenges. Both sides can ask questions of potential jurors in a pretrial ritual known as *voir dire*. If the answers reveal that an individual may be either biased or unable to evaluate the evidence competently, a lawyer can ask the judge to dismiss that person for cause. The judge may do that, or may disagree and rule that sufficient cause has not been demonstrated. In that event, a lawyer can resort to using a peremptory challenge, for which no reason or cause need be

stated. The problem is that each side is limited to only four peremptory challenges. As *voir dire* moves along from one potential juror to the next, at every step
the lawyers on both sides face the question of whether to consume one of the four
precious peremptories now, or save it for later when it may be needed more
urgently to exclude somebody even worse. These decisions are excruciating.

Anita never uses jury consultants. In Anita's view, they don't help. For all their
patina of technical jargon and sophisticated research tools—their socioeconomic
analysis of the local community, their opinion polls, their attitude surveys, their
personality profiles and their focus groups—they can't actually predict how any
given individual is going to react to the presentation of evidence in a specific case.
There are too many variables in the trial itself. At best, consultants can provide
general guidance as to which strategic approaches, arguments and broad categories of juror types offer a more favorable probability of success, and they can help
lawyers hone their presentation techniques. But when it comes right down to it,
jurors are a black box; no one knows what's going on inside their heads. Any
attempt to anticipate how potential jurors will respond to testimony in relation to
the unpredictable demeanor of witnesses, and to the varying styles of the attorneys, and to the manner in which the judge exercises his authority, and to the
interpersonal chemistry among one another—all in the context of what is going
on concurrently and perhaps distractingly in their personal lives—is doomed to
futility. Jury selection is a crapshoot, and that's why Anita hates it. Blyer didn't
use a jury consultant either. Anita likes him the better for it.

But that ordeal is over for now, and she can concentrate on placing the noose
around Ralph Collins' neck. That's speaking figuratively, of course. Massachusetts has no death penalty, and this is something for which Anita is grateful. She
would like to be elected District Attorney some day, and that would be hard for
her in a death penalty state. It's not only that she finds the sanction morally
repugnant as public policy. It is also that empirical studies show it to lack any
deterrent effect. For Anita, that makes it more morally repugnant. She doesn't
think this makes her soft on criminals. She believes that locking up a criminal for
life in prison fully protects society and is plenty hard on the convict too. Her
vision for Ralph Collins is worse, she's convinced, than death: never again the
enjoyment of tasty or satisfying food; gone forever the pleasure of mellowing out
on a scotch before dinner, a glass of fine wine, or a few beers with friends; banished to a distant, frustrating recollection the exhilarating freedom of tooling
around in your own car; relegated to ancient history the satisfaction of doing productive work; banished for all time the ego gratification of purchasing the latest
gear and proudly showing it off; and worst of all, driven by inescapable circum-

stances into nothing more than a memory—a memory always tantalizingly insistent but permanently out of reach—the touch of a woman's skin. That is the fate he deserves: life without possibility of parole. A long ... long ... long ... miserable future of complete material, mental and sensual deprivation, stretching endlessly ahead with no prospect of relief. Sixty years of absolutely nothing doing in the present and absolutely nothing in the future to look forward to. A living death that *seems* eternal, followed by a real death and divine damnation which *is* eternal. A death which is lonely and pathetic, in a prison hospital ward, where nobody notices and nobody cares.

The hour passes quickly and by 9:30 all of the players have arrived in court and settled in place. The bailiff announces in stentorian tones, "All rise. The Superior Court of the Commonwealth of Massachusetts, Middlesex District, is now in session, Judge George Athenas presiding."

Judge Athenas emerges from chambers and trundles towards the bench. The man is huge: about six foot five, at least 300 pounds. He is clean-shaven and well groomed, conventional in appearance but for a startling, outsized helmet of tightly curled and tangled gray hair, like an elderly woman with a perm. Judge Athenas is a commanding presence, no doubt about that. And he uses that command to impose a flinty discipline on the litigations under his supervision. Anita is content with his assignment to this case. She has appeared before him several times previously, and regards him as firm but fair to both sides.

The jury is brought in. "You may begin, Ms. Banks," says the judge, and suddenly the future—so long anticipated, meticulously planned for, and endlessly visualized—is now.

Opening statement. Anita introduces herself to the jury, explains the charges against Ralph, and presents an outline of the case. She stresses the story line of Ralph's gradual descent into the trap of criminal behavior. She wants the jury to understand the human narrative of how an ordinary member of the prosperous, privileged corporate class, with everything seemingly going for him, is reduced to the ignominy of conspiring in the murder of his wife for money. The story is one of a slow but natural progression: from gambling for amusement to a gambling addiction to exhaustion of legitimate sources of funding to involvement with a bookie to the clutches of a vicious loan shark to a crisis of unimaginable peril when the loan shark must be paid, and, finally, tragically, to a desperate attempt to resolve the crisis by the killing of his wife for the insurance benefit, the biggest most fateful wager of a gambler's life.

Anita wraps up her statement with an important teaching for the jury. "Ladies and gentlemen, I expect you to hear Mr. Noche disparage our evidence as 'merely circumstantial'."

"Objection." This from Blyer.

Judge: "To what, Mr. Noche?"

Blyer: "The purpose of opening statements is to preview the evidence and put it into context. Ms. Banks' characterization of how she thinks I will react to the evidence is outside of that purpose."

Judge: "Are you stating for the record that you will not attempt to discredit evidence as being circumstantial?"

Blyer: "No, your honor, just that such issues are appropriately addressed in closing arguments rather than opening statements."

Judge: "Nice try, Mr. Noche. Objection overruled. Proceed, Ms. Banks, but please try to refrain from consulting your crystal ball as to what Mr. Noche might or might not want to say at some future time."

It is a small victory for Anita, but not a defeat for the defense. Blyer knows from the outset that his objection will be swatted away. Attorneys are normally accorded wide latitude in their opening statements as long as they avoid presenting actual evidence. All he wanted was to inject a cloud of suspicion in the minds of the jurors that the prosecution is not above playing questionable games in its zeal to gain a conviction.

"There are three general kinds of evidence," Anita continues, counting off on her fingers. "One is eyewitness, two is physical, and three is circumstantial. Each type has its own strengths and potential weaknesses. I'll give you an example. Let's call it the cookie caper. Say you leave the house for a few hours one afternoon and you tell your son Johnny that the cookies on the top shelf are for the bridge club meeting tonight and under no circumstances may he eat any of them. Later, you come home and some of the cookies are missing. You are hopping mad and you want to bring the cookie crook to justice. But how?

"One possibility is that little brother Billy runs into the kitchen saying, 'Mommy, Mommy, Johnny ate the cookies. I saw him!' That is eyewitness testimony. In this case, there is no problem of mistaken identity; Billy knows what his brother looks like. There is, however, an issue of credibility. Johnny insists, 'Billy's lying, Ma! He's just getting back at me because I wouldn't let him use the video game. He only wants to get me in trouble.' Who's telling the truth? Is Billy's eyewitness testimony credible? That's what you, the jury in the case of the cookie caper, would have to decide. It wouldn't be easy.

"Suppose, alternatively, that Billy is upstairs the whole time. There is no witness. However, you see cookie crumbs on Johnny's mouth. That is physical evidence. In that particular instance, it would be called trace evidence, since traces of a material have been found in a location and at a time that make them incriminating. Does that mean case closed? Not necessarily. There remains the problem of determining what the physical evidence actually is. Johnny insists that the seemingly incriminating crumbs are not from your bridge party batch at all, but instead from a package of cookies he bought at the convenience store. Do you believe him? It depends on the results of expert scientific analysis of the evidence itself: do the crumbs on his lips scientifically match the crumbs on the plate of the bridge party cookies? If so, Johnny is toast. If not, he is free to go.

"Lastly, there may be no crumbs, no witnesses, yet you just *know* that Johnny ate the cookies. Why? Because they were there on the plate when you left the house and they were missing when you returned, and there's no other plausible explanation. Billy is too short to reach the shelf, even standing on a chair. Nobody else but Johnny was in the house. What other explanation could there be? None that makes any sense at all. So you find Johnny guilty beyond a reasonable doubt. The evidence is entirely circumstantial but the common sense conclusion is quite inescapable.

"The evidence in the case against Ralph Collins is similar in nature: circumstantial but overwhelmingly convincing in its totality. That is what you will plainly see. That is why common sense will lead you beyond a reasonable doubt to a verdict of guilty. Thank you."

That was pretty good, Blyer muses. Secretly, he is charged up. Blyer relishes the adrenalin rush of a competitive battle against a worthy opponent, and Ms. Banks appears to be just that.

He briefly considers mocking the notion of a cookie caper, but then thinks the better of it. If the analogy made sense to the jury, the tactic could backfire. Better to play it safe and stick to his original plan. His principal objective at this point is to humanize the perception of Ralph in the minds of the jurors. He is aiming to inoculate Ralph, in some degree at least, against the character assassination he expects will play a prominent role in the prosecution strategy, and he hopes as well to lay the foundation for a contrasting, more sympathetic image of his client. It is better to stick with the plan. Blyer gets up and approaches the jury box.

"Imagine how it feels," he begins, "to be accused of a serious crime that you did not commit. Imagine the worry, the tension, the fear, the sleepless nights, as the enormous weight of the implacable apparatus of law enforcement that belongs to the Commonwealth of Massachusetts bears down upon you in a determined effort to toss you in the slammer and throw away the key." Blyer pantomimes the act of locking a cell door and hurling the key as hard and as far away as he can.

"If you can imagine that level of terror—the night sweats, the panic attacks—if you can feel the pain of being ostracized by family, shunned by friends, avoided by co-workers, then you can begin to understand the true nature of the catastrophe that has befallen the defendant in this case, Ralph Collins. Not only has his beloved, beautiful wife been shot to death in their own home—*in their own bed*—not only has their unborn child, their first, been murdered too, but on top of that he stands falsely accused of having plotted to make it all happen.

"How can that be? How could they arrest the wrong person? How could such a terrible injustice come about? Wouldn't that have to be a freak occurrence of some kind? Ladies and gentlemen, the answer to that question is no, it is not a freak occurrence. The unhappy fact is, it happens all the time. Once in a while you even hear about it on the news: Some poor innocent soul is released from prison because it is determined that there was some error or misconduct in how his trial was handled. But these incidents are merely the very tip of that iceberg. These are the rare instances where an erroneous guilty verdict *can* be corrected due to new evidence becoming available, such as DNA analysis. These cases *are* unusual; that's why they make it to the news. But what doesn't make the news are the much more numerous wrong verdicts which are left to stand because without new evidence those cases can't be reopened. And even those cases constitute no more than a fraction of the iceberg. Most of the buried part of the iceberg of people wrongly sent to jail consists of cases that never come to trial at all. Most arrests, in fact, never do reach the light of day in a courtroom. They are resolved instead by a plea agreement between the prosecution and defense. Many of these agreements involve wholly innocent suspects who nevertheless are induced to plead guilty to something small because they don't want to risk losing at trial on the original, more serious charge. It does not necessarily mean they are guilty of anything; it can just as easily mean they have decided not to fight the system. So the arrest of Ralph Collins, in and of itself, is not evidence of his guilt.

"Now, it came to pass in the normal course of events that my client was in fact offered a plea agreement. It was an attractive one and he was tempted, but in the end he turned it down. He did that on my advice. I told him that I have been in practice for a very long time, and never before have I seen a prosecution case so weak, so lame, so lacking, and so riddled with assumptions, suppositions and unsupported leaps of the imagination.

"It may therefore surprise you that Ms. Banks and I agree on an important point: circumstantial evidence can be as valid and as persuasive as eyewitness testimony or scientific analysis of physical evidence. Where we part company is our assessment of the meager, pitiful excuse for evidence that she has to offer in this specific trial. We are sure that you will see her so-called evidence for what it is: a flimsy house of cards, a concoction of smoke and mirrors, an ephemeral cloud of wishful thinking less solid and substantial than cotton candy. When you hear the evidence she has, you will understand that my client is guilty of nothing more illegal than the peccadillo of gambling with a bookie. And they didn't charge him with that!

"Oh, and, ladies and gentlemen, there is one other thing. Ms. Banks conveniently left it out of her explanation of circumstantial evidence, so I will repair her omission and bring it to your attention. It is a well established principle of law, in Massachusetts as in other states, that when circumstantial evidence can be reasonably interpreted in more than one way, the jury is duty bound—*duty bound*—to accept that interpretation which is most favorable to the defendant. This is no more than a logical application of the standard of reasonable doubt, and we anticipate that Judge Athenas will instruct you on this point before you enter your deliberations. Since *all* of the evidence in this case is circumstantial, and since we will show you how that evidence is clearly subject to alternative explanations, we are confident that you will follow the judge's instructions on the law and return a verdict of not guilty.

"Thank you." Blyer sits down. *Not bad, Anita muses.*

Anita calls her first witness. Her plan for the trial is basic: present the evidence in the context of a narrative that is easy for the jury to understand and retain, then conclude with Brisbane to fit the bits and pieces of incriminating detail together in a damning mosaic whose logic is unassailable. Fleshing out Anita's plan is a design, a structure, a narrative architecture not unlike a play with three acts. Act I is the crime itself, the reason why the jury has been summoned. Act II is the series of events leading up to the crime, the dynamics which explain the reason why the crime was committed. Act III is the investigation which ties Acts I and II together and provides a satisfying denouement: *Who done it? That man right there, the defendant, Ralph Collins.*

Act I opens with the 911 operator. Her role is to set the stage for introduction of the 911 tape as prosecution Exhibit #1. This goes smoothly and the tape is then played for the jury. There is no cross-examination from Blyer; the call is not in dispute, and nothing in it implicates his client.

Next there is testimony from one of the local police officers that responded to the 911 call. He tells about meeting Gladys on front path, seeing the body, alerting his headquarters and the State Police, and securing the house as a crime scene. No cross.

The first beachhead of the defense case is established by Blyer in his cross-examination of Lieutenant Mike O'Mara, head of the state police Crime Scene Unit sent to the house. Anita has called him to describe the physical evidence, or lack of it, and to introduce his report into evidence. Blyer probes on cross: "Lieutenant, your report states that forty seven fingerprints were found in the house and transmitted to the State Police database for identification?"

O'Mara: "That's right."

Blyer: "And your team took fingerprint samples from family and friends who were known to have been in the house at some time?"

O'Mara: "That's right."

Blyer: "And these samples were used to identify the prints found in the house?"

O'Mara: "That's right."

Blyer: "And in due time you received a report back from the State Police Automatic Fingerprint Identification System?"

O'Mara: "That's right."

Blyer picks up two copies of a document from the defense table, hands one to Anita, the other to O'Mara. "This is the document you received?"

O'Mara: "It appears to be, yes."

Blyer: "Request to enter this document as Defense Exhibit #1."

Judge: "Ms. Banks?"

Anita: "No objection."

The Clerk puts an exhibit number sticker on it and returns it to Blyer, who hands it back to O'Mara. "Lieutenant, the report states that all of the prints found in the home were matched with the samples from family and friends, is that right?"

"O'Mara: "That's right."

Blyer: "Lieutenant, as an expert on the forensic analysis of physical evidence, what conclusion do you draw from that fact?"

O'Mara: "That the killer or killers wore gloves."

Blyer: "There are no other possibilities?"

O'Mara: "I don't understand the question."

Blyer: "Is it not possible that the killer was somebody who's prints you did find?"

O'Mara: "*What?* I doubt it."

Blyer: "What is it, exactly, that can be found either in this report or in your own crime scene report that would cause you to doubt that the killing was done by somebody whose prints you found in the house?"

O'Mara: "Not from these reports, but in the context of the entire body of evidence in the case."

Blyer: "Not any evidence found by you?"

O'Mara: "No."

Blyer: "Then I ask you now if the following is a fair summary of your testimony: Nothing you or your team found at the scene contradicts the possibility that the murder was committed by someone whose prints were among the 47 located and identified there. Nevertheless you discount that possibility out of hand and instead infer that there was some unidentified gloved stranger lurking about, basing that view not upon any evidence you discovered but exclusively upon the *cockamamie* theory of the case ginned up by the prosecution. Does that about sum it up?"

O'Mara: "I wouldn't put it that way."

Blyer: "You just did, Lieutenant. Let's turn to the murder weapon. From your own observation of the body at the scene, you could see that Mrs. Collins had been shot?"

O'Mara: "It appeared that way."

Blyer: "And did that appearance cause you and your team to search for a gun?"

O'Mara: "Yes."

Blyer: "Did you find one?"

O'Mara: "No."

Blyer: "In the course of that search, did you find any evidence at all—any bullets, any licenses, any receipts, anything at all—that might have linked Ralph Collins in any way to the murder weapon had you been able to find it?"

O'Mara: "No."

Blyer: "Are you aware of anything that turned up later in the investigation that could possibly have tied Mr. Collins to the gun, had it ever been found?"

O'Mara: "No."

Blyer: "OK, that's clear enough. Did you find signs of a forced entry at the house?"

O'Mara: "A window pane in a basement window had been removed using a glass cutter."

Blyer: "In your opinion as a forensic expert, could a person have reached through the hole to unlock the window, opened the window, and gained entry to the basement through it?"

O'Mara: "Could have, but I doubt that happened."

Blyer: "Oh, more doubts. And why do you doubt that happened?"

O'Mara: "Because we also learned that the burglar alarm had been turned off. Whoever was there knew the alarm code. Why come in through the basement window when they knew how to turn off the alarm? I believe the window was just a diversionary tactic."

Blyer: "But on the other hand, why bother to fake a break in when the killer or killers made no secret at all of the fact that they turned off the alarm?"

O'Mara: "I don't know the answer to that."

Blyer: "Indeed. So, we know that someone turned off the alarm. OK, then, in your expert opinion, who was more likely to know the alarm code: a gloved stranger or one of the forty seven friends and family whose prints you found in the house?"

Anita: "Objection. Calls for a conclusion by the witness not within his field of expertise."

Even as he rules in Anita's favor, Judge Athenas can't quite suppress a fleeting smile of appreciation over the nimble footwook in Blyer's questioning.

Blyer: "No more questions."

Anita attempts some repair work with her witness on redirect: "Lieutenant O'Mara, could the killers have been *told* the alarm code by someone who knew it? Someone, for instance, like Mr. Collins?"

No objection from Blyer, to the surprise of Anita, O'Mara and the judge alike.

O'Mara: "Yes, that could have happened."

Blyer on recross: "Lieutenant, could the killer likewise have been told the alarm code—under completely innocent and unsuspecting circumstances—by someone else who knew it? Someone, for instance, like *Mrs.* Collins? Or, perhaps not so innocently, by an employee of the alarm company?"

Anita can't object since she opened the door with her own question. "Well," says Lieutenant O'Mara carefully, "… I suppose that can't be ruled out."

Blyer: "So here we have more of that doubt of yours, do we not?"

Anita: "Objection. Question asked and answered."

Blyer, before the judge can respond: "Right. Asked and answered. Quite so. Question withdrawn. No further questions for this witness."

The Medical Examiner is called to testify as to manner and cause of death. No cross. And then the day is finished. Blyer feels pretty good. Nothing bad has happened, and he's put a few nicks and scratches in the shiny surface of the prosecution theory. And he's only getting started. He goes home and enjoys dinner with his wife and teenaged son, his youngest and the only one of his children still living at home. Anita goes out to dinner with Brisbane and Mark Bluestein, a junior prosecutor who is assisting her. They review the course of the day and try to anticipate what could happen tomorrow. Their enjoyment of dinner is a few notches lower than Blyer's.

Day two is Gladys. She is rarin' to get started, having spent all of day one sitting on a bench in the hallway outside of 12-G. Potential witnesses are excluded from the courtroom prior to taking the stand so that their testimony isn't influenced by the preceding statements of other witnesses. She understands the need but she still hates having been forced to stay outside.

Now, finally, her chance has arrived to take an active part in putting Ralph away. Anita, always solicitous of Gladys' vulnerability in a time of stress, has emphasized that her appearance is voluntary. She has assured Gladys that it would be possible to find other ways of getting the necessary information in. But Gladys won't hear of it. Gladys *needs* to testify. Having a role in the prosecution, taking a stand by speaking out on the stand, is a necessary step in her healing process. She has assured Anita in return that she is up to the task, and that is true.

This is the opening of Act II: the backstory leading up to the crime. Gladys is sworn in and Anita takes her through the early days of the relationship between Ralph and Bonnie: how they met, the trip to Bermuda, their period of dating, the wedding, and all along her discomfort over the man their daughter decided to marry.

They move on to the period leading up to the murder, the three months between Thanksgiving and the Sunday family dinner. This is the time of Ralph's emotional withdrawal, followed by the restoration of his normal amiability the week after New Year's.

Finally, Gladys relates her ordeal of the Tuesday following that final Sunday dinner when Ralph was in Atlanta: the worrying through Monday night, the call on Tuesday morning to Bonnie's office, the drive to Newton, the absent Impala, the TV going, and the unspeakable horror of finding her daughter's lifeless body with a hole in her temple.

On cross, Blyer's goal is to neutralize the unpalatable image of Ralph that Gladys has created. She has portrayed Ralph as a character whose behavior is somehow out of kilter and who is therefore worthy of suspicion. He will endeavor, starting now, to expose this depiction as unfounded and unreasonable, and replace it with a perception of Ralph as nothing less than a generous, caring and perfectly normal individual who was utterly devoted to his wife. Blyer's core message to the jury throughout the trial will be that Ralph is a regular person like everyone else whose only faults are the defects of his virtues: a surfeit of largess toward his beloved Bonnie impelled by her insatiable thirst for conspicuous consumption in combination with his own unstinting dedication to making her happy.

I know what you're thinking: *Why, that's ridiculous! That can't possibly work! You GOTTA be kidding!* Actually, no. This is not kidding. This is part of what is known as an affirmative defense, and Ralph's lawyer knows what he is doing.

Blyer is circumspect at first and respectful in his questioning of Gladys, but his agenda for Bonnie's mother is critical to Ralph's defense. "Mrs. Legato, please accept my condolences on your loss."

Gladys' deeply ingrained sense of courtesy forces her to nod her head in acknowledgement. Reluctantly.

Blyer: "Mrs. Legato, you testified that your suspicions about Ralph's character arose the very first time he took Bonnie out on a date. Is that right?"

Gladys: "Yes."

Blyer: "Bonnie was living at home at the time?

Gladys: "Yes."

Blyer knows all about the dinner at the Bay Tower from endless conversations with Ralph during their exhaustive preparation of the defense case. "And you were suspicious because Ralph took her to a nice place for dinner?"

Gladys: "It was too nice. Instead of just getting to know each other, he was trying to make an impression with his fancy big shot flash and dash. I thought it was phony."

Blyer: "You thought that. What did Bonnie think?"

Anita: "Objection. Hearsay. Also calls for conclusion of the witness."

Judge. "Sustained."

Blyer: "When Ralph first asked her out, what did Bonnie tell you about where they were going?"

Gladys: "That it was going to be a surprise, but he told her to wear her best dress."

Blyer: "You could see that she was thrilled with anticipation over the date, couldn't you?"

Anita: "Objection. Leading the witness." This is an error pure and simple. Anita can sense where Blyer is heading with his questions and she doesn't like it. But in her apprehension and desire to derail the oncoming freight train her education and experience are momentarily blanked out. As a result, she makes herself look like a rookie. Judge Athenas' eyebrows are arched as he peers at her over his spectacles. "May I remind you that leading questions are permitted on cross, Ms. Banks? Overruled."

Blyer is quick to take advantage of the small gift Anita has given him: the opportunity to repeat the question and thereby fix it in the jurors' memories. "She was thrilled with anticipation, wasn't she?"

Gladys: "She was looking forward to it."

Blyer: "She tried on her dress from her sister's wedding?"

Gladys: "Yes."

Blyer: "It still fit and that was what she wore?"

Gladys: "Yes."

Blyer: "She went out and bought a necklace?"

Gladys: "Yes."

Blyer: "She had her hair done that morning?"

Gladys: "Yes."

Blyer: "When she came home after the date, you and your husband were waiting up?"

Gladys: "Yes."

Blyer: "What word or words did she use to describe the date?"

Gladys scowls. She doesn't want to answer.

Blyer: "Mrs. Legato?"

Gladys: "She said it was 'dreamy'."

Blyer: "Dreamy. That meant she had a good time? She liked the date? She liked him? She liked the place they went to?"

Gladys: "Evidently she did."

Blyer: "So. Your objection to the fancy flash and dash restaurant he took her to is based on *your* evaluation, not Bonnie's. True?"

Gladys: "I was disappointed that she didn't see beyond the shallow, superficial enticement of a $200 dinner."

Good answer thinks Anita, but Blyer is not at all unhappy. It is not especially damaging if the jury regards Ralph as shallow and superficial. That's exactly what he is, after all. But the issue is not what kind of person Ralph is; the issue is how he felt about Bonnie. What's important is that the jury "get it" that Ralph was infatuated with Bonnie, from the day they first met until the shocking tragedy of her death. The jury must "get it" that the very essence of their relationship consisted of his puppy dog devotion to Bonnie along with his unwavering desire to please her. They must "get it" that the joy of Ralph's life was his success in fulfilling her desires. Blyer has to get the jurors to understand that Bonnie was everything Ralph ever dreamed of, and thus everything he ever did was in the interest of making her happy. Moreover, there is not the slightest question in Blyer's mind that Bonnie loved Ralph in return, and that the reason for it was that Ralph understood her thoughts, feelings, desires and pleasures in a way and to a degree that nobody else ever had. To her, his flaws were inconsequential because he was a perfect fit for her needs, and so it mattered not at all to her what her family or anybody else thought of him. In short, it is Blyer's job to convince the jury that Ralph had such a good thing going with Bonnie that the idea he would have her killed makes no sense.

Blyer: "Enticement? Mmmm. Isn't it the case that the purpose of his enticement was to get her to like him as much as he liked her? Was that bad?"

Gladys: "It was the way he went about it."

Blyer: "Which was precisely the way that appealed to Bonnie. What it boils down to is that you're faulting Ralph for courting Bonnie in exactly the way that Bonnie wished to be courted. The way, in fact, the Bonnie responded to most enthusiastically. The only problem is that it was not the way that would appeal to you. Isn't that all you're blaming him for?"

Gladys: "It was all his fancy dancy phony baloney."

Blyer: "I suggest to you the opposite, Mrs. Legato. I suggest to you it was not at all phony but the genuine Ralph Collins, the real unadulterated McCoy. More to the point, it was the genuine Bonnie Legato. I suggest to you that your daughter was no fool. I suggest to you that she married Ralph Collins knowing exactly what he was like. She married him because he understood her so very well, isn't that true?"

Gladys: "I don't know why she married him."

Blyer: "He understood that Bonnie had expensive tastes, would you agree to that?"

Gladys: "I don't know. Maybe a little."

Blyer: "A little? You mentioned the wedding under questioning from Ms. Banks. You said it made you uncomfortable because you thought she was marrying the wrong man. Is that right?"

Gladys: "Yes."

Blyer: "How much did it cost?"

Anita: "Objection. Relevance."

Blyer: "Your Honor, the witness criticized to the cost of a dinner in a restaurant as extravagant and out of proportion. I am going to show that the wedding reception, which was basically a dinner in a restaurant, was similarly extravagant and out of proportion, and it was paid for by the Legatos."

Judge: "I'll allow this line of questioning for a while, but make your point quickly. Answer the question, Mrs. Legato."

Blyer prompts: "The cost of the wedding?"

Gladys: "I don't know. Ken managed the financial end of it."

Blyer: "It cost more than $37,000, didn't it?"

Gladys: "I said, I don't know."

Blyer: "I'll show you then." Blyer picks up two booklets with clear plastic covers from the defense table. Handing one to Anita, he says to the judge: "These are copies of bills for Bonnie's wedding, along with affidavits from the vendors. We've created a summary page in the front. I ask that this document be introduced as Defense Exhibit #2."

Anita: "Objection. Same reason. Relevance. The Legatos are not on trial here."

Judge: "Counsel approach the bench, please." They do. "Mr. Noche?"

Blyer: "Your Honor, Mrs. Legato has lambasted my client for spending too much money on a dinner for Bonnie. The wedding, your honor, was a similar extravagance magnified close to two hundred times. I'm entitled to show that the fancy dancy dinner at Bay Tower was good, not bad, in view of the fact that her parents did essentially the same thing. In addition, it is part of our affirmative defense. Not only are we going to argue that the prosecution evidence does not rise to an adequate level of proof. We are also going to show that Ralph was too much in love with his wife to have her killed, especially when it wasn't necessary. He showed his love in part by spending money on her, which is exactly what her parents did to show their love. Her parents and her husband all spent a ton of money on Bonnie because she had expensive tastes, and that's how they all showed their love."

Anita: "Your Honor, it's ridiculous to compare a wedding to first dinner date. More to the point, Mrs. Legato's testimony was not her discomfort about the cost of the Bay Tower dinner as such, but her discomfort that Mr. Collins spent that much on their very first date, before he had any idea whether Bonnie's tastes were expensive or not."

Judge: "All right, I've heard enough. I am sustaining the objection. Mr. Noche, your line of questioning is legitimate and you may pursue it at another time, but as the subject of cross-examination it has wandered too far afield from the witness' direct testimony. You may recall Mrs. Legato later as a defense witness and explore these matters under questioning then."

Anita: "Thank you, Your Honor."

Blyer also says, "Thank you, Your Honor," and means it. It doesn't matter all that much whether the information gets in now on cross or later in direct testimony, as long as it gets in. And the judge has just promised him it could. Moreover, the judge has in effect blessed the thrust of the overall defense strategy.

Blyer still has to sell it to the jury, but now he knows at least he'll have the chance.

Anita and Blyer return to their places. With the topic of expensive tastes deferred, Blyer has only a few remaining areas to cover on his cross.

Blyer: "Mrs. Legato, you testified that when Bonnie returned from the trip to Bermuda, she related an incident where she thought Ralph was hiding something on his laptop. You testified that you told her that hiding things—keeping secrets—is a dangerous sign in a relationship. Is that correct?"

Gladys: "Yes."

Blyer: "And yet you would describe the relationship you have with your husband as good?"

Gladys. "Very good."

Blyer: "But then that's a contradiction, because you keep secrets from him."

Gladys has no idea where this is coming from. "What do you mean?"

Blyer: "Isn't it true that Chet Townsend, your husband's boss, called the week before last Easter and told you he was going to put your husband on medical leave, and you kept that secret from Ken for a week?"

Gladys is shocked. She glances at Ken in the spectator section, to whom this is news, then turns back to Blyer. "How did you know that?"

Blyer: "Mr. Townsend told us when we interviewed him. He was making the point that you and your husband have such an excellent relationship that you were willing to keep that secret as an act of kindness so as not to ruin Ken's Easter. I would certainly call it an act of kindness. Wouldn't you?"

Gladys. "Yes."

Blyer: "So when you told your daughter that secrets are necessarily wrong in a relationship, you were mistaken, weren't you? They can be an act of love, as with you and Ken. Don't you agree?"

Gladys: "You're twisting everything. The secret I kept from Ken was to protect *him,* not me. The secret Ralph kept was to protect *himself.* That's a big difference"

Blyer: "How can you know that, Mrs. Legato, when you didn't know what the secret was then and you still don't know what it was even now?"

Gladys: "Detective Brisbane believes Ralph was logged onto a gambling site."

Blyer: "Precisely, Mrs. Legato. You had no idea what it was then and even now you depend entirely on the scenario invented by the prosecution, isn't that so?"

Gladys: "I can't imagine what else it could have been."

Blyer: "What if he was looking at pornography. Lot's of people do that but don't want their partners to know about it. That's a possibility, isn't it?"

Gladys: "I suppose ... but I don't think so. He didn't need that. Bonnie told me her ... uh ... (she looks at he judge, then back at Blyer) ... I should say ... physical ... relationship with Ralph was excellent."

Blyer: "Well, Mrs. Legato, as a matter of fact Ralph told me the same thing. So if their physical relationship was excellent, doesn't that sound like a reason for Ralph *not* to have Bonnie killed?"

Gladys: "That was then. This is now."

Blyer: "Did your daughter ever say anything to you to indicate that their physical relationship had deteriorated since then?"

Gladys: "Yes. She told me that between Thanksgiving and New Year's a year ago Ralph was distant and uncommunicative."

Blyer: "We now know that this is the time he found out the magnitude of his gambling debt, isn't that right?"

Judge Athenas makes eye contact with Anita. She knows why. Blyer is again crossing the boundary into subjects unrelated to those covered on direct examination. Anita has the option of objecting, and if she does the judge will shut down this line of questioning. But she decides not to object. She doesn't see how this topic can help Ralph and therefore thinks Blyer is making a mistake. She both acknowledges and responds to the judge's unspoken query with a negative shake of her head. The judge gives a quick shrug in return, as if to indicate, "OK, you've had your chance." Judge Athenas will not intervene on his own initiative. In accord with common practice, he leaves it to the lawyers to blow the whistle when one side or the other strays from the rules of evidence. That is part of their responsibility in the adversary system of American jurisprudence. Should counsel fail to invoke such rules, either inadvertently or as in this instance with intention, then he is content to follow custom and allow the consequences to take their course.

Blyer catches the byplay in his peripheral vision, takes in the meaning, and keeps a straight face to hide the rush of anticipatory pleasure. He is going to be allowed to start building the foundation of his defense *right now*. Gladys, unaware that anything has gone on, answers Blyer's question: "Yes."

Blyer: "So you can understand how he was in emotional turmoil."

Gladys: "I can understand he was too ashamed to tell Bonnie about his problem."

Blyer: "Perhaps, but it also could have been that he wanted to protect Bonnie from worry, isn't that so?"

Gladys: "That doesn't sound like Ralph."

Blyer, feigning astonishment: "It *doesn't?* Mrs. Legato, we now know that Ralph and Bonnie lived on very edge of a financial precipice for years. Did you know that prior to the investigation?"

Gladys: "No."

Blyer: "Bonnie never said anything about that?"

Gladys: "No."

Blyer: "Do you believe that Bonnie was hiding it from you, or that she didn't know herself?"

Anita groans inwardly. It's a 'when did you stop beating your wife' question. Either answer reinforces Blyer's thesis that sometimes people keep secrets for motives that are benign. Anita expects that Gladys will say that Bonnie wasn't aware. The alternative raises too many questions about why Bonnie maintained her spendthrift ways in the face of looming bankruptcy.

Gladys: "I believe that Bonnie didn't know."

Blyer: "So therefore it's fair to say that all along Ralph protected the wife he loved from financial worry, isn't it? Far from 'it doesn't sound like Ralph', it sounds exactly like Ralph, doesn't it?"

Gladys counters adroitly: "It sounds like a *cockamamie* theory ginned up by the defense." Appreciative chuckles from Anita, the judge, some of the jurors, and even Blyer. Score one for Anita.

How did she know to say that, Blyer wonders. Gladys was out in the hallway yesterday when he used those words with Lieutenant O'Mara. Either a family member or Anita must have told her …

In any event, the jape from Gladys is a setback for Blyer but not a serious one. It doesn't matter what Gladys thinks; it matters what the jurors think. And Blyer has at least introduced them to a central theme of the defense case which he will develop as the trial moves forward: Everything that Ralph has ever done is consistent with his being a loving and protective husband who would never, ever consider having any part in the murder of his wife. This is a theme which Blyer wants to cultivate and nurture. He thinks of his sparring with Gladys as the source, the origin, the wellspring of a stream of evidence that he will feed and channel until it develops into a formidable downstream torrent, a gravitational force against which the prosecution has to struggle mightily as it strives to make upstream headway in proving its case beyond a reasonable doubt. The current is not yet strong but at least he has set it in motion, and earlier than he had anticipated.

Blyer's momentum on Ralph's protectiveness is momentarily dissipated, however, so he changes his tack. "Mrs. Legato," he says, "let's go back to Ralph and his laptop in Bermuda. We agreed he *could* have been looking at pornography, despite your doubts on that score. True?"

Gladys: "It's conceivable, though barely."

Blyer: "Could it not also have been an e-mail exchange with another woman from a prior relationship? Someone who was still attached to Ralph even though Ralph had moved on to Bonnie?"

Gladys: "You're watching too many soap operas, Mr. Noche."

Blyer: "Can you rule it out?"

Gladys: "No."

Blyer: "How about some kind of medical condition, a condition that he wasn't ready to reveal to Bonnie so early in their relationship? Can you rule that out?"

Gladys: "I suppose not."

Blyer: "So aren't there a variety of things that Ralph could have been doing on his laptop that had nothing to do with subsequent events related to this case?"

Gladys: "I suppose."

Blyer: "Good. We're almost done now, Mrs. Legato. Just one more area I'd like to ask you about. Let's move on to your testimony that you were uncomfortable about Bonnie's agreeing to marrying Ralph. To your knowledge, did Bonnie herself ever express any such doubts?"

Gladys: "No, not to me, not that I recall."

Blyer: "OK. And at any time since their wedding did you ever hear Bonnie say anything that indicated any regret over marrying Ralph?"

Gladys: "Not that I recall, no."

Blyer: "Thank you. No further questions."

Judge: "This is a good time to break for lunch. Court is in recess until two P.M."

When court reconvenes, Anita has a surprise for the others. At a bench conference, she explains to the judge that Gladys has requested that she be allowed to complete her testimony today in order that she may be present as a spectator for the remainder of the trial. Anita wants to withdraw her objection to the introduction of evidence relating to the wedding and offers to allow Mr. Noche generous freedom in the scope of his cross-examination. "Your Honor," Anita explains, "my thinking on this is that the timing of when these matters are raised—whether now on cross or later on direct questioning by Mr. Noche—will make no difference in the outcome of the case. I therefore can see no reason not to accommodate Mrs. Legato's wish to observe the rest of the trial in the company of her family."

The judge doesn't see any difference either, and given his underlying attitude that the lawyers are the cops when it comes to rules of evidence, he is inclined to go along with this most unusual request. "Mr. Noche?" he inquires.

Blyer: "Fine with me, Your Honor."

Judge: "Then you may resume your cross-examination of Mrs. Legato."

Blyer thinks Anita and the judge are wrong. Since the judge would almost certainly allow Gladys to be classified as a hostile witness, it is true there is no difference between now and later in the specific questions he can ask and the answers that will be given. But exposing Bonnie's expensive tastes and the way the family catered to them at a point so early in the trial will inevitably color the way the jury perceives and registers the remainder of the evidence from the prosecution side. It's another gift.

Gladys is recalled and Blyer gets the booklet documenting the wedding expenses entered as a defense exhibit.

Blyer: "Mrs. Legato, you remember that this morning we discussed your discomfort over the cost of the wedding, and how it cost over $37,000?"

Gladys: "Yes."

Blyer reaches behind his table and pulls out a 30" x 40" foam board. He places it on an easel in view of the jury. "Mrs. Legato, this is a blowup of the first page of defense exhibit two." It looks like this:

Wedding Expenses Paid by Legato Family	
Reception (200 guests @ $120)	$24,000
Reception Gratuities @ 18%	$4,320
Photography	$1,600
Flowers	$1,400
Gown, Veil	$2,200
Video	$1,000
Band	$1,000
Invitations	$450
Transportation	$350
Church Fees	$300
Favors, Attendants' Gifts	$500
	$37,120

Blyer: "It is a summary of the wedding costs. Is it accurate?"

Gladys: "I'll take your word for it."

Blyer: "It was your money as much as your husband's. Don't you know?"

Gladys: "Ken handled the finances."

Blyer: "That's because you were disgusted with how the costs were mounting up, is it not?"

Gladys: "It seemed a bit much."

Blyer: "Isn't 'disgusting' exactly what you told your boss at the gift shop?"

Gladys: "Something like that, perhaps."

Blyer: "We can call Mrs. Robideaux as a witness if we have to. She told us you said to her, quote: 'The cost of this thing is disgusting.' End quote. Is she wrong?"

Gladys: "No. I said that."

Blyer: "And the choices that ran up the disgusting costs were made by Bonnie, were they not?"

Gladys: "Somewhat."

Blyer: "Somewhat? Was it Ralph who said he wanted you to spend $2,200 on her dress and veil? Was it Ralph who said he wanted you to spend $1,400 on flowers? Or was it Bonnie?"

Gladys: "Well, all right, Bonnie."

Blyer: "Just to put this in perspective, how much did you and your husband spend on the wedding of your other daughter Sandy?"

Gladys: "Sandy and Barry insisted on paying for their own wedding."

Blyer: "What did you and Ken contribute?"

Gladys: "We gave them a nice cash wedding present and we paid for the airfare and hotel on their honeymoon."

Barry: "How nice was nice?"

Gladys: "We gave them $5,000."

Blyer: "That's nice. Say the honeymoon hotel and airfare added up to $3,000. That's a total of $8,000, compared to $37,000 for Bonnie. Why the difference?"

Gladys: "They wanted different types of weddings."

Blyer: "The type Bonnie wanted just happened to be disgustingly over the top. So why did your husband go along with all that extravagance, even though you found it disgusting?"

Anita: "Objection. Hearsay."

Blyer: "I'll rephrase. What did your husband tell you about why he went along with it?"

Anita: "Still hearsay."

Blyer: "No, Your Honor. The question is not intended to prove the truth of what Mr. Legato actually thought, but only to indicate what he said. I want to explore how Mrs. Legato felt about what her husband told her."

Judge: "Overruled."

Blyer: "What did he say?"

Gladys: "He said that he wanted her wedding to be the memory of a lifetime."

Blyer: "Did that trouble you?"

Gladys: "Not that. What bothered me was that the value of the memory seemed tied so directly to its cost."

Blyer: "And that feeling was driven by Bonnie, true?"

Gladys sighs: "… yes."

Blyer: "And your husband catered to her expensive desires?"

Gladys: "Yes."

Blyer: "That was one of his ways of showing how he loved her?"

Gladys: "I suppose you could say that."

Blyer: "And that's why you and your husband spent $8,000 on your other daughter's marriage to a guy you liked and $37,000 on Bonnie's marriage to a guy you disliked?"

Gladys: "The circumstances were different."

Blyer: "I'll say. Are you aware that their home in Newton is worth more than yours?"

Gladys: "I have no idea."

Blyer: "On the day you found Bonnie, you had plans to go shopping together with her?"

Gladys: "Yes."

Blyer: "That was not unusual, I understand. You did that, what, three or four times a year?"

Gladys: "About that."

Blyer: "Did you ever shop together in Wal-Mart?"

Gladys: "No."

Blyer: "K-Mart? Target? Sears? Penny's? Macys? Any of those?"

Gladys: "No."

Blyer: "On your own, you have shopped in some of those stores?"

Gladys: "Yes."

Blyer: "But those places weren't upscale enough for Bonnie so together you went to places like the Atrium Mall in Chestnut Hill?"

Gladys: "Sometimes."

Blyer: "More often Copley Place?"

Gladys: "Probably."

Blyer: "That's where they have Neiman Marcus?"

Gladys: "Yes."

Blyer: "Tiffiny's? Ralph Lauren? Louis Vuitton? Gucci? Coach?"

Gladys: "Yes."

Blyer: "OK. There is just one last topic I'd like to cover with you. Mrs. Legato, are you aware of how much money Ralph owed Mr. Mulvaney, the loan shark?"

Gladys: "Ms. Banks told us it was $50,000."

Blyer: "That's correct. Mrs. Legato, did Ralph or Bonnie ever approach you for financial help in paying off the loan shark?"

Gladys: "No."

Blyer: "If Ralph had ever approached you and told you truthfully why he needed $50,000, would you have given it or loaned it to him?"

Anita: "Objection. Calls for speculation by the witness."

Judge: "No. It is a hypothetical, but one that is well within the competence of the witness to answer. She can know what her personal decision would be in a private matter in a given circumstance. Overruled."

Blyer: "Would you have given him the money?"

Gladys: "Of course! If we had known Bonnie was in danger, we would have done whatever it took to keep her safe."

Blyer: "Thank you. No further questions."

Blyer returns to his seat exultant. He appears nonchalant but that is an heroic act of will. He really wants to jump high in the air and click his heels. He really wants to pump his fist up and down and shout '*Yessss!*' Gladys' 'of course' is one of the keystones of his entire case and he has gotten on the record. *And it's only day two.*

Anita has nothing to pursue on redirect, so she moves on to the next witness. She calls the Chief. She wants the Chief to show how Ralph's debt mounted up.

"Please state your name and address for the record."

Chief: "Joseph Siskern. 2044 Majorca Drive, Marblehead, Massachusetts."

After Brisbane's visit to Chelsea, the Chief was induced to provide a statement and testify. He had little choice. Brisbane told him that if he didn't, he—Brisbane—would park on the street in a State Police cruiser in front of his dry cleaning store, wearing a State Police uniform, and would watch calmly as the Chief's customers made themselves scarce and his livelihood cratered. So the Chief, Brisbane and Anita have a deal. He will testify truthfully as to Ralph's gambling activity and the sale of the account to Cap. In return, the Chief will receive transactional immunity, which means he won't be prosecuted on the basis of anything in his statement or testimony. In addition, the State Police and the District Attorney's office won't muck up the delicate ecology of his local arrangements in Chelsea. The Chief had his own attorney present for these negations; Blyer was not involved. Unlike Ralph, the Chief's interests are not entirely aligned with Cap's.

Anita takes the Chief through the history of his dealings with Ralph, culminating in the sale of the account to a "factor."

Anita: "This 'factor', as you call him, was in fact a vicious loan shark, was he not?"

Chief: "He was in the lending business. Vicious is not something I know about one way or the other."

Anita: "He was widely known by the nickname Cap, isn't that true?"

Chief: "I've heard that."

Anita: "And that's because he was known to break people's knee caps if they didn't pay up?"

Chief: "That may be an urban legend."

Anita: "Overall, from start to finish, how much did you lose on your business with Ralph Collins?"

Chief: "A little more than $40,000."

Anita: "So tell me if I have this right. You decide that the prospect of Ralph Collins paying off his debt to you is hopeless. Consequently, you decide to make the best of a bad situation by selling the account, incurring a $40,000 loss in the process. The person you sell it to—'it' being a debt were the debtor has no ability to pay—is an individual widely known for breaking the knee caps of people who can't pay. Does that about sum it up?"

Chief: "I wouldn't put it that way."

Anita swivels around to flash Blyer a quick grin, then swivels back, still grinning: "You just did. No further questions."

Blyer is not the slightest bit perturbed. In fact, the more Cap is portrayed as a feral predator, the happier Blyer is. All he wants to do on cross is nail down a couple of related points.

Blyer: "When you sold the account to Cap, did you wish any harm to come to Ralph?"

Chief: "No."

That's the answer Blyer is looking for but he needs the Chief to explain it in order to make it believable to the jury: "But he cost you $40,000. Wouldn't it be natural for some part of you to want to see him hurt?"

Chief: "No. The deal was strictly business. There was nothing personal in it."

Blyer: "Even though you lost forty grand on the guy?"

Chief: "Mr. Noche, my business is just like any other. Unprofitable as well as profitable customers are a part of every business. What counts is the net profit overall. If business people started taking revenge on their unprofitable customers, they would quickly scare off the profitable ones. No, I had no animosity toward Mr. Collins personally. I simply sold his account to the person who would give me the most for it."

Blyer is satisfied that he has established a foundation of credibility for the testimony to follow, and moves on: "Mr. Siskern, at any time either before or after the deal with Cap was consummated, did Cap ever indicate to you in any way how he planned to recover the money from Ralph?"

Chief: "No."

Blyer: "Did you ever ask him about it?"

Chief: "No.

Blyer: "Weren't you even curious about it?"

Chief: "Not really. Ralph wasn't my problem any more. I was relieved that he was out of my hair."

Blyer: "OK. So, when the time came in early January that Cap established and personally guaranteed a $10,000 line of credit with you on Ralph's behalf, what did you think was going on?"

Chief: "I assumed that Cap had figured out a way to get his money, but I had no idea how."

Blyer: "Even then you weren't curious enough to ask him?"

Chief: "At that point I was more than curious, but I also had enough brains to make absolutely sure I *didn't* know what was going on. Whatever it was, I didn't want to get within a million miles of it. I'm certainly glad now that I didn't."

Blyer has no further questions. Brick by brick, he thinks, he is building an alternate scenario for the jury. Brick by brick.

The Chief is followed by the ramming. To talk about it, Anita calls first the Framingham patrolman, then the Boston detective on the stolen car case, then Brisbane's friend Lieutenant Dunhill, then Gus, then Goon one. Blyer has no cross for any of them. He is not challenging the prosecution hypothesis that Cap not only wanted to recover his investment but to profit from it, nor is he averse to the idea that Cap would stage a little scene to impress upon Ralph the seriousness of his intentions. At the same time, Blyer wants to draw as little attention to the ramming as possible. There are three weaknesses in the defense theory of the case and one of them is the sudden and radical improvement in Ralph's disposition on the day of the ramming. Blyer will argue to the jury that the murder was an unforeseen shock to his client. The dissipation of Ralph's sullen gloom immediately following the ramming might suggest otherwise. It is a topic best glossed over.

The life insurance is the second weakness in his case, and the insurance agent from Dedham comes up next. Blyer has two options for dealing with this, and separation of Ralph from the purchase of the policy is not one of them; the agent will testify to the contrary. That leaves him two alternatives: (1) that Ralph bought it on his own, without involving Bonnie, or (2) that Cap forced Ralph to buy it but did not tell him the reason for it. From Blyer's standpoint, neither is perfect but the second option is much better. The first intrinsically lacks the ring of truth, and furthermore does not account for the fake medical report. So Blyer will acknowledge that Ralph bought the insurance unbeknownst to Bonnie, but will offer an alternative explanation for his doing so. Consequently, neither the insurance agent nor the manager of the credit union in Beverly is subjected to cross examination.

Blyer has some fun with the doctor, however, who is testifying under a grant of transactional immunity of his own. Without it, Dr. Herbert Kroll would have hidden behind the fifth amendment protection against self incrimination relative to the fraudulent medical report on Bonnie submitted to the insurance company.

Blyer: "Dr. Kroll, you've prepared fake medical reports before this one, haven't you?" Blyer doesn't know whether the answer is yes or no, but he is ready for either response; it makes no difference.

Kroll doesn't know that Blyer is bluffing and decides to tell the truth: "Yes."

Blyer is not surprised. It stands to reason that Cap would only approach him to do such a thing if he were confident that Kroll would say yes, and it was hard to see how Cap could acquire that confidence unless Kroll had done it before.

Blyer: "You've done it before at Cap's request?"

Kroll: "Yes."

Blyer: "Is there a standard fee or do the two of you negotiate each time."

Kroll: "It's only been a few times. It's the same amount."

Blyer: "What is that amount?"

Kroll: "Ten thousand."

Blyer: "Did you report that amount on your tax return?"

Kroll: "Yes."

"Yes, of course you did," agrees Blyer dryly. "Dr. Kroll, ten thousand dollars is a lot of money for an hour's work. Is the fee so high because of the risk involved."

Kroll: "I would have to agree with you on that."

Blyer: "The risk that you could lose your license?"

Kroll: "That's true."

Blyer: "It's a fact, is it not, that the District Attorney's office has filed a complaint against you with the Massachusetts Board of Medical Registration?"

Kroll: "Yes."

Blyer: "And the Board could decide to revoke your license?"

Even though Kroll is a contemptible slug, Anita is tired of seeing her witness beaten up. "Objection," she says. "Relevance."

Blyer: "It goes to the character and credibility of the witness."

Judge: "Which is irrelevant, since the substance of his testimony about the falsified medical report is not being challenged. Sustained."

Blyer: "No more questions."

With that, the curtain closes on Anita's Act II. It is the end of the third day of testimony. Anita, not entirely cognizant of the serious wounds Blyer has inflicted on her case, is not so alarmed as she should be. The metaphor she has in mind is of a boxing match. She is aware that they have traded punches and he has landed some good ones, but she feels they are running about even on points and Brisbane is yet to appear to deliver the knockout blow for her side. A better analogy, though, might be the Titanic. Blyer has opened a gouge in the steel cladding of her evidence. The impact at the time has been felt as a minor shudder, its significance underappreciated. The leak is below the surface, down by the engine room, unnoticed. The band is still playing, the passengers still dancing, the waiters still pouring the wine. Anita's case, nevertheless, is taking on water. It is only a matter of time before the extent of the damage becomes apparent.

16

Day four of the trial opens with the launch of Anita's Act III: the investigation following the crime. She starts with Kurt Walsh, Ralph's boss. He is there to set the stage by describing Ralph's unusual detachment and singular lack of participation during the Atlanta meeting. Anita will later argue to the jury that Ralph's radical departure from his normal behavior demonstrates consciousness of guilt.

The point is speculative at best, and so Blyer is not perturbed. He is distressed, however, when Anita uses Walsh to introduce Ralph's hotel bill from Atlanta. It shows no phone calls from Ralph to his home in Newton. Blyer has anticipated this moment with apprehension, and now it has arrived. The third weakness in the defense case is thereby exposed: Ralph never attempted to contact his pregnant wife at any point between the murder and the telephone call to the hotel from Brisbane. He neither tried to reach her nor heard from her all day Monday; having made no contact on Monday, he made no attempt to reach her from his room on Tuesday morning.

Anita is able to get some additional mileage out of the hotel bill by virtue of the fact that Walsh signed off on the expense reimbursement. She enters the exhibit.

Anita: "Mr. Walsh, I show you an expense reimbursement form made out by the defendant, Ralph Collins. Do you recognize this document?"

Walsh: "Yes."

Anita: "You approved this request? That is your signature for approval on the bottom?"

Walsh: "Yes."

Anita: "Could you describe the contents of this particular document?"

Walsh: "It's the standard company expense form. In this case, it's filled out by Ralph, putting in for expense reimbursement related to the Atlanta meeting."

Anita: "Would you describe to the jury the various categories of expenses that are being reimbursed?"

Walsh studies the form: "Well, there's the air fare, the taxis, the hotel bill, airport parking ..."

Anita: "Let's focus on the hotel bill. A copy is stapled to the back of the form?"

Walsh: "Yes."

Anita: "What different types of items do you see listed on it?

Walsh: "OK. There's the room rate. Hotel tax. Sales tax. Minibar ..."

Anita: "Stop there, please. Does your company reimburse for items obtained from the minibar?"

Walsh: "If they're food or soft drinks; not for alcohol."

Anita: "People are expected to abstain from alcohol?"

Walsh: "No, it's not that. It's just that alcohol in the room is a personal relaxation, not a business expense, so the company won't pay for it. That's very different from taking a customer out for a drink."

Anita: "But minibar charges would still appear on the bill, even if he is not reimbursed for them?"

Walsh: "Yes."

Anita: "Are there any such charges on Ralph's bill?"

Walsh: "Yes."

Anita: "Please enumerate them."

Walsh: "There are a bunch on the third night. Five alcoholic beverages from the minibar."

Anita: "The third night would be Monday night?"

Walsh: "Yes"

Anita: "Five alcoholic beverages in his room in one night. How many phone calls all that day"?

Walsh: "None."

Anita: "You reimburse for phone calls, do you not?"

Walsh: "Yes, sure."

Anita: "So if he made any, you would expect them to be on there, so he could get reimbursed. Is that correct?"

Blyer: "Objection. Calls for a conclusion of the witness."

Anita: "I asked what *Mr. Walsh* would expect."

Judge: "Overruled." Blyer knows. He just wants to break Anita's rhythm.

Anita: "If he made phone calls, you would expect them to be on there?"

Walsh: "Yes."

Anita deftly brings it home: "Mr. Walsh, we subpoenaed Ralph's previous expense reports from your accounting department. Would it surprise you to know that on previous business trips during the time he was dating Bonnie or married to her, he called her every single day?"

Walsh: "That's not a surprise."

Anita: "Nothing further."

Walsh is an effective witness but Blyer, on cross, is able attenuate the sting by positing an alternate interpretation. "Mr. Walsh, when you noticed how Ralph was unusually quiet and withdrawn during the meeting, did you ask him about it?"

Kurt: "Yes."

Blyer: "What did he tell you?"

Kurt: "That he had a bad headache."

Blyer: "The whole time?"

Kurt: "He said it must be a migraine."

Blyer: "Did you have any reason to doubt it?"

Kurt: "No."

Blyer: "So you believed he had a headache?'

Kurt: "Yes."

Blyer: "Do you still believe now he had a headache?"

Kurt: "I don't know."

Blyer: "So as far as you're concerned, he could have."

Kurt: "Yes."

Blyer: "Thank you. Nothing further."

Undeterred, Anita continues to bear down on consciousness of guilt by calling Ralph's father to the stand. Both parents are in Boston for the trial and Maureen has been present in the spectator section throughout, while Stuart has been sitting in the hallway awaiting his appearance as a witness. Stuart has only one bit of information to impart but Anita thinks it is significant: after Ralph learned on a Tuesday morning that their daughter-in-law and unborn grandchild had been murdered, he didn't call to tell them about it until Thursday night. Anita is hoping the jury will conclude that the 56 hour delay was a result of their son's guilt over his involvement in her slaying.

Blyer hasn't anticipated Stuart's appearance, having assumed that his inclusion on the State's witness list was a formality. Nevertheless, his intense preparation in getting to know everything there is to know about Ralph and his family pays off now.

Blyer: "Mr. Collins, how often do you and your wife see your son?"

Stuart: "They spend—spent—a whole week with us every summer."

Blyer: "And in between, how often did you speak on the phone."

Stuart: "Every couple of months."

Blyer: "Who initiated the calls?"

Stuart: "Usually Maureen."

Blyer: "So you wouldn't call the relationship between your son and yourselves close, would you?"

Stuart: "We aren't estranged. It depends on how you define close."

Blyer: "Sharing confidences, for example."

Stuart: "Not really, I guess."

Blyer: "Leaning on each other for emotional support?"

Stuart: "I wouldn't say that either."

Blyer: "It's not in Ralph's personality to be open about his emotions with you, is it?"

Stuart: "I would have to say not."

Blyer: "So the fact that he delayed calling you about a personal tragedy does not necessarily indicate that he wasn't suffering from it, does it?"

Stuart: "No, you're right, he doesn't share his feelings with us very much. I don't know why."

Blyer: "Mr. Collins, Ms. Banks has called you to testify because she thinks the delay before he phoned you and your wife with the news shows that Ralph felt guilty about his participation in Bonnie's murder. Did you ever *ask* him why it took so long for him to call?"

Stuart: "Yes."

Blyer: "What did he tell you?"

Anita: "Objection. Hearsay."

Blyer: "I'm merely seeking to find out how Mr. Collins felt about the statement he heard from Ralph."

Judge: "As long as you stick to that, overruled."

Blyer: "What did he tell you?"

Stuart: "That he couldn't bear to break the news because he knew how devastated we'd be, so he just kept putting it off until he had no choice."

Blyer: "Was he right about that? How upset you'd be?"

Stuart: "Absolutely. We loved Bonnie very much. We both thought she was wonderful. More important, it was obvious to us that she was making Ralph happy. And then there was the baby. It would have been our second grandchild. Now we don't even know whether it was going to be a boy or a girl. Can you imagine? There are no words that can describe how we felt. We were devastated."

Blyer: "Then from that perspective alone, wouldn't you say that Ralph had ample reason to dread making that call?"

Stuart: "I would say so."

At that instant, it occurs to Blyer that he can go further than he had planned with this theme. As he told the judge earlier, he is prepared to do more than take shots at the prosecution. He will offer an alternative theory of the crime, which is he counting on to transport the jury deep into the territory of reasonable doubt. Now he sees an opportunity to add another brick to his affirmative defense. "Mr. Collins," he continues, "is it fair to say you know your son quite well?"

Stuart: "I believe so, yes."

Blyer: "You understand his behavior?"

Stuart: "I believe so, yes."

Blyer: "Given that understanding of your son, would you say it is consistent with his character if Ralph delayed calling you about Bonnie for the reason he did in fact feel guilty?"

At this, the focus of every individual in the courtroom snaps to stunned attention. Nobody can figure where Blyer is heading with a question like that. The judge looks to Anita to see if she will object. If she does he will sustain it. In contrast to the hypothetical posed to Gladys about what her own behavior might have been, this question asks the witness to speculate about what somebody else might have done or felt.

Anita is torn. She knows the safe, by the book course is to object. Yet she cannot imagine how a *yes* answer helps the defense. She *wants* the yes answer that she expects Stuart will produce. On that basis she lets the moment pass.

Blyer gets his 'Yes' and ends the cross-examination. He still knows exactly what he is doing.

Anita calls the next witness: me.

Early in the investigation, Brisbane had interviewed each member of the family. When he talked to me, I told him about the strange conversation I had with Ralph in the Legato's den while we were watching football after Thanksgiving dinner. I told him how it was clear to me that Ralph did not want the baby. Now, Anita has me recollect that experience for the benefit of the jury.

On cross, Blyer's knives are fully sharpened. He slices and dices me into slivers faster than one of those tableside chefs at a Japanese steakhouse chops up the veggies.

Blyer: "Did Ralph give you a reason why he didn't want the baby?"

Me: "Yes."

Blyer: "What reason?"

Me: "He said a baby would be too much work and cost too much money. It would put a crimp in their lifestyle."

Blyer: "Lifestyle. Interesting how that theme keeps cropping up. Mr. Thomason, if he didn't want the baby, did he tell you why he was going along with Bonnie having one?"

Me: "Yes. Basically, he said he was willing to *pretend* he was OK about it as a sacrifice because he loved her and wanted to make her happy."

Blyer: "'He loved her ... and wanted to make her happy.' I couldn't have said it better myself. Thank you, Mr. Thomason. No more questions."

And as quickly as that, it's over. It is a far cry from the moment of glory I had envisioned. As I get up, I look over toward Sandy in the spectator section, hoping she isn't thinking that I screwed up. I am relieved when she responds with a *what can you do?* type shrug and makes room next to her on the bench for me to sit.

And then, nearing the end of the fourth day of testimony, it is time for Detective Brisbane. In an extended *tour de force* of skillful questioning, Anita leads him through the entire process of his investigation, from the initial conversation with Gladys in her car and Ken's first reaction to the news, all the way to the review of files on the computer seized from Cap's basement. The jury hears everything: the credit card posting from the restaurant in Chelsea leading to a meeting with the Chief, the calls to financial institutions across Massachusetts leading to the account at the little credit union in Beverly, the follow-up on the partial fingerprint in the stolen car leading to Gus, and the sting with Gus leading to the arrest of Cap. Brisbane's testimony is meticulous, detailed and lucid. His manner is authoritative and professional without a hint of hauteur. He is, in short, a superb witness.

Blyer takes it all in with equanimity. Since he will not quarrel with Brisbane's linkage of the murder to Ralph's gambling debt, little has been said that is harmful to the defense. There are just a few matters to clear up.

Blyer's first question to Brisbane: "Detective, with regard to your testimony about the financial difficulties of Ralph Collins, did you continue to monitor my client's financial activities after his arrest in preparation for your testimony at trial?"

Brisbane: "Yes."

Blyer: "In the course of this continuing investigation, what did you discover about the direction of Mr. Collins' income?"

Brisbane: "It went down."

Blyer: "Did you investigate the reason why it went down?"

Brisbane: "Yes."

Blyer: "What was the reason revealed by your investigation."

Brisbane: "Mr. Collins was put on paid leave of absence by his company."

Blyer: "When he was on paid leave, he continued to receive his base salary but was not eligible for incentive bonuses, is that right?"

Brisbane: "I believe so."

Blyer: "When he lost his incentive bonuses, he lost about twenty percent of his customary total income, isn't that right?"

Brisbane is tempted to remark that while Ralph may have lost twenty percent of his income, he lost fifty percent of his expenses when Bonnie was killed. More, if you count in the kid. But, in deference to the potential reaction of the jury, he resists the temptation. "I didn't calculate," he says.

Blyer: "To your knowledge, with respect to your continuing investigation, did Mr. Collins ever repay any of his debt to Cap, the loan shark?"

Brisbane: "Not that I know of."

Blyer: "So to your knowledge, the interest on his debt of $50,000 is still continuing to accrue at the original rate of one hundred percent per year?"

Brisbane: "Perhaps."

Blyer: "At that interest rate, the debt is more than doubled by now, is that not correct?"

Brisbane: "That interest rate is usurious. It is not legally collectable."

Blyer: "Not by legal methods, no. Isn't that precisely why Mr. Mulvaney has earned the nickname Cap?"

Brisbane: "I wouldn't know."

Blyer: "So since the murder, Mr. Collins has had his income reduced by twenty percent and his debt to Cap has more than doubled. Is there any way in which you can tell this jury that the murder of Bonnie Collins has in fact resulted in any financial benefit whatsoever to Ralph Collins?"

Brisbane: "Not that I know of."

Blyer: "Detective, who were the shooters?"

Brisbane: "We don't know."

Blyer: "In the course of investigation did you ever find anything, anything at all, that connects Ralph Collins to the shooters in any fashion, whoever they may be?"

Brisbane: "No.

Blyer: "Nothing on his computer?"

Brisbane: "No."

Blyer: "Nothing on Cap's computer?"

Brisbane: "No."

Blyer: "No numbers in his telephone records that didn't check out?"

Brisbane: "No."

Blyer: "No indications of any large unexplained financial transactions? Large payments? Large withdrawals?"

Brisbane: "No."

Blyer: "You looked for a connection with the shooters, didn't you?"

Brisbane: "Yes."

Blyer: "And despite your best efforts, found nothing."

Brisbane, annoyed: "I already said, that's correct."

Now Blyer takes a chance and starts down a path whose destination he is not sure of. It's a risk, but a calculated one. "When you examined the file's on Cap's computer after the arrest, did you find any lists or databases with the names of Cap's loan sharking clients?"

Brisbane: "Yes."

Blyer: "In your investigation, was it ascertained whether or not any of Cap's clients were employees, ex-employees or otherwise associated with the burglar alarm company protecting the Collins house?"

Brisbane: "No."

Blyer: "Please describe what attempts were made to investigate the possibility of such a connection."

The situation here is most interesting to Blyer, who delights in the oddities and twists that pop up so often in his cases. An oddity in this case is that there is in fact a connection. One of the clients on Cap's list happens to be a technician on the payroll of the alarm company who might conceivably have been able to obtain the code for Ralph's system. Cap had told Blyer about this early on. Cap had further confided to Blyer that although the technician was completely innocent of any involvement, it was precisely this connection which had provided Cap with the original kernel of the idea that led him to set the scheme in motion in the first place.

With Brisbane's answer comes the crunch. If Brisbane's answer is, 'No attempt was made,' or some variant thereof, then Blyer believes his client will be home free. If the answer is along the lines of 'We checked out the list, there was a connection, but the lead proved out to be a dead end,' then Blyer believes the outcome of the trial remains in doubt; that kind of answer throws the onus of the alarm code back on Ralph. Blyer has considered the evidence presented by the prosecution thus far, the witness list they have submitted, and Brisbane's reaction to his questions up till now, and he has decided that the potential payoff from asking the question outweighs the risk.

It is with enormous relief that Blyer hears Brisbane admit, "We didn't investigate that."

Blyer: "Why not?"

Brisbane: "There was no need. It was obvious that Ralph supplied the code to Cap and Cap passed it along to the shooters."

Blyer: "When you say obvious, what specific evidence did you have to support the chain of events that you're alleging?"

Brisbane: "It was obvious. That was sufficient."

Blyer, feigning shock: "*That's all?* No evidence? Just *'It was obvious?'*"

Brisbane: "Some things are simply obvious. This was one of them. It was obvious that the code was provided by Ralph."

Blyer: "Oh. I see. So, your theory of sound detective practice is to assume the obvious."

Brisbane: "It's not a theory. It's merely that in some situations accepting the obvious makes the most sense."

Blyer: "And this was one of those situations?"

Brisbane: "Yes."

Blyer: "All right, detective. Let's examine the facts in this case a little more closely and see how much sense it makes. Detective Brisbane, are you acquainted with the name Marvin Warnick?"

Brisbane: "I'm not sure. It sounds familiar. I seem to remember it from the list of Cap's clients."

Blyer: "That's right, Detective, it is on that list. If you had not assumed the obvious and instead had checked out the names on that list, you would have discovered something interesting about Mr. Warnick. You would have found out that he is employed by the same security company as provided the alarm for Ralph's house. Does that surprise you?"

Brisbane: "I didn't know that."

Blyer: "Did you know that Mr. Warnick owes Mr. Mulvaney—that is, Cap—approximately $17,000?"

Brisbane: "I don't remember specifically. I must have seen that, since the amounts were posted in Cap's client list."

Blyer: "Would Mr. Warnick have been able to obtain the security code to the system in the Collins house?"

Brisbane: "I don't know."

Blyer: "Well, let's review the things you do know. You know now that there was a man on Cap's client list who owed him $17,000, that this man works for the alarm company, and that he might have access to the Collins security code. In view of all that, do you still think it was sound police practice in this instance to assume the obvious?"

Brisbane: "If I had been aware of his place of employment, I would have checked him out. The client list did not include work place information."

Blyer: "Detective Brisbane, the question is: why didn't you check out all the names on Cap's list as a matter of routine?"

Brisbane: "That would have been impossible. There were 330 names on that list."

Blyer: "You're saying it would have overtaxed the resources of your department?"

Brisbane: "Yes."

Blyer: "Days and days, weeks and weeks, months even, tracking down 330 potential suspects?"

Brisbane: "Something like that."

Blyer: "An impossible burden?"

Brisbane: "I would say so."

Blyer: "Detective, are you familiar with Chapter 93, Section 55 of the Mass. General Laws?"

Brisbane: "I don't recall it specifically."

Blyer: "It provides that if a government agency requests a report on an individual from a credit bureau, they may provide it without violating that individual's rights of privacy. Are you aware that standard credit reports include the individual's employment status?"

Brisbane: "Yes."

Blyer: "Are you familiar with Chapter 93, Section 51?"

Brisbane: "Not specifically."

Blyer: "It provides that if a credit bureau declines a request to provide a credit report, they may be required to do so by a court order. Detective, did you endeavor to obtain the credit reports of the individuals on Cap's client list, either by simple request under Section 55 or by court order under Section 51?"

Brisbane: "No."

Blyer: "Isn't it the case that had you done so, you would have received the reports within a few days, and upon looking through them for a day or two more you would have discovered that Mr. Warnick works for the alarm company?"

Brisbane: "I wouldn't speculate about that."

Blyer: "You wouldn't have passed over that information without acting on it, would you?"

Brisbane: "No."

Blyer: "So it would have been better than assuming the obvious, don't you agree?"

Brisbane: "It wouldn't have made any difference. Ralph provided the alarm code."

Blyer: "Yep. Never you mind the complete lack of evidence: By golly, that's your story and you're sticking to it. All right, let's move on to the audio tape from the wire on Gus. Ms. Banks made much of the statement by Cap which went, "This has to do with the Collins job." You have testified that the 'Collins job' Cap was referring to was the murder of Bonnie Collins. Is that correct?"

Brisbane: "Yes."

Blyer: "And you interpreted the word "job" in that remark to refer to the arrangement of a murder for hire?"

Blyer: "Yes."

Blyer: "On what basis, exactly, did you make that inference?"

Brisbane catches himself this time before saying it was obvious. Upon reflection, he is forced to admit to himself that his interpretation of Cap's remark was indeed gut instinct based on the overall pattern of the case. This, he understands full well, is exactly the point that Collins' slippery lawyer is trying to make. *Assuming the obvious* is how he phrases it. *This pisser Noche is one slick son of a bitch.*

Blyer: "... Detective?"

Brisbane: "My interpretation was based on the totality of the circumstances as I knew them after two months of intensive investigation, and guided by my fifteen years of experience as a police detective."

Blyer: "So you agree: You were assuming the obvious."

You prick, thinks Brisbane. "Nothing of the sort," he says.

Blyer: "Detective, do you recall what it was that triggered Mr. Mulvaney to blurt out his remark about the Collins job?"

Brisbane: "He recognized who Gus was."

Blyer: "Yes, that's right. And what was Mr. Mulvaney's acquaintance with Gus? That is, his one and only acquaintance with Gus?"

Brisbane: "Uh ... let me think ... it was when Gus and his friend delivered the stolen car."

Blyer: "That's right too! And just to be perfectly clear, that was the stolen car that was used to ram into Ralph's Lexus out in Framingham, isn't that right?"

Brisbane: "Yes."

Blyer: "Now ... you don't suspect Gus of being one of the shooters in the murder, do you?"

Brisbane: "No."

Blyer: "So. Could you explain to us why it isn't more logical to interpret Cap's use of the phrase "Collins job" as referring to the ramming rather than to the murder?"

Brisbane: "As you point out, there are two possibilities. It seems more logical to me that Cap was referring to the possibility that was much more significant, which was the murder."

Two possibilities! Blyer rejoices in the phrase. *That was beautifully put, Detective. Thank you very much.*

Blyer: "So, Detective, you're telling the jury that you would ignore completely the fact that the utterance happened at the very moment when Cap saw Gus, who had everything to do with the ramming and nothing—by your own statement—to do with the murder?"

Brisbane: "I am not ignoring that. I'm weighing it in the context of everything else."

Blyer: "Aahhh. I see. Then, it's a matter of judgment."

Brisbane: "Yes."

Blyer: "One last point, Detective. If one were to accept *your* interpretation of Cap's statement about the Collins job, would that—in your opinion—be strong evidence of Cap's own involvement in the murder of Bonnie Collins?"

Brisbane: "Yes."

Blyer: "Now, I'm going to read that statement again. Cap says, 'I get it now. It has to do with the Collins job.' So, Detective, exactly where in that statement is there anything, anything at all, which implicates Ralph Collins in the crime as an accomplice to Cap?"

Brisbane: "Again, it's the totality of all the evidence taken together."

Blyer: "But within that totality, there is nothing in this particular *part* of the totality that points to my client, is there?"

Brisbane: "Not exactly."

Blyer: "Not at all. All that statement does is connect Cap—Mr. Mulvaney—to the murder. Nothing in it points to Mr. Collins. Isn't that true?"

Brisbane: "Taken in isolation, yes."

Blyer: "No further questions."

Anita rises and says: "The prosecution rests, Your Honor."

Blyer is astounded. If *he* had been prosecuting this case, there is one other witness he would have called, definitely, without question. This individual was even on the prosecution's witness list. Blyer thinks that Anita's failure to call her is nothing less than a monumental blunder, and another gift.

The judge addresses Blyer: "Is the defense ready to call its first witness?"

Blyer rises now and says: "Your Honor, we do not intend to call any witnesses. We are ready to proceed directly to closing arguments."

At the far edge of his field of vision, Blyer can sense as much as see the jurors fidgeting uncomfortably. *What does this mean? No witnesses? What's going on? What do we make of that?* It is all anticipated. He will take care of it.

Judge Athenas takes it in stride. Blyer's move is uncommon but not unprecedented. The decision by defense counsel makes perfect sense to him. Typically when the defense calls witnesses, it is to provide an alibi or to refute the prosecution experts' findings with regard to physical evidence; neither of these usual functions has any application in this case. A third common contribution of defense witnesses is to deflate the prosecution theories on motive, but Blyer has already made significant headway on that score. Finally, defense witnesses are sometimes used to provide a portrait of extenuating circumstances: *yes, the defendant did it, but he had more than enough reason, blah blah blah*. That, too, is inapplicable here. So who would Blyer call, anyway, and for what purpose?

But then again, the judge wonders, what the hell *is* Blyer going to do?

Aw, screw it. It's not his problem. Through opening statements and five and a half days of testimony, the defendant has clearly been receiving competent and effective legal representation. From an appeals standpoint, that's what matters.

"Very well. It is now Thursday morning," Judge Athenas says. "I am inclined to schedule closing arguments for Monday morning. Is that satisfactory with counsel?"

"Yes, Your Honor," says Blyer.

"Yes, Your Honor," says Anita.

"I would like to limit the closing on each side to two hours, plus a one hour prosecution rebuttal. Any complaints?"

"No, Your Honor," says Anita.

"No, Your Honor," says Blyer.

The judge announces: "Court is in recess until 9:00 AM Monday morning. The jury is excused until that time. I reiterate my previous instructions: No discussion of the case with anybody, and no TV viewing or newspaper reading about it. Have a good weekend, everyone."

For Blyer and Anita, the weekend is a blur. Each is fully engaged in crafting, refining, honing and rehearsing a closing argument. More than is usual, the outcome of this trial will hinge on how well each of them does. The evidence in the case is uncontested. Everything depends on one's interpretation of the evidence, and that is what closing argument is all about. Anita must overcome the absence of a "smoking gun" and weave a smattering of fragmentary facts into a coherent tapestry that is both vivid and persuasive. Blyer must overcome the prosecution's common sense theory of the crime with an alternate scenario that he can sell as plausible, even if not totally convincing—a scenario from which Ralph is conspicuously absent.

Monday comes too quickly for everyone. Anita goes first. The sequence of closing arguments is at the discretion of the judge, and this judge adheres to conventional practice: the prosecution leads, followed by the defense, and then a prosecution rebuttal. Such a pattern favors the prosecution, which is as it should be, because the State carries the greater burden of proof beyond a reasonable doubt.

Anita lays out the evidence and uses it to paint her picture with clarity, verve and emphasis. She is convinced of Ralph's guilt beyond any doubt at all, so while her language is cool and methodical, her demeanor simmers with damped passion and suppressed anger. The effect is riveting; the attention of the jurors never flags. Blyer, too, is impressed. Momentarily forgetting her missteps during her case in chief, he entertains the thought that if he ever were to consider hiring somebody it could be her.

Anita's peroration is focused and crisp, and Blyer can't help but enjoy it in a spirit of professional admiration:

"Ladies and gentlemen, this case is tragic but not complicated. It's all about money. When you follow the logic of the money, then the logic of what happened to Bonnie Collins and the unborn baby Collins becomes abundantly apparent. The defendant, Ralph Collins, a compulsive gambler, went to a bookie because he ran out of money and exhausted his legitimate sources of credit. The bookie, in turn, dumped Ralph Collins as a client because dealing with him was a money-losing proposition—a loss of $40,000 to be precise. But a financial setback for Mr. Siskern was a financial opportunity for Mr. Mulvaney. Why is that? Because Mr. Mulvaney was in a different business. Mr. Siskern was in the business of assessing risk and evaluating probabilities. Mr. Mulvaney, on the other hand, was in the business of *creating* probabilities. He did this by intimidating the people he dealt with. He did this by instilling fear. People were terrified of him. When he wanted to send a message to Ralph, he didn't leave a voice mail. He didn't send an e-mail or a Fedex or a Western Union telegram. Instead, he dispatched a goon in a stolen car to crash into Ralph as he was driving home from work. Mr. Mulvaney's nickname is a message in itself: Cap, as in 'cross me and your kneecaps are history.' Where Mr. Siskern had clients, Cap did not. Cap had victims.

"Ralph Collins was one of his victims. Ralph was in the clutches of this vicious psychopath. Ralph was cornered, boxed in, under seige. Behind him was a wall of debt, in front of him a snarling Rottweiler of a criminal. Ralph was in a trap, and the trap was closing in on him, inexorably squeezing him tighter and tighter.

"And then, amazingly, Ralph was presented with a way out. All at once, the door of his dark dungeon of hopelessness flew open, and the gloom of despair was banished by the warm, bright rays of a possible route to salvation. *There's a way out!* And that miraculous way out was a helping hand extended by none other than Cap himself!

"Everything would be solved. No more debt. No more Rottweiler. Rescue was in the offing, and barely in the nick of time. There was just one catch, however. The plan involved killing Bonnie. The baby, too. Oh … wait a minute. That second part—about the baby?—that wasn't really a catch. Ralph never wanted the baby anyway. But the part about murdering his wife? That, no doubt, was something Ralph may have found a tad disconcerting.

"We've never maintained that Ralph actually *wanted* to have Bonnie killed, just that he played his role in her murder knowingly and deliberately. So, now, you may be wondering what could Cap possibly have said to Ralph in order to make the killing of Bonnie palatable. We don't know exactly the words he used, because neither Ralph nor Cap is talking. But we have a pretty good idea of the gist of it; we can figure it out from the circumstances. For one thing, first off, he probably would have told Ralph, 'We'll make it easy. You don't have to get your hands dirty. We'll do everything. You don't do anything. In fact, it's better if you're not anywhere around. An out of town business trip is good. Any meetings coming up? February, you say? Atlanta? Perfect.' That is, Cap would have shielded Ralph from what criminals call 'wet work': the shedding of blood. Ralph wouldn't have to go anywhere near it. Cap would make that clear.

"Then Cap would have said to Ralph, 'Listen, pal. I know you're fond of Bonnie and she's sexy and beautiful and all that, but she's no good for you. Admit it. Even if you somehow get the money some other way, you'll just be back in the same predicament later on. No matter how much money you make, Bonnie will spend more. That's never going to change. Bonnie will always have you in the quicksand of deficit spending. If you don't take my offer, you will always be in the position of more money going out than coming in. Forever. I'm handing you a rope, Ralph. It's not a noose, it's your lifeline. I'm your lifeline out of perpetual insolvency.'

"Here's something else Cap would have said to Ralph: 'Think about this, Ralph. If you do what I say, not only do you get me off your back. You also end up with a wad of cash to use any way you want. You can pay off your other bills.

You can go on a trip. You can gamble some more. Anything you please, free and clear. You can start enjoying life again. It's a hell of an opportunity, Ralph.'

"And finally, and perhaps most importantly, Cap would have said to Ralph, 'You don't have to worry about getting caught. The shooters are professionals. They are not going to boast about it to their friends. They are not going to blab about it to some strangers in a bar. They certainly won't tell their wives. As a result, they will never be traced. The police of course will suspect you of involvement because you're the spouse. Police always suspect the spouse. But without the shooters, the police will have no way to trace this thing back to me. And without me, they will never have anything on you. You can relax. You're safe.'

"And so, ladies and gentlemen, taking all these ratiocinations into account, it is easy to see how Ralph's conversion from victim to willing participant in Cap's plan was not merely understandable, it was virtually inevitable.

"And you know what, folks? If that's what Cap told Ralph—and we believe it was very close to that—then he almost got it right. There was just one thing Cap didn't anticipate. And that single unexpected thing, that one surprise that Cap could not foresee, was the diligence and skill of an experienced and dedicated police detective named Arthur Brisbane. Mr. Mulvaney, I am sure, never imagined that a police detective combing through stacks and stacks of financial records would happen to notice a charge for a meal in Chelsea and would happen to wonder *whatever was Ralph Collins doing in Chelsea?* He never imagined the detective following up on that thought and how it would lead to Mr. Siskern, the bookie. And he never imagined, I am sure, how that same police detective would mull over the mention of a partial fingerprint in the report on the Framingham car crash, and how that would lead to Gus, and how Gus would lead to Mr. Mulvaney himself.

"So … it stands to reason that Cap thought he wasn't going to be found without the shooters, but he was wrong. Detective Brisbane found him. Without the shooters.

"Ladies and gentlemen, it is true that the evidence in this case is circumstantial. But when you analyze all of it together it presents a picture that is both complete and damning to the defendant. And by far the most damning piece of evidence, the piece that looms far and away above all others, the piece that links Ralph Collins to the murder of his wife, is the large life insurance policy obtained by the defendant *two* months before her death. A life insurance policy obtained with a fraudulent medical exam so she wouldn't know about it. A life insurance policy paid for out of a hidden bank account. A life insurance policy with a death benefit large enough to pay off Cap and—I repeat, *and*—set Ralph Collins up for the good life all over again. Try as they might, there is no way the defense can get around the awful fact of that life insurance policy. Ralph Collins obtained it and Ralph Collins paid the premiums. That proves conclusively that he was part of the murder plot. The defense can't get around it, and ladies and gentlemen, I trust that neither will you.

"Thank you."

Blyer rises as soon as Anita is seated. His aim is to blunt the effectiveness of her summation by minimizing the time the jury has to absorb it. More than that, he is impatient to begin. He is eager to take advantage of Anita's last and most serious mistake: her failure to call the State's expert witness on the psychology of compulsive behavior.

It is evident to Blyer from Anita's closing statement that this omission was deliberate. She had made a strategic decision to portray Ralph's conduct as a rational response to his objective circumstances, his actions stemming naturally but culpably from an amalgam of financial desperation and physical fear. Blyer is guessing that Anita's choice was based on her estimation that this rational, common sense explanation would be more readily embraced by a jury than some psychological mumbo jumbo about the pathology of compulsive disorders, which they might easily reject as academic flim flam.

Anita's error, Blyer is certain, is in her failure to recognize that Ralph's behavior was not in fact rational, and therefore is not really subject to logical explanation. Quite the contrary. It was the irresistible grip of his compulsive syndrome, his gambling addiction, that determined his illogical course. Either of Ralph's other options—going to his own parents or to Bonnie's—would have secured for him the funds necessary to pay off Cap, and therefore would have solved his immediate problem. But neither of those options would have paved the way for him to satisfy his compulsion to return to gambling. Only the large life insurance payoff would provide the additional funds to make that possible. Without the gambling addiction to drive Ralph's decision-making, the murder of Bonnie would never have been on the table. By obscuring this crucial aspect of the case, by deliberately underplaying the compulsive pathology that drove Ralph over the edge, Anita has deprived herself of any comprehensible narrative to explain Ralph's behavior other than the logic of the money. And when he demolishes that logic, she—and the jury—will be left with nothing but reasonable doubt and his own alternative version of the crime.

Blyer bounds to the space in front of the jury box. "Ladies and gentlemen of the jury, this is the moment I've been waiting for: it is my chance to explain to you why you should—why you *must*—find Ralph Collins not guilty of the crime of murder. But first, let me address a question which, I suppose, must be uppermost in your minds: why did the defense not call any witnesses? It's a good question. The answer is simple. There was nothing more that additional witnesses could add to your knowledge about the case. All possible evidence was already in, put before you by the very able and eloquent Ms. Banks.

"That's all well and good, you may be thinking, but what about the defendant himself? Why didn't he get up there on the stand, take the oath, look us in the eye, and say, 'I am innocent. I had nothing to do with this.' The answer to *that* question is that I advised him not to. So if you have to blame somebody, blame me. But it was sound advice. Why? Because Ralph Collins did not have any evidence to offer. All he could do was get up there and deny his guilt and tell you he didn't do it. That is testimony, but not evidence. Meanwhile, there is simply too much that can go wrong when an innocent defendant testifies. For one thing, a prosecutor could trip him up with sneaky questions. For another, his personality might rub some jurors the wrong way. Unfair? Yes, but it happens. The biggest reason, though, is that a defendant may say something he doesn't mean, or say it in a way that invites misinterpretation.

"That idea, I understand, is counterintuitive. If he's telling the truth, what's the problem? The best way I can explain that is to ask you to think about a time when you said something that made you embarrassed. Everyone has had an experience like that at least once. It's human nature. You blurt out something you don't mean; you wish you could take it back but you can't. The other person is offended and you're embarrassed. Or perhaps you say something in an attempt at humor, and as soon as it comes out of your mouth you regret it because you realize it wasn't funny, it was offensive. And the last thing you intended was to be offensive. So you're embarrassed. Well, that kind of thing can happen to defendants too. The difference is, if it happens to you, you have the opportunity to apologize and smooth things over. If it happens to a criminal defendant, it can shut the prison door behind him for the rest of his life. So a lawyer makes a judgment: is the risk of such an embarrassing mistake worth value of the evidence that can be provided by the defendant. Ralph Collins had no evidence at all to contribute, nor did he have any prior knowledge of the murder. Therefore, the decision this time, for me, was a no-brainer: keep him off the stand.

"OK, now, let's move on to the evidence we do have. Ms. Banks presented to you everything there is, and there is a fair amount of it. And I am not going to quarrel with it. Facts are facts. But—and it's a very big but—the way in which the prosecution *interprets* the evidence is pure malarkey. It's a fantasy. It makes no sense at all.

"For example, let's start with … oh, say … the fact that Ralph Collins didn't want a baby. All right. We stipulate that as a fact. Ralph Collins didn't want a baby. So what? It's a fact of life that children are born all the time in situations where the father doesn't really want a baby. Is that a shocking revelation? Of course not. But in this particular case, Ms. Banks wants you to impute to this fact a singular significance. She wants you to imagine that Ralph's indifference to having a child removed a barrier to the murder of his wife that would otherwise have prevented it. Ms. Banks is trying to impute some sinister significance to it. That notion is pure bunk. It is nothing but smoke and mirrors, a ploy to get you to see something that isn't there. It's bunk because Bonnie Collins wasn't killed because of the baby, she wasn't killed in spite of the baby, she would have been killed anyway if there had been no baby. The baby had nothing whatsoever to do with it. Nothing. Zero. Nada. Zippo. Zilch. Squat. In fact, if the baby had any significance at all in this case, it was exactly what the State's own witness told you. Remember Barry Thomason, Bonnie's brother-in-law? Remember when I asked him what Ralph had said about the baby? And remember what his answer was: Ralph went along with Bonnie's wish for a baby because, quote, *'he loved her and he wanted to make her happy.'* Unquote. Not my witness, remember; Ms. Banks' witness. 'He loved her and he wanted to make her happy.' And remember too, Ralph said this to Mr. Thomason at the Thanksgiving dinner before anything in this case began to unfold. It was before Ralph met ever met Cap. It was even before the fateful meeting in Chelsea when Mr. Siskern told Ralph that he was selling Ralph's account to a loan shark. So there is no reason for you to see any hidden agenda in Ralph's remark. His brother-in-law asked him why, and Ralph told him why. There is nothing more to it."

Blyer continues in this vein for more than an hour, reshaping the jury's perception of the evidence by reminding them of the alternate interpretations he has brought out during testimony. He reminds them that the showboating excess in Ralph's lifestyle that Gladys found so offensive was of great appeal to Bonnie, so much so that she wheedled her parents into funding a $37,000 wedding. Blyer returns to the lack of a phone call from Atlanta, knowing that if even one of the jurors has ever suffered a migraine, that excuse will resonate. He goes back to Brisbane's 'assuming the obvious' and heaps ridicule on the detective's failure to identify Marvin Warnick as a possible member of the conspiracy. He dwells on the testimony of Stuart Collins, who said that both he and Maureen saw how happy Bonnie was making their son. He highlights Brisbane's confirmation of Ralph's loss of income and mounting debt, which followed the murder as an inevitable and predictable consequence of it. And along the way, Blyer proceeds to attack the absence of any physical evidence in the case, as well as any evidence at all tying Ralph to either the shooters or the shooting itself.

Finally, having chopped down most of the sturdiest the trees in Anita's evidentiary forest, Blyer begins using the same testimony to delineate an alternate perspective on the landscape of evidence, one which is radically different from the prosecution's.

"Ladies and gentlemen, what does it all mean? Here is what it means: The reason that the evidence before you has so many contradictory interpretations is that the prosecution's underlying theory of the crime, the fundamental story they want you to believe beyond a reasonable doubt, makes no sense whatsoever.

"Let's start right with the heart of the matter: money. The *logic* of the money, as they phrase it. So what is the logic of the money? It is the *opposite* of what Ms. Banks said it is. The logic of the money is not for Ralph to get it from the insurance; rather, it is to get it from his own family. Let's go back to the testimony of Gladys Legato, the State's own witness. When I asked her if she and her husband would have given Ralph the money if he had told them the truth, what did she say? She said, 'Of course.' Stuart Collins, too—Ralph's dad. The senior Mr. Collins told you he would have just made it an advance on Ralph's inheritance. 'Certainly,' he said. So right there we have the true logic of the money. The logic was for Ralph to simply ask for it, from one side of the family or the other.

"Whoa, not so fast, you might be thinking. Mr. Noche, you might be thinking, what if it was too humiliating for Ralph to confess his weaknesses—his gambling addiction and his poor money management, that is—to his family? What if he knew he could get the money from relatives but his pride wouldn't let him? What if his pride got in the way and he couldn't bring himself to do the logical thing?

"That's a very good question but that theory isn't logical either. It isn't logical because everyone, Ralph included, knows what happens in the aftermath of a domestic murder. Everyone knows the investigation focuses immediately on the people closest to the victim. Ms. Banks suggested to you that Ralph was not afraid of such an investigation because the shooter would never be found. Her point, even if it were valid, would still be irrelevant. What is relevant is the inevitability, the absolute certainty, that a criminal investigation not only would be triggered, but that it would expose both his gambling and his precarious financial circumstances. So Ralph also had to know that if his wife were murdered, his secrets were guaranteed—*guaranteed!*—to be revealed to the very people he wanted most to hide them from.

"The underlying logic of the money, therefore, is totally at odds with the idea that humiliation would prevent Ralph from asking his family. The actual logic was that going to his relatives meant that *one* side of the family would know his secrets, while on the other hand allowing Bonnie to be murdered meant that *both* sides would know. Far from preventing humiliation, murdering Bonnie meant doubling the humiliation. As a matter of fact, it meant increasing the humiliation infinitely, because the whole world would know about it through the press.

"There's more. Yes, it's true, Ralph might get more money from the insurance than he would get from his family. But that potential benefit was offset by incredible costs that he would have been fully aware of from the outset. Let's examine these costs that Ralph would anticipate if, as Ms. Banks alleges, Cap presented him with a murder conspiracy plan and he considered going along with it.

"First of all, he would factor in the cost of losing his beautiful, ebullient and utterly charming wife. You saw it for yourself during the testimony of Gladys Legato when Ms. Banks showed the home videos with Bonnie on them. Ms. Banks was trying to tug at your emotions, trying to get you angry at Ralph for killing such a wonderful person. I was glad she showed the videos. The message of the videos was that Bonnie was a fantastic individual. Why, then, would Ralph choose to lose her if he could get the money from the family? Witness after witness told you he loved her. *Of course* he did. So, perhaps, did *you* when you saw her in the videos. So did I. How could we not? And not only did Ralph love her, but every witness that was asked about it—*every witness*, even Gladys Legato—told you that Bonnie loved him. Consider, too, that there was never anywhere in this case the slightest hint that Ralph had ever strayed from his marriage. Why would there be? Straying from Bonnie Collins could only be a step down from what Ralph already had. After seeing her in the videos, don't you agree? So: losing Bonnie. What a horrendous cost that would be for Ralph.

"On top of that, add the cost of a criminal investigation. I'm not only talking about the cost of hiring me. There would be the dreadful cost to his career, which is now a train wreck. He had to see that coming if Bonnie were killed and he became suspect number A-1. And what about the possibility that he would be charged and convicted? Oh yeah, right, Cap could feed Ralph some soothing line of nonsense about how nothing could be proven. I'm sure he did just that, but let's get real: I don't care what Cap did or didn't say on that subject, Ralph would still have to be afraid of ending up in the penitentiary. There's no way that Ralph could avoid worrying about being charged and getting convicted.

"And what *about* the insurance? Ralph had to know—everybody knows—that insurance won't pay out to a murderer. At the very least, they won't pay until the police investigation bears fruit. And Ralph had to know that if Bonnie were murdered, the prime suspect for the police would be *himself*. So he knew, therefore, the insurance wouldn't pay until he was cleared. How long would that be? Could be a very long time, with Cap's interest charges piling up all the while at an annual rate of 100%. So within a few months of insurance delay, Ralph would easily have to figure, any surplus from insurance over money from his family would simply vanish into interest owed Cap. And that was the bright side. The dark side was the strong possibility that he would be charged, in which case insurance wouldn't pay until the trial was concluded, and if he were convicted, not at all."

"All I ask is that you, the members of the jury, put yourself in Ralph's shoes at the time he was facing the decision that Ms. Banks alleges Ralph faced. I will show you in a few minutes why he never did face that decision, but for the moment just imagine that he did. If Ralph had ever had to decide whether or not to participate in the murder of his wife, the logic of the situation would dictate an obvious answer: No. He would weigh the costs and benefits and the answer would be perfectly clear: No. On the 'yes' side there was the meager and uncertain benefit: the potential to get some extra money beyond what his family would give him. On the 'no' side were the massive, devastating and certain costs, costs known in advance, and costs that would punish him severely regardless of how the criminal investigation turned out. One of these was the cost of humiliation before both sides of his family instead of just one. Another was the cost of losing his fabulous wife. There was also the cost of junking his successful career. There was the cost of exposing his weaknesses to the world. There was the cost of enduring a criminal investigation of which he would be the prime target. And there was, no matter what Cap told him, the possibility that he might spend the rest of his life in jail. And all of those costs had to be weighed against a monetary surplus which might or might not be delivered by the insurance, and which would be wiped out by Cap's interest charges if there were any delay in the insurance payout, which under the circumstances there was guaranteed to be.

"Ladies and gentlemen, if *you* were weighing that possible benefit against those certain costs as Ralph Collins would have seen them at the time, if *you* were in the position Ms. Banks wants you to think Ralph was in, what would you have done? How would *you* have seen the logic of the money in this situation?

"And now I'm going to answer another question which I'm guessing is on your minds right about now. If I were in your place, I would be wondering, 'All right, Mr. Noche, you've told us all about what didn't happen. Now why don't you tell us what did happen?

"It's a fair question and I am not going to disappoint you. To begin, let's go back to the logic of the money and rethink it a little bit. The key question in the logic of the money is: *In whose hands was the money ultimately going to end up?* Not Ralph's hands, not most of it anyway. It was going to land in the hands of Mr. Mulvaney, the notorious Cap. It was Cap who was out the $40,000 cash plus $10,000 credit line for Ralph that he paid to Mr. Siskern. It was Cap who was bound and determined to get his money back with a profit. So number one, we have the true logic of the money. It leads not to Ralph but to Cap.

Number two: the characters of the individuals involved. Who has the character of a murderer? First, is anything wrong with Ralph's character? Let's see, if we think about it real *real hard* maybe we can come up with something. Somebody in all this trial must have said *something* bad about Ralph. Oh, I remember, it was Mrs. Legato. She didn't like it that he took Bonnie out to a fancy dancy restaurant on their first date. Horrors! I apologize if I seem to be mocking Mrs. Legato. I don't mean to do that. But I am mocking the absurd idea that taking Bonnie to a fancy restaurant indicates a character flaw. And that such a criticism comes from one of the parents who spent $37,000 on her wedding. Oh, and Ralph liked the good life. Ms. Banks seems to think that means something bad. Here's a news flash to Ms. Banks: so did Bonnie. The two of them had this in common. They were a matched pair. That's one reason why they were in love with each other: they understood what each other wanted because they wanted the same thing. Yes, and Ralph didn't want a baby. Another news flash to Ms. Banks: neither does half the male population. And like half the male population, he went along with his wife's desire to have one *because he loved her and wanted to make her happy*. Is there anything else bad about Ralph? Not that I heard from any witness. Nothing.

"In contrast to that, we have Cap. Remember why they call him Cap? It's his habit of breaking kneecaps. He is so renown in the Boston underworld for doing that, it has become his nickname. And let's recall what Ms. Banks herself said about Cap. She called him a vicious psychopath. She called him a snarling Rottweiler. In this, the prosecutor was quite right. So number two: character to commit murder. We have Ralph Collins, a man in love with his wife who took her to a fancy dinner on their first date, and we have another man, Mr. Mulvaney, who is a snarling criminal Rottweiler. Which one is more likely to commit murder?

"And number three: we have to ask, who cared about Bonnie? Who loved her and who didn't? Who was proud to be married to her? Who showed her off to his friends and colleagues? Who showered luxuries on her that he couldn't really afford? Who was willing to have that baby to make her happy? That, of course, was Ralph. Who in the picture didn't care one whit about Bonnie? Who in the picture never even met her? That would be … Cap!

"Therefore we have the logic of the money, individual character traits, and the level of relationship with Bonnie that all point to Cap, not Ralph. In those three things alone we have three excellent reasons to interpret the evidence as showing that the murder was *entirely planned and implemented by Cap alone*, with no involvement at all by Ralph. To clarify this in your minds, you need only think about the three famous elements of proof, the very same ones you read about in books and hear about on TV shows: means, motive and opportunity. With logic of the money and with the relationship to Bonnie, it is clear that motive belonged exclusively to Cap, not at all to Ralph. And with his criminal associations, Cap had the means, not Ralph. And with Marvin Warnick on his list of victims, Cap had the opportunity to get the alarm code.

"What else? Oh, yes, the insurance. Ms. Banks said you can't get around the insurance. I agree. It is indeed a key piece of evidence. Fortunately for my client, once again, it points to Cap, not Ralph. True, Ralph obtained the insurance fraudulently and paid for it secretly. And yes, he did that under instructions from Cap. But it was not—I repeat *not*—for the reason alleged by Ms. Banks.

"In the same way that the logic of the money really points to Cap by himself without Ralph, so does the logic of the insurance. In this case, though, we have no actual testimony to guide us through to a conclusion. Only two people know what Cap said to Ralph to get him to buy the insurance, Cap and Ralph. I've already explained why Ralph didn't testify. And neither side called Cap because he maintains to this day that he had no part whatsoever in the murder. Consequently, both Ms. Banks and I expected that if we put him on the stand he would do nothing but lie anyway.

"As a result, all we have to go on is logic. It is true that logic leads us to believe that Cap told Ralph to buy the insurance. After all, Cap provided Doctor Kroll who prepared the bogus medical exam. But was it logical to think that the reason he gave to Ralph as the *purpose* of buying the insurance was so that both of them could profit from the death of his wife? Absolutely not. No logic there. Why not? Because saying that to Ralph would be much too dangerous for Cap. From Cap's point of view, planning the murder jointly with Ralph would have been a major—and more to the point, unnecessary—risk, an unhinged leap in the dark that for Cap would have been entirely pointless. For example, Ralph might go to the cops, who would then be lying in wait to nab the shooters, who would then lead to Cap himself. True, for Ralph to run to the cops would expose his secrets, but remember, so would a murder.

"So think hard about what the prosecution is asking you to believe. It is literally unbelievable. They are asking you to believe that Cap took the risk of planning a murder in conspiracy with a man he had just met, a man with whom he had no bond of trust, a man who had no criminal experience, and a man for whom the inevitable costs of such a venture far outweighed the potential benefits. If you had been in Cap's shoes, would you have taken such a crazy, lunatic risk?

"And more to the same point, there was no need for Cap to take this kind of risk. Cap didn't need Ralph for the killing, just for the insurance. So all he had to do was set Ralph up to buy the insurance without telling him about the murder. How? There are a number of possibilities. Here's one I like: Cap could say to Ralph, 'If you value your kneecaps, you'll do what I tell you. One of the things you'll do is buy life insurance on Bonnie. That's *my* insurance,' Cap would go on, 'because that way she's worth more to me dead than alive. So if you want to keep her alive—and I assume you do—you'll find a way to pay me. The insurance is to motivate you to pay me because if you don't you'll find her dead and I'll get my money from you out of the death benefit.' Under this scenario, the murder of Bonnie is a background threat, the purchase of the insurance an innocent capitulation to Cap's demand, and not a conspiracy in any sense of the word. Is that not a much more logical way to look at it than to think that Cap took the crazy risk of involving Ralph in a conspiracy?

"In the end, ladies and gentlemen, here's what it all boils down to. The prosecution wants you to interpret the evidence as showing a conspiracy which from the standpoint of Ralph Collins was both unnecessary and irrational. They allege a conspiracy in which, for Ralph, the costs exceeded the benefits, which was alien to anything in his personality and history, and which in its core element was to designed to wreak physical and irremediable violence on the loving, successful relationship he shared with his gorgeous and happy wife Bonnie.

"There is, on the other hand, an alternate interpretation of the same evidence which makes perfect sense. The logical interpretation of the evidence is that Mr. Mulvaney—the infamous Cap—acted alone in the planning and direction of the murder of Bonnie Collins, involving Ralph only by duping him to purchase the life insurance under false pretenses. It is Cap, not Ralph, who all along was going to end up with the money. It is Cap, not Ralph, who is the snarling Rottweiler of a career criminal. It was Cap who had never met Bonnie and cared not a whit about her. And it was Cap alone for whom the benefits of the plan outweighed the costs. All Cap had to do was browbeat Ralph into purchasing the insurance and he would be home free. Ralph went along with that because he never imagined that Bonnie would actually be killed, and all he had on his mind was placating the snarling Rottweiler that was tormenting him ever since the ramming.

"Last but not least, even Ralph's delay in calling his parents makes more sense when you realize that he had no part in planning the murder. Remember when I asked Stuart Collins, Ralph's dad, whether Ralph might have felt guilty? And Mr. Collins said yes? Only his innocence in the murder explains why Ralph felt so guilty that he didn't call his parents for days. Think through the logic of that call. If there had been a conspiracy, Ralph would have been prepared to call his parents right away. He would have had a story on file in his mind, a scenario already made up to explain what happened. He would have had a phony act ready to roll. But because the murder was a surprise, he had no story, no act, just genuine shock and ordinary guilt. Sure he felt guilty. It was guilt not from conspiring in the murder but simply from having unwittingly put his wife in a position of danger. It was the kind of guilt felt by a parent who gives his teenager a car and the child is subsequently killed in a traffic accident. It was the kind of guilt felt by a parent who encourages a child to play a sport and then the child is crippled playing that sport. His reluctance to tell his parents was the sign of genuine remorse that his gambling debts had led to such a tragic consequence, rather than the facile prevarication of a conspirator, in which case he would have called right away. It is just another example where Ms. Banks takes a real fact—the delay in Ralph's call to his parents—and gives it an interpretation which is so loony it is as if the prosecution resides in some parallel universe where weirdness prevails.

"Therefore, ladies and gentlemen, I do not rest my argument on the thin reed of reasonable doubt. Rather, I appeal to simple logic. When you apply logic, the prosecution theory of the crime crumbles into a shambles of hopeless nonsense. Instead, I return in conclusion to the elements of proof. Even the prosecution admits that Cap, not Ralph, had the means for murder: he knew the shooters, not Ralph. The only logical interpretation of the costs and benefits revealed in the evidence is that Cap alone, not Ralph, had motive. And with Marvin Warnick on his client list and employed by the security company, Cap had opportunity as well. The only logical interpretation of the evidence is that Cap, and Cap alone, was responsible for this crime.

"Ladies and gentlemen, please follow the logic and find Ralph Collins not guilty. Thank you."

Judge Athenas calls a recess until after lunch so that Anita has a chance to prepare a rebuttal argument. She uses the time to reach a decision.

"Ladies and gentlemen," she commences when the jury returns, "Judge Athenas has granted me an hour to reiterate the reasons why you should find Ralph

Collins guilty. I have decided not to use that time. I believe that the evidence is so compelling, and its meaning so clear, that for me to repeat what I said this morning would be a waste of both my time and yours.

"So, I am going to leave you to your deliberations without further ado. I am just going to add one additional question for you to consider. Here it is. Mr. Noche made a big deal over the fact that the defendant could have gotten the money from his family. That would have been more logical, Mr. Noche said. Well, then, I ask you this: If it was all so gosh darn logical, why didn't he go ahead and do it? All we heard from Mr. Noche was what Ralph could'a, would'a, should'a done. But did Ralph Collins actually ask for the money from his family? No he did not. The question is, why not?

"When you think about that, you will see through all the desperate eyewash the defense has showered you with in this case and you will find Ralph Collins guilty as charged. Thank you."

Hell! thinks Blyer. *Pissshitfuckdamnhell!* Blyer is mad at himself. He had meant to make that connection and had simply forgotten. The explanation is simple. It was humiliating for Ralph to go to his family for money, and so he simply was putting it off until the very last minute when it was absolutely necessary. It's just that he didn't think that moment had arrived yet. In fact, Anita's question *supported* the defense position: Ralph had no idea that Bonnie was about to be killed so there was no reason for him not to put that shameful moment off for as long as possible. But, to his own shame, Blyer had neglected to make that point explicit. The jury would have to figure it out for themselves in the context of everything else. They might do that but then again they might not. If they didn't, they might convict based on misunderstanding the logic of this point and there would be no one to blame but himself. He would have failed Ralph Collins with his dumbhead omission. Worse yet, he would have failed his principal client: Cap.

Just moments ago, Blyer had been feeling wonderful. He was thinking about celebrating his excellent performance in this trial, and his prowess as a lawyer in general, by treating himself and his wife to a nice Italian dinner at Mama Maria's. Now he feels like crap. He is going to go home and make a dent in his inventory of single barrel bourbons.

By mid-afternoon, the judge has given his instructions to the jury, the jury has retired to begin its deliberations, and the courtroom is deserted. The judge is tending to other matters. Blyer has gone home alone. Ralph has gone home to Newton with his parents. The Legatos have all gone to Westborough. Anita, Brisbane and Mark Bluestein have ensconced themselves in the cocktail lounge at the nearby Royal Sonesta to unwind and decompress.

Early the next afternoon, less than 24 hours later, Blyer takes a phone call in his office. It is the bailiff, informing him that the jury has rendered a verdict. The judge will hear it in an hour and a half, giving the defendant time to make it in from Westborough. Blyer leaves immediately and takes a taxi to Thorndike Street, since he can't concentrate on anything else. He arrives with an hour to spare and passes the time shooting the breeze trading gossip with Judge Athenas' clerk of the court.

At the appointed time, all the interested parties are in place and are trying to read the faces of the jurors as they file in and take their seats. The judge addresses the foreman: "Has the jury rendered a verdict?"

"We have, your honor."

◆   ◆   ◆

It comes on eight minutes into the eleven o'clock news.

Brad Sanborn at the anchor desk:

A jury in Cambridge rendered a verdict today in the case of Ralph Collins, accused of murder for helping to arrange the contract killing of his wife Bonnie in their Newton home. The murder took place in February of last year, shocking family, friends and neighbors alike. We have a report from Honor McCorkle on how the trial turned out.

McCorkle, on tape, standing in front of the courthouse:

Brad, I'm reporting from outside the Edwin J. Sullivan Courthouse in Cambridge where a jury today proclaimed Ralph Collins not guilty of murder in the shooting of his wife. Both sides in the case agreed that Mrs. Collins was shot by professional hit men hired by a loan shark to whom Mr. Collins was in debt. Both sides agreed that the motive for the killing was the money from a life insurance policy on Mrs. Collins that would be used to settle the debt. However, the defense insisted that there was no conspiracy because Mr. Collins had no prior knowledge of the murder and played no part it its planning or implementation. The defense argued that the loan shark acted on his own in arranging the hit on Mrs. Collins without informing Mr. Collins. After deliberating for most of a day, the jury sided with the defense.

We talked to Blyer Noche, victorious counsel for the defense.

Cut to Blyer talking into a microphone held by McCorkle:

We were able to demonstrate persuasively that the prosecution theory of the crime was completely illogical. The verdict is a triumph of the American system of justice.

Cut back to McCorkle, facing the camera:

Anita Banks, Assistant District Attorney and lead prosecutor on the case, expressed her disappointment this afternoon.

Anita, speaking into McCorkle's microphone:

We believe with every fiber of our being that Ralph Collins was a full participant in the murder of his wife, but there just wasn't enough evidence to convince a jury. We knew the difficulties going in but we felt that the victim's family deserved the opportunity to see justice served. Unfortunately, the jury didn't see the evidence the way we did.

McCorkle again:

Brad, we were able to talk with one of the jurors after the trial. She helped explain their decision.

McCorkle on camera with juror:

This is Georgine Banfield, who agreed to talk to us about how the jury arrived at their verdict. Mrs. Banfield, can you tell us if there was one deciding factor that tipped the decision in favor of the defendant?

Banfield, into the microphone:

No, like, you know, it was more the combination of everything all together, you know? Like, the prosecutor had her story and the defense lawyer had his, and, like, both stories fit the evidence? And since, like, one version was as good as the other, we couldn't, you know, we couldn't say that guilt was proven beyond a reasonable doubt, even though, you know, like, we all felt bad for the victim's family.

McCorkle, facing the camera:

Thank you, Mrs. Banfield. This is Honor McCorkle for WBOS, reporting from Cambridge.

Blyer and his wife are watching the news from their bed. When McCorkle signs off, his wife turns on her side to face him with her chin cupped in her hand. "I don't know about the American system of justice," she says, "but that defense lawyer they had on there was one sexy hunk!" Blyer grins and tousles her hair. "I was thinking, how about we celebrate tomorrow night? Mama Maria's, maybe?" "Why Mr. Noche," says his wife, "I do believe you're asking me out on a date."

In the den of the house in Westborough, the Legato family—all except Jeff and Sharon who had to return to Portland—has been watching the same newscast. Sandy, Jim and I are too numbed by the verdict to react. Ken growls, "Stupid assholes stupid assholes stupid assholes *stupid assholes*." Gladys bursts into tears again.

17

"Sandykins."

"Jungle Jim!"

The words were familiar but the music wasn't the same. I doubted it ever would be.

It was the Fourth of July, nearly a year and a half since Bonnie's death. We were gathered on the Legato's backyard patio for hamburgers, hot dogs, and my own secret recipe chili. It was the second time that the family had come together since the night of the verdict. The first had been Easter dinner, a glum and downcast affair overhung by frustration over the results of the trial.

On this day, to a stranger, it might have appeared that things were back to normal. Not so. Everyone in the family was sensitive to the welter of emotions that continued to simmer beneath the surface. Each of the Legatos was still dealing with the difficult tasks of mourning in distinct and personal ways. Ken was furthest along in adjusting to his loss and reclaiming some semblance of his previous equanimity; after his moment of clarity in Anita Banks' office, even though the pain of missing Bonnie was still a scalding torment, he was at least able to make his peace with God. For Gladys and the siblings, however, issues remained stubbornly unresolved. For them, even the weather that afternoon presented a problem. It was glorious: sunny, 74 degrees, dry. It was the kind of day that irresistibly seduces you into feeling good. Jim, Jeff and Sandy weren't ready to feel good yet. Gladys, drained and exhausted, was ready to feel better but could not.

As anticipated, Ralph had returned to Kansas City after the trial. One day in June a UPS package was delivered to the Legatos. It contained some personal effects of Bonnie and a note from Ralph saying that the house had been sold. I had thought that this knowledge would provide a modicum of relief to the family, since with Ralph out of sight it might help keep him out of mind. I had been optimistic that his departure could facilitate the arrival of some degree of closure, or if not closure then at least the modest satisfaction of a welcome good riddance. In this I was naive. Quite to the contrary, the news provided instead a new batch of fuel that kept the family's resentment at the boiling point: *He gets to restart his life anew, warmed by the welcoming bosom of his family and the familiar environs of his birthplace. What do we get?*

It was the family's stated intention to use this backyard picnic as a turning point, as the beginning of its collective journey back to a new but tolerable state of normality, as a lever to help get itself unstuck. I was hopeful but skeptical about that. With the bitter aftertaste of a disappointing trial both renewing and compounding the family's abiding misery, I foresaw another afternoon of grim despondency. Therefore, I resolved to make the best of it by trying to reconnect with Jeff. The attempt, I confess, was opportunistic. Ken, Gladys, and Jim—and Sandy to a lesser extent—were all inflamed with a combination of contempt for the prosecution and rage at the jury, a passion that I did not share. Their common outlook was fostering even greater unity and bonding among them than before. As a result, I was feeling a bit marginalized. It was natural, perhaps, that under these circumstances I would gravitate to the only family insider who was equally marginalized. Since the murder, Jeff's characteristic demeanor of doleful brooding had morphed into a sullen moodiness that had even his own family walking on eggs. He was not part of the bonding.

This is not to imply that I had a plan. Having no idea how to be helpful and having been rebuffed several times by his terse unwillingness to respond to my conversational overtures, I had previously given up on attempts to communicate with Jeff. Even our game of jazz one-upmanship had been suspended. Now I thought, what the hell, I'll try again, what have I got to lose?

Jeff was sitting next to Sharon at the picnic table on the back yard lawn. They weren't talking; they were just watching the girls play tetherball. I grabbed a beer from the cooler and sat down across the table from them. "I thought I'd better check up on you guys," I said. "Never can tell what kind of mischief might be brewing with the Portland contingent."

Sharon raised her beer bottle in friendly greeting. "Have a seat. Come join the A-list of carousing revelers. We're a frolicking festival of merriment over here, a veritable Mardi Gras of high spirited exuberance."

Huh? That was unusual. Sardonic is not typical of Sharon's style.

"Hey, Jeff," I said.

He raised his beer in salute but said nothing.

"Guess where we went last Sunday," chirped Sharon. "You won't believe it."

"What won't I believe?"

"I'll let Jeff tell you himself. I'm going to help Gladys mix up the potato salad and leave you two alone."

As Sharon stood up, I turned to Jeff. "What won't I believe?"

"We went to church."

"No! You?"

Jeff shrugged with an expression of wry self-deprecation. "It's true."

"What's going on?"

"I don't know. That's the problem, Barry. I don't know shit any more."

That was unusual too. Foul language is not typical of Jeff's style. It was off key, like hearing Laura Bush tell a joke that was smutty and profane.

"I'm a good listener," I said. Then I sat quietly sipping my beer while he decided.

For whatever reason he chose to open up. "I might have prevented it."

OK! I thought. He's going to talk to me. I realized that perhaps it was because we *weren't* all that close. It didn't matter much to him what I thought. There was small risk for him; little was at stake. But that was fine. I welcomed his trust at whatever level it was being proffered.

"Prevented Bonnie?" I asked.

"Yeah."

"How?"

"She wanted to come up and see me that weekend. She wanted to talk to me about something, she didn't say what. She called earlier in the week, said that Ralph was going to Atlanta on Saturday, she wanted to discuss some things, could she come up that weekend ..."

"... And?" I prompted.

"... And ... and I told her I'd rather she come up some other time, because I had a huge project at work that was coming due. I needed to work night and day through the weekend. That was true. I told her my project would be done by the middle of the next week, it was due on Tuesday, and I would take Thursday or Friday off, whichever she wanted, and drive down to see her. And she said she understood and that would be fine."

I wanted to make sure I interpreted correctly what Jeff was saying. "You think that if you had let her come up that weekend, things would have turned out differently?"

"I don't know. I don't *know!* But maybe. No, not maybe. Yes."

"Jeff," I said mildly. I had to concentrate on speaking gently, on sounding empathic. The truth was, what I felt like was throttling him over the stupidity of what he was saying. Calm down, I had to remind myself, remember he's been traumatized. "Jeff. She was killed in the early hours of Monday morning."

"I know."

"So ... Even if she had come up to see you, she would have been back home by then. She would have had to be back in order to go to work on Monday."

"I know. I mean, I know what you're saying. But that's not what I'm talking about. I'm saying, maybe if we had talked we could have figured out she was in danger. Then we could have taken steps to keep her safe. She could have stayed with Mom and Dad instead of going home to an empty house."

I could hardly believe whom I was hearing this from. If Jeff had heard the same profession of baseless, groundless, unmerited guilt from anybody else, it would have unleashed a gusher of derision. "Wait a minute," I pointed out. "You don't know what she wanted to talk to you about. Maybe it wasn't about Ralph. Maybe it was about the baby. Didn't Sharon invite her to use the two of you as a resource for any questions about the baby?"

Jeff looked startled. Perhaps he hadn't remembered that until now. He gave it some thought. "I don't think that's it. I got the feeling she wanted to talk to me—maybe both of us, Sharon too, I guess—without Ralph being there. He was going to be in Atlanta, remember. If it had been about the baby, she would have wanted Ralph to be there for sure."

"But Jeff," I persisted, "It's like that saying: Hindsight is twenty-twenty. You're looking back on it now with perfect knowledge. But at the time, there was no way you could have had the information you have now. You're blaming yourself now for not knowing something you could not possibly have known then."

"Yeah, yeah. Sharon says the same thing." Shutting down the conversation, Jeff got up and left the table. I was disconsolate. I had offended him. My attempt at helping had been a botch. It had made things worse. What a screw-up I was. I was doing this all wrong. Obviously.

Discouraged, I rose from the picnic table with the intention of rejoining the rest of the family on the patio. Then I realized that Jeff was heading toward the cooler. I watched as he pulled out a bottle of beer, picked up a church key from the serving cart to flick open the top, and start back in my direction. It looked as though I was going to get a second chance. But to do what?

I sat back down but switched to the bench on the side near the hedge, facing the lawn where the girls were still playing tetherball and where the patio was within my field of vision. I sat at one end so that Jeff would have a choice: he could sit across from me to continue our talk or on the same side next to me to allow him to avoid conversation. Naturally, he chose the latter.

It occurred to me then that nobody at all was doing it right for Jeff. Whatever he needed, he wasn't getting from anyone. Not even Sharon, evidently. And whatever it was he needed, it wasn't logic. Jeff is very smart. He had to know that his guilt was illogical, so shoving his face in logic, as I had been doing, was destined to make him feel worse, not better.

"Thanks for coming back," I said as Jeff settled down. Jeff nodded. "Why not? Where else would I go? At least here I can watch the girls. *They're* enjoying themselves, anyway."

I had an idea. I remembered something. I had read about it long ago, in a magazine. Jeff didn't seem in a hurry to go anywhere, so I had some time to think it over, trying to figure out if it made any sense, trying to anticipate how he would react to it. In the end, it boiled down to the realization that I wasn't going to come up with anything better, and if I did nothing at all I was going to feel lousy about it the rest of the day and throughout the next week. It was akin to a Hail Mary pass in football: a desperation play with time running out that has little chance of success but no real downside and a big payoff if it works.

"Jeff," I said tentatively, "Have you ever thought about talking to her?"

"To Sharon?" He was still looking ahead.

"To Bonnie."

Jeff turned and rewarded me with an expression of bottomless scorn. "She's dead, if you hadn't noticed."

I barged ahead. "I'm serious. Hear me out. I'm not yanking your chain. I'm not making this up. It's a serious thing I read about."

Jeff turned his gaze back toward the girls, but did nothing to stop me.

"Look. It seems to me that you're in a terrible trap. You're carrying an awful burden of guilt. Everybody, including me, has tried to talk you out of it by showing you how unreasonable it is. But that doesn't work. It's worse than useless because you already know how unreasonable it is. The problem you have is emotional, not intellectual. When people talk to you that way, the way I did earlier, it's aggravating because in effect they're accusing you of failing to see the obvious. It's frustrating because nobody seems to understand what the real problem is. How'm I doing so far?"

"Keep going," he said.

"All right. It seems to me that if your problem is guilt, what you need is not advice but forgiveness. There's the trap. None of the well-meaning people giving you advice can give you forgiveness. Only two people can do that: yourself and Bonnie."

Still facing straight ahead, Jeff said: "That's what Jim told me. I need to forgive myself. He said it would be easier if I allowed God to help me. That's why I went to church, to see if that could work."

"Catholic church?"

"No, Unitarian Universal."

"Religion lite?"

"Yeah, well, a Catholic Mass wasn't going to work for me, so ..."

"So what happened?"

"I know this may surprise you—it surprised me—but I found it uplifting, in a way. I liked the people there. They seemed so ... I don't know ... especially sweet. I don't really know what I'm saying. I mean, Catholics are nice people too. I can't explain it. There was a feeling of warmth and acceptance. I found it refreshing somehow."

"Did God show up?" I wanted to know.

"No. In fact, they didn't talk about Him all that much. But to your point, I didn't feel His presence in the sense you're asking about. I'm not going back."

"OK," I said, "so let me wind this up. If there is no God to help you, and you're not able to forgive yourself, then that leaves only one other option: Bonnie. I know it sounds nuts to you but give me a chance. Hear me out. Here's how it works: You sit in a chair and talk to her as if she were actually there. Out loud. You tell her everything. What you were doing. How you were feeling at the time. How you feel now. How sorry you are for failing her. How much you miss her. Let it all out. And then, you let her tell you how *she* feels. I know she won't be there physically. But she is already there in your mind. Big time, she's there. The problem is, she's with you all the time, but you've been doing all the talking. Your internal conversation with her memory is a monologue, not a dialog. Now: give her a chance to express what *her* feelings are. Let her have *her* say. Jeff, listen, you need to give her the respect—the *respect*—of paying attention to what *she* thinks, of listening to what she would want to tell you in person if only she could. Why not try it? What's to lose?"

Jeff sat still and seemed to be thinking about it. I had half expected him to stand right up, call me an idiot, and stalk off. But that didn't happen. At length, he drained his beer and said, "Maybe you're on to something."

That was my cue to get up and leave him in peace. So I said, "Cool," and headed back to the patio, where the party had expanded to include neighbors from several nearby houses. This was a longstanding Legato tradition on the Fourth, suspended last year but now reinstated as part of the return to normality. There were other children in the back yard for Sally and Heather to play with, and adults gathered around the grill with other things on their minds besides Ralph and Bonnie. Of course, for the men, those other things revolved mostly around the fate of the Red Sox after the upcoming All Star break: whether they would tank as usual or repeat their spectacular triumph of 2004. But still ...

Forget Kinkade. This scene, on the surface, was Norman Rockwell at his cornball peak.

Sandy noticed my approach and abandoned the buffet set up detail to meet me half way. She was curious, naturally. "What were you two so hot and heavy about," is how she put it. I think she was less interested in the subject of our talk, although she was that as well, than she was wondering how I could have managed to engage her notoriously laconic brother in such an extended interchange. In any event, I told her, "I may have done some good, I think. Would you believe your brother went to church? How about I tell you the whole story on the way home?"

"Deal," she replied, "on one condition: you have to go in now and help my Mom by carrying out the Crock Pots." Knowing I'd be eager to make myself useful, she smiled and turned her face upwards for a kiss. It was an invitation I accepted with pleasure. The kiss lasted until we both became self-conscious; the thought of fifteen sets of eyebrows all raised at the sight of *look at those two over there* had a dampening effect on our ardor.

Sandy is always gorgeous, but that day she looked absolutely stunning in mid-thigh Khaki shorts that showed off her tanned and perfectly proportioned legs, and a white button down collared blouse with shoulders cut back to the curve of her neck, putting on display to best possible advantage those delectable shoulders of hers. Not for the first time, I dwelled on my spectacular good fortune. Only partly in jest, I hold the opinion that my marriage to Sandy is proof positive against the notion of reincarnation. There is no way possible that I could have been sufficiently virtuous enough in any previous life to earn a Karma so marvelous as to include her. And no, it's not just about her legs and shoulders, although I wouldn't pretend that doesn't count. At bottom, at its essence, it's about the way the two of us are a team. To appropriate a word that kids use so much these days, we are awesome together.

But the magic of our marriage was also the root of my conundrum about having a baby. As much as I wanted Sandy to find happiness and fulfillment, I was not sure that wisdom was on the side of heading in that particular direction to seek it. I was too aware of the burdens and pitfalls of parenthood not to be immobilized with trepidation. Beyond that, I felt that our marriage was perfect right then, and I was not keen on risking the upset of that particular applecart through the inevitable stresses that come with raising a child even under the best of circumstances. And I also needed to get past my questions about how her change of heart related to Bonnie's death and her desire to reposition herself within the Legato family constellation.

At the same time, Sandy's point of view was equally compelling. While Sandy was not unmindful of the unknowns that attached to bearing and raising a child, it was characteristic of her unquenchable gusto for life that she was eager to embrace it all. She was intent on living life to the fullest. She could not be satisfied with a glass half full out of caution; she wanted the glass topped off, even if it meant some spillage was the likely consequence. From that perspective, perhaps a baby was something she needed, and perhaps that meant it was something I needed to provide to her. *Because I love her and I want to make her happy.* Well, I do.

It had been more than a year since Sandy's surprise announcement in the car, and she hadn't been pressing the issue. Knowing that the soft sell would work better than the hard push, she hadn't let her yearning intrude on our day to day relationship. She had, however, made sure that I was aware that all the practical obstacles and objections had been cleared away. This was primarily in relation to the purchase of a home. Our condo was too small to raise a child, and we both would want a regular house with a yard for that purpose. So she had asked Ken and Gladys if they would help us out financially with the transition, and perhaps while they were at it a little bit extra to help with the loss of income while she took off from work. "Willing?" they exclaimed in unbridled delight, "It will be our pleasure! You name it!"

Sandy knew this was a radical adjustment for me to make, and there was no actual deadline closing in. Indeed, we had if anything grown closer through the challenge and adversity of the year behind us. Still, I could assume that her forbearance was not infinite, and that the statute of limitations on her patience if not her biological clock would likely be running out. A resolution was going to have come soon, and I had no idea what it should be.

The sound of the screen door banging shut reminded me about the Crock Pots. I gave Sandy a peck on the forehead and headed off for the kitchen. "I'll miss you," she called out. She's funny, too.

One of the Crock Pots contained my chili. The other was filled with Gladys' special for the day: sliced Kielbasa in a scrumptious spicy-sweet tomato sauce. Already on the serving table were the potato salad, which I don't care for, and macaroni salad, which I love; Robust Russet potato chips; homemade coleslaw (Sharon's contribution); rolls for the burgers and dogs; and condiments by the yard: lettuce, tomato, mayonnaise, onions both sliced and chopped, mushrooms, relish, ketchup, yellow and Dijon mustard, half sour and dill pickles, green olives, black olives. The cooler was stocked with a mellow Pino Grigio and old standby Sam Adams but Ken had also included a six-pack of Smutty Nose Brown Dog Ale just for me. Soft drinks were lined up next to an ice bucket: cola, lemon-lime, cream soda, and black cherry. Iced lemonade was waiting in a pitcher.

Plugging the Crock Pots into an outdoor receptacle, amazement at my good luck overtook me for the second time in five minutes. This time I was thinking about Gladys. And no, it wasn't just the cooking, although truth be told I wouldn't pretend *that* doesn't count. But there's more. True, I venerate her wonderful qualities. But there's more than that, too. Much to Sandy's gratified surprise and unbounded delight, Gladys and I had become more than extended family by virtue of marriage. We are, in fact, friends. We *like* each other.

If you insist on putting it under a microscope, if you need reasons why she should like me, I can think of several. For one, her daughter is well loved and has found an emotional safe haven in a secure and durable marriage. The comfort level between Gladys and me is not so much about reasons, though, or even mutual admiration. It is more about having a connection that is visceral, a congruence of perceptions, reactions and attitudes that is intuitive and instinctive. As a result of this innate affinity, Gladys finds it easy to talk to both Sandy and me about things that are difficult for her to discuss with Ken. These are not personal matters but rather quite the opposite: politics, economics, and current events. Gladys has a healthy interest these topics, as does Ken, but the two of them are miles apart in their points of view. Unfortunately for Gladys, Ken lays claim to the domain of political, economic and social policy and practice as properly within his exclusive birthright as a member of the tough minded, unsentimental and rigorously analytical male species; he disparages Gladys' opinions, when contrary to his, as the regrettable progeny of well-intentioned naiveté mated with a lamentable deficit of information. Naturally, under these circumstances, Gladys is loath to discuss the state of the nation with her husband. Consequently, she is parched for real conversation about the larger world beyond the confines of her personal experience. She relishes our visits as opportunities to slake her thirst for exchange of ideas and opinions with folks who appreciate her values and understand her point of view.

Then, too, Sandy and I share with her mother similar aesthetic preferences and tastes in popular culture. We tend to like the same movies, plays and concerts, and often go off together as a threesome. When the three of us do go out, it is with Ken's relieved blessing; the chances of seeing Ken in a movie theater watching "Kissing Jessica Stein" would approximate the probability of finding him kneeling in a Mosque chanting Islam prayers. Besides, our outings together leave him free to putter around his workshop without interruption. Gladys, Sandy and I also recommend books to each other, and discuss them later. We send each other magazine articles and exchange e-mails with links to interesting pages from the web.

Then, too, I credit the prodding and advocacy of Gladys for the fact that I had gradually attained a comfortable level of acceptance by Ken. His early attitude of polite but remote diffidence warmed over time to take on the characteristics of the genial and expansive host, as witness the Smuttynose beer and my assigned role as the official opener of champagne bottles. True, we will never be friends in any meaningful sense of the word. For example, although we both work downtown, it never occurs to either one of us to seek the other out for lunch. Still, my stock had risen steadily over the years in his eyes, and it was largely on the strength of Gladys' recommendation.

Due to my rapport with Gladys, Sandy and I—along with Ken—were the only people at the picnic who had already seen what Gladys was about to unveil to the rest of the family later that afternoon, after the neighbors were gone. This was her year long project, her "opus" as she called it. It was a memorial video preserving forever on DVD the life and legacy of Bonnie Legato Collins. It was called "Nova." The name had been suggested by Sandy, referring to a point of brilliance which lights up the heavens, then, all too quickly, is gone. I, too, thought the title fitting. A nova is the death of a star.

The idea for the video had grown out of Gladys' use of family mementoes as a way to recapture and retain the memories of Bonnie in the early days of mourning. It was suggested by Ken, who alone among us was aware that the technology for making a DVD was available for use on home computers. The result is a compilation of the old VHS cassettes, the even older 8mm films, still photographs, and newly recorded interviews with family and friends. Ken had replaced their home computer with a new one that had the proper features and power to handle the project, and he had patiently, tolerantly taught Gladys how to use the relevant software. Sandy and I had been enlisted as creative consultants. Gladys screened her "rough cuts" for us, and solicited our comments as to sequence, pacing and visual style. We also worked with her in choosing background music. The process had consumed most of Gladys' time when she was not working at the store, and it was, in a quite literal sense, a labor of love. Now it was ready for its premiere showing.

Before the time came for that, however, there was a feast to consume and a walk to take with Jim. When we were ready to go, I retrieved the cigars from the car and we set off on our usual route around the neighborhood.

I hadn't seen Jim since Easter. My impression was that he wasn't feeling any better now than he had then, which was lousy. So, for the second time that day, I said, "I'm a good listener." Hey, it worked with Jeff.

"I know," he answered. We walked some more. We took some puffs on our cigars. Eventually he said, "If I talk to you, can you keep it from the rest of the family? That means Sandy, too."

"That's a promise," I told him.

"I'm considering leaving the priesthood."

I can't say I was shocked. In thinking earlier about why Jim continued to be depressed almost a year and a half after Bonnie's death, that possibility had been foremost in mind. I recalled his homily at the funeral Mass, when I wondered if he was questioning his faith. It had also occurred to me that while Jim was accustomed to dealing with tragedies, they were not his own. They belonged to his parishioners; his experience of calamity was vicarious through them. The enormity of contending with the murder of his sister was not at all like anything his professional life had prepared him to confront.

Jim was waiting to see how I would react. I saw no point in feigning surprise. I said, "Considering it means you haven't decided yet?"

"It's a very hard decision," he replied.

Unwisely making a mockery of my claim to be a good listener, I came back with a question: "Is it the decision that's hard, figuring out what you want to do? Or do you know what you want to do but find it hard to go ahead and do it?" What I had in mind was the difficulty in knowing how to strike a justifiable balance where there is a conflict between having what you desire and the adverse consequences that having it would impose on the people you care about. In other words, I was referring to one of the core, bedrock issues in anybody's life: the struggle in weighing what you owe to others against what you owe to yourself.

Of course my question came out not as philosophical but as impudent, and Jim reacted accordingly. "So tell me, Barry," he said, "remind me when the last time was that you made a decision that was as difficult as this one?"

I was chastened. "I'm sorry. If I sounded like I was minimizing it, I apologize."

As we continued walking, there was silence and I thought I had lost him, that our discussion would retreat to safer but less personal territory. We walked silently for almost half a mile, but then to my extreme relief he was ready to continue. "It's not so simple as you imagine. I know how I feel. I know what I want to do. But that is right now, in my grief. What if what I want now is not right for me in the long run. It's only sixteen months. What if I feel differently a week from now, or a month or a year?"

"If you knew it wouldn't change, you'd leave?"

"Well, I think I would. Here's the thing: the work I used to love most—counseling and comforting my parishioners, God's work—is now the work I dread the most. How can I tell people to trust in the Lord when I don't trust in the Lord myself any more? How can I tell them God is there for them when I don't feel him here for me?"

I had to admit, "I don't know, Jim."

"Exactly. And there's more to it still. It's not just doubts about God. I am wrestling with doubts about myself now too. I have to tell you, it's a weird kind of Catch-22: If I decide to leave the Priesthood, that tells me that my decision to enter the Priesthood was a poor one. But if I made a poor decision like that before, then how do I know that my decision at this point to leave is a good one? My confidence is shaken, and I don't know how to deal with that either."

I didn't know the answer any better than he did, so I changed the subject. "Apart from the situation you'd be leaving, have you thought about where you'd be going? You know what I'm trying to say? I mean, do you have a vision for your future outside the Church?"

"A vision? No. But:" Jim declared with a grin, "I have a job offer!".

"No. *Really?*"

Jim affected his sing-song Irish brogue. "Now Baddy An-d-drew Thomason, me lad, why should ye be sur-purized that somebody other than the Archbishop would want to hire such a fine fellow as me-self?"

I was delighted that he was teasing me again. "Nooooo," I said, "You know that's not what I meant. It's that … well, I didn't think things were that far along. Are you seriously considering taking it?"

"Considering, yes. I wouldn't say seriously. Things are not that far along. This job offer came out of the blue, I didn't seek it out. It's too soon for me. I'm still sorting out the big picture. It's more or less what you were talking about before: clarifying the vision thing."

"What kind of job is it?"

"No, I'd rather put this aside for now. Not that I'm embarrassed or anything; if I take the job, then clearly everyone will know all about it. But in deciding the larger issue, I want to focus on precisely that. I don't want the specifics of a particular job offer to influence the fundamental question of whether I'm staying in the Church."

It seemed to me quite relevant to the big picture and I told him so: "I think it's a huge deal. It shows that you have prospects in the job market. If you leave the church you'll be able to support yourself. That's no small matter."

"No," he said, "You have a point there."

"How long does this offer last? Do you have some time?"

"Some. I think I have a month or two before they move on to hire someone else."

"That sounds patient on their part but still a short time frame for you."

"Yes," Jim agreed. "That's what's dangerous about having a tempting job offer. It puts my decision on a schedule imposed by somebody else."

Although I was learning a lot, the discussion didn't seem to be going anywhere that was useful to Jim and I was starting to feel uneasy about that. It turned into another apology: "I don't think I'm being very helpful to you this afternoon."

Jim was quick to demur. "Untrue. Just talking to you is helpful. Don't forget, I've been thinking about this for a year. It's not surprising that you don't come up with startling and original insights in twenty minutes. You can't offer easy answers because there are none. But you're making a contribution simply by being here for me to use as a sounding board. Who else do I have? Not my family, I'm not ready to share this with them yet. I can't talk to other priests because I don't want word to get around the Archdiocese until I'm quite certain about it. You're it. You and Howard."

That lifted my spirits a bit but I was still feeling inadequate. We walked some more in silence as I tried to think of where to take the conversation next. Jim solved that problem for me by speaking up again. "The truth is, you've helped me quite a bit by taking my problem seriously. A lot of people would have said something like *how could you throw away all those years of training and experience* or *how could you abandon your vocation*. Or *your parishioners need you*. Blah blah blah, as if those things hadn't occurred to me. You were better. At least you tried to grapple with the problem from my frame of reference. I'm grateful for that."

Jim's comment about his frame of reference sent my thinking in a new direction. "There's more to this than Bonnie, isn't there?"

Jim agreed without hesitation: "Yes."

"The pedophile scandals?"

"Not directly."

"Then ... indirectly?"

"I guess you could say that. It's true that I've become disenchanted. The child abuse is part of it, sure, the cover-up and all. But now there's the whole business of closing down churches wholesale."

"They're closing yours?"

"No, it's not that. It's that some are being closed for the wrong reasons. They say it's about the viability of individual parishes, about economic self-sufficiency, sacramental index, that sort of thing, but I think in some cases they're closing parishes based on the real estate value of the church property."

I was puzzled. "Not worth enough?"

"Worth too much to keep."

Now I got it. "They're looking for cash to pay off the abuse settlements?" I ventured.

"Yes. And I understand that too. But the problem is that they are being disingenuous with the lay community. They tell people it's about parish support, and then they close churches with great parish support. So the people don't understand and they get angry and they have sit-ins. As Bonnie used to say, *well duhhh*. I realize the Archdiocese needs cash, but in their panic to maximize the liquidity of their financial assets they are squandering an asset infinitely more precious: the moral authority of the Church as an institution. It's painful for me to see this. I feel like every day I'm carrying around on my back a hundred pound sack of disillusionment."

That is when I realized that Jim had been using the pronoun "they," not "we." In my book, that was a strong signal that deep down, in spirit, he had already left the Church, that emotionally he was already gone. He just wasn't aware of it yet.

There was more. "Ultimately," he went on, "it's not about property values, or pedophiles either. It's still about me and God. I feel that God has put me to a test and so far I have failed it. because I haven't forgiven Ralph, not in any way, not in any degree. And what that means on some level is that I haven't forgiven God. God wants me to forgive Ralph, and if I loved God enough I would be able to do what he wants. I've tried but I can't. So what does that signify? Does it signify that my leaving the church is part of God's plan? That God is guiding me to the right decision, setting me up to fail because His plan for me is outside of the Church? Does that mean I can do anything I choose, because anything I choose, no matter what it is, is God's plan? Where's the sense in that? And where's the free will? It all keeps going around in circles and I can't untangle it. I only know one thing. If I loved God enough, I would be able to forgive Ralph. Since I can't forgive Ralph, that means I don't love God enough. Therefore, I shouldn't be a priest. But then again, that is now. Later, who knows? I tell you, the complexity of it makes my head explode."

I was reminded of something Jim had said during our walk the Thanksgiving before last. *(Was that all? Less than two years ago? It seems like an eternity.)* "Is this along the lines of what you were telling me once about how the peace of God's love and grace is void where prohibited? So, like ... God is there for you but you're not there for him?"

Jim came to a stop and turned in my direction. After a hesitation, he said, "I think that sums it up pretty well. I *want* to be there for God, but I'm not"

I received his compliment with mixed emotions. Naturally, I was pleased that I had been able to grasp the nature of his problem, and that he recognized the same. By the same token, however, that problem was one for which I could not see any way to be helpful. What could I say that could help Jim forgive Ralph? *I* had not forgiven Ralph, that's for sure.

By this time we weren't far from the Legato's driveway. Jim was absorbed in his own thoughts. I was trying to imagine what it must be like to be thrown into a crisis of faith like the one that had been pummeling him for a year and a half. As we turned on to the property, Jim said, "Thanks, Barry." That made me feel better, even though it wasn't clear to me how I had earned it. That being the case, my response was insipid, nothing more than a pathetic platitude: "If there's ever anything I can do to help ..." My inadequacy in the face of his need made me feel like crap all over again.

Abruptly we were swept up in a throng of neighbors pouring out from behind the house. They were on their way home. We exchanged the typical *great to see you again's* and *hope you have a good summer's* and then they were gone. As we rounded the side of the house to the back, the patio came into view. The family, we could see, was already in clean up mode. The time was approaching to see Gladys' opus.

Less than half an hour later, we had assembled in the den. Sharon called the girls in from the back yard, making sure they were included in the experience. Ken gave a very sweet introductory speech, lauding Gladys' effort on the project and glossing over the contributions of Sandy and me. I didn't take that as an affront. Rather, I attributed it to a motive of kindness, of not wanting Jim, Jeff and Sharon to feel left out of something the two of us had been such a part of.

The DVD was splendid. A loving portrait of Bonnie's life, painted in two hours worth of cherished memories, it brought laughter, tears, repeated exclamations of *oh my I had forgotten that* and many requests for Ken to *stop, I'd like to see that part again.*

When it was over, the room was quiet. We were all groping to find a way to express adequately our appreciation of what Gladys had accomplished. Sandy found the way. She stood, said "Hear hear!," and started clapping. As one, the rest of us rose and joined in a standing ovation. When it died out, Gladys thanked us briefly, as befits her unassuming ways, and then floated a proposal: "Why don't we go in the kitchen and polish off what's left of the banana cream pie?" The motion was adopted by unanimous acclamation.

When the pie plates were empty and the supply of Edy's Ice Cream exhausted, it was time to go. That's when something else happened that was nice. Jeff, who had never before been the initiator of a conversation between us, came over to me and said, "The best three ballads in the jazz songbook."

The game was back on! I scrambled for answers and came up with good ones: "Number three: *My Funny Valentine*; number two: *Send in the Clowns*; and number one, no question, hands down: *'Round Midnight*.

He nodded his head in acknowledgement. "Not bad, not bad at all. But how can you leave out *Bess You Is My Woman Now* or *Someone to Watch Over Me?*"

"You specified three," I countered. Which one of my three would you remove to put in *Bess?*"

"Good point," he allowed. "Why don't we expand it to five and toss in *September Song* for good measure."

My dad likes *September Song*. He says he identifies with it. "Deal," I said, and we shook hands ceremonially.

As Sandy and I took off in the car, she was bursting with curiosity. I told her all about Jeff's expedition to a church, his guilt over the visit from Bonnie that didn't happen, and my suggestion that he allow Bonnie herself to grant him absolution. Sandy then made my day complete. "That's interesting," she said, "because while you were out on your walk with Jim, Jeff disappeared into the house for quite a while. Maybe he was upstairs doing what you suggested."

"Could be," I told her, and related how Jeff had resumed our jazz challenge just before we left.

"Now tell me about Jim," Sandy persisted.

"I can't," I protested. "Jim opened up to me today, but only on condition that I make a strict promise not to talk about it to anybody else. That included you, specifically."

I was expecting Sandy to employ her considerable wiles to try to drag the secret out of me, but I was wrong. She merely said, "You gonna' keep your promise?"

"I am," I insisted. "I really have to."

At that, she patted my knee and said, "You're a good man, Charlie Brown."

18

In retrospect, the Fourth of July marked a turning point. It signaled the beginning of an adjustment to the new reality of life without Bonnie, and resignation to the destruction of our faith in the criminal justice system. Beatific we were not; the process would be irregular and slow. Progress was halting. Nevertheless, some kind of emotional gravitational force had switched poles and now was working in the Legato's favor. A positive momentum was beginning to build and the recovery was starting to nourish itself.

For Sandy and me, the summer proved a quiet balm. It was for the most part relaxing and it was over too soon. We were even able to enjoy our annual vacation week in Bar Harbor, returning rested and refreshed. This was in marked contrast to the previous year, during the period of heartsick tension following Ralph's arrest but before the trial, when we should have stayed home and saved the money.

We spent a night in Portland on our way up north, having dinner with Jeff and Sharon. Sharon happily related that Jeff was finally doing better, and we could see that for ourselves. The girls, too, had returned to normal. They had never been told the true circumstances of Bonnie's death. All they knew was that their daddy had become detached and aloof because his sister had died. With his recovery, an enormous weight of worry had been lifted from their shoulders. *Their daddy was back!*

The girls were also growing up with a speed that was astonishing, as if in a film with time-lapse photography. This was most particularly the case with Heather, who, now eleven, was well into her "tween" years. The change was so dramatic that I couldn't resist tweaking her parents: "What happens, guys, when she wants her navel pierced? Or better yet, a tattoo?" At this, Sharon held her head in her hands in a theatrical display of mock despair. Jeff didn't see the humor. "Don't go there," he pleaded. Clearly, they were already worried about such things. Kids, I thought. *Worry is part of the package.*

Amidst the good news, Gladys was the exception. She was stranded. Working on the DVD had helped her to cope but finishing it had not helped her to move on. It had merely left her without a project upon which she could focus her energies. Now more than ever, the memory replayed itself as an endless loop in her mind: *No car in the garage. Calling out. The TV. Her feet at the end of the bed. The bullet hole in her head.*

Gladys and Ken had taken a vacation of their own. The idea occurred to Ken a few days after the picnic. He'd been hoping that with the completion of the DVD, Gladys would find closure and would be able to start weaning herself from her obsession with the past. When that magic failed to materialize on July 5, Ken began to think about what he might do to move the process along more quickly. He remembered then that Gladys had for some time expressed an interest in visiting San Francisco. He had lots of frequent flier miles and hotel points that he could cash in. Maybe a vacation there would do the trick.

Ken made the suggestion a few days later. Gladys was dubious but willing. She, too, was emotionally ready to move on with her life, but could not imagine what she might move on *to*. Maybe Ken was right, she thought. Maybe a vacation, while not a permanent solution, might prove diversion she needed to get her mind unstuck. Ken proposed that they schedule the trip for the last week in August, leaving seven weeks for Gladys to become absorbed in the planning and to relish the anticipation. This, too, would allow Ken to clear his calendar at work, in which he had long since become fully re-engaged.

The trip was not a success.

The plan Gladys devised was crammed with activities on the theory that unstructured idleness would create a vacuum that could only be filled with sorrow. One day they toured the wine country, then dined along the waterfront in Sausalito on their way back. Another day they headed south to browse the boutiques in Monterrey and the art galleries of Carmel-By-The-Sea. On the days when they left the rental car in the garage, they took in Ghirardelli Square, Chinatown, Fisherman's Wharf, Nob Hill, Union Square, and Hayes Valley. They went on the tour of Alcatraz. They checked out Haight-Ashbury, amused to see how the 1960's epicenter of flower power had devolved into disappointingly conventional, if still slightly funky, commercial district. They agreed that The Castro was something they could skip.

But of course Bonnie was there with them anyway. In a restaurant or while they were walking, they would discuss what the family had been through and how everyone was coping. In a store they would see an item that reminded them of Bonnie—something she would have loved or something she would have hated. A young woman who bore a passing resemblance to Bonnie would be walking on the sidewalk, and Gladys and Ken would look at each other without having to say a thing. Sometimes on these occasions they could talk about their memories and feelings calmly, acknowledging the pain and loss but without picking off the scab and exposing the raw open wound all over again. More often, these discussions proved counterproductive as they caused Gladys to descend into a despondent funk. When they returned from San Francisco, Gladys was still stranded.

◆　　◆　　◆

There are certain days in Boston when the air is crystal clear and the light just before dusk takes on a mellow, velvety glow. It was an early September evening such as that when Sandy and I found ourselves heading on foot toward EJ's. We were going there at the invitation of Howard, who had offered to treat us to dinner. We spent most of the walk speculating as to what might be the occasion for Howard's hospitality. It wasn't our anniversary, and neither of us had birthdays in the offing.

Dufus that I am, I had no inkling of what was happening even as we ambled inside to find Jim standing by the lectern, chatting casually with Howard. It was no surprise to see Jim in EJ's, given the friendship that had developed between them. Normally, though, Howard would have let us know that Sandy's brother would be joining us.

As we passed through the front door, Howard's face lit up with his patented 150-watt smile, as it usually did when we stopped by. His pleasure was not over seeing me, I assure you. I am a realist. The radiance of Howard's greeting had taken a quantum leap after Sandy and I started dating. Howard is smitten with Sandy. Not that I blame him.

"Hey!" Howard exclaimed, "The birds are here."

That's what he calls us now: the birds. It's a term of endearment. He explained it to us the first time: "You bill and coo like pair of lovebirds. You eat like hummingbirds. That makes you strange birds." Hummingbirds are petite but have enormous appetites relative to their size, so when you think about it, Howard has a point. Billing, cooing and eating: that's us, all right.

"Jungle Jim," said Sandy, "what's up?"

Jim gave a quick shrug—he didn't know—and said, "I didn't expect to see you either."

We all turned toward Howard. His eyes bore a mischievous twinkle as he suggested, "Let's go in back. Then I explain." Asking his assistant manager to take over the lectern, he led us to a table in a corner. We endured some small talk until our drinks were served and we had ordered our meals from the menu. At last it was time for Howard to come clean.

"This dinner, it's a bribe."

Immediately, Jim's hand swatted his forehead in the universal *of course* gesture. He "got it," but we were still in the dark. Jim spoke up before Howard could continue. "Let me see if I can solve the puzzle. I think Howard wants you two to talk me into changing my mind about the job offer. Howard, am I right?"

Howard: "Bull's eye."

That's when I caught on. "Is this the job you were telling me about on the Fourth of July?"

Jim: "Ahh-yep."

Sandy chimed in with a slight edge of exasperation: "Will one of you Three Amigos please tell me what is going on?"

I turned in her direction. "At this point I don't know any more about it than you do. Jim told me at the picnic he had a job offer but wouldn't say what it was." I looked at Jim. "What is it?"

Jim: "Howard is planning to open a second location. He wants me to manage the new unit."

Sandy, genuinely shocked, said, "How can a priest have another ... Oh ... Howard wants you to leave the priesthood?"

"No, it's not about what Howard wants, not at all. I've already made that decision, independent of Howard or the job."

"What? You have? Barry, you knew about this?'

"The Fourth of July."

"Do Mom and Dad know?"

Jim answered. "Not yet. As of now it's just you three."

Sandy: "When were you going to tell people?"

Jim: "After I give official notice to the Church."

"And when is that"

"I'm sitting with the decision for a while. I'm waiting until I'm sure I won't want to change my mind."

"Does this have to do with Bonnie? Stupid question. Of course, it must."

Giving in to Sandy's prodding, Jim shed his reticence and began to describe his feelings in the same terms he had laid them out for me. He did this in considerable detail, and the dinner plates were cleared by the time he was finished. No longer shocked, Sandy now felt dejected and disheartened on her brother's behalf. Jim used to have a purpose in his life, a spiritual home, a vocation. Now he didn't. Ralph Collins stole it from him, the rotten piece of shit, and with it her brother's zest for life. It had to leave a massive empty hole, how could it not? Nothing wrong with managing a restaurant, she was thinking, but how could it hope to provide a life of meaning and consequence in comparison with serving the Lord and the community as a priest?

On the other hand, the thought flashed through her mind as they perused the dessert menus, maybe he could meet a good woman and fall in love.

My mind was on something else. "Jim," I asked, "do you know anything about the restaurant business?"

"No," he answered.

"Not a problem!" interjected Howard. "Everything he needs to know, I teach him."

Jim expanded on that. "Howard and I have been over this in depth. He says that my lack of experience is irrelevant, because he will teach me everything. He'll mentor me. Everything will be the same as here. It'll be the same architect, the same builder, the same interior design, the same menu, the same suppliers, the same computer system, everything down to the same stationery and business cards. The point is, he has a successful formula here at EJ's, and I just have to follow it. I don't need to figure any of these things out. The other area where experience helps is in business relationships, and again, he already has those: the suppliers, the bankers, the advertising agencies, the lawyers, the accountants, they're all in place. I wouldn't have to deal with any of that."

Sandy was shaking her head. "It can't be that easy."

Howard answered first: "People."

Again, Jim expanded: "Howard is recruiting me because I'm good with people."

Howard: "Not *good*. Superb! The best."

Jim: "Howard's theory on this is that he doesn't need experience, he needs a human relations genius to make his formula work when he's not physically present. He needs somebody who is alert and responsive in making customers happy, and sensitive and adroit in managing the staff. He thinks that I'm that somebody."

Sandy: "And?"

Jim: "And what?"

Sandy: "Are you that somebody?"

Jim: "Maybe, but I'm turning down the job just the same. Howard, I've been thinking about nothing else ever since you asked me to reconsider. I still come to the same conclusion every time. What I need is not just to work with people, but to help them. I need to feel I'm doing more than serving steaks; I need to feel I'm serving humanity. I don't mean to sound lofty or holier than thou. I'm not putting down the restaurant business, or what other people do. I'm simply recognizing my own personal needs. And I know I can't change the world. I just need to contribute to making it better. So I've made my second decision. I'm going to be looking for work in the non-profit sector. I don't know if it will be a charity, or a group that pushes for social change, but it's going to be something that makes me feel good about myself. Howard, besides my family, our friendship is one of the most valued parts of my life. I hope this doesn't change that."

Howard was gracious. "Of course not. I'm disappointed, sure, but that's just business. You'll always be my good friend."

I glanced at Sandy, to see how she was taking all this. She was glowing. She had just been reminded why she loved each and every one of the Three Amigos.

We indulged in dessert, thanked Howard for a great dinner, and began our walk toward home. Within a few minutes, we were passing through the square near the corner of Water and Kilby, where Sandy and I had first met. As usual, my eyes came to rest on the statue: the revolutionary holding a baby aloft *(the future!)* in triumph above the pain and death of the Hungarian uprising. But this time the experience was different. This time I saw the baby and everything just clicked. In an overdue but still unexpected burst of self-awareness, it was suddenly all both obvious and inevitable. It was going to happen.

We were already holding hands. All I said was, "I'm ready," and she knew exactly what I meant. We're a team, don't forget. She stopped, grabbed my other hand, and holding on to both of them, said, "Really? This is definite?"

"This is definite," I told her, and meant it, and tears formed in her eyes. Her voice choking with emotion, she asked, "Can you possibly imagine how much I love you?"

The rest of the way home she was euphoric, and when we got there we performed a small but emblematic ceremony. It was a burial at sea, so to speak: we dumped her supply of birth control pills down the toilet. We kissed to the tune of the flush. Then, even though her pill from that morning was still working, we agreed that it wouldn't hurt to get in a little practice.

The next morning, Sandy's elation was unabated. This helped me greatly, as I was thus reassured that I was in fact doing the right thing for her, and, it occurred to me, perhaps for Gladys too. I was convinced of exactly how right it was when we left for work in the morning and she gleefully greeted Alexander by name as we reached the sidewalk. This was the first time Sandy had done that since the murder. "Hello, Alexander!" she bellowed with radiant zest. "Top o' the mornin' to ya!"

There is a stormwater drain along the curb in front of the building where our condo is located. The top of the drain is covered by a cast iron fitting that has parallel bars at the pavement level to let water flow in and keep debris out. It was this cast iron piece of public works that Sandy was talking to. She had given it a name on the day after we moved in. She named it Alexander, as in: *Alexander the grate*.

I very much hope our kid inherits Sandy's sense of humor. With the world as it is today, he—or she—is surely going to need it.

978-0-595-43587-6
0-595-43587-4

CPSIA information can be obtained
at www.ICGtesting.com
Printed in the USA
FSHW012005110321
79407FS

9 780595 435876